ALFRED A. KNOPF

1915 · 100 YEARS · 2015

Notes from a Dead House

FYODOR DOSTOEVSKY

Notes from a Dead House

Translated by

Richard Pevear &
Larissa Volokhonsky

ALFRED A. KNOPF   NEW YORK   2015

THIS IS A BORZOI BOOK
PUBLISHED BY ALFRED A. KNOPF

Translation copyright © 2015 by Richard Pevear and Larissa Volokhonsky
Foreword copyright © 2015 by Richard Pevear

Library of Congress Cataloging-in-Publication Data
Dostoyevsky, Fyodor, 1821–1881, author.
[Zapiski iz mertvogo doma. English (Pevear and Volokhonsky)]
Notes from a dead house / by Fyodor Dostoevsky ;
translated by Richard Pevear and Larissa Volokhonsky.
pages ; cm
ISBN 978-0-307-95959-1 (hardcover) — ISBN 978-0-307-95960-7 (eBook)
I. Pevear, Richard, [date] translator.
II. Volokhonsky, Larissa, translator. III. Title.
PG3326.Z3   2014
891.73'3—dc23   2014018194

Jacket design by Peter Mendelsund

Manufactured in the United States of America
First Edition

Contents

Foreword

Late in the night of April 22–23, 1849, the young Fyodor Dostoevsky was awakened in his apartment in Petersburg and informed that he was under arrest for his participation in a secret utopian socialist society. The other members of the society, including its founder, Mikhail Petrashevsky, a follower of the French socialist thinker Charles Fourier, were arrested at the same time. The emperor Nicholas I had been alarmed by the series of revolutions that broke out in Europe in 1848, the year of the *Communist Manifesto*, and had decided to move against the radical intellectuals. The "Petrashevists" were confined in the Peter and Paul Fortress in Petersburg for eight months while the investigation was carried out. In the end, the judicial commission recommended death by firing squad, but the military court commuted the sentence to eight years at hard labor in Siberia.

Dostoevsky was specifically charged with circulating a letter by the liberal literary critic Vissarion Belinsky that was "filled with impertinent expressions against the Orthodox Church and the sovereign power" and with attempting to set up a clandestine printing press.[*] The emperor himself revised his sentence to four years at hard labor followed by four years of military service in Siberia. But he also decided to stage a little drama for the prisoners—a mock execution on the Semyonovsky parade ground, to be interrupted at the last moment by an imperial reprieve and the reading of the actual sentences. Konstantin Mochulsky notes that the emperor "entered personally into all the details: the scaffold's dimensions, the uniforms to be worn by the condemned, the priest's

---

[*] See *Dostoevsky, His Life and Work*, by Konstantin Mochulsky, translated by Michael A. Minihan (Princeton, NJ: Princeton University Press, 1967), p. 140.

vestments, the escort of carriages, the tempo of the drum roll, the route from the fortress to the place of shooting, the breaking of the swords, the putting on of white shirts, the executioner's functions, the shackling of the prisoners."* On December 22, 1849, the performance took place. Petrashevsky was in the first group of three to be "executed"; Dostoevsky was in the second. He had just turned twenty-eight.

In a letter to his brother Mikhail written that same evening, Dostoevsky declared:

> As I look back upon the past and think how much time has been spent to no avail, how much of it was lost in delusions, in mistakes, in idleness, in not knowing how to live; what little store I set upon it, how many times I sinned against my heart and spirit—for this my heart bleeds. Life is a gift, life is happiness, every moment could have been an age of happiness. *Si jeunesse savait!*† Now, on changing my life, I am being born again in a new form. Brother! I swear to you I will not lose hope and will preserve my spirit and my heart in purity. I'll be reborn to the better. This is all my hope, all my consolation!

That rebirth did take place, but more slowly than Dostoevsky may have thought and through experiences he could not have imagined before the years he spent at hard labor. His *Notes from a Dead House* give an account of it.

In February 1854, Dostoevsky was released from the prison in Omsk and sent to serve as a private in the fortress of Semipalatinsk, in Kazakhstan, some four hundred miles further east. There for the first time he was allowed to contact his family. In a letter to his brother written on February 22, 1854, a week after his release, Dostoevsky described the horrors of prison life and in particular the hatred of the peasant convicts for the nobility, to which he belonged by birth, though his sentence deprived him of his legal rights as a nobleman. The details in the letter are more shocking than anything we find in *Notes from a Dead House*. Yet he could say in the same letter, referring "even to

---

* Mochulsky, p. 140.
† If youth only knew! (French).

robber-murderers": "Believe me, there were deep, strong, beautiful natures among them, and it often gave me joy to find gold under a rough exterior." The intensity of that contradiction was at the heart of Dostoevsky's prison experience. The struggle to understand its implications would inform all his future works.

Dostoevsky arrived in Semipalatinsk filled with plans for writing. He felt that he had enough material in him for many volumes, and though as an exile he was forbidden to publish, he hoped that situation would change in some six years, if not sooner. While still in Omsk, a week after his release, he had asked his brother to send him books. The list is interesting: "I need (very necessary) ancient historians (in French translations); modern historians: Guizot, Thierry, Thiers, Ranke, and so forth; national studies, and the Fathers of the Church . . . and church histories . . . Send me the Koran, Kant's *Critique of Pure Reason* . . . and Hegel, especially his *History of Philosophy*. My whole future depends on this . . ." He was clearly intent on rethinking his former utopian socialism both historically and philosophically. "I won't even try to tell you what transformations went on in my soul, my faith, my mind, and my heart in those four years," he wrote in the same letter. "That perpetual escape into myself from bitter reality has borne its fruit. I now have many new needs and hopes of which I never thought in the old days."

In Semipalatinsk, Dostoevsky made the acquaintance of the young Baron Alexander Egorovich Vrangel (1833–1915), who was sent there in 1854 as the district procurator. By an odd coincidence, Vrangel happened to have witnessed the mock execution of the Petrashevists in 1849; he had also read Dostoevsky's early works and admired them. The two became friends and eventually shared a house, and Vrangel also interceded with the authorities several times on the author's behalf. The baron's memoirs of those years, published in 1912, give a detailed and moving portrait of Dostoevsky. He describes their first meeting: "He had on a soldier's greatcoat with red stand-up collar and red epaulettes. Morose, with a sickly pale face covered with freckles, he wore his light-blond hair cut short; in height he was taller than average. Staring intently at me with his intelligent grey-blue eyes, it seemed he was trying to peer into my soul."* Through Vrangel, Dostoevsky was intro-

---

* Mochulsky, p. 156.

duced to the commanding officers of the fortress and was received in society, where he met his future wife, Marya Dmitrievna Isaeva.

Vrangel recalled Dostoevsky working on his prison memoirs while they lived together. "I was happy to see him during the moments of his creative work," he wrote, "and I was the first person who listened to the notes of this outstanding work of art." Vrangel also recorded a curious incident that occurred one day while they were sitting on the terrace having tea. His servant announced that a young woman was asking to see Dostoevsky. She was invited to the garden, and Dostoevsky recognized her at once as the daughter of a Gypsy woman who had been sent to prison for murdering her husband. The girl herself had been involved in the escape of two convicts from the prison in Omsk. Their plan—"completely illogical and fantastic," according to Vrangel—was to make their way eastward, join the khan's army, and come back to free their fellow prisoners. He says that the girl's sudden reappearance inspired Dostoevsky to write a new chapter, "The Escape," the next to last in *Notes from a Dead House* and the book's thematic culmination.

The emperor Nicholas I died in the spring of 1855 and in September his son, Alexander II, who came to be known as the Tsar-Liberator, ascended the throne. The liberal spirit of the new government made itself felt rather quickly and, perhaps owing to it, Dostoevsky was promoted from private to noncommissioned officer in the autumn of that same year. A year later, in October 1856, he was made a commissioned officer and his rights as a nobleman were restored. This improvement in his position made it possible for him to marry Marya Dmitrievna the following February. His official work and the turmoil of his courtship and eventual marriage had interfered with his writing, but after his marriage he went back to it more steadily. He worked on some of his prison sketches, then set them aside in order to write two long stories, *Uncle's Dream* and *The Village of Stepanchikovo*, which he thought would be better suited to his reappearance as a writer. In fact, they are more or less the same as his pre-prison works. The deep change that was going on in him had not yet found its form and voice.

In 1858 Dostoevsky asked for permission to retire from the service and return to Russia. The permission was granted, but the order took more than a year to reach him, and it did not allow him to live in

Moscow or Petersburg. In the summer of 1859, he left Semipalatinsk for the city of Tver, a hundred miles north of Moscow, where his literary plans and the idea of collaborating with his brother Mikhail on a weekly magazine took clearer shape. The two stories were published in reputable journals that same year, and in mid-December, after more petitions, Dostoevsky was finally allowed to return to Petersburg.

During the spring and summer of 1860, while he and Mikhail were going through the complicated process of starting their magazine, Dostoevsky set to work on the final version of *Notes from a Dead House*. Surprisingly, however, in the fall the first two chapters were published in another magazine, *The Russian World*, an "obscure weekly," as Joseph Frank describes it.* Frank suggests that Dostoevsky wanted to make "a preliminary trial of the censors' response." He was afraid that, despite the liberal atmosphere of the time, his portrayal of life at hard labor would not be approved for publication. The editor of *The Russian World* offered to take the matter into his own hands, submitted the early chapters to the censors, and the Central Censorship Authority passed them. The magazine published the next three chapters in its January numbers and promised more to come, but there would be no more. The Dostoevskys' magazine *Vremya* ("Time") had begun to appear that same January, and the whole of *Notes from a Dead House*, including the opening chapters, was published there in 1861–62.

The *Notes* made a very strong impression on the reading public, especially the radical youth. For Dostoevsky it indeed marked a triumphant return to literature. As Joseph Frank observed: "No writer was now more celebrated than Dostoevsky, whose name was surrounded with the halo of his former suffering, and whose sketches only served to enhance his prestige as a precursor on the path of political martyrdom."† He was invited to give talks and readings to student groups and charitable organizations, opportunities he always accepted gladly, because they brought him into direct contact with his readers. His fellow writers also admired the *Notes:* Turgenev likened the book to Dante's *Inferno*,

---

* Joseph Frank, *Dostoevsky: The Stir of Liberation* (Princeton, NJ: Princeton University Press, 1988), p. 28.
† Frank, p. 140.

and Tolstoy thought it not only Dostoevsky's finest work, but one of the best books in all of Russian literature.

Notes from a Dead House was the first published account of life in the Siberian hard-labor camps. It initiated the genre of the prison memoir, which unfortunately went on to acquire major importance in Russian literature. But the book was innovative not only in its subject matter, but in its composition. Dostoevsky left the prison in Omsk with a collection of notes he had managed to take during those four years. In them he had recorded the unusual words and expressions of the peasant convicts, their arguments, their play-acting, their songs and stories, entrusting the pages to one of the medical assistants in the prison hospital, who duly returned them to him when he was released. These notes supplied the unique voicing of the book. While still in Tver, in the summer of 1858, Dostoevsky wrote to his brother that he now had "a complete and definite plan" in mind. "My personality will disappear from view. These are the notes of an unknown man; but I vouch for their interest . . . Here there will be the serious, the gloomy, and the humorous, and *folk conversation with its particular hard-labor colorings.*"*

In the semi-fictional form he chose to give his narrative, Dostoevsky places himself at a third remove. The fictional author-narrator of the *Notes*, Alexander Petrovich Goryanchikov, is a former nobleman serving a ten-year sentence for murdering his wife in a fit of jealousy. His *Notes* are presented to us, in the introduction and in one brief intrusion in part two, chapter VII, by another first-person narrator, the "editor" of Goryanchikov's manuscript. He tells us, with a mixture of heavy irony and underlying sympathy, about Goryanchikov's reclusive life in Siberia after prison and his sudden death—a closure that is in sharp contrast to the ending of the book itself. This fictionalizing was in part a mask for the censors: the notes of a man serving a sentence for a common-law crime were more likely to be passed for publication than the notes of a political criminal. But the mask is dropped rather quickly. By the second chapter, we hear a fellow nobleman say, in response to the narrator's first impressions of the peasant prisoners: "Yes, sir, they don't

---

* Mochulsky, p. 184; emphasis in original.

like noblemen . . . especially political criminals." Though he keeps the
persona of Alexander Petrovich throughout, the narrator's thoughts,
his preoccupations, and his conscience are not at all those of a man
who has murdered his wife. Dostoevsky's personality does not disappear from view; he is present as the observer of the life around him, but
also as the protagonist of the inner transformation that the experience
of prison brings about in him. It is Dostoevsky, not Goryanchikov, who
says towards the end: "I outlined a program for the whole of my future
and resolved to follow it firmly. A blind faith arose in me that I would
and could fulfill it all . . . I waited, I called for freedom to come quickly;
I wanted to test myself anew, in a new struggle."

The fictional editor of Goryanchikov's notes ends his introduction by describing his own fascination with them, but then says rather
casually: "Of course, I may be mistaken. I will begin by selecting two
or three chapters; let the public judge . . ." There is nothing loose or
casual about the structure of the book itself, however. It is divided into
two parts. Part One, as we can see from the chapter titles, is made up
of first impressions. It is filled with vivid details that both repulse and
intrigue the narrator as he tries to settle into his new circumstances.
He moves about freely in time, but keeps coming back to his initial
experiences. By the end of Part One we are still in his first month of
captivity, rounded off with Christmas and the brief respite of the theater performance. Part Two is constructed differently. Here the narrator speaks more generally of prison life—the hospital, various kinds
and degrees of corporal punishment, the officers, certain of his prison
"comrades," the prison animals—and even includes an inset story told
by another prisoner. But again there is an underlying unity to this
seemingly random sampling, an inner unity, in the author's deepening
perception of the people he has been thrown together with. He begins
to fathom their difference not only from himself but from his former
assumptions about the "Russian peasant"—an abstract figure idealized
by the radical intelligentsia. As a result of this synchronic structure,
there is no sense in the book of time passing. "The prison is immo-
bile," as Mochulsky observes, "it is a 'dead house' frozen in perpetu-
ity, but the author moves."* It is the movement of his own increasing

---

* Mochulsky, p. 186.

penetration and comprehension, which passes through his first Easter, through the release of the hurt eagle at the end of the chapter on prison animals, through the drama of the escape, to culminate on his last day of captivity in a sudden assertion: "I must say it all: these people are extraordinary people. They are perhaps the most gifted, the strongest of all our people. But their mighty strength perished for nothing, perished abnormally, unlawfully, irretrievably. And who is to blame?"

This inner change in Dostoevsky's perception of the people began during his first Easter in prison with the surprise recollection of a forgotten moment from his childhood, which came to him while he was lying on his bunk with his eyes closed, trying to forget the vileness of his surroundings. Interestingly enough, he did not include this "awakening" in _Notes from a Dead House_, though its effects are central to the book; he wrote about it only fifteen years later, in the issue of his _Writer's Diary_ for February 1876, in an entry entitled "The Peasant Marey," which we include here as an appendix. It tells of how the frightened nine-year-old Dostoevsky was comforted by one of his father's serfs.

Now suddenly, twenty years later, in Siberia, I remembered this whole encounter with such clarity, to the very last detail. Which means that it had embedded itself in my soul imperceptibly, on its own and without my will, and I suddenly remembered it when it was needed . . . And so, when I got off my bunk and glanced about, I suddenly felt that I could look at these unfortunate men with totally different eyes, and that suddenly, by some miracle, all the hatred and anger in my heart had vanished completely.

What he saw in these "simple people" was a complexity of character, a capacity for extremes of both evil and good, that destroyed the basic assumptions of the utopian socialism he had embraced as a young man. "What had been a pitying sentimentalism towards weak and basically unassertive characters," Joseph Frank writes, "now took on a tragic complexity as Dostoevsky's sympathies with the unsubjugated peasant convicts stretched the boundaries of official morality to the breaking point."* Early in *Notes from a Dead House*, the author meditates on a complex riddle that pursued him all the while he was in prison: the sameness of the crime and the sameness of the sentence, faced with the enormous variety of human characters and motives and of the effects on different characters of the same punishment. "True, there are variations in the length of the sentences. But these variations are relatively few; while the variations in one and the same crime are a numberless multitude. For each character there is a variation." This riddle comes up again five years later in *Crime and Punishment*, where the remarkable investigator, Porfiry Petrovich, says to Raskolnikov:

> It must be observed that the general case, the one to which all legal forms and rules are suited, and on the basis of which they are all worked out and written down in books, simply does not exist, for the very reason that every case, let's say, for instance, every crime, as soon as it actually occurs, turns at once into a completely particular case, sir; and sometimes, just think, really completely unlike all the previous ones, sir.

Still later, in *The Brothers Karamazov*, Dmitri Karamazov confesses to his brother Alyosha:

> Too many riddles oppress man on earth. Solve them if you can without getting your feet wet ... Besides, I can't bear it that some man, even with a lofty heart and the highest mind, should start from the ideal of the Madonna and end with the ideal of Sodom. It's even more fearful when someone who already has the ideal of Sodom in his soul does not deny the ideal of the Madonna either, and his heart burns with it, verily, verily burns, as in his young, blameless years. No, man is broad, even too broad, I would narrow him down. Devil knows what to make of him, that's the thing!

---

* Joseph Frank, *Dostoevsky: A Writer in His Time* (Princeton, NJ: Princeton University Press, 2009), p. 214.

The epilogue of *Crime and Punishment* is set in a Siberian hard-labor prison closely resembling the prison in Omsk, where Raskolnikov, like the narrator of *Notes from a Dead House*, confronts "a new, hitherto completely unknown reality" and undergoes a "gradual regeneration." In the early drafts of *The Brothers Karamazov*, Dostoevsky gave Dmitri Karamazov the name of Ilyinsky. Dmitri Ilyinsky was one of his fellow prisoners in Omsk; in the *Notes* he is not named; the narrator refers to him only as "the parricide." He had been sentenced to twenty years at hard labor for murdering his father, but after serving ten years of his sentence, he was found to be innocent. Dostoevsky, who never believed in his crime, says in the *Notes* that he was haunted by his memory, and his last novel bears him out. In his early drafts of *Crime and Punishment*, Dostoevsky called the depraved immoralist Svidrigailov by the name of Aristov. Aristov was the A—v of *Notes from a Dead House*, "an example of what the carnal side of man can come to, unrestrained by any inner norm, any lawfulness . . . Add to that the fact that he was cunning and intelligent, good-looking, even somewhat educated, and not without abilities. No," says the narrator, "better fire, better plague and famine, than such a man in society!"

All of Dostoevsky's later work grew out of his meditation on the extremes he met with in the "hitherto completely unknown reality" of the dead house. It is, finally, a meditation on human freedom. The radical social thought of his time had trouble finding a place for freedom; given the right social organization, freedom was really no longer necessary. It also excluded the irrational; it reduced good and evil to the useful and the harmful; it removed the metaphysical dimensions of human life. But Dostoevsky had seen that the extremes of good and evil, the breadth that Mitya Karamazov talks about, were innate even in the crudest men, and that they would never renounce the need to assert their freedom, bizarre and deformed as the results might be. "The prisoner himself knows that he is a prisoner, an outcast . . . ," he writes, "but no brands, no fetters will make him forget that he is a human being."

—*Richard Pevear*

Part One

Introduction

In the remote parts of Siberia, amidst steppes, mountains, or impenetrable forests, you occasionally happen upon small towns of one or, at the most, two thousand inhabitants, wooden, unsightly, with two churches—one in town, the other in the cemetery—towns that look more like a good-sized village near Moscow than a town. They are usually quite well supplied with police officers, assessors, and all other subaltern ranks. In general, serving in Siberia, despite the cold, is extremely warm and snug. People live simply, unprogressively; the customs are old, firm, sanctified by the ages. The officials, who by rights play the role of the Siberian aristocracy, are natives, deep-rooted Siberians, or transients from Russia, mostly from the capitals,[1] enticed by the payment of tax-free wages, the double travel allowance, and tempting hopes for the future. Those who are able to solve the riddle of life almost always stay in Siberia and delight in taking root there. Later on they bear sweet and abundant fruit. But others, light-minded folk, unable to solve the riddle of life, soon weary of Siberia and ask themselves in anguish why on earth they ended up there. They impatiently serve out their term of office, three years, and once it expires, they immediately put in for a transfer and go back where they came from, denouncing Siberia and laughing at it. They are wrong: not only from the point of view of service, but from many others, one can be blissfully happy in Siberia. The climate is excellent; there are many remarkably rich and hospitable merchants, and many extremely well-to-do non-Russians. The young ladies blossom like roses and are moral in the highest degree. Wildfowl fly down the streets and right into the hunters' arms. Unnatural quantities of champagne are drunk. The caviar is astonishing. The harvest is fifteenfold in some places . . . Generally, it is a blessed land. You need only know how to take advantage of it. In Siberia they know how.

In one such merry and self-contented little town, with the most charming inhabitants, the memory of which will remain forever fixed in my heart, I met Alexander Petrovich Goryanchikov, a settler, a Russian-born gentleman and landowner, who was later sent to second-degree hard labor for the murder of his wife, and, on the expiration of the ten-year term laid down by the law, was living out his life humbly and inaudibly as a settler in the town of K.[2] In fact, he had been assigned to the suburbs, but he lived in town, which provided him with the opportunity of earning at least some sort of living by teaching children. In Siberian towns one often meets with teachers who are exiled settlers; they are not scorned. For the most part they teach French, so necessary for making one's way in life, and of which no one in the remote parts of Siberia would have any notion without them. I first met Alexander Petrovich in the house of Ivan Ivanovich Gvozdikov, an old-fashioned, distinguished, and hospitable official, who had five very promising daughters of various ages. Alexander Petrovich gave them lessons four times a week, at thirty silver kopecks a lesson. His appearance interested me. He was an extremely pale and thin man, not yet old, about thirty-five, small and frail. He was always dressed quite neatly, European style. When you talked to him, he would look at you very fixedly and attentively, listen to your every word with strict politeness, as if pondering it, as if by asking him a question you were setting him a task or trying to worm some secret out of him, and in the end he would answer clearly and briefly, but weighing every word of his answer so much that you would suddenly feel awkward for some reason and would finally be glad yourself that the conversation was over. I asked Ivan Ivanovich about him right then and learned that Goryanchikov led an irreproachable and moral life, and that otherwise Ivan Ivanovich would not have invited him for his daughters, but that he was terribly unsociable, hid himself from everyone, was extremely learned, read a great deal, but spoke very little, and that generally it was rather difficult to get into conversation with him. Some insisted that he was positively mad, though they also found that essentially that was not such an important failing, that many of the respected members of the town were ready to show Alexander Petrovich every kindness, that he could even be of use in writing petitions, and so on. It was supposed that he must have many relations in

Russia, maybe even not among the least of people, but it was known that since his exile he had resolutely broken off all connections with them—in short, he only harmed himself. Besides, we all knew his story, knew that he had killed his wife in the first year of their marriage, had killed her out of jealousy and then turned himself in (which had lightened his punishment considerably). Such crimes are always considered a misfortune and are looked upon with pity. But despite all that, the odd fellow stubbornly shunned everyone and appeared among people only to give lessons.

At first I paid no special attention to him, but, I don't know why myself, he gradually came to interest me. There was something enigmatic about him. To get into conversation with him was quite impossible. Of course, he always answered my questions and even looked as if he considered it his foremost obligation; but after his answers, I found it hard to ask him anything more; besides, after such conversations, his face always showed some sort of suffering and fatigue. I remember walking home with him from Ivan Ivanych's once on a beautiful summer evening. It suddenly occurred to me to invite him to my place for a moment to have a cigarette. I cannot describe the look of horror that came to his face; he was completely at a loss, started to mutter something incoherent, and suddenly, casting an angry glance at me, rushed off in the opposite direction. I was even surprised. From then on, whenever we met, he looked at me as if with some sort of fright. But I did not let up; something drew me to him, and a month later, for no reason at all, I went to see Goryanchikov myself. Of course, it was a stupid and indelicate thing to do. He lodged on the outskirts of town, with an old tradeswoman who had a consumptive daughter, who in turn had an illegitimate daughter, a child of about ten, a pretty and cheerful little girl. Alexander Petrovich was sitting with her and teaching her to read when I came in. Seeing me, he became as confused as if I had caught him at some crime. He was completely taken aback, jumped up from his chair, and stared at me all eyes. We finally sat down; he followed my every glance intently, as if he suspected each of them of having some special, hidden meaning. I realized that he was suspicious to the point of madness. He looked at me with hatred, all but asking: "Will you leave soon?" I began talking to him about our little town, about the current news; he kept silent and smiled angrily; it turned out that he not only did not know the most ordinary town news known to everyone, but was not even interested in knowing it. After that I talked about our region, its needs; he listened to me silently and looked into my eyes so strangely that I finally began to be ashamed of our conversation. However, I almost managed to tease him out with new books and magazines; I had them with me, just arrived in the mail, and offered them to him still uncut. He cast a greedy glance at them, but changed his mind at once and declined the offer for lack of time. I finally took leave of him and, on going out, felt that some intolerable burden had been lifted from my heart. I was ashamed, and it seemed extraordinarily stupid of me to pester a man who has made it his chief task to hide as far away as possible from the whole world. But the deed was done. I remember noticing almost no books in his room, which meant they were wrong when they said that he read a lot. However, driving past his windows once or twice very late at night, I noticed light in them. What was he doing, sitting there till dawn? Could he be writing? And, if so, what precisely?

Circumstances took me away from our little town for about three months. Returning home when it was already winter, I learned that Alexander Petrovich had died that autumn, had died in solitude and had not even once sent for a doctor. They had already nearly forgotten him in town. His lodgings stood vacant. I immediately made the acquaintance of the deceased man's landlady, with the aim of finding out from her what in particular her tenant had been occupied with, and whether he had been writing anything. For twenty kopecks she brought me a basket full of papers that the deceased had left behind. The old woman confessed that she had already used up two notebooks. She was a sullen and taciturn woman, from whom it was hard to draw anything sensible. Of her lodger she could tell me nothing particularly new. It seemed from what she said that he hardly ever did anything and for months did not open a book or pick up a pen; instead he paced up and down his room all night, thinking about something and sometimes talking to himself; that he loved her granddaughter Katya very much and was very affectionate with her, especially after he learned that her name was Katya; and that on St. Catherine's day he always went to have a memorial service offered for somebody. He could not stand visitors; he left the house only to teach children; he even looked askance at her, the old woman, when she came once a week to tidy his room a least a little, and hardly ever said so much as a word to her in all those three years. I asked Katya if she remembered her teacher. She looked at me silently, turned to the wall, and began to cry. So the man had been able to make at least somebody love him.

I took his papers and spent a whole day sorting them. Three-quarters of these papers were empty, insignificant scraps, or his pupils' exercises in penmanship. But there was one notebook, a rather voluminous one, filled with small handwriting and unfinished, perhaps abandoned and forgotten by the author himself. It was a description, though a disjointed one, of the ten years of life at hard labor that Alexander Petrovich had endured. At times this description was interrupted by another sort of narrative, some strange, horrible memories, jotted down roughly, convulsively, as if under some sort of constraint. I reread those passages several times and was almost convinced that they had been written in madness. But the notes on hard labor—"Scenes from a Dead House," as he himself calls them somewhere in his manuscript—seemed to me not without interest. The totally new world, unknown till then, the strangeness of some facts, certain particular observations about those lost people, fascinated me, and I read some of it with curiosity. Of course, I may be mistaken. As a test, I will begin by selecting two or three chapters; let the public judge . . .

I

The Dead House

Our prison stood at the edge of the fortress, right by the fortress rampart. You could look at God's world through the chinks in the fence: wouldn't you see at least something? But all you could see was a strip of sky and a high earthen rampart overgrown with weeds, and on the wall sentries pacing up and down day and night, and right then you would think that years would go by, and you would come in the same way to look through the chinks in the fence and see the same rampart, the same sentries, and the same little strip of sky, not the sky over the prison, but a different, far-off, free sky. Picture to yourself a large yard, some two hundred paces long and a hundred and fifty wide, surrounded on all sides, in the form of an irregular hexagon, by a high stockade, that is, a fence of high posts (palings) dug deeply into the ground, their ribs pressed firmly against each other, fastened together by crosswise planks, and sharpened at the tips: this was the outer wall of the prison. On one side of the wall sturdy gates had been set in, always locked, always guarded day and night by sentries; they were opened on demand to let people out to work. Beyond those gates was the bright, free world; people lived like everybody else. But on this side of the wall, you pictured that world as some sort of impossible fairy tale. Here you were in a special world, unlike anything else; it had its own special laws, its own clothing, its own morals and customs, an alive dead house, a life like nowhere else, and special people. It is this special corner that I am setting out to describe.

Once inside the wall, you see several buildings. On both sides of the wide inner yard stretch two long, one-story log houses. These are the barracks. Here the prisoners live, sorted by categories. Then, deeper into the enclosure, there is another similar house: this is the kitchen, divided into two sections; further on there is another building where there are cellars, barns, and sheds, all under the same roof. The middle of the yard is empty and forms a rather large, level space. Here the prisoners line up for head count and roll call morning, noon, and evening, and occasionally several more times a day—depending on the suspiciousness of the sentries and their ability to count quickly. Round about, between the buildings and the fence, there is still quite a lot of space. There, behind the buildings, some inmates of a more unsociable and gloomy character like to walk in their off-hours, shielded from all eyes, and think their own thoughts. Meeting them during these strolls, I liked to peer into their sullen, branded faces, trying to guess what they were thinking about. There was one prisoner whose favorite occupation during his free time was counting the posts. There were about fifteen hundred of them, and he had them all counted up and marked off; each post signified a day for him; each day he counted off one post and in that way, by the number of posts left uncounted, he could actually see how many days of prison he had left before his term was served. He was sincerely glad when he finished some one side of the hexagon. He still had many years to wait; but in prison there was time enough to learn patience. I once saw a prisoner taking leave of his comrades before being released after twenty years in prison. There were people who remembered him entering the prison for the first time, young, carefree, mindful neither of his crime nor of his punishment. He was leaving a gray-haired old man with a sad and gloomy face. He went silently around our six barracks. On entering each barrack, he recited a prayer before the icons, then made a low bow to his comrades, asking them not to remember evil against him.[1] I also remember how one prisoner, formerly a well-to-do Siberian peasant, was called to the gates once towards evening. Six months earlier he had received news that his former wife had remarried, and he had been deeply saddened. Now she herself came to the prison, sent for him, and gave him alms. They talked for about two minutes, wept a little, and said good-bye forever. I saw his face when he came back to the barrack . . . Yes, you could learn patience in that place.

When darkness fell, we were all brought to the barracks, where we were locked in for the night. I always found it hard to go back to our barrack from outside. It was a long, low, and stuffy room, dimly lit by tallow candles, with a heavy, stifling smell. I don't understand now how I survived for ten years in it. Three planks on the bunk: that was all my space. Some thirty men shared the same bunk in our room alone. In winter they locked up early; it was a good four hours before everybody fell asleep. Meanwhile—noise, din, guffawing, swearing, the clank of chains, fumes and soot, shaven heads, branded faces, ragged clothes, everything abused, besmeared . . . yes, man survives it all! Man is a creature who gets used to everything, and that, I think, is the best definition of him.

Altogether there were about two hundred and fifty of us in the prison—a nearly constant figure. Some came, others finished their terms and left, still others died. And they were all kinds! I think each province, each region of Russia had its representatives here. There were non-Russians, there were even exiles from the Caucasian mountaineers. All this was sorted out according to the severity of the crime and, consequently, to the number of years they were condemned to serve. It must be supposed that there was no crime that did not have its representative here. The main core of all the prison populace consisted of deported convicts of the civilian category (*departed* convicts, as they naïvely mispronounced it). These were criminals totally deprived of all civil rights, cut-off slices of society, their faces branded in eternal witness to their outcast state. They were sent to hard labor for terms of eight to twelve years and then distributed around various Siberian districts as settlers. There were also criminals of the military category, who were not deprived of civil rights, as is generally the case in penal companies of the Russian army. They were sent for short terms, at the end of which they went back where they came from to serve as soldiers in Siberian battalions of the line. Many of them returned to prison almost at once for repeated serious offenses, not for a short term now, but for twenty years. This category was called "perpetual." But the "perpetuals" were still not totally deprived of civil rights. Finally, there was yet another special category of the most terrible criminals, a rather numerous one, mainly from the military. It was called the "special section." Criminals were sent to it from all over Russia. They themselves considered that they were lifers and did not know their term at hard labor. According to the law, their tasks were to be doubled and tripled. They were kept in prison until the heaviest hard-labor sites were opened in Siberia. "You're in for a term, but we're in for the long haul," they used to say to other inmates. Later I heard that this category had been abolished. Besides that, the civilian order has also been abolished in our fortress, and a single military-prisoner company has been set up. Naturally, along with that the superiors have also been changed. In other words, I am describing old times, things long past and gone . . .

This was long ago now; I see it all as if in a dream. I remember how I entered the prison. It was on an evening in the month of December. Darkness was already falling; people were coming back from work; they were preparing for the roll call. A mustached sergeant finally opened the door for me to this strange house, in which I was to spend so many years, to endure so many sensations, of which, if I had not experienced them in reality, I could never have had even the vaguest notion. For example, could I ever have imagined how terrible and tormenting it would be that, in all the ten years of my term, not once, not for a single minute, would I be alone? . . . At work always under guard, at home with my two hundred comrades, and never once, never once alone! . . . However, that was not all I had to get used to!

Here there were chance murderers and professional murderers, robbers and gang leaders. There were petty thieves, and tramps who lived by holdups or by breaking and entering. There were those about whom it was hard to decide what could have brought them there. And yet each of them had his own story, hazy and oppressive, like the fumes in your head after last night's drunkenness. Generally, they spoke little of the past, did not like to tell and clearly tried not to think about what had been. I even knew murderers among them so cheerful, so never-thoughtful, that you could wager their conscience had never reproached them at all. But there were also the gloomy ones, who were almost always silent. Generally, it was rare that anyone told about his life, and curiosity was not in fashion, was somehow not the custom, was not acceptable. Though on rare occasions someone would start talking out of idleness, and another man would listen coolly and gloomily. No one could surprise anyone here. "We're literate folk!" they often said, with some strange self-satisfaction. I remember how a drunken robber (you could occasionally get drunk in prison) once began telling about how he killed a five-year-old boy, how he lured him first with a toy, took him to some empty shed, and there put a knife in him. The whole bar-rack, which until then had laughed at his jokes, cried out like one man, and the robber was forced to shut up; they did not cry out in indigna-tion, but just so, because he *shouldn't* have talked *about that;* because it was not acceptable to talk *about that.* I will note by the way that these people were indeed literate and that not in a figurative but in the literal sense. Certainly more than half of them could read and write. In what other place where Russian folk gather in large numbers could you find a group of two hundred and fifty people more than half of whom were literate? As I heard later, someone concluded from similar data that literacy ruins the people. That is a mistake: the causes here are quite different, though it is impossible not to agree that literacy develops self-assurance in people. But that is by no means a shortcoming. The cat-egories were distinguished by their clothing: some had jackets half dark brown and half gray, and their trousers as well—one leg gray, the other dark brown. At work once, a girl who sold rolls came up to the prison-ers, studied me for a long time, and then suddenly burst out laughing. "Pah, what a sight!" she cried. "Not enough gray cloth, and not enough black!" There were some whose jackets were all of gray cloth, and only the sleeves were dark brown. Our heads were also shaved differently: some had half the head shaved lengthwise, and others crosswise.

At first glance you could notice a rather strong similarity in this strange family; even the most distinct, most original personalities, who reigned over the others involuntarily, tried to fall into the general tone of the whole prison. In general I must say that all these people, with the exception of a few inexhaustibly cheerful ones, who were held up to universal scorn because of it, were gloomy, envious, terribly vain, boastful, touchy, and formalists in the highest degree. The ability to be surprised at nothing was considered the greatest virtue. They were all mad about keeping up appearances. But not infrequently the most arrogant look changed with lightning speed to the most pusillanimous. There were several truly strong men; they were simple and unaffected. But, strangely enough, among these truly strong men there were a few who were vain to the utmost degree, almost to the point of sickness. In general, vanity and appearances took the foreground. The major-ity were depraved and terribly degenerate. There was ceaseless gossip and scandal-mongering: it was hell, pitch-darkness. Yet no one dared to rebel against the internal statutes and accepted customs of the prison; everyone submitted. There were outstanding characters who submitted with difficulty, with effort, but submitted all the same. Such men came to the prison as had gone all too far, who had leaped beyond all measure in freedom, so that in the end they committed their crimes as if not of themselves, as if not knowing why, as if in delirium, in a daze; often out of a vanity chafed in the highest degree. But with us they were reined in at once, though some of them had been the terror of whole villages and towns before coming to prison. As he looked around, the newcomer would soon realize that he had landed in another place, that here there was nobody to surprise, and he would humble himself imperceptibly and fall in with the general tone. Outwardly, this general tone consisted of a sort of special personal dignity that pervaded almost every inhabitant of the prison. As if the title of convict, of condemned man, constituted some sort of rank, and an honorable one at that. No signs of shame and repentance! However, there was also a sort of outward, so to speak, official humility, a sort of calm philosophizing: "We're lost folk," they would say. "You didn't know how to live in freedom, now stroll down the green street and inspect the ranks."[2] "You didn't listen to your father and mother, now you can listen to the drumhead's leather." "You thought gold embroidery was no fun, now crush stones till your time is done." This was all oft repeated, both by way of admonition and as ordinary proverbs and sayings, but never seriously. It was all just words. Hardly a one of them acknowledged his lawlessness to himself. Let someone who was not from among the convicts try reproaching a prisoner for his crime and abusing him (though it's not in the Russian spirit to reproach a criminal)—there would be no end of cursing. And what masters at cursing they all were! Theirs was a refined, artistic cursing. They raised cursing to the level of a science; they tried to bring it off not so much by an insulting word as by an insulting meaning, spirit, idea—that was more subtle, more venomous. Incessant quarrels had developed this science still more among them. All these people worked under the lash, consequently they were idle, consequently they were depraved: if they were not depraved before, they became so at hard labor. They had not gathered here by their own will; they were all strangers to each other.

"The devil wore out three pair of boot soles before he got us heaped together!" they said of themselves; and therefore gossip, intrigue, old wives' slander, envy, squabbles, and spite were always in the foreground of this hellish life. No old wife could be so much an old wife as some of these murderers. I repeat, there were strong men among them, characters who all their lives were accustomed to crushing and domineering, hardened, fearless. These men were somehow involuntarily respected; they, for their part, though often very jealous of their reputation, generally tried not to be a burden to anyone, did not get into empty quarrels, behaved with extraordinary dignity, were reasonable and almost always obedient with the authorities—not on principle, not out of a sense of duty, but just so, as if by some sort of contract, a sense of mutual advantage. However, they were also treated with caution. I remember how one of these prisoners, a fearless and resolute man, known to the authorities for his brutal inclinations, was summoned once to be punished for some offense. It was a summer day, during off-hours. The officer who was most immediately and directly in charge of the prison came in person to the guardhouse, located just by our gates, to be present at the punishment. This major was a sort of fatal being for the prisoners; he reduced them to trembling before him. He was insanely strict, he "hurled himself at people," as the convicts used to say. What they feared most in him was his penetrating, lynx-like gaze, from which nothing could be concealed. He somehow saw without looking. When he entered the prison, he already knew what was going on at the other end. The prisoners called him "Eight-eyes." His system was wrong. He only made the already embittered men more bitter by his furious, malicious acts, and if it had not been for the commandant over him, a noble and reasonable man, who occasionally tempered his savage escapades, his administration would have caused much harm. I do not understand how he could have ended happily; he retired alive and well, though he was, incidentally, brought to trial.

The prisoner turned pale when he was summoned. Usually he lay down silently and resolutely under the rods, silently endured the punishment, got up after the punishment all dishevelled, looking upon the misfortune that had befallen him with philosophic equanimity. They always treated him cautiously, however. But this time for some reason he considered himself in the right. He turned pale and, in secret from the convoy, managed to slip a sharp English cobbler's knife into his sleeve. Knives and other sharp instruments were frightfully forbidden in prison. Searches were frequent, unexpected, and thorough; the punishments were harsh; but as it was difficult to find something when a thief decided to hide it, and as knives and tools were a permanent necessity in prison, there was never any lack of them, despite the searches. And if they were taken away, new ones immediately appeared. The whole prison rushed to the fence and looked with bated breath through the chinks in the paling. They all knew that this time Petrov would not lie down under the rods and that the major's end had come. But at the most decisive moment, our major got into his droshky and drove away, entrusting the carrying out of the punishment to another officer. "God himself saved him!" the prisoners said afterwards. As for Petrov, he quite calmly endured the punishment. His wrath departed along with the major. A prisoner is obedient and submissive up to a certain point; but there is a limit that should not be overstepped. Incidentally, nothing could be more curious than these strange fits of impatience and rebelliousness. Often a man endures for several years, resigns himself, suffers the harshest punishments, and suddenly explodes over some small thing, a trifle, almost nothing. From one point of view, he could even be called mad; and so they do call him.

I have already said that in the course of several years I did not see the least sign of repentance among these people, nor the least heavy brooding on their crime, and that the majority of them inwardly considered themselves perfectly in the right. That is a fact. Of course, vanity, bad examples, swagger, false shame are mostly responsible for that. On the other hand, who can say he has probed the depths of these lost hearts and read in them what is hidden from the whole world? Yet it should have been possible, in so many years, to notice, to catch, to grasp at least some feature in those hearts that would testify to inner anguish, to suffering. But there was no such thing, decidedly no such thing. No, crime, it seems, cannot be comprehended from given, ready-made points of view, and its philosophy is a bit more difficult than people suppose. Of course, prisons and the system of forced labor do not correct the criminal; they only punish him and ensure society against the evildoer's further attempts on its peace and quiet. In the criminal himself, prison and the most intense forced labor develop only hatred, a thirst for forbidden pleasures, and a terrible light-mindedness. But I am firmly convinced that the famous system of solitary confinement also achieves only a false, deceptive, external purpose. It sucks the living juice from a man, enervates his soul, weakens it, frightens it, and then presents this morally dried-up, half-crazed mummy as an example of correction and repentance. Of course, a criminal who has risen against society hates it, and almost always considers himself right and society wrong. Besides, he has already suffered its punishment, and he almost considers he has come out clean, has evened the score. Finally, from such points of view, one might reckon that the criminal himself ought to be all but vindicated. But, despite all possible points of view, everyone will agree that there are crimes which always and everywhere, by all possible laws, from the beginning of the world, have been considered indisputable crimes and will be considered so as long as man remains man. Only in prison did I hear stories of the most horrible, most unnatural deeds, the most monstrous murders, told with the most irrepressible, the most childishly merry laughter. The memory of one parricide in particular will not leave me. He was of the nobility, served in the government, and to his sixty-year-old father was something of a prodigal son. His behavior was completely wayward, and he ran deeply into debt. His father tried to curb him, to reason with him; but his father had a house, a farm, was suspected of having money, and—the son killed him, hungry for the inheritance. The crime was discovered only a month later. The murderer himself reported to the police that his father had disappeared no one knew where. He spent the whole month in the most depraved fashion. Finally, in his absence, the police found the body. A sewage ditch covered with boards ran the whole length of the courtyard. The body was lying in that ditch. It was dressed and neat, the gray head had been cut off and put back on the body, and the killer had placed a pillow under it. He did not confess; he was stripped of his nobility and rank, and sent to hard labor for twenty years. All the time I lived with him, he was in the merriest, the most excellent of spirits. He was a whimsical, light-minded, highly unreasonable man, though not at all stupid. I never noticed any particular cruelty in him. The prisoners despised him, not for his crime, which nobody ever mentioned, but for his foolishness, for not knowing how to behave. In conversation he occasionally remembered his father. Once, talking about the healthy constitution hereditary in his family, he added: "*My parent* now, he never complained of any illness, right up to his death." Such brutal insensitivity is, of course, impossible. It is phenomenal; there is some lack in the man's constitution here, some bodily and moral defect still unknown to science, and not merely a crime. Of course, I did not believe in that crime. But people from his town, who supposedly knew all the details of his story, told me the whole case. The facts were so clear, it was impossible not to believe them.

The prisoners heard him cry out once in his sleep at night: "Hold him, hold him! Cut his head off, his head, his head! . . ."

Almost all the prisoners talked and raved in their sleep. Curses, thieves' jargon, knives, axes most often came from their mouths when they raved. "We're beaten folk," they used to say, "we're all beaten up inside; that's why we shout in our sleep."

Government-imposed forced labor was a duty, not an occupation: the prisoner finished his assignment or served his allotted hours of work and went back to prison. The work was looked upon with hatred. Without his own special, personal occupation, to which he was committed with all his mind, with all his reckoning, a man could not live in prison. And how, then, could all these people, intelligent, having lived intensely and wishing to live, forcibly heaped together in this place, forcibly torn away from society and normal life, have a normal and regular life here, by their own will and inclination? From idleness alone, such criminal qualities would develop in a man here as he had no notion of before. Without work, and without lawful, normal property, a man cannot live, he becomes depraved, he turns into a brute. And therefore each person in prison, owing to natural need and some sense of self-preservation, had his own craft and occupation. The long summer days were almost entirely taken up with government work; in the short nights there was barely enough time for sleep. But in winter the prisoners, according to the rules, had to be locked up as soon as it got dark. What is there to do during the long, dull hours of a winter evening? And therefore almost every barrack, despite the prohibition, turned into an enormous workshop. Work itself, being occupied, was not forbidden; but it was strictly forbidden to have tools with you in prison, and without them work was impossible. But people worked on the quiet, and it seems the authorities, in some cases, did not look into it very closely. Many of the convicts came to the prison knowing nothing, but they learned from others and later went out into freedom as good craftsmen. There were bootmakers, and shoemakers, and tailors, and cabinetmakers, and locksmiths, and woodcarvers, and gilders. There was a Jew, Isai Bumstein, a jeweler, who was also a moneylender. They all worked and earned their two cents. Orders for work came from town. Money is minted freedom, and therefore, for a man completely deprived of freedom, it is ten times dearer. Just to have it jingling in his pocket half comforts him, even if he cannot spend it. But money can be spent always and everywhere, the more so as forbidden fruit is twice sweeter. And in prison you could even get hold of vodka. Pipes were strictly forbidden, but everybody smoked them. Money and tobacco saved them from scurvy and other diseases. Work saved them from crime: without work the prisoners would have devoured each other like spiders in a jar. In spite of which, both work and money were forbidden. Surprise searches were often carried out at night, everything forbidden was confiscated, and well hidden as the money was, it still sometimes ended up in the searchers' hands. That was partly why it was not saved, but quickly spent on drink; that was why vodka also found its way into the prison. After each search, the guilty ones, besides being deprived of all their property, would most often be painfully punished. But, after each search, the losses were quickly replenished, new things were obtained at once, and everything went on as before. The authorities knew that, and the prisoners did not murmur against the punishments, though such a life was like setting up house on Mount Vesuvius.

Those who had no craft went into other kinds of business. There were rather original ways. Some, for instance, went into secondhand dealing, and sometimes sold such things as it would never occur to people outside prison walls not only to buy and sell, but even to consider as things. But the prison was very poor and the trade was brisk. The least rag had value and was good for something. From poverty, money also acquired a totally different value in prison than outside it. A big and complicated piece of work was paid for in pennies. Some even made a success of moneylending. An indebted or bankrupt prisoner would take his last possessions to the moneylender, to get a few copper coins from him at frightful interest. If he did not redeem the things in time, they would be sold without delay and without mercy. Moneylending flourished so much that even government-issued things—government linens, footwear, things necessary to every prisoner at every moment— were accepted as pledges. But in the case of such pledges, matters could take a different, though not entirely unexpected, turn: the man who left the pledge and got the money would go at once, without another word, to the senior sergeant, the man immediately in charge of the prison, and report the pledging of government things, and they would at once be taken away from the moneylender, without even informing the higher authorities. Curiously enough, there was sometimes even no quarrel involved: the moneylender would silently and sullenly return what he had to, as if he had even expected it to turn out that way. Maybe he could not help admitting to himself that in the pledger's place he would have done the same. And therefore, if he did curse afterwards, it was without any malice, just so, to clear his conscience.

Generally, they all stole terribly from each other. Almost everybody had his own chest with a lock for keeping government things. This was permitted; but the chests were no salvation. I suppose one can imagine what skillful thieves we had there. One prisoner, a man sincerely devoted to me (I say that without any exaggeration), stole my Bible, the only book we were allowed to have in prison. He confessed it to me the same day, not out of repentance, but out of pity for me, because I spent so long looking for it. There were people who sold vodka and quickly became rich. I will tell about that trade separately sometime; it is quite remarkable. There were many who wound up in prison for smuggling, and therefore it is no surprise that, despite the searches and guards, vodka was brought into the prison that way. Incidentally, smuggling is by nature a special sort of crime. Can you imagine, for instance, that for some smugglers money, profit, plays a secondary role, that it does not come foremost? And yet it is sometimes precisely so. A smuggler works by passion, by vocation. He is something of a poet. He risks all, faces terrible danger, dodges, invents, extricates himself; he sometimes even acts by a sort of inspiration. It is a passion as strong as card-playing. I knew a certain inmate in prison, externally of colossal dimensions, but so meek, quiet, humble, that it was impossible to imagine how he ended up in prison. He was so mild and easy to get along with that in all his time in prison he never quarreled with anybody. But he was from the western border, got put away for smuggling, and, naturally, could not help himself and started running vodka. So many times he was punished for it, and how afraid he was of the rod! And this running of vodka brought him a most negligible income. Only the entrepreneur got rich from it. The odd fellow loved art for art's sake. He was tearful as an old woman, and so many times, after being punished, he would promise and swear to give up smuggling. He would control himself manfully, sometimes for a whole month, but in the end he still could not keep away from it . . . Thanks to such persons, there was no lack of vodka in prison.

Finally, there was another source of income, which, while it did not make the prisoners rich, was constant and beneficial. This was almsgiving. The upper class of our society has no idea how merchants, tradesmen, and all our people care for the "unfortunate." The almsgiving is almost continuous, and almost always in the form of bread, rolls, and kalachi,[3] far more seldom in money. Without these alms, in many places prisoners, especially those awaiting trial, who are kept much more strictly than those who have been sentenced, would have a hard time of it. The alms are religiously shared out among the prisoners. If there is not enough to go around, the rolls are cut into equal parts, sometimes even as many as six parts, so that each prisoner is sure to get his piece. I remember the first time I was given alms in money. It was soon after my arrival in prison. I was coming back from the morning's work alone, with a convoy soldier. I crossed paths with a mother and her daughter, a girl of about ten, pretty as a little angel. I had already seen them once. The mother was a soldier's wife, a widow. Her husband, a young soldier, had been on trial and had died in the prisoners' ward of the hospital while I, too, was lying sick there. His wife and daughter came to take leave of him; they both wept terribly. When she saw me, the girl blushed and whispered something to her mother; the mother stopped at once, rummaged in her purse for a quarter kopeck, and gave it to the girl. The girl rushed after me . . . "Here 'unfortunate,' take a little kopeck for Christ's sake," she cried, running ahead of me and putting the coin in my hand. I took her little kopeck, and the girl went back to her mother perfectly content. I held on to that little kopeck for a long time.

II

First Impressions

The first month and generally the beginning of my life in prison are vividly present now in my imagination. My subsequent prison years flit through my memory much more dimly. Some seem completely effaced, merged together, leaving a single overall impression: heavy, monotonous, stifling.

But everything I experienced in the first days of my hard labor stands before me now as if it happened yesterday. And so it should be.

I clearly remember that, when I first stepped into that life, I was struck that I seemed to find nothing especially striking, unusual, or, better to say, unexpected in it. It all seemed to have flashed by me before in my imagination when, on my way to Siberia, I tried to figure out my destiny ahead of time. But soon a huge number of the strangest surprises, of the most monstrous facts, began to stop me at almost every step. And only later on, after living in prison for quite a long time, did I fully comprehend all the exclusiveness, all the unexpectedness of such an existence, and I marveled at it more and more. I confess that this astonishment accompanied me throughout my long term at hard labor; I could never be reconciled to it.

My first general impression on entering prison was extremely repulsive; but despite that—strangely!—it seemed to me that it was much easier to live in prison than I had imagined on the way there. Though the prisoners were in fetters, they walked freely about the whole prison, swore, sang songs, did their own work, smoked pipes, and even drank vodka (at least a few did), and at night some got down to playing cards. The labor itself, for instance, did not seem to me so very punishing, so *hard*, and only much later did I realize that the punishment and *hardness* of this labor lay not so much in its difficulty and ceaselessness as in its being *forced*, imposed, under the lash. In freedom a peasant most likely works incomparably more, sometimes even at night, especially in summer; but he works for himself, works with a reasonable purpose, and it is incomparably easier for him than for a convict doing forced labor that is totally useless to him. It occurred to me once that if they wanted to crush, to annihilate a man totally, to punish him with the most terrible punishment, so that the most dreadful murderer would shudder at this punishment and be frightened of it beforehand, they would only need to give the labor a character of complete, total uselessness and meaninglessness. If present-day hard labor is uninteresting and boring for the convict, it is still reasonable in itself, as labor: the prisoner makes bricks, digs the earth, plasters, builds; there is meaning and purpose. The worker sometimes even gets carried away by it, wants to do it better, more quickly, more skillfully. But if he were forced, for instance, to pour water from one tub into another and from the other into the first, to grind sand, to carry a pile of dirt from one place to another and back again—I think the prisoner would hang himself after a few days, or commit a thousand crimes, to die rather than endure such humiliation, shame, and torment. To be sure, such a punishment would turn into torture, revenge, and would be meaningless, because it would achieve no reasonable purpose. But since a portion of that torture, meaninglessness, humiliation, and shame is unfailingly present in any labor that is forced, hard labor is incomparably more tormenting than any free labor, precisely for being forced.

However, I came to prison in the winter, in December, and had no idea yet of the summer work, which was five times more difficult. In winter there was generally little government work in our fortress. The prisoners went to the Irtysh[1] to break up old government barges, worked in workshops, shoveled snow around government buildings after blizzards, baked and crushed alabaster, and so on and so forth. The winter day was short, the work was soon done, and our people all returned to prison early, where there was almost nothing for them to do, if they did not happen to have some work of their own. But maybe only a third of the prisoners were busy with their own work; the rest twiddled their thumbs, sauntered aimlessly around all the barracks, cursed, schemed and plotted among themselves, got drunk if some money turned up, at night gambled away their last shirt at cards—and all that from anguish, from idleness, from having nothing to do. Later I understood that, besides the lack of freedom, besides the forced labor, there was one more torment in prison life that was almost worse than all the others. This was *forced communal cohabitation*. Of course, there is also communal cohabitation in other places; but not everybody would want to live with the sort of people that wind up in prison, and I am sure that every convict felt that torment, though, of course, for the most part unconsciously.

The food also seemed quite sufficient to me. The prisoners insisted that there was nothing like it in the penal companies of European Russia. Of that I cannot venture to judge: I have never been there. Besides that, many had the possibility of acquiring their own food. Beef cost half a kopeck a pound, in the summer three kopecks. But the only ones who could buy their own food were those who had a steady supply of money; the majority in the prison ate institutional food. However, when the prisoners praised their food, they were speaking only of the bread and blessing the fact that our bread was held in common, and not given out by weight. The latter horrified them: if it had been given out by weight, a third of them would have gone hungry; if collectively, everybody had enough. Our bread was somehow especially tasty and was famous all over town. This was ascribed to the fortunate construction of the prison ovens. The shchi,[2] though, was very plain. It was cooked in a common cauldron, with the addition of a little grain, and, especially on weekdays, came out watery and thin. I was horrified by the enormous number of cockroaches in it. But the prisoners paid no attention to that.

The first three days I did not go to work, as was done with all new-comers: they were allowed to rest after the journey. But the next day I had to leave the prison to have my irons changed. My fetters were non-regulation, made of chain links, or "clinkers," as the prisoners called them. They were worn over the clothes. The regulation prison fetters, adapted to work, were made not of rings but of four iron rods almost as thick as a finger, connected by three rings. They were worn under the trousers. A strap was fastened to the middle ring, and was in turn attached to the belt at the waist, which was worn immediately over the shirt.

I remember my first morning in the barrack. The drum in the guardhouse by the gate sounded reveille, and some ten minutes later the sergeant on duty began to unlock the barracks. People began to wake up. By the dim light of a cheap tallow candle prisoners, shivering with cold, got up from their bunks. Most of them were silent and sullen with sleep. They yawned, stretched, and wrinkled their branded foreheads. Some crossed themselves, others were already starting to squabble. It was terribly stuffy. Fresh winter air burst through the door the moment it was opened, and billows of steam raced around the barrack. The prisoners crowded around the water buckets; they took the dipper by turns, filled their mouths with water, and washed their hands and faces with it. The water was prepared the evening before by the slop man. According to the rules, each barrack had a prisoner elected by the whole group to serve in the barrack. He was called the slop man, and he did not go out to work. He was charged with seeing to the cleanliness of the barrack, with washing and scrubbing the bunks and the floors, with bringing in and taking out the slop pail, and with providing fresh water in two buckets—for washing in the morning and drinking during the day. Over the dipper, of which there was only one, quarreling broke out immediately.

"Where're you sticking yourself, brand-head!" growled a tall, sullen prisoner, lean and swarthy, with some strange bulges on his shaven skull, shoving another one, fat and squat, with a merry and ruddy face. "Stay put!"

"What're you shouting about! If you stay, you pay! Get lost! Look at this elongated monument! Not a drop of hetiquettanity in the man, brothers!"

"Hetiquettanity" produced a certain effect: many laughed. That was all the merry fat man needed. He was obviously a sort of volunteer buffoon in the barrack. The tall prisoner looked at him with the profoundest contempt.

"Rollicky little cow," he said, as if to himself. "Fattened up on our clean prison bread.* He'll drop a dozen sucking pigs by Christmas, if we're lucky."

The fat man finally got angry.

"And what kind of bird are you!" he suddenly shouted, turning all red.

"The bird kind!"

---

* "Clean prison bread" means bread made from pure flour, with no admixtures. *Author.*

"What kind?"

"That kind."

"What's that kind?"

"Like I said, that kind."

"But what kind?"

The two fastened their eyes on each other. The fat man was waiting for an answer and clenched his fists as if he wanted to throw himself into a fight at once. I really thought there would be a fight. This was all new to me, and I watched with curiosity. Later on I learned that all such scenes were perfectly innocent and were played out, as in a comedy, for the general amusement. They almost never led to a fight. This was all quite characteristic and represented the custom of the prison.

The tall prisoner stood there calm and majestic. He felt they were looking at him and waiting to see whether or not he would shame himself with his reply; he had to hold up his end, to prove that he was indeed a bird, and to show precisely what kind of bird. With inexpressible contempt, he cast a sidelong glance at his adversary, trying, for greater offense, to look somehow over his shoulder, from above, as if he were examining him like a bug, and uttered slowly and distinctly:

"Kagan! . . ."

Meaning that he was the bird Kagan.[3] A loud burst of laughter greeted the prisoner's resourcefulness.

"You're no Kagan, you're a scoundrel!" bellowed the fat man, sensing that he had flunked on all points, and verging on a blind rage.

But once the quarrel turned serious, the fellows were immediately pulled up short.

"What's this racket!" the whole barrack shouted at them.

"Better to fight it out than split your gullets," someone hollered from the corner.

"Fight, yeah, just wait!" came the answer. "Our lads are feisty, uppity; when it's seven against one, they're fearless . . ."

"They're good ones, the both of them! One got to prison for a pound of bread, and the other's a pantry whore, ate some old woman's curds and was whipped for it."[4]

"Well, well, enough of that!" cried the invalid soldier who lived in the barrack to keep order and therefore slept on a special cot in the corner.

"Water, lads! Ninvalid Petrovich is awake! Greetings, Ninvalid Petrovich, our dear brother!"

"Brother . . . What kind of brother am I to you? We never drank up a rouble together, and now it's 'brother'!" grumbled the invalid, putting his arms through the sleeves of his overcoat . . .

They were preparing for roll call; dawn was breaking; a dense, impenetrable crowd of people gathered in the kitchen. The prisoners in their sheepskin jackets and two-colored hats crowded around the bread, which one of the cooks was cutting. The cooks were elected by the whole group, two for each kitchen. They also had charge of the kitchen knife for cutting bread and meat, one for the whole kitchen.

The prisoners placed themselves in all the corners and around the tables, hats and jackets on, belts tied, ready to go straight out to work. Before some of them stood wooden bowls of kvass.[5] They crumbled bread into the kvass and sipped it. The noise and din were unbearable; but some talked sensibly and quietly in the corners.

"Greetings and welcome to you, dear old Antonych!" said a young prisoner, sitting down beside a scowling and toothless prisoner.

"Well, greetings to you, if you mean it," the man said, not raising his eyes and trying to chew his bread with his toothless gums.

"And here I thought you was dead, Antonych, I really did."

"No, you die first, and me after . . ."

I sat down beside them. On my right two grave prisoners were talking, obviously trying to maintain their dignity before each other.

"No fear they'll steal from me," said one. "The fear, brother, is that I'll do the stealing."

"Well, don't go touching me with your bare hand: I'll burn you."

"As if you'll burn me! You're a mucker same as us; there's no other name for it . . . She'll fleece you without so much as a thank-you. I dunked my last little kopeck here, too. The other day she came herself. Where was I to go with her? I began asking to go to Fedka the hangman's: he had a house on the outskirts, bought it from mangy Solomon, the Yid, the one who strung himself up later . . ."

"I know. He used to smuggle vodka for us three years ago. We called him Dark Pothouse Grishka. I know."

"No, you don't. Dark Pothouse was somebody else."

"The hell he was somebody else! A fat lot you know! I'll bring you as many witnessaries as you . . ."

"You will, will you! You're what, and I'm who?"

"Who? I don't want to brag, but I used to beat you—that's who!"

"You beat me? The man who could beat me hasn't been born yet, and whoever tried is eating dirt."

"You Moldavian plague!"

"The Siberian pest on you!"

"Go talk to a Turkish saber!"

And the abuse took off.

"All right, all right, enough racket!" people around them shouted. "They didn't know how to live in freedom; here they're glad to get clean bread . . ."

Things quieted down at once. Verbal abuse, "tongue lashing," was allowed. It was partly an amusement for everybody. But it usually did not lead to fighting, and only rarely, in exceptional cases, did enemies come to blows. A fight would be reported to the major; there would be inquiries, he would come himself—in short, it would be bad for everybody, and therefore fights were not allowed. And the enemies themselves abused each other more for diversion, as an exercise of style. Often they deceived themselves, they began in a terrible fever, frenziedly. You think: they're going to fall on each other. Nothing of the sort: they reach a certain point and break it off at once. In the beginning all this was extremely surprising to me. I have purposely given examples here of the most ordinary prison conversations. I could not imagine at first how it was possible to curse for the pleasure of it, to find amusement in it, a nice exercise, gratification. However, we also must not forget vanity. A cursing dialectician was respected. He was all but applauded, like an actor.

Just the evening before I had noticed them looking askance at me.

I had already caught several dark looks. Other prisoners, on the contrary, circled around me, suspecting I had brought money with me. They immediately started to fawn on me, began teaching me how to wear my new fetters, got me—for money, of course—a little chest with a lock for putting away the prison things I had already received and some of the linen I had brought to prison with me. The very next day they stole it and drank up the money. One of them later became very devoted to me, though he never stopped stealing from me on every suitable occasion. He did it without any embarrassment, almost unconsciously, as if out of duty, and it was impossible to be angry with him.

Among other things, they taught me that I should have my own tea, that it would not be bad if I acquired a teapot for myself, and meanwhile they borrowed someone else's for me and recommended me a cook, saying that for thirty kopecks a month he would cook whatever I liked, if I wished to eat separately and buy my own provisions . . . Naturally, they borrowed money from me, and on the first day alone they each came to borrow three times.

In prison they generally took a dark and unfavorable view of former noblemen.

Even though they were already stripped of all their property rights and were completely equal to all the other prisoners—the prisoners would never recognize them as their comrades. This happened not even from conscious prejudice, but just so, quite sincerely, unconsciously. They sincerely considered us noblemen, even though they themselves liked to taunt us with our fall.

"No, enough now! Knock it off! Through Moscow Pyotr used to strut, now Pyotr's stuck here on his butt"—and suchlike pleasantries.

They loved to watch our sufferings, which we tried not to let them see. In the beginning it was especially hard for us at work, because we were not as strong as they were, and we could not do our full share. There is nothing more difficult than entering into the simple people's confidence (especially such people) and earning their love.

There were several noblemen in the prison. First of all, there were five Poles. I will speak of them sometime separately. The convicts disliked the Poles terribly, even more than the noble Russian prisoners. The Poles (I am speaking only of the political criminals) treated them with a sort of refined, offensive politeness, were extremely uncommunicative, and were quite unable to conceal their loathing for them, and the latter realized it very well and paid them back in kind.

It took me almost two years of living in the prison before I gained the sympathy of some of the convicts. But the greater part of them finally came to like me and recognized me as a "good" man.

Of Russian noblemen, besides myself, there were four. One was a mean and scoundrelly little creature, terribly depraved, a spy and informer by profession. I had heard about him even before I got to prison and from the first days broke off all relations with him. Another was that same parricide I have already spoken of in my notes. The third was Akim Akimych; rarely have I seen such an odd bird as this Akim Akimych. He is sharply imprinted in my memory. He was tall, lean, weak-witted, terribly illiterate, extremely pedantic, and punctilious as a German. The convicts laughed at him; but some were even afraid to have anything to do with him, because of his carping, demanding, and cantankerous character. From the first step he chummed them up, swore at them, even fought. He was phenomenally honest. He would notice some injustice and immediately mix into it, though it was none of his business. He was naïve in the extreme; for instance, he sometimes scolded the prisoners, reproaching them for being thieves, and earnestly entreated them not to steal. He had been a sublieutenant in the Caucasus. He and I fell in with each other from the first day, and he told me his case at once. He had started in the Caucasus as a junker[6] in an infantry regiment, ground away for a long time, was finally made an officer, and was sent to some fortress as a senior commander. One allied princeling in the neighborhood set fire to his fortress and attacked it by night, but the attack failed. Akim Akimych played it clever and did not give any sign that he knew who the malefactor was. The affair was blamed on hostile princes, and a month later Akim Akimych invited the princeling for a friendly visit. The man came, suspecting nothing. Akim Akimych drew up his detachment, exposed and rebuked the prince publicly, proved to him that setting fire to fortresses was shameful. Then he read him a most detailed exhortation on how allied princelings should behave in the future, and in conclusion he had him shot, which he immediately reported to the authorities in full detail. For all that he was tried and sentenced to death, but the sentence was mitigated and he was sent to Siberia, to hard labor of the second degree, to twelve years in prison. He was fully aware that he had acted wrongly, told me that he knew it even before he had the princeling shot, knew that an ally should be tried according to the law; but, though he knew it, he seemed quite unable to understand the real nature of his guilt:

"For pity's sake! He set fire to my fortress! What should I do, bow down to him for it?" he said in response to my objections.

But, though the prisoners made fun of Akim Akimych's lunacy, they still respected him for his precision and skill.

There was no craft that Akim Akimych did not know. He was a joiner, a bootmaker, a shoemaker, a house painter, a gilder, a locksmith—and he had learned all that in prison. He was self-taught in everything: one glance and he did it. He also made various boxes, baskets, lanterns, children's toys, and sold them in town. In that way he picked up a little money, and he immediately spent it on extra linen, on a softer pillow, installed a folding mattress. He lived in the same barrack with me and did me many good turns during my first days at hard labor.

Coming out of the prison to go to work, the prisoners formed two rows in front of the guardhouse; before and behind the prisoners, convoy soldiers lined up with loaded muskets. An officer of the engineers appeared, a sergeant, and several lower-ranking engineers attached to the works. The sergeant counted the prisoners and sent them off in parties where they were needed for work.

I was sent along with others to the engineering workshop. It was a low stone building that stood in a large yard heaped with various materials. Here was the smithy, the locksmith's shop, the joiner's, the painter's, and so on. Akim Akimych used to come there and work in the painter's shop, boiled linseed oil, mixed paints, and finished tables and furniture in imitation walnut.

While waiting for my fetters to be changed, I got to talking with Akim Akimych about my first impressions of prison.

"Yes, sir, they don't like noblemen," he observed, "especially political criminals, they devour them gladly, and no wonder, sir. First, you and the people are different, not like them at all, and, second, they're all former serfs or from the ranks. Judge for yourself, how could they like you? Life is hard here, I can tell you. But in Russian penal companies it's harder still, sir. We have some from there. They can't praise our prison highly enough, as if they'd gone from hell to paradise. The trouble isn't the work, sir. They say there, in the first category, the authorities aren't entirely military, or at least they act differently from ours. There, they say, convicts can live in their own little houses. I've never been there, but that's what they say, sir. They don't get their heads shaved; they don't wear uniforms; though, by the way, it's good that we dress in uniforms here and get shaved; in any case there's greater order, and it's more pleasing to the eye. Only they don't like it. And then just look what rabble they are, sir! One's a cantonist, another a Circassian, the third a schismatic,[7] the fourth an Orthodox peasant, his family and dear children left behind, the fifth a Jew, the sixth a Gypsy, the seventh who knows what, and they all have to live together anyhow, to get along, to eat from the same bowl, to sleep on the same bunk. And here's your freedom: you can eat an extra bit only on the sly, every penny has to be hidden in your boot, and there's nothing but prison and more prison . . . Like it or not, you get foolish in the head."

But that I already knew. I especially wanted to ask about our major. Akim Akimych kept no secrets, and, I recall, my impression was not entirely pleasant.

But I was doomed to live for two years under his command. Everything Akim Akimych told me about him turned out to be perfectly correct, with the difference that the impression of reality is always stronger than the impression from a mere account. He was a dreadful man, precisely because such a man had almost unlimited power over two hundred souls. In himself he was only disorderly and malicious, nothing more. He looked upon the prisoners as his natural enemies, and that was his first and greatest mistake. He actually had some abilities; but everything, even what was good, came out in some distorted form. Unrestrained, malicious, he would burst into the prison sometimes even at night, and if he noticed that a prisoner was sleeping on his left side or on his back, he would punish him in the morning: "Sleep on your right side, as I ordered." In the prison he was hated and feared like the plague. He had a purple, spiteful face. Everyone knew that he was entirely in the hands of his orderly, Fedka. Most of all he loved his poodle, Tresorka, and he nearly lost his mind from grief when Tresorka fell ill. They say he sobbed over him as over his own son; he drove one veterinarian out and, as his habit was, nearly gave him a beating, and, hearing from Fedka that there was a convict in the prison who was a self-taught veterinarian whose treatments were very successful, he immediately sent for him.

"Save us! I'll shower you with gold if you cure Tresorka!" he shouted at the prisoner.

This was a Siberian muzhik, actually a very able veterinarian, but cunning, shrewd, a perfect little muzhik.

"I take a look at Tresorka," he told the prisoners later, though it was a long while after his visit to the major, when the whole thing had been forgotten. "I look: the dog's lying on a sofa, on a white pillow; and I can see he's got an inflammation, that he needs a bloodletting, and he'll recover, by gorry, I say to myself! Then I think, 'But what if I don't cure him, what if he croaks?' 'No, Your Honor,' I say, 'you called me too late. If it was at this same time yesterday or the day before, your dog would be cured; but now I can't cure him . . .'"

So Tresorka died.

I was told in detail how someone had wanted to kill our major. There was a certain inmate in the prison. He had been living with us for several years already and was distinguished by his meek behavior. It was also noticed that he almost never spoke to anyone. So he was considered something of a holy fool.[8] He was literate and for the whole last year constantly read the Bible, read it day and night. When everyone had fallen asleep, he would get up at midnight, light a wax church candle, climb onto the stove,[9] open the book, and read till morning. One day he went and announced to the sergeant that he did not want to go to work. This was reported to the major; the man boiled over and immediately came galloping himself. The prisoner rushed at him with a previously prepared brick, but he missed. He was seized, tried, and punished. It all happened very quickly. Three days later he died in the hospital. As he lay dying, he said that he held no evil against anyone, but only wanted to suffer. By the way, he did not belong to any schismatic sect. He was remembered with respect in the prison.

They finally changed my fetters. Meanwhile several kalach girls had come to the workshop one after another. Some were quite little girls. They usually came with kalachi until they were of age; their mothers baked them, and they sold them. Once they were grown up, they kept coming, but now without kalachi; that is how it almost always happened. There were some who were no longer girls. A kalach cost half a kopeck, and almost all the prisoners bought them.

I noticed one prisoner, a joiner, already gray-haired, but ruddy-faced and smilingly flirtatious with the kalach girls. Before they came, he wrapped a red calico scarf around his neck. One fat and completely pockmarked wench set her tray down on his workbench. A conversation began.

"Why didn't you come there yesterday?" the prisoner began with a smug little smile.

"That's a good one! I did come, and it was you that played hooky," the pert wench replied.

"We were called for, otherwise I'd have showed up without fail . . . And two days ago all your friends came to me."

"Who's that, then?"

"Maryashka, and Khavroshka, and Chekunda, and Two-penny . . ."

"What is this?" I asked Akim Akimych. "Can it be? . . ."

"It happens, sir," he replied, modestly lowering his eyes, because he was an extremely chaste man.

It did happen, of course, but very rarely and with the greatest difficulty. Generally, there were more lovers of drink, for instance, than of that sort of thing, despite all the natural burden of this forced life. It was hard to get hold of a woman. You had to choose the time, the place, make arrangements, set up a meeting, hunt for seclusion, which was especially difficult, win over the guards, which was still more difficult, and generally spend a heap of money, relatively speaking. But all the same I did manage, later on, to be a witness to occasional love scenes. I remember once in the summer there were three of us in some shed on the bank of the Irtysh, firing up a brick-baking oven. The guards were nice fellows. Finally, two "prompters," as the prisoners call them, showed up.

"Well, where were you sitting so long? At the Zverkovs', I bet," the prisoner they had come to see greeted them, having waited a good while already.

"Sat for a long time, did I? That magpie just sat longer on the post than I did at their place," the girl replied merrily.

She was the dirtiest girl in the world. This was Chekunda. Two-penny came with her. She was beyond all description.

"And it's a long time since I've seen you," the philanderer went on, turning to Two-penny. "Seems you've lost weight."

"Maybe so. I used to be real fat, but now—it's like I swallowed a needle."

"So you keep company with soldiers, eh?"

"No, it's wicked people fed you that about us—but anyhow, what of it? Though I go without a rib, I love the soldiers, that's no fib."

"Drop them and love us; we've got money . . ."

To complete the picture, imagine this philanderer, head shaved, fettered, in stripes, and under guard.

I said good-bye to Akim Akimych and, learning that I could go back to the prison, took my guard and went home. People were already gathering. The first to come back were those who worked at set tasks. The only way to make a prisoner work diligently was to give him a set task. Sometimes these tasks were enormous, but even so they got done twice sooner than if a man was made to work until the dinner drum. Once the task was done, the prisoner went home without hindrance, and no one could stop him.

We did not eat together, but haphazardly, whoever came first; besides, the kitchen had no room for everybody at once. I tried the shchi, but, being unaccustomed, was unable to swallow it, so I made myself some tea. We sat down at the end of the table. I had a comrade with me, a nobleman like myself.

Prisoners came and went. However, there was room enough, not everyone had gathered yet. A group of five men seated themselves separately at a big table. The cook poured them two bowls of shchi and set a whole skillet of fried fish on the table. They were celebrating something and were eating their own food. They looked askance at us. A Pole came in and sat down beside us.

"I wasn't at home, but I know everything!" a tall prisoner shouted loudly, coming into the kitchen and glancing around at everyone there.

He was about fifty, muscular and lean. There was something sly and at the same time merry in his face. Especially remarkable was his thick, pendulous lower lip: it gave his face an extremely comical look.

"So you had a good night? Why don't you say good day? To our Kurskis!" he added, sitting down beside the men eating their own food. "Greetings! Welcome your guest."

"We're not from Kursk, brother."

"Tambov, then?"

"Not from Tambov either. We've got nothing for you, brother. Go find a rich muzhik and ask him."

"I've got Ivan-Rumble and Marya-Hiccup in my belly today, brothers—where does he live, this rich muzhik?"

"Gazin's a rich muzhik: go to him."

"Gazin's on a drinking binge today, brothers; he's drinking up his whole purse."

"That's twenty roubles," another man observed. "It's profitable, brothers, selling vodka."

"So you won't receive a guest? Well, then we'll gulp from the common bowl."

"Go and ask for tea. The gentlemen there are having tea."

"What gentlemen, there are no gentlemen here; they're just like us now," one prisoner who was sitting in the corner observed gloomily. Until then he had not uttered a word.

"I'd like some tea, but I'm ashamed to ask: I've got my anbishin," the prisoner with the thick lip said, looking at us good-naturedly.

"I'll give you tea, if you like," I said, inviting the prisoner. "Want some?"

"Want some? How could I not!" He came over to the table.

"See, at home he was just a clodhopper, but here he's learned about tea; wants to drink with gentlemen," the gloomy prisoner pronounced.

"Does nobody drink tea here?" I asked him, but he did not deign to answer.

"Here come the kalachi. Honor us with a little kalach!"

They brought the kalachi. A young prisoner brought a whole string of them and sold them all over the prison. The kalach girl gave him every tenth one for it; that one kalach was what he counted on.

"Kalachi, kalachi!" he cried, coming into the kitchen. "Hot Moscow kalachi! I'd eat plenty, but my pocket's empty. Well, lads, here's the last of them: has anybody got a mother?"

This appeal to maternal love made them all laugh, and they took several kalachi from him.

"You know, brothers," he went on, "Gazin's going to carouse himself into trouble today. By God! Found a good time for a binge. Eight-eyes is bound to turn up."

"They'll hide him. What, is he badly drunk?"

"Far gone! He's turning mean."

"Well, it'll come to fists then . . ."

"Who are they talking about?" I asked the Pole who was sitting beside me.

"Gazin, a prisoner. He deals in vodka here. Once he makes enough money, he drinks it away at once. He's cruel and malicious. He's quiet enough when he's sober, but when he's drunk, it all comes out. He goes for people with a knife. Then they calm him down."

"How do they do that?"

"Ten or so prisoners fall on him and beat him terribly, till he's lost all consciousness, that is, till he's half-dead. Then they put him on a bunk and cover him with a coat."

"But mightn't they kill him?"

"It would kill another man, but not him. He's terribly strong, stronger than anybody here in prison, and of the sturdiest constitution. The next morning he gets up feeling perfectly fine."

"Tell me, please," I went on questioning the Pole, "I see them eating their own food, while I'm drinking tea. And yet they look at me as if they envy this tea. What does it mean?"

"It's not about the tea," the Pole replied. "They're angry with you because you're a nobleman and not like them. Many of them would like to pick on you. They'd like very much to insult you and humiliate you. You're going to see a lot more unpleasantness here. It's terribly hard here for all of us. For us it's harder in all respects. It takes a lot of indifference to get used to it. You'll meet with unpleasantness and abuse more than once over tea and your own food, though quite often quite a lot of them here have their own food, and some drink tea all the time. They can, but you can't."

Having said that, he got up and left the table. A few minutes later, his words came true . . .

III

First Impressions

M—cki (the Pole who talked to me)[1] had only just left when Gazin, completely drunk, barged into the kitchen.

A drunken prisoner, in broad daylight, on a weekday, when everybody was obliged to go out to work, with a strict superior who might turn up in the prison at any moment, with a sergeant who was in charge of the prisoners and never left the prison, with the guards, the invalids—in short, with all this strictness—completely confused the notions of the prisoners' everyday life that had been taking shape in me. I had to spend a long time in prison before I could explain to myself all these facts that puzzled me so much in the first days of my term.

I have already said that the prisoners always had their own work and that this work was a natural need in the life at hard labor; that, apart from this need, a prisoner passionately loves money and values it above everything, almost on a par with freedom, and that it is enough to have it jingling in his pocket for him to be comforted. On the other hand, he is gloomy, sad, restless, and dispirited if he has none, and then he is ready to steal or do anything at all only so as to get it. But, though money was so precious in prison, it never stayed long with the lucky fellow who had it. First of all, it was hard to keep it from being stolen or confiscated. If the major laid hands on it during surprise searches, he immediately confiscated it. He may have used it to improve the prisoners' food; in any case it was turned over to him. But most often it was stolen: you could not rely on anyone. Later on we discovered a way of keeping money in total security. We gave it for safekeeping to an old man, an Old Believer, who came to us from the Starodubsky settlements, and before that from Vietka . . . [2] I cannot help saying a few words about him, though it takes me away from my subject.

He was a little old man of about sixty, small, gray-haired. He made a distinct impression on me from the first glance. He was so unlike the other prisoners: there was something so serene and gentle in his gaze that I remember looking with special pleasure at his clear, bright eyes, surrounded by small, radiating wrinkles. I often talked with him, and rarely in my life have I met such a kind, good-natured being. He was sent up for an extremely serious crime. Among the Starodubsky Old Believers some converts to Orthodoxy began to appear. The government strongly encouraged them and began making every effort to further the conversions of other dissenters. The old man together with other fanatics resolved to "stand for the faith," as he put it. The building of a church for the reconciled was begun, and they burned it down. The old man was sent to hard labor as one of the instigators. He had been a well-to-do tradesman; he left a wife and children behind; but he went into exile firmly, because in his blindness he regarded it as "suffering for the faith." After living with him for some time, you would involuntarily wonder: how could this man, humble, meek as a child, be a rebel? I spoke with him several times "about faith." He never yielded anything in his convictions; but there was never any anger or any hatred in his objections. And yet he had destroyed the church and did not deny it. It seemed that, with his convictions, he must regard his act and the "suffering" he endured for it as a glorious deed. But however attentively I looked, however I studied him, I never noticed any sign of vanity or pride in him. We had other Old Believers with us in prison, most of them Siberians. They were highly developed folk, cunning muzhiks, great Bible readers and dogmatists, and, in their own way, strong dialecticians; haughty, arrogant folk, devious and intolerant in the highest degree. The old man was a completely different sort of person. Though maybe a greater Bible reader than all of them, he avoided arguments. In character he was highly gregarious. He was mirthful, laughed frequently—not with the coarse, cynical laughter of the convicts, but with a serene, gentle laughter that had much childlike artlessness in it and that somehow especially suited his gray hair. I may be mistaken, but it seems to me that you can know a man by his laughter, and if from the first encounter you like the laughter of some completely unknown person, you may boldly say that he is a good man. The old man gained universal respect throughout the prison, which did not make him vainglorious in the least. The prisoners called him "grandpa" and never offended him. I partly understood how he was able to influence his fellow believers. But despite the apparent firmness with which he endured his hard labor, a deep, incurable sadness lay hidden in him, which he tried to conceal from everybody. I lived in the same barrack with him. Once during the night, past two o'clock, I woke up and heard a quiet, restrained weeping. The old man was sitting on the stove (the same one on which the Bible-reading prisoner used to pray at night, the one who had wanted to kill the major) and praying from his handwritten book. He was weeping, and I heard him say from time to time: "Lord, do not abandon me! Lord, give me strength! Children, my little ones, my dears, I'll never see you again!" I cannot tell you how sad I felt. So it was to this old man that almost all the prisoners gradually began to give their money for safekeeping. Almost all the men in the prison were thieves, but for some reason everybody suddenly became convinced that the old man simply could not steal. They knew that he hid the money entrusted to him somewhere, but it was in such a secret place that nobody was able to find it. Later he explained his secret to me and to some of the Poles. There was a knot in one of the posts that looked as if it was firmly embedded in the tree. But it could be taken out, and there was a deep hollow behind it. Grandpa hid the money in it and put the knot back in place, so that nobody could ever find anything.

But I have digressed from my story. I stopped at why money never stayed long in a prisoner's pocket. But, apart from the difficulty of safeguarding it, there is so much anguish in prison, and a prisoner is by nature a being who yearns so much for freedom, and, finally, by his social position, is so light-minded and disorderly, that he is naturally inclined to suddenly "go all out," to carouse away all his capital, with noise and music, so as to forget his anguish if only for a moment. It was even strange to watch some of them work without letup, sometimes for several months, solely in order to squander all their earnings in one day, clean themselves out, and then drudge away for several more months until the next binge. Many of them liked buying new clothes, which were unfailingly of the civilian sort: non-uniform black trousers, vests, Siberian kaftans. Calico shirts and metal-studded belts were also very popular. On feast days they would dress up, and the dressed-up man unfailingly went about all the barracks showing himself to everybody.

The self-satisfaction of a well-dressed man was almost childish—and in many ways the prisoners were perfect children. True, all these fine things somehow suddenly left their owner, were sometimes pawned and let go for nothing the same evening. However, a binge unfolded gradually. It was usually timed to a feast day or the binger's name day. The prisoner would get up in the morning, light a candle before the icon and pray; then he would dress up and order himself a dinner: beef and fish would be bought, Siberian dumplings prepared; he would eat like a horse, almost always alone, rarely inviting comrades to share his meal. Then vodka would appear: the name-day man would get plastered and unfailingly walk around the barracks, reeling and stumbling, trying to show everybody that he was "on a spree," and thereby earn universal respect. Everywhere among Russian people a certain sympathy is felt for a drunk man; but in prison a man on a spree was even shown deference. Prison carousing had its own sort of aristocratism. In making merry, a prisoner unfailingly hired music. There was a little Pole in the prison, a runaway soldier, quite a vile little fellow, but who played the fiddle and had his own instrument—it was all he possessed. He did not know any craft and thus his only earnings came from getting hired by carousers to play merry dances. His duty consisted in constantly following his drunken master from barrack to barrack and sawing away at his fiddle for all he was worth. Boredom and anguish often showed on his face. But the cry "Play, you've been paid for it" made him saw away again and again. A prisoner setting out on a spree could be firmly assured that, if he got very drunk, he would unfailingly be looked after, put to bed in time, and always be hidden somewhere if the authorities appeared, and all that quite disinterestedly. For their part, the sergeant and the invalids who lived and kept order in the prison could also be completely at ease: the drunk man could not cause any disorder. The whole barrack looked after him, and if he got noisy or rowdy—he would be pacified at once, even simply tied up. And therefore the lower-ranking prison authorities turned a blind eye on drunkenness and declined to notice it. They knew very well that if they forbade vodka, there would be something worse. But where did the vodka come from?

Vodka was bought right in the prison, from so-called taverners.[3] There were several of them, and they carried on their trade continuously and successfully, even though there were generally few drinkers and "carousers," because carousing called for money, and prisoner money was hard to come by. The trade began, went on, and was concluded in a rather original way. Suppose a prisoner has no craft and no wish to work (there were such), but wants to get money and besides is an impatient man, who wants to make a quick fortune. He has some money to start with, and he decides to deal in vodka: a bold venture, involving great risk. You could pay for it with your hide and lose both goods and capital straight off. But the taverner goes into it. He has little money to start with, so the first time he brings the vodka to the prison himself and, naturally, sells it for a good profit. He repeats the experiment a second and third time, and if he is not caught by the authorities, he quickly sells out, and only then does he establish a real business on broad foundations: he becomes an entrepreneur, a capitalist, keeps agents and assistants, risks much less, and earns more and more. His assistants take the risks.

In prison there are always many people who have squandered, gambled, or caroused away everything to the last kopeck, people without a craft, pitiful and bedraggled, but endowed with a certain degree of boldness and resolution. Such people have nothing left for capital, nothing intact but their hide; it can still serve for something, and it is this last capital that the spendthrift carouser decides to invest. He goes to an entrepreneur and hires himself out to smuggle vodka into the prison; a rich taverner has several such employees. Somewhere outside the prison there exists such a person—a soldier, a tradesman, sometimes even a wench—who, on the entrepreneur's money and for a certain reward, comparatively rather decent, buys vodka in a pothouse and hides it in a secluded spot where the prisoners go to work. The supplier almost always begins by testing the quality of the vodka and sips some—mercilessly topping it up with water; take it or leave it, the prisoner cannot be too choosy: it is already enough that his money has not been lost altogether and the vodka has been delivered; whatever it is, it is still vodka. The smuggler, pointed out to the supplier beforehand, comes to him from the prison taverner with bulls' guts. These guts have first been washed out, then filled with water to keep them in their original moist and pliant state, so as to be suitable in due time for holding vodka. Having filled the guts with vodka, the prisoner ties them around himself, as far as possible in the most hidden parts of his body. Naturally, the contrabandist here shows all his adroitness, all his thievish cunning. It is partly a matter of honor: he has to fool both the guards and the sentries. And he does fool them: a guard, often a new recruit, will always be outsmarted by a good thief. Naturally, the guard is studied beforehand; the time and place of work are also taken into consideration. The prisoner, a stove maker, for instance, will climb up on a stove: who is going to see what he's doing there? The guard is not going to follow after him. Coming to the prison, he keeps a coin in his hand—fifteen or twenty silver kopecks, just in case—and waits for the corporal at the gates. Each prisoner coming back from work is searched and felt all over by the corporal of the guards, who then unlocks the prison gates for him. The vodka smuggler usually counts on his being ashamed to feel too thoroughly in certain places. But sometimes the shrewd corporal gets to those places as well and feels out the vodka. Then there remains one last resort: the smuggler, silently and in secret from the guards, slips the hidden coin into the corporal's hand. It may happen that by means of this maneuver he passes through safely and brings in the vodka. But sometimes the maneuver does not succeed, and then he has to settle accounts with his last capital, that is, his hide. A report is made to the major, the capital is whipped, and whipped painfully, the vodka is confiscated, and the smuggler takes it all on himself, without betraying the entrepreneur, but, let us note, not because he scorns informing, but solely because informing is not profitable for him: he would be whipped anyway; his only consolation would be that they both got whipped. But he still needs the entrepreneur, though, by prior arrangement, the smuggler does not get a kopeck from him for his whipped back. As for informing in general, it usually flourishes. In prison an informer is not subject to the least humiliation; to be indignant at him is even unthinkable. He is not shunned, people are friends with him, so that if you were to start proving to the prisoners all the vileness of informing, you would meet with complete incomprehension. That inmate from the nobility, depraved and base, with whom I broke all relations, was friends with the major's orderly Fedka and served him as a spy, and Fedka told the major everything he heard about the prisoners. We all knew it, and it never even occurred to anyone to punish or even reproach the scoundrel.

But I digress. Of course, it happens that vodka is brought in safely; then the entrepreneur receives the delivered guts, pays for them, and begins to calculate. The calculation shows that his goods have already cost him very dearly; and so, for greater gain, he decants it again, diluting it again almost by half with water, and, now quite prepared, awaits a buyer. The next Sunday, and sometimes on a weekday, a buyer appears: he is a prisoner who has worked like an ox for several months and saved a bit of money in order to drink it all up on a prearranged day. The poor toiler has been dreaming about this day long before its arrival, in sleep and in happy reveries over his work, and its charm has kept up his spirits in the dull course of prison life. At last the dawn of the bright day shows in the east; the money has been saved, not confiscated, not stolen, and he takes it to the taverner. The man first serves him vodka as pure as possible, that is, only diluted by half; but as the vodka is drunk, the bottle immediately gets topped up with water. A glass of vodka costs five or six times more than in a pothouse. Imagine how many such glasses you have to drink, and how much you have to pay, in order to get drunk! But, being unaccustomed to drinking and having abstained for a long time, the prisoner gets tipsy rather quickly, and usually goes on drinking until he drinks up all his money. Then all the new things go: the taverner is at the same time a usurer. First the most recently bought personal things go to him, then it gets on to old junk, and, finally, the government things. Having drunk up everything to the last rag, the drunkard goes to sleep, and waking up the next day with the unavoidable din in his head, he begs the taverner in vain for at least one sip of vodka for the hair of the dog. He sadly endures his adversity, and sets to work again the same day, and again works for several months without letup, thinking of the happy day of his binge, which has irrevocably sunk into oblivion, and gradually beginning to take heart and wait for another such day, which, though still far off, is sure to come in due course.

As for the taverner, having finally earned the enormous sum of several dozen roubles, he gets a last supply of vodka and now does not dilute it with water, because he intends it for himself: enough dealing, it's time to celebrate! Carousing, drinking, eating, music begin. He has great means; even the nearest, lowest prison authorities have been buttered up. The binge sometimes goes on for several days. Naturally, the supply of vodka is soon drunk; then the carouser goes to other taverners, who are already expecting him, and drinks until he has drunk up every kopeck. However well the prisoners protect the carouser, he is sometimes noticed by the higher authorities, the major or the duty officer. He is taken to the guardhouse, his capital, if any is found on him, is confiscated, and in conclusion he is whipped. He shakes himself, goes back to the prison, and a few days later again takes up his profession of taverner. Some carousers, the rich ones, naturally, also dream about the fair sex. For big money, instead of working, they sometimes make their way from the fortress to the outskirts, accompanied by a bribed guard. There, in some remote little house, somewhere on the very edge of town, a great feast is thrown, and really big money is squandered. Even a prisoner is not scorned if he has money; a guard who knows the business is somehow chosen beforehand. Such guards are usually future candidates for prison themselves. However, everything can be done for money, and such excursions almost always remain secret. It should be added that they occur quite rarely; they require a good deal of money, and lovers of the fair sex resort to other means that are totally without danger.

From the first days of my prison life, one young prisoner, an extremely pretty boy, aroused a special curiosity in me. His last name was Sirotkin. He was a rather mysterious being in many respects. I was struck first of all by his beautiful face; he was no more than twenty-three years old. He was in a special section, without a term, which meant he was considered one of the most important military criminals. Gentle and meek, he spoke little, laughed rarely. His eyes were blue, his features regular, his face clean, tender, his hair a light brown. Even his half-shaven head did little to disfigure him, such a pretty boy he was. He had no skills, but he managed to get money, not much, but often. He was noticeably lazy and went about looking slovenly. Unless someone else dressed him nicely, sometimes even in a red shirt, and Sirotkin would obviously be glad of the new clothes: he would go about the barracks, showing himself off. He did not drink, did not play cards, hardly ever quarreled with anyone. He used to stroll behind the barracks—hands in his pockets, quiet, pensive. What he could have been thinking about was hard to imagine. You would sometimes call to him out of curiosity and ask him about something, and he would answer at once and even somehow deferentially, not prisoner-fashion, but always briefly, tersely; and he would look at you like a ten-year-old boy. When he happened to have money, he did not buy something necessary, did not have his jacket mended or get himself new boots, but would buy a kalach or a gingerbread and eat it up—just as if he were seven years old. "Hey, Sirotkin," the prisoners used to say, "you orphan from Kazan!"[4] During off-hours he usually hangs around the other barracks; almost everybody is busy doing something, he alone does nothing. They would say something to him, almost always in mockery (he and his comrades were often made fun of)—he says nothing, turns, and goes to another barrack; but sometimes, if they teased him badly, he would blush. I often thought: what has this quiet, simple-hearted being done to wind up in prison? Once I was lying in the hospital, in the prisoners' ward. Sirotkin was also sick and lay next to me. One evening he and I got to talking; he became unexpectedly animated and, incidentally, told me how he had been sent for a soldier, how his mother had wept over him, seeing him off, and how hard it had been for him as a recruit. He added that he had been unable to endure life as a recruit, because everyone was so angry there, so stern, and the commanders were almost always displeased with him . . .

"How did it end?" I asked him. "What did you do to land here? And in the special section at that . . . Ah, Sirotkin, Sirotkin!"

"I spent only a year in the battalion, Alexander Petrovich; and I came here because I killed Grigory Petrovich, my company commander."

"So I heard, Sirotkin, but I don't believe it. How could you kill anybody?"

"That's what happened, Alexander Petrovich. It was so-o hard for me."

"But how do other recruits live through it? Of course, it's hard at first, but then they get used to it, and, lo and behold, out comes a fine soldier. Your mother must have pampered you, fed you on milk and gingerbread till you were eighteen?"

"It's true my dear mother loved me very much, sir. When I went as a reecruit, she took to her bed, and I've heard she never got up again . . . Life as a reecruit got very bitter for me towards the end. The commander didn't like me and kept punishing me—and what for? I'm obedient in everything, live properly, don't drink, don't borrow money; and that's a bad business, Alexander Petrovich, if a man borrows money. Everybody around is so hardhearted—there's no place to go and weep. I used to slip around a corner somewhere and cry there. So once I was standing guard. It was nighttime; they put me on watch at the guardhouse by the gun racks. Wind: it was autumn, dark as could be. And I felt so heartsick, so heartsick! I set my gun by my foot, unfixed the bayonet and laid it aside, kicked off my right boot, aimed the muzzle at my chest, leaned against it, and pulled the trigger with my toe. Misfire! I examined the gun, cleaned the touchhole, poured in new primer, rubbed the flint a little, and put the gun to my chest again. What then, sir? The powder flashed, but again no shot! What's this? I think. I put my boot on, fixed the bayonet, and paced about silently. It was then that I decided to do this thing: anywhere at all, so long as it's out of the reecruits! Half an hour later the commander arrives; he was making the main round. He comes straight at me: 'Is that any way to stand guard?' I grabbed my gun and stuck the bayonet into him up to the muzzle. Got four thousand,[5] and then came here, to the special section . . ."

He was not lying. Why else would they have sent him to the special section? Ordinary crimes are punished much more lightly. However, Sirotkin alone among all his comrades was such a good-looking boy. As for the others like him, of whom we had as many as fifteen, it was even strange to look at them; only two or three faces were more or less tolerable; the others were all lop-eared, ugly, slovenly; some were even going gray. If circumstances permit, I will tell about this group in more detail some day. Sirotkin was often friendly with Gazin, the same one apropos of whom I began this chapter, recalling how he had barged into the kitchen drunk and that this had confused my first notions of prison life.

This Gazin was a terrible creature. He made a ghastly, tormenting impression on everybody. It always seemed to me that nothing could be more ferocious, more monstrous, than he. In Tobolsk I saw the robber Kamenev, famous for his evildoings; later I saw Sokolov, a runaway soldier, in prison awaiting trial as a hideous murderer. But neither of them made such a repulsive impression on me as Gazin. I sometimes imagined that I saw before me an enormous, gigantic spider the size of a man. He was a Tatar; terribly strong, the strongest man in the prison; of above average height, of Herculean build, with an ugly, disproportionately huge head; he walked with a stoop and wore a perpetual scowl. Strange rumors about him circulated in the prison: it was known that he was from the military; but the talk among the prisoners, whether true or not I don't know, was that he had escaped from Nerchinsk;[6] that he had been sent to Siberia more than once, had escaped more than once, had changed his name, and had finally landed in our prison, in the special section. It was also told of him that he used to like putting the knife to little children just for the pleasure of it: he would take the child to some convenient place, frighten and torment him first, and then, having fully enjoyed the terror and trembling of the poor little victim, would put the knife to him, quietly, slowly, with enjoyment. All of that may have been invented, owing to the generally painful impression Gazin made on everybody; but these inventions somehow suited him, they went well with him. And yet, when he was not drunk, he usually behaved quite reasonably in prison. He was always quiet, did not quarrel with anybody and avoided quarrels, but as if out of contempt for the others, as if he considered himself above the rest; he spoke very little and was somehow deliberately uncommunicative. All his movements were slow, calm, self-confident. You could see by his eyes that he was far from stupid and extremely cunning; but there was always something haughtily mocking and cruel in his face and in his smile. He traded in vodka and was one of the most prosperous taverners in the prison. But a couple of times a year he would get drunk himself, and it was then that the whole bestiality of his nature would come out. Getting drunk gradually, he first started picking on people with little jibes, very vicious and calculated, and as if prepared long in advance; finally, getting completely drunk, he became horribly violent, grabbed a knife, and threw himself at people. The prisoners, knowing his terrible strength, scattered and hid; he threw himself at anyone he met. But they soon found a way to handle him. Some ten men from his barrack would suddenly throw themselves on him all at once and start beating him. It is impossible to imagine anything more cruel: they beat him in the chest, under the heart, in the pit of the stomach, in the belly; they beat him hard and long and stopped only when he lost all consciousness and became like a dead man. They would not have ventured to beat anyone else that way: it would have killed another man, but not Gazin. After beating him completely unconscious, they wrapped him in a sheepskin jacket and laid him on the bunk: "He'll sleep it off." And in fact he would get up the next morning almost well and go silently and sullenly to work. And each time Gazin got drunk, everybody in the prison knew that the day was bound to end for him with a beating. He knew it himself, and still he got drunk. Several years passed like that. Finally, they noticed that Gazin was starting to cave in. He complained of various pains, grew noticeably more sickly, went to the hospital more and more often . . . "He's caving in!" the prisoners said among themselves.

He came into the kitchen in the company of that vile little Pole with the violin that carousers usually hired to fill out their revelry, and stopped in the middle of it, looking silently and attentively at everyone there. They all fell silent. Finally, seeing me and my comrade, he looked at us spitefully and mockingly, smiled smugly, seemed to have figured something out for himself, and, reeling badly, came over to our table.

"Allow me to ask," he began (he spoke Russian), "on what sort of income are you pleased to be drinking tea here?"

I silently exchanged glances with my comrade, realizing that it would be best to keep silent and not answer him. The first contradiction would send him into a rage.

"So you've got money?" he went on asking. "So you've got heaps of money, eh? Came to hard labor just to sit and sip tea? Came to sit and sip tea, did you? Speak up, or else! . . ."

But seeing that we were resolved to keep silent and not notice him, he turned purple and trembled with fury. Beside him, in the corner, stood a big tray, where all the bread cut for the prisoners' dinner or supper was placed. It was so big that it could hold bread enough for half the prison, but now it was empty. He seized it with both hands and brandished it over us. A little more and he would have smashed our heads. Despite the fact that murder or intended murder threatened the whole prison with extreme unpleasantness: there would be investigations, interrogations, reinforced strictness, and therefore the inmates generally did everything they could not to reach the point of such extremes—despite that, they all now sat hushed and expectant. Not a word in our defense! Not a cry against Gazin!—so strong was their hatred of us! Our dangerous situation obviously pleased them . . . But the affair ended well: he was just about to bring the tray down, when someone shouted from the front hall:

"Gazin! The vodka's been stolen! . . ."

He slammed the tray on the floor and rushed out of the kitchen like a madman.

"Well, God saved them!" the prisoners said among themselves. And they went on talking about it long afterwards.

I was unable to find out afterwards whether this news of the stolen vodka was true or had been invented on the spot to save us.

That evening, already in the dark, before they locked the barracks, I wandered near the fence, and a heavy sadness fell on my soul, and never again did I experience such sadness in all my prison life. It was hard to endure the first day of imprisonment, wherever it might be: in a prison, in a fortress, at hard labor. But I remember being occupied most of all by one thought, which afterwards constantly pursued me during all my life in prison—a partly insoluble thought, insoluble for me even now: about the inequality of punishment for the same crime. True, crimes cannot be compared with each other, even approximately. For instance, two criminals each killed a man; the circumstances of both cases are weighed, and both wind up with the same punishment. Yet look at the difference between the crimes. One, for instance, put a knife into a man just like that, for nothing, for an onion: he came out on the high road, put a knife into a muzhik, and all the man had was an onion. "Look, man! You sent me out to rob: so I put a knife in a muzhik and all I found on him was an onion." "Fool! An onion's a kopeck! A hundred men—a hundred kopecks. There's a rouble for you!" (A prison legend.) But another killed defending the honor of his bride, his sister, his daughter from the lust of a tyrant. One killed as a vagrant beset by a whole regiment of pursuers, defending his freedom, his life, often dying of hunger; another cuts little children's throats for the pleasure of it, to feel their warm blood on his hands, to enjoy their fear, their last dove-like trembling under his knife. And what then? They both go to the same hard labor. True, there are variations in the length of the sentences. But these variations are relatively few; while the variations in one and the same crime are a numberless multitude. For each character there is a variation. But suppose it's impossible to reconcile, to smooth over this difference, that it's an insoluble problem—sort of like squaring the circle—let's suppose so! But even if this inequality did not exist—look at another difference, the difference in the consequences of the punishment . . . Here is a man who languishes at hard labor, who melts down like a candle; here is another who, before he got to hard labor, did not even know there was such a rollicking life, such a pleasant club of jolly fellows. Yes, there are such men in prison. Here, for instance, is an educated man, with a highly developed conscience, with awareness, with heart. The aching of his own heart will kill him with its torment before any punishments. He will condemn himself for his crime more mercilessly, more pitilessly than the most terrible law. And here next to him is another man, who will not think even once of the murder he has committed all the while he is in prison. He even considers himself in the right. And there are some who commit murders on purpose, so as to get to hard labor and thus rid themselves of an even harder life in freedom. There he lived in the last degree of humiliation, never ate his fill, and worked for his entrepreneur from morning till night; at hard labor the work is easier than at home, there is more than enough bread, and such as he never saw before; on holidays there is beef, there are alms, there is the possibility of earning a kopeck or two. And the company? Crafty, cunning, all-knowing folk. And so he looks at his comrades with respectful amazement; he has never seen the like; he considers them the best society there could be. Can the punishment of these two be felt in the same way? But, anyhow, why occupy oneself with insoluble problems? There's the drum, it's time for the barracks.

IV

First Impressions

The last head count began. After this head count, the barracks were locked, each with its own padlock, and the prisoners remained shut in till daybreak.

The head count was carried out by a sergeant and two soldiers. Sometimes the prisoners were lined up in the yard for it and the guards officer would come. But most often the whole ceremony took place informally in the barracks. So it was this time. The counters frequently made mistakes, counted wrong, left and then came back. At last the poor guards came up with the desired figure and locked the barrack. It held some thirty prisoners packed rather tightly on the bunks. It was too early to sleep. Each of them obviously had to busy himself with something.

Of authorities, only the one invalid I mentioned earlier was left in the barrack. In each barrack there was also a senior prisoner, appointed by the major himself—for good conduct, of course. It very often happened that the senior prisoners in their turn were caught at some serious mischief; then they were whipped, immediately demoted to the juniors, and replaced by others. The senior in our barrack turned out to be Akim Akimych, who, to my surprise, not infrequently shouted at the prisoners. The prisoners usually responded to him with mockery. The invalid was smarter than he and did not interfere in anything, and if he ever did happen to open his mouth, it was more out of propriety, for the sake of a clear conscience. He sat silently on his cot, mending his boot. The prisoners paid almost no attention to him.

On that first day of my prison life I made an observation and later became convinced that it was right. Namely, that all the non-prisoners, whoever they might be, from those directly involved with the prisoners, such as convoy soldiers, guards, down to everyone in general who had anything to do with prison life, had a somehow exaggerated view of the prisoners. As if they were nervously expecting every moment that a prisoner might throw himself at them with a knife. But the most remarkable thing was that the prisoners themselves were aware that they were feared, and it obviously gave them a sort of bravado. Yet for prisoners the best superior is precisely one who is not afraid of them. And in general, despite the bravado, prisoners themselves like it much better when they are trusted. They can even be won over that way. It happened during my term in prison, though extremely rarely, that some one of the superiors would come to the prison without an escort. You should have seen how that struck the prisoners, and struck them in a good sense. Such a fearless visitor always aroused respect for himself, and even if something bad might actually happen, it would not happen in his presence. The fear inspired by prisoners exists wherever there are prisoners, and I really do not know what in fact causes it. There are, of course, some grounds for it, starting from the outward appearance of the prisoner, the acknowledged criminal; besides that, anyone approaching a prison senses that this whole mass of people has been gathered here against their will, and that, whatever the measures taken, a living man cannot be made into a corpse: he will be left with his feelings, with a thirst for revenge and life, with passions and the need to satisfy them. But, despite that, I am firmly convinced that there is still no need to fear prisoners. A man does not so easily and so quickly attack another man with a knife. In short, if the danger is possible, if it does sometimes happen, then, from the rarity of such unfortunate occurrences, one can conclude directly that the risk is negligible. Naturally, I am speaking now only of prisoners who are already sentenced, many of whom are even glad that they have finally made it to prison (a new life is sometimes so good!), and are therefore disposed to live quietly and peacefully; besides, they would not allow the really troublesome among them to show much bravado. Every convict, however bold and impudent he may be, is afraid of everything at hard labor. A prisoner awaiting judgment is another matter. He really is capable of attacking a stranger just like that, for nothing, solely because, for instance, he is going to be punished the next day, and if there is a new trial, the punishment will be postponed. Here there is a reason, a purpose for the attack: it is "to change his lot" at all costs and as soon as possible. I even know a strange psychological case of this sort.

In our prison, in the military category, there was a prisoner, a former soldier, not stripped of his rights, who had been sentenced to two years in prison, a terrible braggart and a remarkable coward. Generally, braggadocio and cowardice are met with extremely rarely in a Russian soldier. Our soldiers always look so busy that, even if they were so inclined, they would have no time for braggadocio. But if he is already a braggart, then he is almost always a do-nothing and a coward. Dutov (the prisoner's name) finally served his short term and went back to a battalion of the line. But since everyone like him, sent to prison for correction, is definitively spoiled there, it usually happens that, after enjoying their freedom for no more than two or three weeks, they are taken to court again and turn up back in prison, only not for two or three years now, but in the "perpetual" category, for fifteen or twenty years. And so it happened. Some three weeks after leaving prison, Dutov committed a burglary; on top of that, he was rude and rowdy. He was tried and sentenced to severe punishment. Terrified in the extreme, to the utmost, by the forthcoming punishment, pitiful coward that he was, on the eve of the day he was to run the gauntlet, he attacked a guards officer with a knife as he came into the prisoners' cell. Naturally, he knew very well that by such an act he would greatly increase his sentence and his term at hard labor. But he was precisely counting on putting off the terrible moment of punishment for at least a few days, a few hours! He was such a coward that, in attacking the officer with a knife, he did not even wound him, but did it all for the sake of form, only so that there would be a new crime, for which he would again stand trial.

The time before punishment is, of course, terrible for the sentenced man, and over several years I got to see a good number of them on the eve of their fatal day. I usually met with sentenced prisoners in the hospital, in the prisoners' ward, where they would be lying sick, as happened quite often. It is known to all prisoners all over Russia that the people who sympathize most with them are doctors. They never make any distinction between prisoners, as almost everyone on the outside involuntarily does, except perhaps for simple folk, who never reproach a prisoner for his crime, however terrible it was, and forgive him everything on account of the punishment he endures and in general for his misfortune. Not for nothing do folk all over Russia call crime misfortune and criminals unfortunates. That is a profoundly significant definition. It is all the more important for being made unconsciously, instinctively. As for doctors—they are a veritable refuge for prisoners in many cases, especially for those under sentence, who are kept in worse conditions than the ordinary convicts . . . And so the sentenced man, having calculated the probable time until his terrible day, often gets to the hospital, wishing to put the difficult moment off a while longer. When he is discharged, knowing that tomorrow is almost certainly the fatal day, he is almost always in great agitation. Some try to conceal their feelings out of vanity, but their awkward, affected bravado does not deceive their comrades. They all understand what it is about and say nothing out of human sympathy. I knew a prisoner, a young man, a murderer, a former soldier, who was sentenced to the maximum number of rods. He was so frightened that on the eve of the punishment he decided to drink a jug of vodka infused with snuff. Incidentally, vodka always turns up for a condemned prisoner before his punishment. It is smuggled in long before the appointed day, is obtained for big money, and the condemned man would sooner go six months without necessities so as to save up the sum needed for a half pint of vodka to be drunk fifteen minutes before the punishment. There is a general conviction among prisoners that a drunk man does not feel the rods or lashes as badly. But I am digressing from my story. The poor fellow, having drunk his jug of vodka, in fact became sick at once; he began to vomit blood and was taken to the hospital nearly unconscious. This vomiting so damaged his lungs that after a few days he showed symptoms of real consumption, from which he died six months later. The doctors who treated him for consumption had no idea what had caused it.

But, since I am telling about the faintheartedness frequently met with in prisoners awaiting punishment, I must add that, on the contrary, some of them astonish the observer by their extraordinary fearlessness. I recall several examples of courage that reached the point of a sort of insensibility, and these examples were not that rare. I particularly recall my encounter with one frightful criminal. One summer day rumor spread through the prisoners' wards that in the evening the famous brigand Orlov, a runaway soldier, was to be punished, and after the punishment he would be brought to the ward. Waiting for Orlov, the sick prisoners affirmed that he was to be cruelly punished. They were all in some agitation, and, I confess, I also awaited the famous brigand's appearance with great curiosity. I had long been hearing wonders about him. He was an evildoer such as few are, who put his knife cold-bloodedly into old people and children—a man with a formidable strength of will and a proud consciousness of his strength. He pleaded guilty to many murders and was sentenced to run the gauntlet. It was already evening when he was brought. The ward was dark, and candles had been lit. Orlov was nearly unconscious, terribly pale, with thick, disheveled, pitch-black hair. His back was swollen and of a bloody blue color. The prisoners tended to him all night, changed the water for him, turned him from side to side, gave him medicine, as if they were caring for some near and dear one, or some benefactor. The very next day he came fully to his senses and paced up and down the ward a couple of times! That amazed me: he had been so weak and exhausted when he arrived in the hospital. He had made it at one go through half the total number of rods he was sentenced to. The doctor had stopped the punishment only when he saw that to continue it threatened the inevitable death of the criminal. Besides, Orlov was a small man and of weak constitution, and what's more he had been worn out by being kept on trial for a long time. Anyone who has ever happened to meet with prisoners on trial will probably long remember their worn-out, gaunt, and pale faces, their inflamed eyes. Despite that, Orlov was quickly recovering. Obviously, his spirit, his inner energy, was a great help to nature. In fact, this was not at all an ordinary man. I became more closely acquainted with him out of curiosity and studied him for a whole week. I can say positively that I have never in my life met a man of stronger, more iron character than he. Once, in Tobolsk, I saw a celebrity of this kind, the former chief of a band of brigands. He was a wild beast in the fullest sense, and standing next to him and not yet knowing his name, you sensed instinctively that you had a frightful creature beside you. But for me the horrible thing in him was his spiritual torpor. The flesh had won out over all his inner qualities so much that from the first glance you could see by his face that the only thing left in him was one savage craving for physical gratification, sensuality, fleshly indulgence. I am sure that Korenev—the name of this brigand—would even have lost heart and trembled with fear in the face of punishment, though he was capable of killing without even batting an eye. Orlov was the complete opposite of him. This was manifestly a total victory over the flesh. You could see that the man had limitless control of himself, despised all tortures and punishments, and had no fear of anything in the world. You saw in him only an infinite energy, a thirst for activity, a thirst for revenge, a thirst for attaining a set goal. Among other things, I was struck by his strange haughtiness. He looked upon everything from some incredible height, though without any effort to stand on stilts, but just so, somehow naturally. I think there was no being in the world who could have had an effect on him by authority alone. He looked at everything with a sort of unexpected calm, as if there was nothing in the world that could surprise him. And though he fully realized that the other prisoners looked at him with respect, he did not pose before them in the least. Yet vanity and arrogance are characteristic of almost all prisoners without exception. He was not at all stupid and was somehow strangely frank, though by no means a babbler. To my questions he replied directly that he was waiting to recover, the sooner to get through the rest of the punishment, and that he had been afraid at first, before the punishment, that he would not survive it. "But now," he added, winking at me, "the matter's settled. I'll get through the rest of the strokes and set off at once with a party to Nerchinsk, but I'll escape on the way. Escape for sure! If only my back heals quickly!" And all those five days he waited greedily until he could ask to be discharged. During the wait, he was sometimes full of laughter and merriment. I tried to talk with him about his adventures. He frowned a little at these questions, but always answered frankly. When he realized that I was getting at his conscience and probing for some repentance in him, he looked at me with such contempt and haughtiness, as if I had suddenly turned in his eyes into a silly little boy, with whom it was impossible to reason as with a grown-up. Something like pity for me even showed in his face. A moment later he burst into the most simple-hearted laughter at me, without any irony, and I'm sure, when he was left alone and recalled my words, he laughed maybe several more times. He was finally discharged with his back not quite healed; I, too, was discharged just then, and we happened to return from the hospital together: I to the prison, he to the guardhouse next to our prison, where he had been kept before.

Saying good-bye, he shook my hand, and this was a sign of great trust on his part. I think he did it because he was very pleased with himself and the present moment. At bottom he could only have despised me and certainly must have looked at me as at a submissive creature, weak, pathetic, and beneath him in all respects. The next day he was led out to his second punishment . . .

Once our barrack was locked, it suddenly acquired a special look— the look of a real dwelling, a domestic hearth. Only now could I see the prisoners, my comrades, as if quite at home. During the day, the sergeants, the guards, and the authorities in general could turn up in the prison at any moment, and therefore the inhabitants of the prison all behaved somehow differently, as if not quite at ease, as if expecting something every moment, in some sort of apprehension. But as soon as the barrack was locked, they all settled down calmly at once, each in his own place, and nearly everyone took up some handiwork. The barrack was suddenly lit up. Each man had his own candle and candlestick, most often a wooden one. Some began to stitch boots, some to sew clothes. The mephitic atmosphere of the barrack became worse by the hour. A bunch of revelers squatted in a corner over cards on a spread rug. In almost every barrack there was such a prisoner, who kept a flimsy three-foot rug, a candle, and an incredibly dirty, greasy pack of cards. All this together was known as a maidan.[1] The keeper was paid by the gamblers, some fifteen kopecks a night; that was his cut of the deal. The card players usually played blackjack, draw poker, and so on. They were all games of chance. Each player spilled a pile of copper money in front of him—all he had in his pocket—and got up only when he was cleaned out or had beaten his comrades. The game ended late at night, or sometimes went on till daybreak, till the moment when the barrack was unlocked. In our room, as in all the other barracks of the prison, there were always destitute men, *baygushi*, who had gambled or drunk away everything, or who were simply destitute by nature. I say "by nature," and I put special emphasis on the expression. Indeed, among our people everywhere, in whatever surroundings, in whatever conditions, there are and always will be certain strange persons, placid and often not at all lazy, who are destined by fate to remain eternally destitute. They are always solitary, they are always slovenly, they always look somehow downtrodden and depressed by something, and they are eternally ordered about by somebody, run somebody's errands, usually a carouser or a man suddenly become rich and eminent. Any undertaking, any initiative is a grief and a burden for them. It seems they were born on the condition that they never begin anything themselves and only serve others, that they not live by their own will, that they dance to another's tune; their purpose is only to do for others. To crown it all, no circumstances, no upheavals can make them rich. They are always destitute. I have noticed that such persons exist not only among simple people, but in all companies, estates, parties, journals, and associations. So it was in every barrack, in every prison, and as soon as a maidan was set up, one of them immediately appeared with his services. In general, no maidan could do without a servant. He was usually hired by all the players together, at five silver kopecks for the whole night, and his main duty was to stand watch all night. Most of the time he froze for six or seven hours in the dark, in the entryway, at thirty degrees below zero, listening to every tap, every clank, every footstep outside. The major or the guards sometimes appeared in the prison quite late at night, came in quietly, and caught the gamblers, and the workers, and the extra candles, which could be seen from outside. In any case, when the lock suddenly began to rattle on the door to the yard, it was already too late to hide, put out the candles, and lie down on a bunk. But since the servant on watch caught it badly afterwards from the maidan, the cases of such mishaps were extremely rare. Five kopecks was, of course, absurdly insignificant pay, even for prison; but I was always struck, in this and all other cases, by the severity and mercilessness of the prison employers: "You took the money, so do the job!" This was an argument that brooked no objections. For the kopecks paid, the employer took all he could take, took, if possible, even something extra, and still considered that he had done the hired man a favor. A carouser, drinking, throwing money around right and left without counting, unfailingly cheated his servant, and that I noticed in more than one prison, in more than one maidan.

I have already said that almost everyone in the barrack settled down to some handiwork: besides the gamblers, there were no more than five totally idle men; they went to sleep at once. My place on the bunk was just by the door. On the other side of the bunk, head to head with me, was Akim Akimych. He worked till ten or eleven, gluing together some multicolored Chinese lantern commissioned from him in town for rather good pay. He was an expert at making lanterns, worked methodically, without getting distracted; when he finished work, he put everything away neatly, spread out his mattress, said his prayers, and lay down properly in bed. He extended this propriety and orderliness, evidently, to the most petty pedantry; he obviously must have considered himself an extremely intelligent man, as all dull and limited people generally do. I disliked him from the very first day, though, I remember, on that first day I mused about him a great deal and marveled most of all that such a person, instead of succeeding in life, had wound up in prison. Later on I shall have to speak more than once about Akim Akimych.

But I will briefly describe the composition of our whole barrack. I was to live in it for many years, and these were my future roommates and comrades. Understandably, I studied them with greedy curiosity. To the left of my place on the bunk was a little group of Caucasian mountaineers, sent up mostly for robberies and with varying terms. There were two Lezgins, one Chechen, and three Daghestan Tatars.[2] The Chechen was a gloomy and sullen creature; he hardly ever spoke with anyone and always looked around him with hatred, furtively, and with a venomous, maliciously mocking smile. One of the Lezgins was already an old man with a long, fine, hooked nose—an inveterate brigand by the look of him. But the other, Nurra, made a most delightful, pleasing impression on me from the very first day. He was still a young man, not tall, of Herculean physique, perfectly blond, with pale blue eyes, a pug nose like a Finnish woman's, and bowlegs from a life spent on horseback. His body had been cut and wounded all over by bayonets and bullets. In the Caucasus he had belonged to the allies, but he kept going on the quiet and joining the opposition mountaineers, and made raids with them on the Russians. Everyone in the prison liked him. He was always cheerful, friendly to everyone, worked without a murmur, was calm and serene, though he often looked indignantly at the vileness and filth of the prisoners' life and was fiercely outraged by any sort of stealing, swindling, drunkenness, and dishonesty in general; yet he never quarreled, but only turned away in indignation. He himself, during all his time in prison, never stole anything or committed a single bad act. He was extremely devout. He said his prayers piously; during the fasts before the Muslim holy days he fasted fanatically and stood for whole nights in prayer. Everyone liked him and believed in his honesty. "Nurra's a lion," the prisoners used to say; and the nickname of "lion" stuck to him. He was absolutely convinced that, once he had finished his appointed term in prison, he would be sent home to the Caucasus, and he lived only in that hope. I think he would have died if he had been deprived of it. I noticed him distinctly on my first day in prison. It was impossible not to notice his kind, sympathizing face among the angry, sullen, and jeering faces of the other prisoners. Within the first half hour of my arrival in prison, he patted me on the shoulder as he walked past me and laughed good-naturedly in my face. At first I could not understand what this meant. He spoke Russian very poorly. Soon after that he came up to me again, and again smiled and gave me a friendly pat on the shoulder. Then again and again, and so it went on for three days. On his part, as I guessed and later learned, this meant that he was sorry for me, that he felt how hard this first acquaintance with prison was for me, that he wanted to show me his friendship, cheer me up, and assure me of his protection. Kind and naïve Nurra!

The Daghestan Tartars were three in number, and they were all brothers. Two of them were middle-aged, but the third, Alei, was no more than twenty-two and looked younger still. His place on the bunk was next to mine. His beautiful, open, intelligent, and at the same time good-naturedly naïve face won my heart at first sight, and I was very glad that fate had sent me him and not some other man as a neighbor. His whole soul was expressed in his handsome—one might even say beautiful—face. His smile was so trustful, so childishly simple-hearted; his big, dark eyes were so gentle, so tender, that I always felt a special pleasure, even a relief from anguish and sadness, in looking at him. I say it without exaggeration. At home one day his older brother (he had five older brothers; two others ended up in some sort of mill) told him to take his saber and get on his horse to go on an expedition with him. In mountaineer families respect for one's elders is so great that the boy not only did not dare, but did not even think of asking where they were going. The brothers did not find it necessary to tell him. They were all setting out on a robbery, to waylay a rich Armenian merchant and hold him up. And so it went: they killed the convoy, put a knife into the Armenian, and stole his goods. The affair was discovered: all six were seized, tried, found guilty, flogged, and sent to hard labor in Siberia. The only mercy granted Alei by the court was the shortening of his term; he was sent up for four years. The brothers loved him very much, and more with a sort of fatherly than brotherly love. He was their comfort in exile, and they, who were usually gloomy and sullen, always smiled looking at him, and when they talked to him (though they talked to him very little, as if they considered him still a boy with whom there was no point in talking about anything serious), their stern faces softened, and I guessed they were saying something jocular, almost childish—at least they always exchanged glances and chuckled good-naturedly when they heard his reply. He hardly ever dared to address them himself: so respectful he was. It is hard to imagine how this boy, through the whole time of his imprisonment, was able to preserve such gentleness of heart, to form in himself such strict honesty, such sincerity and attractiveness, and not become coarse and depraved. His, however, was a strong and harmonious nature, for all its apparent gentleness. I got to know him well later on. He was as chaste as a pure maiden, and if someone in prison committed a nasty, cynical, dirty, or unjust and violent act, the fire of indignation lit up in his beautiful eyes, which made them still more beautiful. But he avoided quarrels and abuse, though he was not one of those who let themselves be insulted with impunity and knew how to stand up for himself. But he had no quarrels with anyone: everyone liked him and everyone was nice to him. At first he was merely polite with me. I gradually began to converse with him; after a few months he learned to speak excellent Russian, which his brothers never accomplished in all their time in prison. He seemed to me an extremely intelligent boy, extremely modest and tactful, and already quite capable of reasoning. In general, I will say beforehand: I consider Alei a far from ordinary being, and I remember my meeting with him as one of the best meetings in my life. There are people so beautiful by nature, so richly endowed by God, that the mere thought that they might ever change for the worse seems impossible to you. You are always at peace about them. I am at peace about Alei even now. Where is he now? . . .

Once, already long after my arrival in prison, I was lying on the bunk and thinking about something very painful. Alei, who was always busy and liked to work, was not occupied with anything this time, though it was too early to go to sleep. It was one of their Muslim holy days, and they were not working. He was lying with his hands behind his head and also thinking about something. Suddenly he asked me:

"So, is it very hard for you now?"

I looked him over with curiosity, and this quick, direct question from Alei, always tactful, always discerning, always intelligent of heart, seemed strange to me; but looking more attentively, I saw in his face so much anguish, so much suffering from his memories, that I realized at once that for him, too, it was very hard and precisely at that moment. I told him my guess. He smiled and sighed sadly. I liked his smile, always tender and heartfelt. Besides, when he smiled, he showed two rows of pearl white teeth, the beauty of which might have been envied by the most beautiful woman in the world.

"So, Alei, you must have been thinking of how they're celebrating this holy day at home in Daghestan? It must be good there?"

"Yes," he replied rapturously, and his eyes shone. "But how did you know I was thinking about that?"

"How could I not know! So it's better there than here?"

"Oh, why do you say that! . . ."

"What flowers there must be there now, what a paradise! . . ."

"O-oh, better not to speak of it." He was in great agitation.

"Listen, Alei, did you have a sister?"

"I did, and what of it?"

"She must be a beauty, if she's like you."

"Forget about me! She's such a beauty, there's no better in all Daghestan. Ah, what a beauty my sister is! You've never seen anything like it! My mother was also a beauty."

"And your mother loved you?"

"Ah! What are you saying! She must have died of grief for me by now. I was her favorite son. She loved me more than my sister, more than anyone . . . She came to me in my sleep last night and wept over me."

He fell silent and did not say another word that evening. But from then on he kept trying to talk to me, though out of the respect which for some unknown reason he felt for me, he never addressed me first.

But he was very glad when I addressed him. I asked him about the Caucasus, about his former life. His brothers did not prevent him from talking to me; they were even pleased. Seeing that I was growing more and more fond of Alei, they, too, became much friendlier towards me.

Alei helped me at work and did me all the service he could in the barrack, and you could see that he was very pleased to oblige me and to make things easier for me in some way, though in this effort to oblige there was not the slightest humiliation or profit-seeking, but only a warm, friendly feeling for me, which he no longer concealed. Among other things, he had considerable manual ability; he learned to sew linens rather well, stitched boots, and later did his best to learn joinery. His brothers praised him and were proud of him.

"Listen, Alei," I said to him once, "why don't you learn to read and write in Russian? Do you know how useful it might be for you here in Siberia later on?"

"I'd like to very much. But who will teach me?"

"As if there aren't enough literate people here! Do you want me to teach you?"

"Oh, please do!" And he even sat up on the bunk and clasped his hands pleadingly, looking at me.

We started the next evening. I had a Russian translation of the New Testament—a book that was not forbidden in prison. Without an ABC, with this book alone, Alei learned to read excellently in a few weeks. After some three months, he understood the printed language perfectly. He studied with ardor, with enthusiasm.

Once he and I read through the whole of the Sermon on the Mount. I noticed that he seemed to recite certain passages from it with particular feeling.

I asked him if he liked what he had read.

He gave me a quick glance and color came to his face.

"Oh, yes!" he answered. "Yes, Isa is a holy prophet, Isa speaks the words of God. How good!"

"What do you like most of all?"

"Where he says: forgive, love, do not offend, and love your enemies. Ah, how well he speaks!"[3]

He turned to his brothers, who were listening to our conversation, and ardently began saying something to them. They talked among themselves long and seriously, nodding their heads in agreement. Then with a gravely benevolent, that is, a purely Muslim, smile (which I like so much, and what I like is precisely the gravity of this smile), they turned to me and confirmed that Isa was God's prophet and that he performed great miracles, that he fashioned a bird out of clay, blew on it, and it flew . . . and that they have it written in their books. In saying this, they were fully convinced that they were giving me great pleasure by praising Isa, and Alei was perfectly happy that his brothers had decided and wished to give me this pleasure.

Writing also went extremely well for us. Alei got hold of some paper (and did not allow me to pay for it), pens, ink, and in some two months he learned to write exceedingly well. His brothers were even struck by it. Their pride and satisfaction knew no limits. They did not know how to thank me. At work, if we happened to be working together, they vied with each other in helping me and counted it their own good fortune. To say nothing of Alei. He loved me maybe as much as his brothers. I will never forget how he left the prison. He took me behind the barrack, threw himself on my neck and wept. He had never kissed me or wept before. "You've done so much for me, so much," he said. "My father and mother could not have done so much: you have made a man of me. God will reward you, and I will never forget you . . ."

Where is he, where is he now, my good, dear, dear Alei! . . .

Besides the Circassians, there was also a whole group of Poles in our barracks, who made up a completely separate family and hardly communicated with the other prisoners. I have already said that, for their exclusiveness, for their hatred of the Russian prisoners, they were hated in their turn by everybody. These were sick, tormented natures; there were six of them. Some of them were educated people. I will talk about them separately and in detail further on. It was from them that I occasionally obtained some books during the last years of my life in prison. The first book I read made a strong, strange, and singular impression on me. I will speak in particular about those impressions another time. They are all too curious for me, and I am sure they will be totally incomprehensible for many. It is hard to judge about certain things if you have not experienced them. I will say one thing: that moral privations are more painful than any physical torments. A simple man, going to hard labor, lands in his own society, or perhaps one even more developed. He has lost a great deal, of course—his birthplace, his family, everything—but his milieu remains the same. An educated man, who is subject by law to the same punishment as the simple man, often loses incomparably more. He has to stifle in himself all his needs, all his habits, to move into a milieu that is insufficient for him, to get used to breathing a different air . . . He is a fish out of water . . . And the same punishment imposed by law on everyone turns out to be ten times more tormenting for him. This is true . . . even if it is only a matter of sacrificing material habits.

But the Poles made up a special closed group. There were six of them, and they stuck together. Of all the prisoners in our barrack, they liked only the Jew, and that maybe only because he amused them. However, the other prisoners also liked our little Jew, though all of them without exception laughed at him. He was our only one, and even now I cannot recall him without laughing. Whenever I looked at him, I was always reminded of Gogol's little Jew Yankel, from *Taras Bulba*,[4] who, when he got undressed to go and spend the night with his wife in some sort of closet, at once bore a terrible resemblance to a chicken. Isai Fomich, our Jew, was as like a plucked chicken as two drops of water. He was no longer a young man, around fifty, short and weak, cunning, and at the same time decidedly stupid. He was impudent and arrogant, and at the same time a terrible coward. He was all little wrinkles, and his brow and cheeks bore the brands he had received on the scaffold. I simply cannot understand how he could have survived sixty lashes. He came on the accusation of murder. He had a recipe hidden away, which his Jewish friends had obtained for him from a doctor immediately after the scaffold. With this recipe an ointment could be prepared which could make his brands go away in two weeks. He did not dare use this ointment in prison and waited for the end of his twelve-year term at hard labor, after which, having settled in exile, he firmly intended to use the recipe. "Othervise it vill be impossible to get marryet," he said to me once, "and I absolutely vant to get marryet." He and I were great friends. He was always in excellent spirits. Life in prison was easy for him; he was a jeweler by trade, was buried in work from town, where there was no jeweler, and was thus delivered from heavy work. Naturally, he was also a moneylender and provided all the prisoners with money at interest and against pledges. He had come before me, and one of the Poles described his arrival for me in detail. It is a very funny story, which I will tell further on; I will be speaking of Isai Fomich more than once.

The rest of the people in our barrack consisted of four Old Believers, old men and Bible readers, among them the old man from the Starodubsky settlements; two or three Ukrainians, gloomy fellows; a young prisoner with a fine little face and a fine little nose, about twenty-three years old, who had already killed eight souls; a group of counterfeiters, one of whom was the entertainer of our whole barrack; and finally several gloomy and sullen persons with shaved skulls and disfigured faces, silent and envious, who looked around themselves with lowering hatred, and intended to go on looking like that, silently scowling and hating, for long years to come—for their whole term at hard labor. All this only flashed past me on that first cheerless evening of my new life—flashed amidst the smoke and soot, the curses and inexpressible cynicism, in the mephitic atmosphere, in the clanking of fetters, amidst oaths and shameless guffawing. I lay down on the bare bunk, put my clothes under my head (I had no pillow as yet), covered myself with my sheepskin coat, but was unable to fall asleep for a long time, worn out though I was and broken by all the monstrous and unexpected impressions of that first day. But my new life was only beginning. Much still lay ahead of me that I had never thought of, that I had not anticipated . . .

The First Month

Three days after my arrival in prison, I was ordered to go to work. That first day of work is a very memorable one for me, though nothing extraordinary happened to me in the course of it, at least taking into consideration all that was extraordinary in my situation to begin with. But this, too, was one of my first impressions, and I still went on greedily observing everything. All those first three days I had spent in the most painful feelings: "This is the end of my wanderings: I am in prison!" I repeated to myself every moment. "This is my refuge for many long years, my corner, which I enter with such a mistrustful, such a morbid feeling . . . But who knows? Maybe many years from now I'll be sorry when I have to leave it! . . . ," I would add, not without an admixture of that gleeful feeling which sometimes reaches the point of a need to deliberately chafe your own wound, as if you wish to admire your own pain, as if the consciousness of the extent of your misfortune indeed affords pleasure. The thought of being sorry to leave this corner in time struck me with horror: even then I already had a presentiment of the monstrous degree to which a man grows accustomed to things. But that still lay ahead of me, and meanwhile everything around me now was hostile and—frightening . . . or maybe not everything, but naturally it seemed so to me. That savage curiosity with which my new fellow convicts looked me over, their redoubled severity towards a novice from the gentry who had suddenly appeared in their corporation, a severity that at times almost reached the point of hatred—all this tormented me so much that I myself wanted to start work all the sooner, the sooner to learn and experience the whole of my calamity at once, so as to begin to live as they all did, the sooner to fall into the same rut with them. Naturally, I did not notice then and did not suspect much that was right under my nose: amidst the hostile I had as yet to divine the comforting. However, in the meantime the few affable, gentle persons I met in those three days greatly encouraged me. The most gentle and affable with me was Akim Akimych. Among the sullen and hate-filled faces of the other prisoners, I could not help noticing several that were kind and cheerful. "There are bad people everywhere, and among the bad some good ones," I hastened to think, consoling myself. "Who knows? Maybe these people are not so much worse than the *remainder*, who *remained* there, *outside the prison*." I was thinking that, and shook my head at the thought myself, and yet—my God!—if I had only known then how true that thought was!

There was a man here, for example, whom I came to know fully only after many, many years, and yet he was with me and constantly around me during almost all my time in prison. This was the prisoner Sushilov. Just now, when I mentioned convicts who were *no worse* than others, I involuntarily recalled him at once. He served me. I also had another servant. From the very beginning, from the first days, Akim Akimych recommended to me a prisoner named Osip, saying that for thirty kopecks a month he would cook special food for me every day, if I found the prison fare so disgusting and had the means to buy my own. Osip was one of the four cooks appointed for our two kitchens by election among the prisoners, though, incidentally, they remained perfectly free to accept or reject the appointment; and having accepted it, they could reject it again even the next day. The cooks did not go out to work, and all their duty consisted in baking bread and cooking shchi. They were called not cooks but cookies (in the feminine)—not out of disdain for them, by the way, the less so as the most sensible and, if possible, honest men were chosen for the kitchen, but just so, as a friendly joke, at which our cooks were not offended in the least. Osip was almost always chosen, and for several years in a row he was our constant cooky, and occasionally refused, only for a time, when he was quite overcome by anguish and, along with it, the wish to smuggle in vodka. He was a man of rare honesty and meekness, though he got there for contraband. He was that same contrabandist, the tall, sturdy fellow I have already mentioned; a coward, afraid of everything, especially birching, placid, uncomplaining, gentle with everyone, who *never* quarreled with anyone, but who could not help smuggling vodka, despite all his cowardice, out of a passion for contraband. He and the other cooks also dealt in vodka, though, of course, not on the same scale as Gazin, for instance, because he did not have the courage to risk so much. I always got along very well with this Osip. As for the means for having your own food, very little was needed. I won't be wrong if I say that my food cost me only one silver rouble a month, apart from bread, naturally, which was government issue, and sometimes shchi, if I was very hungry, despite my aversion to it, which, however, went away almost completely later on. I usually bought a piece of beef, a pound a day. In winter it cost half a kopeck. Beef was brought from the market by one of the invalids, of whom we had one in each barrack to keep order, and who voluntarily took upon themselves the duty of going to the market every day to buy things for the prisoners, and did not take any pay for it, except perhaps something trifling. They did it for the sake of their own peace; otherwise it would have been impossible for them to live in the barracks. They used to bring tobacco, bricks of tea, beef, kalachi, and so on and so forth, with the one exception of vodka. They were not asked to bring vodka, though they were occasionally treated to some. For several years in a row, Osip cooked for me one and the same piece of fried beef. How it was fried is another question, and that was not the point. Remarkably enough, for several years I hardly exchanged two words with Osip. I tried to talk with him many times, but he was somehow unable to keep up a conversation: he would smile, or answer yes or no, and that was all. It was even strange to look at this seven-year-old Hercules.

But, besides Osip, another of the people who helped me was Sushilov. I did not ask him or seek him out. He somehow found me himself and attached himself to me; I don't even remember when or how it happened. He began doing laundry for me. A big cesspit was dug behind the barracks for that purpose. The prisoners' linen was laundered over that pit in wooden tubs. Besides that, Sushilov himself invented thousands of different duties to please me: he prepared my tea kettle, ran various errands, found things I needed, took my jacket to be mended, tarred my boots four times a month; he did it all zealously, bustlingly, as if God knows what sort of duty lay on him—in short, he bound his fate with mine completely, and took all my affairs upon himself. For instance, he never said, "You have so many shirts, your jacket is torn," and so on, but always, "*We* now have so many shirts, *our* jacket is torn." He tried to read my eyes, and seemed to have taken that as his main purpose in life. He had no sort of handicraft, and it seems he got his kopecks only from me. I paid him as much as I could, that is, in small change, and he always remained uncomplainingly satisfied. He could not help serving somebody, and it seems he chose me in particular because I was more well-mannered than the others and more honest about payments. He was one of those who can never get rich and set themselves up, and who would accept to stand watch for a maidan, spending whole nights in freezing entryways, listening to every sound outside in case it was the major, and for it took five silver kopecks for almost a whole night, and if they failed they lost everything and answered for it with their hide. I have already spoken about them. The characteristic of these people is the annihilation of their own person always, everywhere, and before almost everyone, and in group activities to take not even a secondary but a tertiary role. All this is simply in their nature. Sushilov was a very pitiful fellow, totally uncomplaining and humiliated, even downtrodden, though nobody in our barrack had trod on him, he was just downtrodden by nature. I always pitied him for some reason. I could not even glance at him without that feeling; but why I pitied him, I could not say myself. I also could not converse with him; nor did he know how to converse, and it was obviously a great difficulty for him, and he would only liven up when, to end the conversation, I would give him something to do, ask him to go, to run somewhere. I even became convinced, finally, that I was giving him pleasure by it. He was neither tall nor short, neither good- nor bad-looking, neither stupid nor smart, neither young nor old, slightly pockmarked, somewhat blond. It was never possible to say anything too definite about him. One thing only: it seems to me, as far as I could guess, that he belonged to the same company as Sirotkin, and that solely because he was downtrodden and uncomplaining. The prisoners occasionally chuckled at him, mainly because he had *exchanged* on the way to Siberia with his party, and had done so for a red shirt and one silver ruble. It was the negligible price he had sold himself for that made the prisoners laugh at him. To exchange means to change names, and therefore fates, with someone. Strange as this fact may seem, it is true, and in my time it was still in full force among prisoners sent to Siberia, hallowed by tradition and defined by well-known forms. At first I simply could not believe it, though I finally came to accept the obvious.

Here is how it was done. For instance, a party of prisoners is being sent to Siberia. All sorts are going: to hard labor, to the mills, to penal settlements; all going together. Somewhere along the way, say in Perm province, one member of the party decides to exchange with another. For instance, some Mikhailov, sentenced for murder or some other capital offense, finds going to hard labor for many years unbeneficial. Suppose he's a clever fellow, an old hand, who knows his business; so he's on the lookout for somebody in the same party who is of a simpler, more downtrodden, more uncomplaining sort, and whose sentence is comparatively lighter: a few years in a mill or a settlement, or even at hard labor, only for a shorter term. Finally, he comes across Sushilov. Sushilov is a house serf and is simply being sent to a settlement. He has already gone a thousand miles, naturally without a kopeck to his name, because Sushilov will never have a kopeck—he goes on, exhausted, worn-out, eating only government rations, without a fleeting bite of something good, in nothing but government clothes, serving everybody for pitiful small change. Mikhailov strikes up a conversation with Sushilov, makes his acquaintance, even becomes friends with him, and finally, at some stopping place, treats him to vodka. He finally makes the suggestion: how would he like to exchange? "I, Mikhailov, this and that, I'm going to hard labor, not really to hard labor, but to a 'special section.' It's hard labor, but special, meaning better." This special section, for as long as it existed, was not even known to all the authorities—for instance, those in Petersburg. It was such a separate and special little corner, in one of the little corners of Siberia, and held so few people (in my time there were about seventy men in it), that it was even hard to find a trace of it. Later I met people who worked in Siberia and knew it well, who first heard about the existence of a "special section" from me. In the Code of Law there are only six lines about it: "There is instituted in such-and-such prison a Special Section for the most serious criminals, until such time as camps for the heaviest hard labor are opened in Siberia." Even the prisoners themselves did not know whether it was for good or for a fixed term. No term was mentioned; it only said until the opening of the heaviest labor, meaning "for the long haul."

No wonder that neither Sushilov nor anyone in his party knew about it, not excluding the convict Mikhailov himself, who could only have a notion of this special section judging by his crime, which was all too serious and for which he had already gone through his three or four thousand. Consequently, he was not being sent to a very nice place. Whereas Sushilov was going to a settlement; what could be better? "How would you like to exchange?" Sushilov is a bit tipsy, a simple soul, filled with gratitude for Mikhailov's kindness to him, and therefore does not dare to refuse. Besides, he has already heard from the prisoners in his party that it is possible to exchange, that others do it, consequently there is nothing extraordinary and unheard-of about it. They come to an agreement. The shameless Mikhailov, taking advantage of Sushilov's extraordinary simplicity, buys his name from him for a red shirt and a silver rouble, which he gives him on the spot in front of witnesses. The next day Sushilov is no longer drunk, but he is given drink again, and, well, it's bad to back out: the silver rouble has already been drunk up, a little later the red shirt has been, too. If you don't like it, pay back the money. And where is Sushilov to get a whole silver rouble? And if he doesn't pay it back, his group will make him: they take a strict view of these things. Besides, if you've made a promise, keep it—that the group will insist on. Otherwise they'll chew you to pieces. Beat you to death, maybe, or simply kill you, or at least scare the hell out of you.

In fact, if the group granted indulgence even once in a matter like this, that would put an end to the custom of exchanging names. If it is possible to go back on your promise and break a deal that has already been concluded and paid for—who will keep it after that? In short, this is a group, a common cause, and therefore the party is very strict about it. Sushilov finally sees that he cannot plead his way out, and decides to give his full consent. The deal is announced to the whole party; well, and there may be others there who ought to be given gifts and drinks, if need be. For them, naturally, it's all the same whether Mikhailov or Sushilov lands in some hellhole, but they've drunk vodka, they've been given a treat—consequently, they'll keep mum. At the very first stopping place, for instance, they call the roll; they come to Mikhailov: "Mikhailov!" "Here!" shouts Sushilov. "Sushilov!" "Here!" shouts Mikhailov—and they go on. Nobody even mentions it anymore.

In Tobolsk the exiles are sorted out. Mikhailov goes to a settlement, and Sushilov under reinforced convoy to the special section. No further protest is possible; and what in fact can be proved? For how many years would such a case drag out? What would come of it? Where, finally, are the witnesses? If any are found, they will deny it all. And so the result remains that, for a red shirt and a silver rouble, Sushilov winds up in the "special section."

The prisoners laughed at Sushilov—not because he exchanged (though they generally despise those who exchange lighter work for heavier, as they do any fools who get taken in), but because all he got for it was a red shirt and a silver rouble: the price was too insignificant. Exchanges are usually done for big sums, again relatively speaking. They sometimes even charge several dozen roubles. But Sushilov was so uncomplaining, unassuming, and insignificant for them all, that he wasn't even worth laughing at.

I lived for a long time with Sushilov, several years. He gradually became extremely attached to me; I could not help noticing it, and so I also became quite used to him. But once—I can never forgive myself for it—he did not do something I asked him to do, and meanwhile he had just taken money from me, and I had the cruelty to say to him: "So, Sushilov, you take the money but don't do the work." Sushilov said nothing, ran and did my errand, but then suddenly grew sad. Two days passed. I thought: it can't be because of my words. I knew that one prisoner, Anton Vasiliev, kept demanding some paltry debt from him. He probably had no money, but was afraid to ask me. On the third day I said to him: "Sushilov, it seems you want to ask money from me for Anton Vasiliev? Here." I was sitting on the bunk then; Sushilov was standing in front of me. He seemed to be very struck that I myself offered him money, that I myself remembered his difficult position, the more so as, in his opinion, he had taken too much from me recently, so that he did not dare hope I would give him more. He looked at the money, then at me, suddenly turned and left. I was very struck by it all. I followed him and found him behind the barracks. He was standing by the prison stockade, his face pressed to the palings and his arms leaning against them. "What's the matter, Sushilov?" I asked. He did not look at me, and I noticed, to my great astonishment, that he was on the verge of tears. "Alexander Petrovich . . . you think," he began in a breaking voice, trying to look away, "that I . . . for you . . . for the money . . . but I . . . I . . . a-a-ah!" Here he turned to the stockade again, so that he even bumped his forehead against it, and broke into sobs! . . . It was the first time I had seen a man in prison cry. I had a hard time comforting him, and though after that he began to serve me and "look after me" still more zealously, if that was possible, I noticed by certain almost imperceptible signs that his heart could never forgive me my reproach. And yet others laughed at him, picked on him at every opportunity, sometimes abused him badly—and he lived peacefully and amicably with them and never got offended. Yes, it can be very hard to make a man out, even after long years of acquaintance!

That is why prison could not present itself to me in its true light at first glance, as it did later on. And that is why I said that, even if I did look at everything with such greedy, heightened attention, I still did not perceive many things that were right under my nose. Naturally, I was struck in the beginning by the big, sharply distinguished features, but I may have perceived them wrongly as well, so that they left only an oppressive, hopelessly sad impression in my soul. My meeting with A—v contributed a great deal to that. He was also a prisoner, who had come to hard labor not long before me, and who made an especially painful impression on me during my first days in prison. However, I knew even before I came to prison that I would meet A—v there. He poisoned that first difficult time for me, making my inner torment more intense. I cannot pass him over in silence.

He was the most repulsive example of the baseness and vileness a man can sink to, and how far he can go in killing all moral feeling in himself, with no effort and with no regret. A—v was that young man of the nobility whom I have already mentioned briefly, saying that he reported everything that happened in the prison to our major and was friends with his orderly Fedka. Here is his history in brief: without finishing his studies anywhere, and having quarreled with his family in Moscow, who were appalled by his dissolute behavior, he arrived in Petersburg, and, to get money, decided on a vile denunciation, that is, decided to sell the blood of ten people for the immediate satisfaction of his unquenchable thirst for the most coarse and dissolute pleasures, for which, seduced by Petersburg, its pastry shops and lowlife he had become so greedy that, while being no fool, he risked a mindless and senseless act. He was soon exposed; he had involved innocent people in his denunciation, had deceived others, and for that he had been sent to Siberia, to our prison, for ten years. He was still quite young, life was only just beginning for him. It would seem that such a terrible change in his fate should have shocked him, should have called up some resistance, some change in his nature. But he accepted his new fate without the least embarrassment, even without the least revulsion, was not morally outraged at it, was not frightened of anything in it, except perhaps the necessity of working and of parting with the pastry shops and lowlife. He even fancied that the status of prisoner only gave him a freer hand for still greater meanness and vileness. "A convict is a convict; if you're a convict, you can act meanly and not be ashamed of it." That was literally his opinion. I recall this nasty creature as a phenomenon. I lived for several years among murderers, profligates, and inveterate villains, but I can say positively, never in my life have I met such total moral degradation, such decisive depravity, and such insolent baseness as in A—v. With us there was a parricide from the nobility; I have already mentioned him; but I was convinced by many details and facts that even he was incomparably more honorable and humane than A—v. Before my eyes, during my life in prison, A—v turned into and remained a piece of meat with teeth and a stomach, and with an unquenchable thirst for the coarsest, most brutish carnal pleasures, and to satisfy the least and most whimsical of these pleasures, he was capable of cold-blooded murder, cutting throats, anything so long as it left no traces. I am not exaggerating; I got to know A—v well. He was an example of what the carnal side of man can come to, unrestrained by any inner norm, any lawfulness. And how revolting it was for me to look at his eternally mocking smile! He was a monster, a moral Quasimodo.[1] Add to that the fact that he was cunning and intelligent, good-looking, even somewhat educated, and not without abilities. No, better fire, better plague and famine, than such a man in society! I have already said that everything in prison was so corrupt that spying and informing flourished and the prisoners were not at all angry about it. On the contrary, they were all very friendly with A—v and treated him much more amicably than they did us. Our drunken major's favor towards him lent him importance and weight in their eyes. Among other things, he persuaded the major that he could paint portraits (he also persuaded the prisoners that he had been a lieutenant in the guards), and the major demanded that A—v be sent to work in his house—to paint his portrait, of course. There he became close with the orderly Fedka, who had great influence over his master, and consequently on everybody and everything in the prison. A—v spied on us at the request of that same major, who, when drunk, slapped his face and called him a spy and an informer. It happened, even quite often, that right after slapping him, the major would sit down and order A—v to go on with the portrait. It seems our major really believed that A—v was a remarkable artist, all but a Briullov,[2] whom he had heard of, but even so he considered he had the right to slap his face, because, say, you may be an artist now, but you're also a convict, and even if you were Briullov three times over, I'd still be your superior, and therefore I'll do whatever I like to you. Among other things, he made A—v take his boots off and empty the chamber pots, and even so for a long time he could not give up the thought that A—v was a great artist. The portrait dragged on endlessly, for almost a year. Finally, the major realized that he was being hoodwinked, and once he became fully convinced that the portrait, instead of getting finished, looked less and less like him every day, he got angry, thrashed the artist, and sent him to do dirty work in the barracks. A—v obviously regretted it, and it was hard for him to give up his idle days, the handouts from the major's table, his friend Fedka, and all the pleasures the two of them had concocted for themselves in the major's kitchen. Once A—v was sent away, the major at least stopped persecuting M., a prisoner whom A—v was constantly denouncing to him, and this is why. At the time of A—v's arrival in prison, M. was alone. He was in great anguish; he had nothing in common with the other prisoners, looked at them with horror and loathing, did not notice and failed to see in them all that might have had a reconciling effect on him, and did not approach them. They repaid him with the same hatred. Generally, the position of people like M. in prison was terrible. M. did not know the reason why A—v had landed in prison. On the other hand, A—v, having realized who he was dealing with, at once convinced him that he had been exiled for something quite the opposite of informing, for almost the same thing as M. M. was terribly glad to find a comrade, a friend. He looked after him, comforted him during his first days in prison, supposing that he must be suffering very much, gave him his last money, fed him, and shared the most necessary things with him. But A—v at once conceived a hatred for him, precisely because the man was noble and looked upon any baseness with horror, precisely because he was totally unlike him, and he hastened at the first opportunity to inform the major of everything M. had told him about the prison and the major in their conversations. The major hated M. terribly for that and persecuted him, and, had it not been for the commandant's influence, would have brought him to grief. A—v not only was not embarrassed when M. later learned of his baseness, but even liked to meet him and look at him mockingly. This obviously gave him pleasure. M. pointed this out to me himself several times. The vile creature later escaped with another prisoner and a guard, but I will speak of their flight in what follows. He fawned upon me very much in the beginning, thinking I had not heard his story. I repeat, he poisoned my first days in prison with a still greater anguish. I was horrified at the terrible vileness and meanness I had been thrown into and found all around me. I thought everything here was just as vile and mean. But I was wrong: I was judging everything by A—v.

During those three days I loitered about the prison in anguish, lay on my bunk, asked a trustworthy prisoner, pointed out to me by Akim Akimych, to sew some shirts out of the government linen issued to me, for payment of course (a few kopecks a shirt); acquired for myself, on Akim Akimych's insistent advice, a folding mattress (of felt with a linen cover), flat as a pancake, and a pillow stuffed with wool, terribly hard when you're not used to it. Akim Akimych got into a great flutter arranging all these things for me and took part in it himself, sewing a quilt for me with his own hands, put together from scraps of old prison broadcloth trousers and jackets, which I bought from other prisoners. Government things that had outlived their time became the prisoners' property; they were sold at once right there in prison, and no matter how worn-out a thing was, there was still hope of getting it off your hands at some sort of price. In the beginning I was very surprised by it all. Generally, this was my first encounter with simple people. I myself suddenly became just as simple, just as much of a convict as they were. It was as if their habits, their notions, opinions, customs also became mine, at least formally, by the rules, though I did not share them in essence. I was astonished and embarrassed, as if I had never suspected any of it before and had never heard of it, though I had known and heard. But reality makes quite a different impression than knowledge and hearsay. For instance, could I ever have suspected before that such things, such old castoffs, could also be considered belongings? Yet I did have a quilt sewn for me from these old castoffs. It is hard to imagine the sort of cloth prison clothes were made of. It looked as if it was indeed thick army broadcloth; but once you wore it a bit, it turned into some sort of fishnet and tore outrageously. Anyhow, broadcloth clothes were issued yearly, but it was hard to get them to last even that long. A prisoner works, carries heavy loads; his clothes wear and tear quickly. Sheepskin coats were issued every three years, and usually served during that time as clothing, blanket, and bedding. But sheepskin coats are strong, though it was no rarity to see somebody at the end of the third year, that is, of the wearing period, in a sheepskin coat patched with plain canvas. Despite that, even very worn-out sheepskins, at the end of the appointed period, were sold for around forty silver kopecks. And some better preserved ones sold for sixty or even seventy, which was big money in prison.

Money—I have already spoken of this—was of terribly great importance and power in prison. I can say positively that a convict who had at least some money in hard labor suffered ten times less than one who did not have any, though the latter was also provided with everything by the prison, and what on earth should he have money for?—so our authorities reasoned. Again I repeat, if the prisoners had been deprived of all possibility of having their own money, they would either have gone crazy, or dropped dead like flies (despite their being provided with everything), or, finally, gotten themselves into unheard-of villainies, some from anguish, others the sooner to be somehow executed and annihilated, or to somehow "change their fate" (a technical expression). If a prisoner who has all but sweated blood to earn his kopeck, or ventured upon unheard-of ruses to obtain it, sometimes involving theft and swindling, then spends it so unreasonably, with such childish senselessness, that by no means proves that he does not value it, though it may seem so at first sight. A prisoner is greedy for money to the point of convulsions, to a darkening of the mind, and if he does indeed throw it away like wood chips when he carouses, he does it for something he considers on a higher level than money. What is higher than money for a prisoner? Freedom, or at least the dream of freedom. And prisoners are great dreamers. I will say something about that later, but while I'm at it, believe me, I have seen men exiled for *twenty years* who would quite calmly say to me such phrases as "Just wait, God grant I'll finish my term, and then . . ." The whole meaning of the word "prisoner" is a man with no will; but in wasting money, he is acting by *his own will.* In spite of any brands, fetters, and the hateful palings of the prison that screen him off from God's world and close him in like a beast in a cage—he can get hold of some vodka, which is a fearfully forbidden pleasure, treat himself to a bit of philandering, sometimes (though not always) bribe his immediate overseers, the invalid soldier and even the sergeant, to look the other way while he violates law and discipline; to top it all off, he can even display his bravado before them, and a prisoner loves terribly to display his bravado, that is, to show off before his comrades, and even persuade himself, *at least for a time*, that he has much more freedom and power than it may seem—in short, he can carouse, brawl, reduce somebody to dust, and prove to him that he *can do* all this, that it is all "in our own hands," that is, persuade himself of something the poor fellow cannot even dream of. Incidentally, that may be why one notices among prisoners, even in a sober state, a general inclination to bravado, to boasting, a comical and very naïve aggrandizing of themselves, illusory though it be. Finally, this carousing involves some risk—meaning there is at least some illusion of life in it, at least a remote illusion of freedom. And what will one not give for freedom? What millionaire, his throat squeezed by a noose, would not give all his millions for one breath of air?

The authorities are sometimes surprised that some prisoner who for several years has been so quiet, so well-behaved, has even been made an overseer on account of his praiseworthy behavior, suddenly, out of the blue—as if some devil has gotten into him—turns mischievous, carouses, makes a row, and sometimes even risks some criminal offense:

shows disrespect for his superiors, kills or rapes someone, and so on. They look at him in amazement. And yet maybe the whole reason for this sudden outburst in a man from whom it could be least expected is the anguished, convulsive display of his personality, an instinctive longing for his own self, a desire to declare himself, his humiliated self, which appears suddenly and reaches the point of anger, rage, a darkening of the mind, fits, convulsions. So, perhaps, a man buried alive wakes up in his coffin, bangs on the lid and tries to throw it off, though of course reason could convince him that all his efforts will be in vain. But the point is that he is no longer reasoning: it's convulsions. Let us also take into account that almost any self-willed display of personality in a prisoner is considered a crime; and in that case it is naturally all the same to him whether it is a big or a small display. If it's carousing, let it be carousing; if it's a risk, let it be an all-out risk—even murder. It's enough just to begin: once a man is drunk, there's no holding him back! And therefore it would be better in every way not to drive him that far. It would be more peaceful for everyone.

Yes, but how to do it?

VI

The First Month

When I entered prison, I had some money; I carried very little on me, for fear it would be confiscated, but just in case I had several roubles hidden away, that is, glued under the cover of a Gospel, which could be brought to prison. This book with money glued into it had been given to me back in Tobolsk, by those who also suffered in exile and already counted their time in decades, and who had long been accustomed to seeing a brother in every unfortunate.[1] There are in Siberia, and they have almost never been lacking, a number of persons who seem to have made their purpose in life a brotherly care for the "unfortunate," a totally disinterested, saintly compassion and commiseration for them as for their own children. I cannot help briefly recalling here one such encounter. In the town where our prison was there lived a certain lady, Nastasya Ivanovna, a widow.[2] Naturally, none of us, while in prison, could have made her acquaintance personally. It seems she had chosen it as the purpose of her life to help the exiles, but most of all she took care of us. Whether there had been a similar misfortune in her family, or someone especially near and dear to her heart had suffered for such a crime, in any case she seemed to consider it a special happiness to do all she could for us. Of course, she could not do much; she was very poor. But we, sitting in prison, felt that there outside we had a very devoted friend. Among other things, she often brought us news, which we had great need of. When I left prison and was on my way to another town, I managed to call on her and make her personal acquaintance. She lived somewhere on the outskirts with one of her close relations. She was neither old nor young, neither good- nor bad-looking; it was even impossible to tell if she was intelligent or educated. The one thing noticeable in her at every step was an infinite kindness, an overwhelming desire to please, to make things easier, to be sure to do something nice for you. All this could be seen in her gentle, kind eyes. Together with one of my comrades from prison, I spent almost a whole evening with her. She tried to read our eyes, laughed when we laughed, hastened to agree with everything we said; she fussed over treating us to whatever she could. She served us tea, snacks, some sweets, and if she had had thousands, it seems she would have been glad, if only because she could please us better and make things easier for our comrades left behind in prison. As we were saying good-bye, she gave us cigarette cases as mementos. She had glued them together for us out of cardboard (they were glued up God knows how) and stuck some colored paper on them, the way they bind arithmetic books for children in schools (and maybe some arithmetic book had actually been used for the covering). The edges were decorated with a thin border of gilt paper, for which she had probably gone on purpose to a shop. "You do smoke cigarettes, so maybe you'll find it useful," she said timidly, as if apologizing for her gift . . . Some people say (I've heard and read it) that the loftiest love of one's neighbor is at the same time the greatest egoism.[3] Where the egoism was in all this, I fail to understand.

Though I did not have a lot of money when I came to prison, I somehow could not be seriously annoyed by those prisoners who, almost in the first hours of my prison life, having already deceived me once, came quite naïvely a second, a third, and even a fifth time to borrow from me. But I will confess one thing frankly: I found it very annoying that all these people with their naïve ruses certainly must, as it seemed to me, have considered me a simpleton and a fool and been laughing at me precisely because I gave them money a fifth time. It certainly must have seemed to them that I was falling for their tricks and ruses, and if, on the contrary, I had refused them and chased them away, I'm sure they would have had much greater respect for me. But, annoyed as I was, I still could not refuse. I was annoyed because in those first days I was seriously preoccupied with how and on what footing I was going to establish myself in prison, or, better, on what footing I ought to stand with them. I felt and understood that this whole milieu was completely new to me, that I was completely in the dark, and that it was impossible to live in the dark for so many years. I had to prepare myself. Of course, I decided that above all I had to act directly, as inner feeling and conscience dictated. But I also knew that this was only an aphorism, and the most unexpected experience still lay before me.

And therefore, despite all the petty cares of my settling into the barrack, which I have already mentioned, and which I was drawn into for the most part by Akim Akimych, despite the fact that they also distracted me somewhat—a terrible gnawing anguish tormented me more and more. "A dead house!" I would say to myself, in the evening sometimes, on the porch of our barrack, studying the prisoners, who had already gathered after work and were lazily loitering about the prison yard, from the barrack to the kitchen and back. I studied them and from their faces and movements tried to find out what sort of people they were and what sort of characters they had. They loafed about in front of me either with scowling brows or much too merry (those two looks were most often met with and almost characteristic of prison), cursing or simply talking, or, finally, strolling alone, as if lost in thought, gliding quietly, some with a tired and apathetic look, others (even here!) with a look of defiant superiority, hats cocked, coats thrown over their shoulders, with bold, sly eyes and an impudent grin. "All this is my milieu, my present-day world," I thought, "which I've got to live with, like it or not . . ." I kept trying to ask questions and find out about them from Akim Akimych, with whom I liked very much to drink tea, so as not to be alone. I will say in passing that tea, in that first time, was almost my only nourishment. Akim Akimych did not refuse the tea, and he himself set up our funny, homemade little tin samovar, which M. had lent me. Akim Akimych usually drank one glass (he also had glasses), drank it silently and ceremoniously, handed the glass to me, and at once set to work on my quilt. But of what I needed to find out he could not inform me, nor did he even understand why I was so especially interested in the characters of the convicts around us and close to us, and he listened to me with a sort of sly little smile, which I remember very well. "No, clearly, I must experience it myself and not keep asking questions," I thought.

On the fourth day, just like that time when I went to have my fetters changed, the prisoners lined up early in the morning, in two rows, on the little square in front of the guardhouse, by the prison gates. Ahead, facing them, and behind, soldiers were drawn up, guns loaded and bayonets fixed. A soldier has the right to shoot a prisoner if he attempts to escape from him; but at the same time he has to answer for his shooting if it was not in a case of extreme necessity; and it is the same in the case of an open mutiny of the convicts. But who would venture to escape in plain sight? The engineers officer, the sergeant, some lower-ranking engineers and soldiers assigned to supervise the work appeared. The roll was called; the group of prisoners going to the tailor's shops left before the rest; the engineers were not concerned with them; they worked for the prison itself and made clothes for it. Then some went off to the workshops, and the rest to do ordinary dirty work. I went with twenty other prisoners. Outside the fortress, on the frozen river, there were two government barges, which were no longer usable and had to be dismantled, so that at least the old timbers would not go to waste. Though it seems all this old material was worth very little, almost nothing. Firewood was sold in town at a very low price, and there were enough forests around. Prisoners were sent there only so that they would not sit with idle hands, and they understood that very well themselves. They always did such work sluggishly and apathetically, and it was almost totally different when the work itself was sensible, worthwhile, and especially when they could get it on assignment. Then they became as if inspired, and though they gained nothing at all from it, I saw how they spared no effort to finish sooner and better; their self-esteem was even somehow involved in it. But it was hard to get an assignment for this present work, done more for the sake of form than of need, and it was necessary to work right up till the drum beat the call to go home at eleven o'clock in the morning. The day was warm and misty; the snow was nearly melting. Our whole group went out of the fortress to the riverbank, with a slight clanking of fetters, which, though hidden under our clothes, still gave out a high and piercing metallic sound at each step. Two or three men detached themselves to fetch the necessary tools from the storeroom. I walked with the rest and even became as if animated: I wanted all the sooner to see and find out what the work was. What was this hard labor? And how would it be for me to work for the first time in my life?

I remember everything to the last detail. On the way some tradesman with a little beard met us, stopped, and put his hand in his pocket. A prisoner immediately stepped out of our group, took his hat off, received the alms—five kopecks—and quickly returned to us. The tradesman crossed himself and went on his way. We spent those five kopecks the same morning on kalachi, dividing them equally among our party.

Of this whole group of prisoners, some were sullen and taciturn, as usual, others were indifferent and sluggish, still others chattered lazily among themselves. One was terribly pleased and merry about something, sang and all but danced on the way, his fetters clanking at every leap. It was the same short and stocky prisoner who, on my first morning in prison, had quarreled with another man by the water buckets, during wash-up time, because the other man senselessly insisted that he was the bird Kagan. This rollicking fellow's name was Skuratov. Finally, he began to sing some dashing song, of which I remember the refrain:

They married me off without me there—
I was down at the mill.

The only thing lacking was a balalaika.

Of course, his extraordinarily merry state of mind at once aroused indignation in some of our party, and was even taken as all but offensive.

"Hear him howl!" one prisoner said reproachfully, though it was none of his business.

"The wolf only had one song, and that he stole, the Tula-man!" one of the gloomy ones observed with a Ukrainian accent.

"Suppose I am a Tula-man," Skuratov immediately objected, "but you in your Poltava—you choked on a dumpling."

"Lies! And you, what do you eat? You slurp shchi from a bast shoe!"

"And now it's like the devil's feeding him cannonballs," a third one added.

"It's true I'm a pampered man, brothers," Skuratov responded with a little sigh, as if regretting his pamperedness, addressing everyone in general and no one in particular. "Since childhood I've been wrought up" (meaning "brought up"—Skuratov deliberately distorted the word) "on prunes and little white rolls. My dear brothers own a shop in Moscow even now, selling wind in the passageway. Rich merchants."

"And what were you selling?"

"Oh, I've come down through various qualities. It was then, brothers, that I got my first two hundred . . ."

"Not roubles!" one curious listener picked up, even jumping as he heard about so much money.

"No, my dear man, not roubles—rods. Luka, hey, Luka!"

"For some it's Luka, but for you it's Luka Kuzmich," a small and skinny prisoner with a sharp little nose responded reluctantly.

"Well, Luka Kuzmich, then, devil take you."

"For some it's Luka Kuzmich, but for you it's Uncle."

"Well, devil take you and your uncle, there's no point talking to you! And it was a good word I wanted to say. Well, so you see, brothers, as it happened I didn't spend long in Moscow. They gave me fifteen lashes for the road and threw me out. So I . . ."

"Why did they throw you out?" interrupted one prisoner, who had been diligently following the story.

"Don't break the quarantine, don't drink bung-juice, don't play blubberlips—so, brothers, I didn't manage to get properly rich in Moscow. And I wanted verry, verry much to get rich. I wanted it so much, I can't tell you."

Many burst out laughing. Skuratov was obviously one of those voluntary jokers, or, better, buffoons, who seemed to make it their duty to amuse their sullen comrades, and who, naturally, got nothing but abuse for it. He belonged to a particular and remarkable type, whom I may have occasion to talk about again.

"Even now you could be shot for a sable," observed Luka Kuzmich. "Why, your clothes alone are worth a good hundred roubles."

Skuratov was wearing a most shabby, worn-out sheepskin coat, with patches sticking out on all sides. He looked the man up and down quite indifferently but attentively.

"But the head, brothers, the head's worth a lot!" he replied. "As I was bidding farewell to Moscow, my only comfort was that my head was coming with me. Farewell, Moscow, thanks for the hot time, for the breath of freedom, for the good lambasting! And the sheepskin, my dear man, is nothing for you to look at . . ."

"So it's your head I should look at?"

"His head isn't even his, it was handed out to him," Luka mixed in again. "They gave it to him as alms when his party passed through Tyumen."

"But still, Skuratov, you must have had some trade?"

"Trade, hah! He was a blind beggar's guide, led the moles around, pinched pennies from them," observed one of the scowling ones. "That's all he had for a trade."

"I actually tried stitching boots," Skuratov replied, completely ignoring the barb. "I only made one pair."

"Did anybody buy them?"

"Yes, I ran into a man who clearly didn't fear God or honor his father and mother: the Lord punished him—he bought them."

Everybody around Skuratov roared with laughter.

"I worked again, here already," Skuratov went on with perfect composure, "for Stepan Fyodorovich Pomortsev, the lieutenant, making uppers for his boots."

"Was he pleased?"

"No, brothers, he wasn't. He cursed me to kingdom come, and also gave me a knee in the backside. He was verry angry. Eh, you're a cheat, my life, a cheat, my prison life!"

And then a little later on
Ak-kulina's man turned up . . .

He unexpectedly dissolved in song again and started skipping and beating his feet in rhythm.

"What an outrageous man!" growled the Ukrainian walking beside me, looking askance at him with spiteful contempt.

"A useless man!" another observed in a definitive and serious tone.

I decidedly did not understand why they were angry with Skuratov, and why all merry people in general, as I had already managed to notice in those first days, seemed to be held in a certain contempt. I ascribed the anger of the Ukrainian and the others to personal reasons. But it was not personal; it was anger at the fact that Skuratov had no self-control, had no stern, affected air of his own dignity, with which the whole prison was infected to the point of pedantry; in short, at his being, in their own expression, a "useless" man. Yet they were not angry with all the merry ones and did not slight them all as they did Skuratov and others like him. It depended on how a man allowed himself to be treated: a good-natured, guileless man would at once be subjected to humiliation. I was even shocked by it. But among the merry ones there were also some who could and would bite back, and who gave no quarter to anybody: these they were forced to respect. Here, in this same group of people, there was one of these snappish ones, essentially the merriest and nicest of men, but I got to know that side of him only later—a tall, imposing fellow, with a big wart on his cheek and a most comical expression on his face, who was, however, rather handsome and keen-witted. He was known as "the pioneer," because he once served in the pioneers;[4] now he found himself in the special section. I will come back to him later.

However, not all the "serious" ones were as expansive as the Ukrainian made indignant by merriment. There were several men in the prison who aimed at preeminence, a knowledge of all things, resourcefulness, character, intelligence. Many of them were in fact intelligent people, with character, and in fact achieved what they aimed at, that is, preeminence and considerable moral influence over their comrades. Among themselves these clever ones were often great enemies—and they each had many who hated them. They looked upon the other prisoners with dignity and even condescension, picked no unnecessary quarrels, were in good standing with the authorities, behaved like managers at work, and none of them would find fault, for example, with singing; they did not stoop to such trifles. With me all this sort were remarkably polite all the while I was in prison, but not very talkative—also, it seems, out of dignity. Of them I will also have to speak in more detail.

We came to the riverbank. On the river below, frozen into the ice, stood the old barge that had to be broken up. On the other side of the river lay the bluish steppe; the view was gloomy and deserted. I expected everyone to throw themselves into work, but they did not even think of it. Some sat on logs that lay on the bank; almost all of them pulled from their boots pouches of local tobacco, sold in leaves at the market for three kopecks a pound, and stubby willow pipes with little homemade wooden stems. The pipes began to puff; the convoy stretched out in a line around us and with an utterly bored look began to guard us.

"And whose bright idea was it to break up this barge?" one man muttered as if to himself, not addressing anyone. "Do they need wood chips or something?"

"Somebody who's not afraid of us thought it up," observed another.

"Where are all these muzhiks flocking to?" the first asked after a brief silence, not noticing, of course, the answer to his previous question, and pointing at a crowd of muzhiks in the distance making their way somewhere in single file over the untouched snow. Everybody turned lazily in that direction and, having nothing better to do, started making fun of them. One of the muzhiks, the last one, walked in a somehow extraordinarily funny way, spreading his arms and hanging his head sideways in its conical felt hat. His whole figure was fully and distinctly outlined against the white snow.

"Look how brother Petrovich got hisself all wrapped up," one man observed, mocking the muzhiks' way of talking. It is remarkable that the prisoners generally looked down somewhat on the muzhiks, though half of them were muzhiks themselves.

"That last one walks like he's planting turnips, eh, lads?"

"He's heavy-minded, got lots of money," a third one observed.

They all laughed, but also somehow lazily, as if unwillingly. Meanwhile a kalach seller came up, a pert and saucy wench.

They spent the five kopecks of alms on kalachi and divided them up equally on the spot.

A young fellow who sold kalachi in prison took two dozen and started arguing hotly that he should get three extra and not just two, according to the usual arrangement. But the woman would not agree.

"Well, then give me a little of that?"

"That what?"

"What the mice don't eat."

"Bite your tongue!" the wench shrieked and laughed.

Finally, a sergeant with a swagger stick came to inspect the work.

"Hey, you, what are you all sitting around for! Get moving!"

"Come on, Ivan Matveich, give us an assignment," one of the "superior" men said, slowly getting up.

"Why didn't you ask earlier, before you were sent out? Take the barge apart, there's your assignment."

Somehow the men finally rose and went down to the bank, barely dragging their feet. The "managers" emerged from the crowd at once, at least verbally. It turned out that the barge was to be broken up not just anyhow, but preserving the timbers as far as possible, and in particular the ribs fastened all along the barge's keel with wooden pins—slow and tedious work.

"First off, we've got to pull out this little timber here. Let's set to it, lads," observed one prisoner, not a manager or superior, but a simple laborer, a reserved and quiet fellow, who had been silent up to then, and, bending over, he took hold of a thick timber, waiting for helpers. But nobody helped him.

"Yeah, sure you'll pick it up! You'll never pick it up, and if your grandpa bear comes along, he won't pick it up either!" someone grumbled through his teeth.

"Well then, brothers, how do we begin? I really don't know . . . ," said the upstart, puzzled, abandoning the beam and raising himself.

"You can't work your way through all this work . . . What are you popping up for?"

"He couldn't feed three chickens without losing count, and here he's the first . . . Squawker!"

"I didn't mean anything, brothers," the puzzled man tried to talk his way out of it, "I just . . ."

"What am I supposed to do, put dust covers on you or something? Pickle you for the winter?" the officer shouted again, looking in perplexity at the twenty-headed crowd that did not know how to set to work. "Get moving! Quick!"

"You can't go quicker than quick, Ivan Matveich."

"And so you don't do anything, eh? Saveliev! Yammer Petrovich! It's you I'm talking to: What are you standing there pawning your eyes for! . . . Get moving!"

"What can I do by myself? . . ."

"Give us an assignment, Ivan Matveich."

"I told you—there won't be any assignment. Take the barge apart and go home. Get moving!"

They finally set to work, but sluggishly, reluctantly, clumsily. It was even vexing to look at this robust crowd of stalwart workmen who seemed decidedly perplexed about how to get down to business. They were just starting to remove the first, smallest rib, but, as it happened, it kept breaking, "breaking by itself," as they reported in justification to the officer; consequently, it was impossible to work that way, and they had to go about it somehow differently. There followed a long discussion among themselves on how to go about it differently and what to do. Of course, it gradually reached the point of cursing and threatened to go even further . . . The officer shouted and waved his stick again, but again the rib broke. It finally turned out that there were not enough axes and that more tools had to be fetched. Two fellows were detached at once, under convoy, to bring tools from the fortress, while the rest quite calmly sat down on the barge, took out their pipes, and started smoking again.

The officer finally spat.

"Well, so you're still hard at it! Eh, what people, what people!" he muttered angrily, waved his hand, and went off to the fortress swinging his stick.

An hour later the sergeant came. After calmly hearing the prisoners out, he announced that he was giving them an assignment to remove four more ribs, but to make sure that they came out whole and not broken, and on top of that he marked out a sizable section of the barge to be dismantled, after which they could go home. It was a big assignment, but Lord, how they set to it! Where was their laziness, where was their perplexity! Axes whacked, wooden pegs got pulled out. Others shoved thick poles underneath and, pressing down on them with twenty hands, nimbly and skillfully wrenched out the ribs, which, to my astonishment, now came out perfectly whole and undamaged. Work was at the boil. Everyone suddenly became somehow remarkably intelligent. There was no unnecessary talk, no cursing; everyone knew what needed to be said or done, where to stand, what advice to give. Exactly half an hour before the drum, the given assignment was finished, and the prisoners went home tired, but perfectly content, though they had gained only a mere half hour against the appointed time. But as for me, I noticed one particular thing: no matter where I tried to join in and help them with the work, I was out of place everywhere, I was a hindrance everywhere, they all but drove me away with curses everywhere.

Even the lowest ragamuffin, who was himself the worst of workmen and did not dare make a peep before the other sharper and more sensible convicts, considered it his right to yell at me and chase me away if I stood next to him, under the pretext that I was hindering him. Finally one of the sharp ones said to me directly and rudely:

"What are you doing here? Get out! Don't butt in where you're not invited."

"Got himself in a fix!" another chimed in at once.

"Better take yourself a cup," a third said to me, "and go around collecting money for stone construction or tobacco destruction. You've got nothing to do here."

I had to stand apart, and to stand apart when everybody was working was somehow embarrassing. But when I actually did go and stand at the end of the barge, they shouted at once:

"See what workers they've given us! What can you do with them? Nothing, that's what!"

All of this, naturally, was deliberate, because they were all amused by it. They had to crow over the former gentleman, and, of course, they were glad of the chance.

It is now quite understandable why, as I already said earlier, my first question on entering prison was how to behave, on what footing to put myself with these people. I sensed beforehand that I would often have such clashes with them as now, at work. But, despite any such clashes, I decided not to change my plan of action, which I had already partly thought out at the time; I knew it was right. Namely: I decided that I must behave as simply and independently as possible, by no means to betray any effort to get closer with them; but not to reject them if they themselves wished to get closer. By no means to fear their threats and hatred and, as far as possible, to pretend I did not notice it. By no means to side with them on certain points, and not to cater to some of their habits and customs—in short, not to invite myself into their full friendship. I realized at first glance that they would be the first to despise me for it. However, by their way of thinking (and I later learned this for certain), I still had to maintain and even show respect for my noble origin before them, that is, to pamper myself, put on airs, disdain them, turn up my nose at everything, and keep my hands clean. That was precisely how they understood a nobleman to be. Naturally, they would abuse me for it, but deep down they would still respect me. Such a role was not for me; I had never been a nobleman according to their notions; but instead I promised myself never to belittle my education or my way of thinking before them by any concession. If, to please them, I were to start fawning on them, agreeing with them, being familiar with them, entering into their various "qualities" in order to gain their sympathy—they would at once assume I was doing it out of fear and cowardice, and would treat me with contempt. A—v was not an example: he visited the major, and they were afraid of him themselves. On the other hand, I did not want to withdraw from them into a cold, inaccessible politeness, as the Poles did. I saw very well now that they despised me for wanting to work as they did, for not pampering myself and putting on airs before them; and though I knew for certain that later on they would be forced to change their opinion of me, still the thought that they now seemed to have the right to despise me, thinking that I was trying to ingratiate myself with them at work, upset me very much.

That evening, when the afternoon's work was done and I returned to the prison, tired and worn-out, a terrible anguish came over me again. "How many thousands of days like this lie ahead of me," I thought, "all the same, all just the same!" It was already dusk, and I was wandering alone, silently, along the fence behind the barracks, when suddenly I saw our Sharik running straight towards me. Sharik was our prison dog, just as there are company, battery, and squadron dogs. He had been living in the prison from time immemorial, did not belong to anyone, considered everyone his master, and fed on scraps from the kitchen. He was a rather big dog, black with white spots, a mongrel, not very old, with intelligent eyes and a bushy tail. Nobody ever petted him, nobody paid any attention to him. Already on the first day I stroked him and let him eat bread from my hand. When I stroked him, he stood still, looked at me affectionately, and, as a sign of contentment, quietly wagged his tail. Now, not having seen me for a while—me, the first one in years who had thought of petting him—he ran around looking for me among them all, and finding me behind the barracks, ran with a squeal to meet me. I don't know what came over me, but I rushed to kiss him and hugged his head. He put his front paws on my shoulders and started licking my face. "So here is the friend fate has sent me!" I thought, and afterwards, during that first oppressive and gloomy time, whenever I came back from work, the first thing I did, before going anywhere, was to hurry behind the barracks with Sharik leaping ahead of me and squealing for joy, to hug his head and kiss it, kiss it, with some sort of sweet and at the same time tormentingly bitter feeling wringing my heart. And I remember it was even pleasant for me to think, as if flaunting my own hurt to myself, that now I had one being left in the whole world who loved me and was attached to me, my friend, my only friend—my faithful dog Sharik.

VII

New Acquaintances. Petrov

But time passed and I gradually began to feel myself more at home. With each day I was less and less confused by the commonplace occurrences of my new life. The events, the surroundings, the people—it all became somehow familiar to my eyes. To be reconciled with this life was impossible, but it was long since time to recognize it as an accomplished fact. All the misapprehensions that still remained in me I hid away in myself and stifled as much as possible. I no longer wandered about the prison like a lost man, nor did I betray my anguish. The wildly curious gazes of the convicts no longer rested on me so often, no longer followed me with such deliberate insolence. I also obviously became familiar to them, for which I was very glad. I already walked about the prison as if I was at home, knew my place on the bunk, and even apparently got used to things I had never in my life thought of getting used to. I went regularly every week to have half my head shaved. Every Saturday during our free time each of us was summoned from the prison to the guardhouse for that purpose (anyone who did not get shaved had to answer for it), and there a battalion barber lathered our heads with cold lather and mercilessly scraped them with the dullest of razors, so that even now I get chills all over just remembering that torture. However, a remedy was soon found: Akim Akimych pointed out to me a prisoner from the military category who charged a kopeck for shaving anyone with his own razor and made a business of it. Many of the convicts went to him to avoid the official barbers, and yet they were not pampered folk. Our prisoner-barber was called *major*—why, I don't know, and how he resembled a major I also can't say. Now, as I write, I keep picturing this major, a tall, lean, and taciturn fellow, rather stupid, eternally immersed in his occupation, and unfailingly with a strop in his hand on which, day and night, he sharpened his utterly worn-down razor, and seemed to be totally absorbed in this occupation, obviously taking it for the purpose of his whole life. In fact, he was extremely pleased when the razor was good and somebody came for a shave: his lather was warm, his hand light, his shaving like velvet. He obviously enjoyed his art and was proud of it, and he accepted his earned kopeck with nonchalance, as if it was indeed a matter of art and not of a kopeck. A—v caught it badly from our real major when he was ratting to him once about the prison and, mentioning the name of our prison barber, carelessly referred to him as "the major." The real major flew into a rage and was offended in the highest degree. "Do you know, you scoundrel, what a major is?" he shouted, foaming at the mouth, dealing with A—v in his own way. "Do you have any idea what a major is!? And suddenly there's some scoundrel of a convict, and you dare call him a major to my face, in my presence?! . . ." Only A—v could get along with such a man.

From the very first day of my life in prison I began to dream of freedom. Calculating when my prison term would be over, in a thousand different forms and methods, became my favorite occupation. I could not even think of anything otherwise, and I am sure that anyone who is deprived of freedom for a term does the same. I don't know whether the other convicts thought and calculated as I did, but the astonishing light-mindedness of their hopes struck me from the first step. The hope of an inmate, deprived of freedom, is of a completely different sort from that of a man living a real life. A free man has hopes, of course (for instance, for a change in his lot, for success in some undertaking), but he lives, he acts; the whirl of real life carries him away entirely. Not so the inmate. Here, let's say, there is also life—the life of prison, of hard labor; but whoever the convict may be and whatever his term of punishment, he is decisively, instinctively, unable to take his lot as something absolute, definitive, as part of real life. Every convict feels that he is not *at home*, but as if on a visit. He looks at twenty years as if they were two, and is completely convinced that when he leaves prison at fifty-five he will be as fine a fellow as he is now at thirty-five. "We've still got a life to live!" he thinks and stubbornly drives away all doubts and other vexing thoughts. Even exiles without a term, in the special section, sometimes reckoned that an order might suddenly come from Petersburg: "Send to the mines in Nerchinsk and set a term." Then it will be fine: first, it takes almost six months to get to Nerchinsk, and life in a transport party is so much better than life in prison! And later he'll finish his term in Nerchinsk, and then . . . Some gray-haired men even reckoned that way!

In Tobolsk I saw men chained to the wall. He sits like that on a chain seven feet long; his cot is right there. He has been chained up for something uncommonly horrible, which he did already in Siberia. They sit like that for five years, for ten years. Most of them are robbers. I saw only one among them who seemed to be of the gentry; he had been in government service somewhere. He spoke as meekly as could be, with a lisp; he had a sweet little smile. He showed us his chain, showed how to lie comfortably on the cot. What a rare bird he must have been! In general, they all behave meekly and appear to be content, and yet each of them wants so very much to get through his term quickly. Why would that be? Here is why: he would then leave his stuffy, dank room with its low brick ceiling, walk in the prison yard, and . . . and that's all. He will never be let out of prison. He knows himself that those who have been chained up are kept in prison forever, till they die, and in fetters. He knows it, and still he wants terribly to finish his term on the chain. For without that wish, how could he sit for five or six years on a chain and not die or go out of his mind? Would anyone sit it out?

I felt that work might save me, fortify my health, my body. Constant inner anxiety, nervous agitation, the stuffy air of the barrack could destroy me completely. "Let me be outside often, get tired each day, learn to carry heavy loads—and at least I'll save myself," I thought. "I'll fortify myself, come out in good health, cheerful and strong, not yet old." I was not mistaken: work and activity were very good for me. I looked with horror at one of my comrades (a nobleman), how he dwindled away in prison like a candle. He entered it together with me, still young, handsome, cheerful, and left half-ruined, gray-haired, crippled, short of breath. "No," I thought, looking at him, "I want to live, and I will live." But I did catch it at first from the convicts for my love of work, and for a long time they taunted me with scorn and mockery. But I took no notice of anyone and cheerfully set off somewhere, for instance to bake and crush alabaster—one of the first tasks I learned. That was easy work. The chief engineers were prepared, as far as possible, to make the work easier for the noblemen, which, however, was not at all indulgence, but merely fairness. It would be strange to demand of a man who was twice weaker and had never worked the same assignment as was normally given to a real worker. But this "pampering" was not always done, and when it was, it was done as if stealthily: these things were kept under strict observation. Quite often we had to do hard work, and then, naturally, it was twice as hard for the noblemen as for the other workers. Usually three or four men, old or weak, were sent to the alabaster works, and so, naturally, we were among them; and on top of that, one real worker was attached who knew the job. Usually, over the course of several years, it was the same man, Almazov, a stern, swarthy, and lean man, already on in years, unsociable and squeamish. He deeply despised us. However, he was very taciturn, so much so that he did not even bother to grumble at us. The shed in which the alabaster was baked and crushed also stood on the deserted and steep riverbank. In winter, especially on a bleak day, it was dismal to look at the river and the distant bank opposite. There was something melancholy and heart-wrenching in that wild and deserted landscape. But it was almost worse when the sun shone brightly on the endless white mantle of snow; you wanted to fly off somewhere into that steppe, which began on the other bank and spread southwards in an unbroken sheet for a thousand miles. Almazov usually started work silently and sternly; we were as if ashamed that we could not help him in any real way, and he purposely managed everything alone, purposely did not ask for any help from us, as if to make us feel all our guilt before him and regret our own uselessness. And the whole thing amounted to nothing more than heating the oven for baking the alabaster we brought and put into it. The next day, when the alabaster was thoroughly baked, we began to unload the oven. Each of us took a heavy mallet, filled a special box with alabaster, and set about crushing it. This was lovely work. The fragile alabaster quickly turned into white, sparkling dust, it crumbled so readily, so well. We swung the heavy mallets and raised such a racket that we enjoyed it ourselves. We would get tired, finally, but at the same time we became light; our cheeks flushed, our blood circulated more quickly. Here Almazov even began to look at us indulgently, as one looks at little children; he puffed indulgently at his pipe, but still could not help grumbling when he had to speak. However, he was like that with everybody, and it seems he was in fact a kind man.

Another job I was assigned to was turning the flywheel in the workshop. It was a big, heavy wheel. To spin it called for great effort, especially when the turner (an artisan from the engineers) was turning something like a stairway banister or a leg for a big table to furnish some functionary's office, which required nearly a whole log. In that case one man's strength was not enough, and two were usually assigned to it—myself and B., another nobleman. This work was left to us for several years, whenever some turning needed to be done. B. was a weak, frail man, still young, suffering from a chest ailment. He came to prison a year before me, along with two other comrades—one an old man who prayed to God day and night all the while he was with us (for which the prisoners respected him greatly) and who died while I was still there; the other still a very young man, fresh, ruddy, strong, brave, who, when B. became exhausted in the middle of their journey, carried him for the remaining five hundred miles. The friendship between them was something to see. B. was a man of excellent education, noble, with a magnanimous character, but spoiled and exasperated by illness. We handled the flywheel together, and it even amused us both. It gave me first-rate exercise.

I also especially liked shoveling snow. This usually came after blizzards, which were not rare in winter. After a twenty-four-hour snowstorm, some houses were covered halfway up the windows, and some were almost completely buried. When the storm was over and the sun came out, they drove us out in big gangs, sometimes the whole prison, to shovel the snowdrifts away from the government buildings. Each of us was given a shovel, the assignment was for all of us, sometimes so big that you had to wonder how we could handle it, and we all set to work together. The crumbly snow, only just fallen and slightly frozen on the surface, was easily taken up by the shovel in huge lumps and scattered about, turning into sparkling dust while still in the air. The shovel cut freely into the white mass glistening in the sun. The prisoners almost always did this work cheerfully. The fresh winter air, the movement excited them. They all grew merry; they laughed, shouted, joked. They started throwing snowballs, though, naturally, the sensible ones yelled at them after a few minutes, indignant at the laughter and merriment, so that the general enthusiasm usually ended in curses.

I gradually began to widen the circle of my acquaintances. However, I was not thinking about making acquaintances myself: I was still uneasy, gloomy, and mistrustful. My acquaintances began by themselves. One of the first to visit me was the prisoner Petrov. I say "visit" and give special emphasis to the word. Petrov was in the special section and lived in the barrack furthest away from mine. There obviously could be no connections between us; we also had decidedly nothing in common and could not have. And yet in those first days Petrov seemed to consider it his duty to come to my barrack almost every day or to stop me during our free time, when I would be walking behind the barracks, as far from all eyes as possible. At first I found it unpleasant. But he was somehow able to do it so that his visits soon even began to divert me, though he was not an especially gregarious or talkative man. In appearance he was of medium height, strongly built, adroit, fidgety, with a rather pleasant face, pale, broad cheekbones, a bold gaze, small, closely set white teeth, and an eternal pinch of snuff behind his lower lip. Holding snuff behind one's lip was a custom among many of the convicts. He looked younger than his years. He was about forty, but seemed only thirty. He always talked to me with extreme ease, and behaved on an equal footing in the highest degree, that is, extremely decently and tactfully. If he noticed, for instance, that I was seeking solitude, he would talk to me for a couple of minutes, leave me at once, and thank me each time for my attention—certainly something he never did with anyone else in the prison. It is curious that these relations between us lasted not only for the first few days, but over the course of several years, and almost never became closer, though he really was devoted to me. Even now I cannot decide what he wanted from me, why he thrust himself upon me every day. Though he did happen to steal from me later on, he did it somehow *inadvertently*; but he almost never asked me for money, which means he did not come for money or for any other profit.

Again I don't know why, but it always seemed to me as if he did not live in the same prison with me, but somewhere far off in another house, in town, and only came to the prison in passing, to find out the news, to visit me, to see how we all lived. He was always hurrying somewhere, as if he had left someone waiting for him somewhere, as if he had not finished doing something. And yet he never seemed very flustered. His gaze, too, was somehow strange: intent, with a shade of boldness and a certain mockery, but he gazed somehow into the distance, through the object; as if he were trying to make out, beyond the object in front of his nose, some other more distant one. This gave him an absent-minded look. I watched on purpose sometimes to see where Petrov would go after me. Where was it that he was so expected? But he would hurry off somewhere to the barracks or the kitchen, sit down there by one of the talkers, listen attentively, occasionally enter into the conversation himself, even very vehemently, and then would suddenly break off and fall silent. But whether he talked or sat silently, still you could see that he was there just so, in passing, that he had something to do elsewhere and was expected. The strangest thing was that he never had anything to do; he lived in complete idleness (apart from prison work, of course). He knew no handicrafts, and almost never had any money. But he was not much worried about money either. And what did he talk about with me? His conversation was as strange as he was. He would see, for instance, that I was walking behind the barracks and would suddenly turn abruptly in my direction. He always walked quickly, always turned abruptly. He came at a walk, but seemed to be running.

"Hello."

"Hello."

"Am I bothering you?"

"No."

"I wanted to ask you about Napoleon. Isn't he a relative of the one from the year twelve?" (Petrov was a cantonist and could read and write.)

"He is."

"Then how come they say he's a president?"[1]

He always asked questions quickly, curtly, as if he needed to find something out as soon as possible. As if he was inquiring into a very important matter that could brook no delay.

I explained what sort of president he was and added that he might soon become an emperor.

"How is that?"

I explained that, too, as well as I could. Petrov listened attentively, with perfect understanding and a quick grasp, even inclining his ear towards me.

"Hm. And here's something I wanted to ask you, Alexander Petrovich: is it true what they say, that there are apes whose arms reach their heels, and who are as tall as the tallest man?"

"Yes, there are such apes."

"What sort are they?"

I also explained as much as I knew about that.

"Where do they live?"

"In hot countries. There are some on the island of Sumatra."

"That's in America, isn't it? Don't they say the people there walk upside down?"

"Not upside down. You're talking about the antipodes."

I explained what America was and, as well as I could, what the antipodes are. He listened as attentively as if he had come running on purpose for the antipodes alone.

"Ahh! And I read last year about the countess La Vallière. Arefyev brought the book from the adjutant. So is it true, or just made up? Dumas wrote it."[2]

"Of course it's made up."

"Well, good-bye. My thanks to you."

And Petrov vanished, and essentially we almost never talked in any other way.

I began to make inquiries about him. M., learning of this acquaintance, even warned me. He told me that many of the convicts had struck terror into him, especially at the beginning, during his first days in prison, but none of them, not even Gazin, had made such a terrifying impression on him as this Petrov.

"He's the most resolute, the most fearless of all the convicts," said M. "He's capable of anything; he'll stop at nothing, if the fancy takes him. He'll put the knife to you, too, if it occurs to him, just so, simply put the knife to you, without wincing, without remorse. I even think he's not in his right mind."

This opinion interested me greatly. But somehow M. could not account for why it seemed so to him. And, strangely enough, for several years after that, I knew Petrov, talked with him almost every day; in all that time he was sincerely attached to me (though I decidedly do not know why)—and all through those several years, though he lived sensibly in prison and did absolutely nothing terrible, each time I looked at him and talked with him, I felt certain that M. was right and that Petrov was perhaps the most resolute and fearless of men, and knew no constraint. Why it seemed so to me, I also cannot account for.

I will note, however, that this Petrov was the same one who had wanted to kill the major when he was summoned to be punished, and when the major was "saved by a miracle," as the prisoners said, having left just before the moment of punishment. Another time, before he came to prison, it happened that a colonel struck him at drill. He had probably been beaten many times before that; but this time he refused to take it and stabbed his colonel openly, in broad daylight, before the drawn-up ranks. However, I don't know his whole story in detail; he never told it to me. Of course, these were only outbursts, when his nature revealed itself all at once, fully. But still they were very rare in him. He really was sensible and even placid. There were hidden passions in him, even strong, burning ones; but the hot coals were always covered with ashes and smoldered quietly. I never noticed in him, as I did, for instance, in others, even the shadow of braggadocio or vanity. He rarely quarreled, but on the other hand he was not particularly friendly with anyone, except for Sirotkin, and then only when he needed him. Once, however, I saw him become seriously angry. He had not been given something, some object or other; he had not gotten his share. His quarrel was with a prison strongman, tall, spiteful, a bully, a jeerer, and far from a coward—Vassily Antonov, a common-law criminal. They had been shouting for a long time, and I thought the matter would end at most with simple blows, because occasionally, though very rarely, Petrov fought and swore like the lowest convict. But this time something else happened: Petrov suddenly went pale, his lips trembled and turned blue, he had difficulty breathing. He got up and slowly, very slowly, with the inaudible steps of his bare feet (he liked to go barefoot in the summer), approached Antonov. All at once everybody in the whole noisy and clamorous barrack became hushed; you could have heard a fly buzz. Everybody waited for what would happen. Antonov leaped up to meet him; he looked awful . . . I couldn't stand it and left the barrack. I expected to hear the cry of a murdered man before I stepped off the porch. But this time, too, the matter ended in nothing: before Petrov had time to reach him, Antonov silently and hastily threw him the contested object. (The matter had to do with a most pitiful rag, some sort of foot cloth.) Naturally, a couple of minutes later Antonov cursed him a little anyway, for the sake of propriety and his conscience, to show he was really not all that frightened. But Petrov paid no attention to the curses, and did not even respond: the matter was not about curses, and it had been decided in his favor; he was left very pleased and took his rag. Fifteen minutes later he went back to his loitering about the prison with a look of complete idleness and as if searching out some curious conversation somewhere, so that he could poke his nose in and listen. He seemed to be interested in everything, but it somehow happened that he mostly remained indifferent to it all and just loitered about the prison doing nothing, as if tossed now here, now there. He might also be compared with a worker, a stalwart worker, who could work at a cracking pace, but who for the time being has not been given any work, and meanwhile sits there playing with little children. I also couldn't understand why he stayed on in prison, why he didn't escape. He wouldn't have thought twice, if he had wanted to badly enough. Reason holds sway over people like Petrov only until they want something. Then nothing on earth can hinder their desire. And I'm sure he could have escaped handily, fooled everybody, gone for weeks without bread somewhere in the forest or in the bulrushes. But he evidently had not hit upon this thought yet and did not desire it *fully*. I never noticed any great reasoning, any particular common sense in him. These people are born with one idea, which unconsciously moves them here and there all their lives; so they rush about all their lives until they find something they really want to do; then they are ready to risk their heads. I was sometimes surprised at how it was that such a man, who had killed his superior for striking him, could lie down so unprotestingly under the rods. He was sometimes whipped when he was found with vodka. Like all convicts without a trade, he occasionally undertook to smuggle vodka. But he lay down under the rods as if of his own accord, that is, as if he acknowledged that he deserved it; otherwise he wouldn't have done it for the life of him. I also marveled at him when, despite his obvious attachment to me, he stole from me. It came over him somehow in spells. It was he who stole my Bible from me, which I gave him only to carry from one place to another. He had to go just a few steps, but he managed to find a buyer on the way, sold it, and drank up the money at once. He evidently wanted very much to have a drink, and what he wanted very much *had* to be fulfilled. Such a man kills another for twenty-five kopecks, so as to drink a dram of vodka on those kopecks, though another time he would let a man with a hundred thousand pass right by. That evening he told me about the theft himself, with no embarrassment or remorse, quite indifferently, as if it were the most ordinary incident. I tried to give him a good scolding; I was also sorry about my Bible. He listened without annoyance, even very meekly; he agreed that the Bible was a very useful book, was sincerely sorry that I no longer had it, but did not regret stealing it at all; he looked at me with such self-confidence that I at once stopped scolding him. He put up with my scolding, probably reasoning that the man could not do without yelling at him for such an act—so, all right, let him give vent to it, amuse himself, yell; but essentially it was all nonsense, such nonsense that it was embarrassing for a serious man to talk about it. It seems to me he generally considered me a sort of child, almost an infant, who did not understand the simplest things in the world. If, for instance, I started talking to him about something other than learning and books, he did answer me, true, but as if only out of politeness, confining himself to the briefest replies. I often wondered what this bookish knowledge that he usually asked me about meant to him. Every now and then, during these conversations, I would glance at him out of the corner of my eye to see if he was laughing at me. But no, he usually listened seriously, attentively, though not very, in fact, and this last circumstance sometimes annoyed me. He asked his questions precisely, pointedly, but was somehow not very surprised at the information he received from me and even took it absent-mindedly . . . It also seemed to me that he had decided, without racking his brains too long, that it was impossible to talk with me as with other people, that apart from talking about books, I would not understand anything and even could not understand anything, so there was no use bothering me.

I'm convinced that he even loved me, and that always amazed me greatly. Whether he regarded me as an immature, incomplete man, whether he felt that special sort of compassion for me that any strong creature instinctively feels for a weaker one, once he had recognized me as such . . . I don't know. And though that did not prevent him from stealing from me, I'm convinced that he felt sorry for me even as he stole from me. "Eh, really!" he may have thought, laying hands on my goods, "what sort of man is he, if he can't even protect his own goods!" Yet that seems to be what he loved me for. He once said to me himself, somehow inadvertently, that I was "all too kindhearted a man" and that I was "so simple, so simple, it was even a pity to see. Only don't be offended, Alexander Petrovich," he added a moment later. "I said it from the heart."

It sometimes happens in the lives of such people that they suddenly reveal and distinguish themselves sharply and prominently in a moment of abrupt mass action or upheaval, and thus hit at once upon their full activity. They are not men of words, and cannot be the instigators or main leaders of the affair; but they are its main executors and the first to begin. They begin simply, without special pronouncements, but they are the first to leap over the main obstacle, without reflection, fearlessly making straight for all the knives—and everybody rushes after them and goes on blindly, goes on till the last wall, where they usually lay down their lives. I don't believe Petrov has ended well; in some one moment it will be all over for him at once, and if he has not perished so far, it means his time has not come yet. Who knows, though? Maybe he will live to have gray hair and die most peacefully of old age, drifting about aimlessly here and there. But I think M. was right when he said that he was the most resolute man in the whole prison.

VIII

Resolute Men. Luchka

About the resolute it is hard to say much; in prison, as everywhere, there were very few of them. By the looks of him, he is a horrible man; you think over what other people tell about him and even steer clear of him. Some unaccountable feeling made me avoid these people at first. Later my views of even the most horrible murderers changed in many ways. A man may not be a murderer, but he may be more horrible than another who got there for six murders. There were crimes of which it was hard to form even the most elementary notion: there was so much strangeness in the way they were committed. I say that precisely because here, among our simple people, some murders proceed from the most astonishing causes. There exists, for instance, and even quite frequently, the following type of murderer. The man lives quietly and meekly; he has a hard lot, but he bears it. Suppose he's a muzhik, or a house serf, a tradesman, a soldier. Suddenly something in him comes unhinged; he can't control himself and sticks a knife into his enemy and oppressor. It's here that the strangeness begins: for a while the man suddenly leaps beyond all limits. The first man he killed was an oppressor, an enemy; that is a crime, but understandable; he had a reason; but then he kills not an enemy but the first man he meets, kills him for fun, for a rude word, for a glance, for a trifle, or simply "Out of my way, don't cross me, I'm coming." It's as if the man is drunk, as if he's in a feverish delirium. As if, having leaped over a line that was sacred to him, he begins to admire the fact that nothing is holy for him anymore; as if he feels an urge to leap over all legality and authority at once, and to revel in the most boundless and unbridled freedom, to revel in this thrill of horror, which it is impossible for him not to feel. He also knows that a terrible punishment awaits him. All this may resemble the sensation when a man on a high tower feels drawn to the depths below him, so that he is finally glad to throw himself down headlong: do it quickly and there's an end to it! And all this happens even with the most meek and hitherto inconspicuous people. Some of them, when so bedazed, even start prancing. The more downtrodden he was before, the stronger now is his urge to show off, to strike terror into people. He enjoys this terror, he likes the very revulsion he arouses in others. He affects some sort of *desperation*, and such a "desperate man" is sometimes just waiting for a quick punishment, just waiting to be *finished off*, because it is finally hard for him to keep up this affected *desperation*. It is curious that in most cases all this mood, all this affectation, lasts right up to the scaffold, and then is cut off just like that: as if this term were somehow formal, set out beforehand according to the rules. Here the man suddenly becomes submissive, effaces himself, turns into a sort of rag. On the scaffold he whimpers—asks people's forgiveness. He gets to prison, and you look: such a driveler, such a sniveler, so downtrodden you're even astonished at him: "Can this be the same one who put the knife to five or six people?"

Of course, even in prison some don't become submissive so soon. They still maintain a certain swagger, a certain boastfulness: as if to say, Look, I'm not what you think, I "did in six souls." But in the end he becomes submissive all the same. Only sometimes he amuses himself, recalling his wild fling, his once-in-a-lifetime binge, when he was "desperate," and he loves it when he finds some simpleton and can play-act before him with the proper seriousness, boasting and telling him of his exploits, though without letting it be seen that he himself wants to tell about them. As if to say, See what sort of a man I was!

And with what refinement this touchy caution is observed, how lazily negligent such a story can sometimes be! What studied foppishness shows in the tone, in the storyteller's every word! Where do these people learn it!?

Once during those first days, on a long evening, lying idle and anguished on my bunk, I listened to one of these stories and, in my inexperience, took the storyteller for some colossal, horrible villain, for an unheard-of iron-willed character, while at the same time I all but made fun of Petrov. The theme of the story was how he, Luka Kuzmich, for nothing else but his own pleasure, had *packed away* a major. This Luka Kuzmich was that same small, skinny, sharp-nosed young prisoner in our barrack, a Ukrainian, of whom I have already made some mention.

He was, in fact, a Russian, but born in the south, a house serf, I think. There actually was something sharp and insolent in him: "Small bird, sharp claw." But prisoners instinctively figure a man out. He was shown very little respect, or, as they say in prison, "hisself was shown very little respect." He was terribly vain. That evening he was sitting on the bunk sewing a shirt. Sewing linens was his trade. Next to him sat a dull and limited fellow, but a kind and gentle one, sturdy and tall, his neighbor on the bunk, the prisoner Kobylin. Luchka, being his neighbor, often quarreled with him and generally treated him with condescension, mockingly and despotically, which Kobylin, in his simple-mindedness, did not quite notice. He was knitting a woolen sock and listened indifferently to Luchka. The latter was telling his story rather loudly and clearly. He wanted everybody to hear it, though he tried to pretend, on the contrary, that he was telling it to Kobylin alone.

"So, brother, they sent me away from our parts," he began, poking with his needle, "to Ch—ov, for vagrancy, I mean."[1]

"When was that, long ago?" Kobylin asked.

"It'll be two years come pea harvest. Well, so we got to K—v, and they put me in prison there for a little while. I look: there are some twelve men locked up with me, all Ukrainians, tall, strong, hefty as bulls. And so peaceable: the food is bad, the major twists them around as suits his hawnor" (Luka deliberately distorted the word). "I sit there one day, two days: I see—they're cowardly folk. 'Why do you give the fool such an easy time of it?' I say. 'Just go and try talking to him!'—and they even grin at me. I say nothing."

"There was this funny Ukrainian there, brothers," he added suddenly, abandoning Kobylin and addressing everyone in general. "He told how he was sentenced in court, and how he talked in court, and he cried his heart out; said he left his children behind, and his wife. And himself such a manly fellow, gray-haired, fat. 'I says to him: no! But the devil's son goes on writing, writing. Well, I says to myself, you can drop dead, and I'll just watch! But the man goes on writing, writing, like a song! . . . And so my head rolled!' Give me some thread, Vasya, this prison stuff's rotten."

"From the market," said Vasya, handing him the thread.

"Ours from the tailor's shop is better. The other day we sent Ninvalid, he must've bought it from some vile wench," Luchka went on, threading the needle against the light.

"Must be a sweetie of his."

"Must be."

"So what about that major?" the completely forgotten Kobylin asked.

That was just what Luchka wanted. But he did not go on with his story at once, and even seemed to pay no attention to Kobylin. He calmly smoothed out the thread, calmly and lazily shifted his legs under him, and then finally began:

"I finally stirred up my Ukrainians, and they demanded to see the major. That morning I had already asked my neighbor for a sharper,[*] took and hid it—just in case, I mean. The major was furious. He came. 'Well,' I say, 'don't chicken out, lads.' But their hearts were already in their heels; they were shaking all over. The major came running in, drunk. 'Who's this! What's this! I'm the tsar, I'm God!'

"When he said, 'I'm the tsar, I'm God,' I stepped forward," Luchka went on, "the knife up my sleeve."

"'No, Your Honor,' I say, gradually getting closer and closer to him, 'how can it be, Your Honor,' I say, 'that you're our tsar and God?'

"'Ah, so it's you, is it?' the major shouted. 'You're the rebel!'

"'No,' I say (getting closer and closer), 'no, Your Honor, as may be known to you, our God is one, almighty and ever-present,' I say. 'And our tsar is one, set over us all by God himself. He is a monarch, Your Honor. And you, Your Honor,' I say, 'are still only a major—our superior, Your Honor, by the tsar's mercy and your own merits.'

"'Wha-wha-wha-wha-at!' He just clucked, he couldn't speak, he was choking. He was very amazed.

"'Here's what,' I say, and I suddenly made a rush for him and stuck the whole knife right into his stomach. It was a skillful job. He rolled over and only jerked his legs a little. I threw down the knife.

"'There, lads,' I say, 'pick him up now!'"

. . .

---

[*] A knife. *Author.*

Here I will make a digression. Unfortunately, the expression "I'm the tsar, I'm God" and many others like them were much in use among many commanders in the old days. It must be admitted, however, that there are not many such commanders left, perhaps none at all. I will also note that the ones who especially flaunted and liked to flaunt such phrases were mostly commanders who had risen from the ranks themselves. Officer's rank seems to churn up all their insides, and their heads as well. Having long groaned in harness and gone through all the degrees of subordination, they suddenly see themselves officers, commanders, ennobled, and being unaccustomed and in that first intoxication, they exaggerate the notion of their power and significance—naturally, only in relation to the lower ranks subordinate to them. Towards the higher ranks they are still as servile as before, which is totally unnecessary and even disgusts many of their superiors. Some of these servile ones even hasten with particular feeling to show their superior officers that, though they are officers themselves, they come from the lower ranks and "always remember their place." But with regard to the lower ranks they turn into all but absolute monarchs. Now, of course, it is unlikely that any such officers exist and that any could be found who would shout "I'm the tsar, I'm God." But, despite that, I will still note that nothing so irritates prisoners, and all the lower ranks in general, as such phrases from their superiors. This brazen self-aggrandizement, this exaggerated opinion of their impunity, provokes hatred in the most obedient man and drives him out of all patience. Fortunately, this is almost entirely a thing of the past, and even in the old days was severely prosecuted by the authorities. I know several instances of it.

And in general the lower ranks are irritated by any supercilious negligence, any disdain in their treatment. Some think, for instance, that if the prisoners are well fed, well kept, treated according to the law, the matter ends there. That is also a mistake. Every man, whoever he may be and however humiliated, still requires, even if instinctively, even if unconsciously, respect for his human dignity. The prisoner himself knows that he is a prisoner, an outcast, and he knows his place before his superior; but no brands, no fetters will make him forget that he is a human being. And since he is in fact a human being, it follows that he must be treated as a human being. My God! *Humane* treatment may make a human being even of someone in whom the image of God has faded long ago.[2] These "unfortunates" need to be treated all the more humanely. That is their salvation and their joy. I have met such kind, noble commanders. I have seen the effect they have had on these humiliated people. A few gentle words—and the prisoners all but resurrected morally. They rejoiced like children, and, like children, they began to love. I will note one more strange thing: the prisoners themselves do not like to be treated too familiarly and *too* kindly by their superiors. They want to respect their superior, and here they somehow cease to respect him. The prisoner likes it, for instance, that his superior has decorations, that he looks distinguished, that he is in favor with some still higher superior, that he is strict, and important, and just, and maintains his dignity. Prisoners like such an officer more: it means that he preserves his own dignity, and does not offend them, therefore everything is good and beautiful.

"They must have given you a hot time for that," Kobylin remarked calmly.

"Hm. A hot time, brother, it was hot all right. Alei, hand me the scissors! What, brothers, no maidan today?"

"They drank up all their money," Vasya observed. "If they hadn't, there might have been."

"If! In Moscow they pay a hundred roubles for an 'if,'" Luchka observed.

"How many did they give you, Luchka, all in all?" Kobylin asked again.

"A hundred and five, my good friend. And I'll tell you, brothers, they all but killed me," Luchka went on, abandoning Kobylin again. "Once they handed down the hundred and five, they drove me out in full dress. And I'd never tasted a whip before. Huge numbers of people poured out for it, the whole town came running: a robber's going to be punished, a murderer, that is. They're stupid, these people, there's no telling how stupid. Timoshka* stripped me, laid me down, and shouted:

---

* The executioner. *Author.*

'Hold on now, it stings!' I wait for what'll happen. So he smacks me once—I wanted to cry out, opened my mouth, but there was no cry in me. The voice wasn't there. So he smacks me a second time, and believe it or not I didn't hear them count *two*. And when I came to my senses, I heard them count seventeen. They took me off the rack four times for a half-hour rest, brothers, and poured water on me. I look at them all goggle-eyed and think, 'I'm about to die . . .'"

"But you didn't?" Kobylin asked naïvely.

Luchka looked him up and down with a highly contemptuous glance; guffaws were heard.

"What a numbskull!"

"Nothing upstairs," observed Luchka, as if he regretted even having to talk to such a man.

"Lacks brains," Vasya clinched.

Luchka had killed six people, but nobody in the prison was afraid of him, though it may have been his heart's desire to be known as a horrible man . . .

IX

Isai Fomich. The Bathhouse. Baklushin's Story

Christmas was approaching. The prisoners were awaiting it with a sort of solemnity, and, looking at them, I also began to wait for something extraordinary. Four days before the holiday, we were taken to the bathhouse. In my time, especially in my first years, prisoners were rarely taken to the bathhouse. Everybody rejoiced and started getting ready. We were supposed to go after lunch, so there would be no work in the afternoon. The one who rejoiced and bustled about the most in our barrack was Isai Fomich Bumstein, a Jewish convict, whom I already mentioned in the fourth chapter of my story. He liked to steam himself to the point of stupefaction, of unconsciousness, and now, each time I happen to go through my old memories and remember our prison bathhouse (which is worthy of being remembered), the face of the most blessed and unforgettable Isai Fomich, my comrade at hard labor and neighbor in the barrack, appears before me. Lord, what a hilarious and droll man he was! I've already said a few words about his appearance: some fifty years old, puny, wrinkled, with terrible brand marks on his cheeks and forehead, skinny, weak, with a white chicken's body. In the expression of his face you could see a constant, unwavering self-satisfaction and even bliss. It seems he was not at all sorry to have wound up at hard labor. Since he was a jeweler, and there was no jeweler in our town, he worked constantly for the gentry and the town officials just doing jewelry work. They paid him something all the same. He was not in want, he was even *rich*, but he saved his money and lent it on pledges and at interest to all the convicts. He owned a samovar, a good mattress, cups, a complete dinner set. The town's Jews kept up an acquaintance with him and patronized him. On Saturdays he went under convoy to their prayer house in town (which was allowed by law), and lived in complete clover, though waiting impatiently for the end of his twelve-year term in order "to get marryet." There was a most comical mixture in him of naïveté, stupidity, cunning, boldness, simple-mindedness, timidity, boastfulness, and insolence. I found it very odd that the convicts did not laugh at him at all, except to make little jokes just for the fun of it. Isai Fomich evidently served as a diversion and a permanent amusement for everybody. "He's our only one, don't lay a finger on Isai Fomich," the prisoners said, and Isai Fomich, though he realized what was going on, was clearly proud of his significance, which the prisoners found very amusing. He arrived in prison in a hilarious fashion (before my time, but I was told about it). Suddenly one day, before evening, after work, the rumor spread through the prison that a Jew had been brought and was being shaved in the guardhouse and was about to come in. There was not a single Jew in our prison then. The prisoners waited impatiently for him and surrounded him at once as he came through the gate. The prison sergeant led him to the civilian barrack and pointed to a place on the bunk. In his hands Isai Fomich had a sack with the government things issued to him and his personal property. He laid down the sack, climbed onto the bunk, and sat with his legs tucked under, not daring to raise his eyes to anybody. There were sounds of laughter around him and prison jokes directed at his Jewish origin. Suddenly a young prisoner pushed his way through the crowd, carrying in his hands some very old, dirty, and tattered summer trousers, with prison foot rags on top of them. He sat next to Isai Fomich and slapped him on the shoulder.

"Well, my dear friend, it's six years I've been waiting here for you. Look, how much will you give me for these?"

And he laid out before him the rags he had brought.

Isai Fomich, who had been so timid when he entered the prison that he had not even dared raise his eyes to this crowd of mocking, disfigured, and terrible faces that had formed a tight ring around him, and had been so frightened that he had not managed to say a word, suddenly roused himself on seeing the pledge and quickly began to finger the rags. He even held them up to the light. Everybody waited for what he would say.

"So, how's about a silver rouble? They're worth it!" the customer began, winking to Isai Fomich.

"A silver rouble, never, but seven kopecks would do it."

These were the first words Isai Fomich uttered in prison. Everybody just rocked with laughter.

"Seven! Well, give me seven, then; the luck's on you! Watch out, take good care of that pledge; you'll answer for it with your head."

"With three kopecks interest, it'll be ten kopecks," the Jew went on in a trembling and faltering voice, going to his pocket for the money and looking around fearfully at the prisoners. He was terribly frightened, but he did want to do the business.

"What, three kopecks a year in interest?"

"No, a month, not a year."

"You're a tight-fisted one, Jew. What's your name?"

"Isai Fomitz."

"Well, Isai Fomich, you'll go far with us here! Good-bye."

Isai Fomich looked the pledge over once more, folded it, and carefully put it into his sack, to the ongoing laughter of the prisoners.

Everybody really even seemed to like him, and nobody offended him, though almost all of them owed him money. He himself was as inoffensive as a chicken, and, seeing the universal sympathy for him, even strutted a bit, but with such simple-hearted comicality that he was forgiven for it at once. Luchka, who had known many Jews in his time, often teased him, not at all out of malice, but just so, for amusement, as people amuse themselves with a little dog, a parrot, a trained animal, and the like. Isai Fomich knew that very well, was not offended in the least, and joked back rather cleverly.

"Hey, Jew, I'm gonna beat you!"

"You give me one, and I'll give you ten," Isai Fomich retorts dashingly.

"Mangy devil!"

"So I'm mangy!"

"Mangy Jew!"

"So what if I am. I itch, but I'm rich. I've got money."

"You sold Christ."

"So you say."

"Bravo, Isai Fomich, fine fellow! Don't lay a finger on him, he's our only one!" the prisoners shout, laughing.

"Hey, Jew, you'll get the knout and go to Siberia."

"I'm already in Siberia."

"They'll send you further."

"And is the Lord God there?"

"That he is."

"Well, so what, then. As long as there's God and money, it's good anywhere."

"Fine fellow, Isai Fomich, what a fine fellow!" they cry out around him, and Isai Fomich, though he can see they're laughing at him, is in good spirits; the general praise gives him visible pleasure, and he starts to sing in a high treble, for the whole barrack to hear: "La-la-la-la-la!"—a song without words, to some absurd and ridiculous tune, the only one he sang all the while he was in prison. Later, when he became more closely acquainted with me, he assured me under oath that it was the same song and the same tune that all six hundred thousand Jews, big and small, sang as they crossed the Red Sea,[1] and that every Jew was supposed to sing it at the moment of triumph and victory over his enemies.

On the eve of Saturday, each Friday evening, men came to our barrack from the other barracks on purpose to see Isai Fomich celebrate his Sabbath. Isai Fomich was so innocently boastful and vain that this general curiosity also gave him pleasure. With pedantic and affected pomposity he covered his tiny little table in the corner, opened the book, lit two candles, and, muttering some mysterious words, began to array himself in his vestment ("veshtment," as he pronounced it). It was a multicolored woolen shawl, which he kept carefully in his chest. He tied bands on both arms and attached a little wooden box to his head with a strap, right on his forehead, so that it looked as if Isai Fomich's forehead had sprouted a ridiculous horn. Then the prayer began. He read it in singsong, cried out, spluttered, swung around, made wild and ridiculous gestures. Of course, all this was prescribed by the rites of prayer, and there was nothing ridiculous or strange in it, but the ridiculous thing was that Isai Fomich seemed purposely to display and flaunt his rites before us. He would suddenly cover his head with his hands and start reading in sobs. His sobbing increases and, exhausted and all but wailing, he lowers his head crowned with the ark onto the book; but suddenly, amidst the most violent sobbing, he begins to laugh and to chant in singsong, in a voice somehow tenderly solemn, somehow weak from overflowing happiness. "See how worked up he is!" the prisoners would say. I once asked Isai Fomich what was the meaning of this sobbing and then suddenly this solemn transition to happiness and bliss. Isai Fomich was awfully fond of these questions of mine. He immediately explained to me that the weeping and sobbing meant thinking about the loss of Jerusalem, and that the law prescribed that one weep and beat one's breast as hard as possible at the thought of it. But at the moment of the bitterest weeping, he, Isai Fomich, *must suddenly*, as if inadvertently, recall (this *suddenly* is also prescribed by the law) that there exists a prophecy about the return of the Jews to Jerusalem. Here he must immediately burst into joy, singing, laughter, and start saying his prayers so that his voice expresses the greatest possible happiness, and his face the greatest possible solemnity and nobility. This *sudden* change, and the obligatory character of it, Isai Fomich liked very much: he saw it as an especially clever trick, and he told me about this intricate rule of the law with a boastful air. Once, in the very heat of his prayer, the major came into the room, accompanied by the guards officer and some convoy soldiers. All the prisoners stood to attention by their bunks; only Isai Fomich began to shout and grimace still more. He knew that prayer was permitted, that it could not be interrupted, and that he was of course not risking anything by shouting in the major's presence. But he found it extremely pleasing to strike a pose before the major and show off before us. The major came and stood one step behind him: Isai Fomich turned his back to his little table and, waving his arms, started reciting his solemn prophecy in singsong right into the major's face. Since it was prescribed for him that at that moment his face should express exceedingly much happiness and nobility, he immediately did so, squinting his eyes somehow peculiarly, laughing, and nodding his head at the major. The major was surprised; but he finally snorted with laughter, called him a fool right to his face, and left, while Isai Fomich intensified his shouting still more. An hour later, when he was having supper, I asked him: "And what if the major, stupid as he is, had gotten angry with you?"

"What major?"

"What do you mean, what major? Didn't you see him?"

"No."

"Why, he was standing two feet away, right in front of your face."

But Isai Fomich began to assure me in the most serious way that he had decidedly not seen any major, and that while saying these prayers he falls into some sort of ecstasy, so that he no longer sees or hears anything that happens around him.

I can see Isai Fomich as if it were now, when he loiters idly around the whole prison, trying as hard as he can to do nothing, as the Law prescribes for Saturday. What impossible stories he told me each time he came back from his prayerhouse; what outlandish news and rumors from Petersburg he brought me, assuring me that he had gotten it from his Jews, and they had gotten them at first hand.

But I'm talking too much about Isai Fomich.

There were only two public bathhouses in the whole town. The first, kept by a Jew, had separate rooms, at fifty kopecks per room, intended for high-flown people. The other was primarily for simple folk, decrepit, dirty, small, and it was to this bathhouse that our prison was taken. It was cold and sunny; the prisoners were glad to leave the fortress and have a look at the town. There was ceaseless joking and laughter on the way. An entire platoon of soldiers accompanied us with loaded rifles, to the wonder of the whole town. In the bathhouse we were at once divided into two shifts: the second waited in the cold vestibule while the first was washing, which was necessary because the bathhouse was small. But, despite that, the bathhouse was so small that it was hard to imagine how even half of us could fit into it. Petrov never left my side; even without my asking, he hastened to help me and even offered to wash me. Along with Petrov, Baklushin also volunteered to serve me; he was that prisoner from the special section who was nicknamed "the pioneer" and whom I have already mentioned as the merriest and nicest of the prisoners, which in fact he was. He and I were already slightly acquainted. Petrov even helped me to undress, because, being unaccustomed, it took me a long time, and the vestibule was almost as cold as outside. Incidentally, it is very difficult for a prisoner to undress, if he has not yet fully learned how. First, he has to learn how to quickly unlace his under-fetters. These under-fetters are made of leather, about seven inches long, and are worn over the drawers, just under the iron

ring around the leg. A pair of under-fetters costs no less than sixty silver kopecks, and yet every prisoner acquires them at his own expense,
because it is impossible to walk without them. The ring of the fetters
does not fit tightly around the leg; you can put your finger between
ring and leg; as a result the ring hits against the leg, chafes it, and without under-fetters a prisoner will manage to rub himself raw in a single
day. But removing the under-fetters is not so difficult. More difficult is
learning how to skillfully remove your drawers from under the fetters.
That's a real trick. Having pulled your drawers down, say, on your left
leg, you first have to pass them between your leg and the iron ring;
then, once your leg is free, the drawers have to be pulled back through
the same ring; then everything that has been taken off the left leg has
to be pulled through the ring on the right leg; and after that everything
that has been pulled through the ring has to be pulled back up again.
It's the same story with putting on fresh drawers. For a novice it's even
hard to figure out how to do it. The first one to teach us all that was the
prisoner Korenev, in Tobolsk, the former robber chief who had spent
five years on a chain. But prisoners get used to it and manage without
the slightest difficulty. I gave Petrov several kopecks to provide soap
and some bast; true, each prisoner was also issued prison soap, as big as
a two-kopeck piece and as thick as a slice of cheese served as an evening
snack among people of the "middling sort." Soap was sold right there in
the vestibule, along with spiced tea, kalachi, and hot water. By arrangement with the bathhouse owner, each prisoner was allotted only one
basin of hot water; for half a kopeck whoever wanted to wash himself
cleaner could get another basin, which would be passed inside from the
vestibule through a special window. Having undressed me, Petrov even
led me under the arm, noticing that I had great difficulty walking in fetters. "Pull them up on your calves," he kept saying, supporting me like
an attendant, "and be careful, there's a step here." I was even somewhat
ashamed; I wanted to assure Petrov that I could walk by myself, but
he would not have believed me. He treated me decidedly like a child,
immature and clumsy, whom everyone was obliged to help. Petrov was
by no means a servant; he was anything but a servant; if I had offended
him, he would have known how to deal with me. I never promised him
money for his services, and he did not ask for any. What induced him
to tend to me like that?

When we opened the door to the bathhouse itself, I thought we were entering hell. Imagine a room some twelve paces long and the same in width, in which maybe up to a hundred men are packed at once, and certainly at least eighty, because the prisoners were divided into just two shifts, and in all about two hundred of us had come to the bathhouse. Steam clouding your eyes, soot, filth, such crowdedness that there was nowhere to set your foot down. I was frightened and wanted to turn back, but Petrov immediately reassured me. Somehow, with the greatest difficulty, we forced our way to the benches over the heads of people sitting on the floor, asking them to bend down so that we could pass. But all the places on the benches were taken. Petrov announced to me that we had to buy places and at once entered into negotiations with a prisoner who had a place by a window. The man gave up his place to me for a kopeck, immediately took the money from Petrov, who had had the foresight to bring it with him to the bathhouse clenched in his fist, and darted at once under the bench right under my place, where it was dark, dirty, and there was a layer of sticky slime almost half a finger thick. But the places under the benches were all taken, too; people were also creeping around there. On the whole floor there was no space bigger than the palm of your hand not occupied by prisoners sitting hunched up and splashing themselves from their basins. Others stood between them and, holding their basins, washed themselves standing up; the dirty water poured straight onto the shaven heads of those sitting under them. On the top shelf and all the steps leading to it, men sat, cramped and hunched up, washing themselves. But little washing went on. Simple folk don't wash much with soap and hot water; they steam themselves terribly and then douse themselves with cold water—that's their bath. Some fifty birch besoms rose and fell together; they all whipped themselves to the point of intoxication. More steam was added every moment. This was no longer heat; it was the fiery furnace. All was a bawling and roaring to the noise of a hundred fetters dragging on the floor . . . Some, wishing to pass by, got entangled in the chains of others and themselves struck against the heads of those sitting below them, falling, cursing, bringing the struck ones down with them. Filthy water came pouring from all sides. Everybody was in some sort of excited, intoxicated state of mind; shrieks and shouts rang out. At the window to the vestibule, where water was dispensed, there was cursing, jostling, a real scramble. The hot water spilled on the heads of those sitting on the floor before it reached its destination. Now and then the mustached face of a soldier, gun in hand, peeked in the window or the slightly opened door to see if there was any disorder. The shaven heads and steamed red bodies of the prisoners looked uglier than ever. Old scars from whipping or flogging usually stand out more vividly on a steamed back, so that now all those backs seemed newly covered with wounds. Frightful scars! I got chills looking at them. They pour on more—and steam veils the whole room in thick, hot clouds; it's all roaring, shouting. Through the clouds of steam flash beaten backs, shaven heads, doubled-up arms and legs; and to crown it all, Isai Fomich roars full-throatedly on the highest shelf. He steams himself into oblivion, but it seems no heat can satisfy him; for a kopeck he hires a man to birch him, but the man finally can't stand it, abandons the besom, and runs to douse himself with cold water. Isai Fomich does not give up and hires a second man, a third: he's resolved to overlook the cost on such an occasion and goes through five replacements. "There's a healthy steaming! Bravo, Isai Fomich!" the prisoners shout to him from below. Isai Fomich himself feels that at that moment he is higher than them all and has outdone them all; he is triumphant and in a shrill, crazed voice screams out his aria: "La-la-la-la-la," which drowns all other voices. It occurred to me that if we should all wind up in the fiery furnace together, it would very much resemble this place. I could not help conveying this conjecture to Petrov; he only looked around and said nothing.

I wanted to buy him a place next to me, but he sat down at my feet and declared that he was very comfortable. Meanwhile Baklushin kept buying water for us and bringing it as needed. Petrov said he would wash me from head to foot, so that "you'll be all nice and clean," and urgently invited me to steam myself. I did not risk that. Petrov soaped me up all over. "And now I'll wash your *little feet*," he added in conclusion. I was about to say that I could wash them myself, but did not contradict him and surrendered myself completely to his will. The diminutive "little feet" had absolutely no servile tone to it; Petrov simply could not call my feet "feet," probably because other, real people had feet, while mine were still only little feet.

Having washed me, he conveyed me to the vestibule with the same ceremony, that is, supporting me and cautioning me at every step as if I were made of porcelain, helped me into my drawers, and, when he was completely done with me, rushed back to steam himself.

When we came home, I offered him a glass of tea. He did not refuse the tea, drank it, and thanked me. It occurred to me to loosen my purse strings and treat him to a dram of vodka. Vodka was found in our barrack. Petrov was highly delighted, drank it, grunted, and, observing that I had revived him completely, hurried off to the kitchen, as if there were something there that could not possibly be decided without him. Instead of him another interlocutor arrived, Baklushin (the pioneer), whom I had also invited for tea while we were still in the bathhouse.

I don't know of a character sweeter than Baklushin's. True, he gave no quarter to others, even quarreled often, did not like anyone to interfere in his affairs—in short, he could stand up for himself. But he never quarreled for long, and everybody in the prison seemed to like him. Wherever he went, he was greeted with pleasure. He was known even in town as the most amusing man in the world and one who never lost his joviality. He was a tall fellow, around thirty, with a dashing and simple-hearted face, quite handsome, and with a wart. He sometimes distorted that face of his so killingly, impersonating somebody or other, that the people around him could not help laughing. He was one of the jokers himself; but he gave no leeway to our scornful haters of laughter, and therefore nobody denounced him for being an "empty and useless" man. He was full of fire and life. He got acquainted with me during the very first days and announced to me that he had been a cantonist, had then served in the pioneers, and had even been noticed and liked by some highly placed persons, of which, for old times' sake, he was very proud. He immediately started questioning me about Petersburg. He even read books. Having come to me for tea, he first of all made the whole barrack laugh, telling how Lieutenant Sh. had given our major a dressing down that morning, and, sitting beside me, he announced to me with a pleased look that it seemed the theater was going to take place. They were planning to have theater in the prison during the holidays. Actors had turned up; scenery was being prepared little by little. Some townspeople promised to give their clothes for the actors' roles, even the female ones; there was even hope of obtaining, by means of an orderly, an officer's uniform with epaulettes. If only the major doesn't decide to forbid it like last year. Last year at Christmas the major had been in a bad mood: he had lost at cards somewhere, and there had been some mischief in the prison, so he had forbidden it out of spite, but now maybe he won't want to hinder things. In short, Baklushin was excited. It was clear that he was one of the chief initiators of the theater, and I promised myself then and there that I would go to the performance without fail. Baklushin's simple-hearted joy over the success of the theater delighted me. One thing led to another, and we got to talking. Among other things, he told me that he had not served in Petersburg all the time; that he had done something wrong and had been sent, albeit as a sergeant, to a garrison battalion in R.[2]

"It's from there that I was sent here," said Baklushin.

"What for?" I asked him.

"What for? What do you think it was for, Alexander Petrovich? For falling in love!"

"Well, you don't get sent here for that," I objected, laughing.

"True," Baklushin added, "true, along with that I also turned my pistol on a German there. But, judge for yourself, is it worth exiling a man over a German?"

"How was it, though? Tell me, I'm curious."

"A very funny story, Alexander Petrovich."

"So much the better. Go on, tell me."

"Shall I? Well, listen, then . . ."

What I heard was not really funny, but rather the very strange story of a murder . . .

"It was like this," Baklushin began. "So they sent me to R. I see it's a nice, big town, only there are lots of Germans. Well, naturally, I'm still a young man, in good standing with the superiors, I go around with my hat cocked—passing the time, you know. Winking at the German girls. And I liked one of the German girls there. Luisa. They were laundresses, of rich people's linen, she and her aunt. The aunt was old, all puffed up with herself, and they lived well. At first I kept strolling past their windows, but then we became real friends. Luisa spoke Russian well, only she swallowed her *r*s a little—such a sweetheart, I'd never met anyone like her. At first I tried a little of this and that, but she says to me: 'No, that you can't do, Sasha, because I want to preserve all my innocence so as to make you a worthy wife,' and she was just sweet with me—such a ringing laugh she had . . . and such a clean little thing, I'd never seen anyone like that except for her. It was she who lured me into marriage. Well, how could I not marry, just think! So I was getting ready to go to the lieutenant colonel with my request . . . Suddenly I look—Luisa didn't come to meet me once, didn't come a second time, didn't show up a third time . . . I sent her a letter: no answer. What's this, I think? I mean, if she'd wanted to deceive me, she'd have managed it, she'd have answered the letter and come to see me. But she didn't even know how to lie; she just broke it off. It's the aunt, I thought. I didn't dare go to the aunt; she knew about us, but we pretended—I mean, we trod softly. I went around like in a daze, wrote her a final letter and said, 'If you don't come, I'll go to your aunt myself.' She got frightened and came. She cries; she says a certain German, Schultz, a distant relation, a watchmaker, rich and already elderly, has expressed a wish to marry her—'in order to make me happy, he says, and not to be left without a wife in his old age; and he says he loves me and has long been meaning to do it, but said nothing and kept preparing himself. So, Sasha,' she says, 'he's rich, and for me that's happiness; can you want to deprive me of my happiness?' I look: she's crying, she embraces me . . . Eh, I think, she's talking reason! What's the use of marrying a soldier, even if he's a sergeant? 'Well, good-bye, Luisa,' I say. 'God be with you. I mustn't deprive you of your happiness. And, what, is he handsome?' 'No,' she says, 'he's old, he's got a long nose . . .' She even laughed herself. I left her there. So, I think, it's not fated to be! The next morning I went to his shop—she had told me the address. I look through the window: a German's sitting there making watches, about forty-five, hook-nosed, bug-eyed, in a tailcoat and with a standing collar, a real high one, so pompous. I just spat; wanted to smash his window on the spot . . . but no, I think, don't lay a finger on him, what's lost is lost! I went to the barracks in the evening, lay on my cot, and—would you believe it, Alexander Petrovich?—burst out crying . . .

"Well, so a day passes, a second, a third. Not a glimpse of Luisa. And meanwhile I heard from one of her friends (an old woman, also a laundress, Luisa sometimes went to see her) that the German knew about our love, and that was why he decided to speed up his proposal. Otherwise he'd have waited another couple of years. He supposedly made Luisa swear that she'd have nothing to do with me; and meanwhile he supposedly kept a firm grip on Luisa and the aunt, meaning he could still change his mind, he was not entirely decided yet. She also told me that in two days, on Sunday, he had invited them both for coffee in the morning, and that there would be another relation, an old man, who used to be a merchant, but was now poor as could be and worked as a watchman in some basement. When I learned that they might settle the whole business on Sunday, I got so angry I couldn't control myself. And all that day and the next I did nothing but think about it. I think I could have eaten that German up.

"On Sunday morning I still didn't know anything, but once the Sunday services were over, I jumped up, put on my overcoat, and went to the German. I thought I'd find them all there. Why I went to him and what I wanted to say, I didn't know myself. But I put a pistol in my pocket just in case. I had this worthless little pistol with an old-fashioned lock; I used to shoot it when I was a boy. You couldn't even shoot anything with it. But I put a bullet in it anyway; I thought: they'll be rude, they'll want to throw me out—I'll draw the pistol and scare them. I arrive. There's nobody in the shop, they're all sitting in the back room. There's not a soul besides them, no servants. All he had for servants was a German maid, who also did the cooking. I go through the shop; I see—the door there is shut, an old door held by a hook. My heart is pounding. I stopped to listen: they were talking in German. I shoved as hard as I could with my foot, and the door opened at once. I look: the table is set. On the table there's a big coffee pot, and coffee is simmering on a spirit lamp. There are rusks; on another tray, a decanter of vodka, herring, sausage, and also a bottle of some sort of wine. Luisa and her aunt, both gussied up, are sitting on a sofa. Facing them on a chair sits the German fiancé himself, brushed up, in a tailcoat and a standing collar sticking out in front. On a chair to one side sits another German, an old man, fat, gray-haired, who says nothing. When I came in, Luisa went pale. The aunt started up, then sat down again, and the German frowned. He was angry; he rose to meet me.

" 'What do you want?' he says.

"I was disconcerted, but anger took strong hold of me.

"'What do I want?' I say. 'Receive me as a guest, offer me vodka. I've come to you as a guest.'

"The German thought a little and said:

"'Zit down.'

"I sat down.

"'Give me some vodka,' I say.

"'Here iss vodka,' he says. 'Trink, if you please.'

"'So you won't give me good vodka?' I say. It's because I'm very angry.

"'That iss good vodka.'

"I was offended that he took such small account of me. And the more so because Luisa was looking. I drank and then said:

"'What makes you so rude, German? You should be friends with me. I've come to you out of friendship.'

"'I cannot be your friend,' he says. 'You are a simple soldat.'

"Well, here I flew into a rage.

"'Ah, you scarecrow,' I say, 'you sausage maker! Do you know that right now I can do whatever I want with you? Want me to shoot you with this pistol?'

"I drew the pistol, stood in front of him, and put the barrel right to his head, point-blank. The rest of them sit there neither dead nor alive; afraid to make a peep; the old man is shaking like a leaf, says nothing, turns all pale.

"The German was surprised, but he pulled himself together.

"'I'm not afraid of you,' he says, 'and I ask you as a noble man to abandon this joke at once, and I am not afraid of you at all.'

"That's a lie,' I say. 'You *are* afraid!' And what else! He didn't dare move his head from under the pistol; he just sat there.

"'No,' he says, 'ziss you do not dare to do.'

"'And why do I not dare to do ziss?' I say.

"'Because,' he says, 'it is strictly forbitten, and you vill be severely punished for it.'

"Devil knows about this fool of a German! If he hadn't fired me up, he might still be alive; all it took was an argument.

"'So you think I don't dare?' I say.

"'No-o!'

"'I don't dare?'

"'You appsolutely do not dare to do ziss to me . . .'

"'Take that, then, sausage!' I fired, and he rolled off the chair. The others cried out.

"I pocketed the pistol and took off, and when I got to the fortress, I threw the pistol into the nettles by the gate.

"I came home, lay on the cot, and thought: they'll take me right now. An hour went by, then another—nothing happened. And before dark such anguish came over me; I went out; I simply had to see Luisa. I walked past the watchmaker's. I look: there are people there, police. I rushed to her old friend: call Luisa out! I wait a little, I see: Luisa comes running, throws herself on my neck, weeps. 'It's all my fault,' she says. 'I was wrong to listen to my aunt.' She also told me that the aunt went home right afterwards and was so scared she got sick and—kept mum. 'She didn't tell anybody herself and told me not to; she was afraid; let them do as they like. "Nobody saw us then, Luisa," she said. 'He sent his maid away, because he was afraid. She'd have scratched his eyes out, if she'd learned he wanted to get married. None of his shop assistants were there either; he sent them all away. He made the coffee and prepared the snacks himself. And his relative has been silent all his life, he's never said a word, and after what just happened, he grabbed his hat and was the first to leave. He'll probably also keep quiet,' said Luisa. And so it was. For two weeks nobody arrested me and I wasn't under any suspicion. Believe it or not, Alexander Petrovich, in those two weeks I experienced all my happiness. Luisa and I met every day. She became so attached to me! She wept: 'I'll follow you wherever they send you,' she said. 'I'll give up everything for you!' I thought it would be the life of me, she moved me so much. Well, but after two weeks they arrested me. The old man and the aunt got together and testified against me . . ."

"But wait," I interrupted Baklushin, "the most they could give you is ten years, maybe twelve, a full term in the civilian category, but you're in the special section. How can that be?"

"Well, that was for something else again," said Baklushin. "When they brought me to court, the captain used foul language against me in front of the judges. I couldn't stand it and said to him: 'What are you swearing for, you scoundrel! Don't you see you're sitting in front of the zertsalo?'[3] Well, things took a different turn then; they started the trial over and tried me for all of it together: four thousand rods, and then here to the special section. When I was taken out to be punished, the captain was also taken out: for me it was down the green street, and him they stripped of his rank and sent to the Caucasus as a common soldier. Good-bye, Alexander Petrovich. Come and see our performance."

X

Christmas

The holidays finally came. On Christmas Eve hardly any of the prisoners went to work. A few went to the tailor's shop or the workshop; the rest only came for the assignments; then, though they were sent here and there, almost all of them, alone or in groups, returned at once to the prison, and after dinner nobody left it. In the morning, too, the greater part went on their own business, not the prison's: some to see about smuggling vodka and ordering more; others to see some chums, or to collect some debts before the feast for work done earlier; Baklushin and other participants in the theater to visit acquaintances, mostly officers' servants, and get the necessary costumes. Some went about with a preoccupied and bustling air solely because others were bustling and preoccupied, and, though they had no money coming to them from anywhere, looked as if they, too, would be getting money from somebody. In short, it was as if they were all expecting some change the next day, something extraordinary. Towards evening the invalids whom the prisoners had sent to the market came back bringing all sorts of eatables: beef, pork, even geese. Many prisoners, even the most modest and thrifty, who had been saving up their kopecks all year, felt obliged to open their purses on such a day and celebrate the breaking of the fast in a proper way.[1] The next day the prisoners held a genuine feast, inalienable and formally recognized by law. On that day a prisoner could not be sent to work, and there were only three such days in the year.

And, finally, who knows how many memories must have been stirred in the souls of these outcasts at the coming of such a day! The days of major feasts are sharply imprinted in a simple man's memory from childhood. These are days of rest from their heavy labors, days of family gatherings. In prison they were bound to be remembered with pain and longing. For the prisoners, respect for the solemn day even turned into a sort of formal ritual; few caroused; everyone was serious and as if busy with something, though many had almost nothing to do. But both the idle ones and the carousers tried to maintain a certain gravity ... It was as if laughter were forbidden. The general mood reached a sort of punctiliousness and irritated intolerance, and if anyone disrupted the general tone, even accidentally, they reined him in with shouts and curses, and were angry with him as if he had shown disrespect for the feast itself. This mood among the prisoners was remarkable, even touching. Besides innate reverence for the great day, the prisoner unconsciously felt that by observing the holiday he was as if in contact with the whole world, that he was therefore not entirely an outcast, a lost man, a cut-off slice, that things in prison were the same as among other people. They felt it; it was obvious and understandable.

Akim Akimych was also preparing very much for the feast day. He had no family memories, because he had grown up as an orphan in a strange house and had been doing hard work almost from the age of fifteen; nor had he had any special joys in his life, because his whole life had been regular, monotonous, for fear of stepping even a hair's breadth outside his prescribed duties. Nor was he especially religious, because propriety seemed to have swallowed up in him all his other human gifts and particularities, all passions and desires, bad and good. As a result of all that, he was preparing to meet the solemn day not fussing, not worrying, not confused by melancholy and totally useless memories, but with a quiet, methodical propriety, exactly enough to fulfill the duties of the ritual established once and for all. In general he did not like to think much. The meaning of a fact seemed never to enter his head, but the rules once pointed out to him he fulfilled with sacred precision. If he had been ordered the next day to do exactly the opposite, he would have done it with the same obedience and thoroughness as he had done the opposite the day before. Once, once only in his life, had he attempted to follow his own mind—and he had landed in prison. The lesson had not been wasted on him. And though he was destined never to understand exactly what he was guilty of, he had deduced a salutary rule from his adventure—never to reason in any circumstances, because "he had no head for it," as the prisoners used to say among themselves. Blindly devoted to ritual, he looked with a sort of anticipatory reverence even at his festive suckling pig, which he stuffed with kasha and roasted (with his own hands, because he also knew how to roast), as if it were not an ordinary suckling pig, which one could always buy and roast, but some sort of special, festive one. Maybe he had been accustomed since childhood to seeing a suckling pig on the table on that day, and deduced that a suckling pig was necessary for that day, and I'm certain that if even once he went without eating suckling pig on that day, he would be left all his life with a certain remorse over an unfulfilled duty. Before the feast, he went about in his old jacket and trousers, decently mended, but completely worn-out despite that. It now turned out that he had kept the new suit issued to him four months earlier carefully tucked away in his chest and had not touched it, with the smiling thought of solemnly putting it on for the first time at Christmas. And so he did. In the evening he took out his new suit, unfolded it, examined it, brushed it, blew on it, and, having done all that, tried it on beforehand. It turned out that the suit was a perfect fit; everything was as it should be, it buttoned tightly all the way up, the stiff, braid-trimmed collar held the chin high; at the waist it even had something of a uniform's trimness, and Akim Akimych grinned with pleasure and turned jauntily before his tiny mirror, to which he had long ago glued gold borders with his own hands in his spare time. Only one little hook on the jacket collar seemed to be slightly out of place. Having realized it, Akim Akimych decided to move the hook; he moved it, tried it again, and it turned out to be just right. Then he folded it as before and, with his mind at peace, put it back in the chest until the next day. His head was shaved satisfactorily; but, looking himself over attentively in the little mirror, he noticed that his head did not seem perfectly smooth; barely visible sprouts of hair showed, and he immediately went to "the major" to have himself shaved decently and according to form. And though nobody was going to inspect Akim Akimych the next day, he had himself shaved solely for the peace of his conscience, so as to fulfill all his duties for the sake of such a day. Reverence for a little button, for an epaulette, for a bit of braid, had been indelibly imprinted in his mind since childhood as an unquestionable duty, and in his heart as the image of the height of beauty a decent man can attain. Having put everything right, he, as the senior prisoner in the barrack, ordered hay brought in and watched attentively as it was spread on the floor. The same thing was done in the other barracks. I don't know why, but they always spread hay in our barracks for Christmas.[2] Then, having finished all his labors, Akim Akimych said his prayers, lay down on his cot, and fell at once into a child's untroubled sleep, so as to wake up as early as possible the next morning. All the prisoners acted the same way, however. They went to bed much earlier than usual in all the barracks. The usual evening work was stopped; there was no mention of maidans. Everyone waited for the next morning.

It finally came. Early, before dawn, just after the morning drums, the barracks were opened and the sergeant, who came to count the prisoners, wished us all a Merry Christmas. We responded with the same, responded affably and kindly. After quickly saying their prayers, Akim Akimych and many others, who had their geese and suckling pigs in the kitchen, hastened to go and see what was being done with them, how they were being roasted, where things stood, and so on. From the small windows of our barracks, plastered with snow and ice, you could see through the darkness that bright fires, started before dawn, were blazing in both kitchens, in all six ovens. Prisoners were already darting about the yard, in the dark, with their sheepskin jackets on or just thrown over their shoulders; they were all rushing to the kitchen. But some, though very few, had already managed to visit the tavern-ers. These were the most impatient ones. Generally, they all behaved themselves decorously, peaceably, and with unusual ceremony. You did not hear the usual cursing and quarreling. Everybody understood that it was a big day and a great feast. There were some who went to other barracks to wish certain people a Merry Christmas. There was a show of something like friendliness. I will note in passing that there was almost no friendship to be observed among the prisoners, I don't mean in general—that goes without saying—but in particular, when some one prisoner became friends with another. There was almost none of that among us, and it is a remarkable feature: it is not that way in free-dom. Among us, with very rare exceptions, we generally treated each other callously, drily, and this sort of formal tone was established and accepted once and for all. I also left the barrack; dawn was just breaking; the stars were fading; a thin, frosty steam was rising. Columns of smoke poured from the kitchen chimneys. Some of the prisoners I came across readily and affably wished me a Merry Christmas. I thanked them and responded in kind. Certain of them had not said a word to me before then for that whole month.

Just by the kitchen a prisoner from the military barrack caught up with me, a sheepskin coat thrown over his shoulders. He had noticed me when I was halfway across the yard and started shouting: "Alexander Petrovich! Alexander Petrovich!" He was running to the kitchen and in a great hurry. I stopped to wait for him. He was a young fellow, with a round face, a gentle expression in his eyes, very taciturn with everybody, and he had not yet said a single word to me and up to then had not paid any attention to me since my arrival in prison; I didn't even know his name. He came running up to me and stood, breathless, right in front of me, looking at me with a sort of dumb but at the same time blissful smile.

"What is it?" I asked him, not without surprise, seeing him standing in front of me, smiling, staring wide-eyed at me, and not saying anything.

"But . . . it's Christmas . . . ," he murmured and, realizing that there was nothing more to say, he abandoned me and hurried into the kitchen.

I will note here, incidentally, that after that he and I never had any relations and hardly ever said a word to each other up to my leaving prison.

In the kitchen, around the hot, burning stoves, there was bustling and jostling—a real crush. Everybody watched over his own goods; the cookies were beginning to prepare the prison meal, because dinner was supposed to be earlier that day. No one had started to eat yet, however, though some would have been glad to, but they observed appearances in front of the others. They were waiting for the priest, and only after that was the fast to be broken. Meanwhile, it was not yet full daylight when the summoning cries of the corporal began to resound outside the prison gates: "Cooks!" These cries resounded almost every minute and went on for nearly two hours. The cooks were summoned from the kitchens to receive the offerings brought to the prison from all over town. They were brought in extraordinary quantities, in the form of kalachi, bread, cheesecakes, suet cakes, flatbread, pancakes, and other baked goods.

I don't think there was a single merchant's or tradesman's wife in the whole town who did not send her bread and best wishes on the great feast day to the "unfortunate" prisoners. There were rich offerings—fancy breads of the whitest flour, sent in large quantities. There were very poor offerings—a two-penny little kalach and a couple of wretched suet cakes slightly smeared with sour cream: this was a gift of the poor to the poor, from their last. Everything was received with equal gratitude, without distinction of gifts and givers. The prisoners who received them took their hats off, bowed, gave their best wishes, and brought the offerings to the kitchen. When whole heaps of the offered bread had accumulated, seniors from each barrack were sent for, and they distributed everything equally among the barracks. There was no arguing, no cursing; it was done honestly, equally. What came to our barrack was then divided among us; this was done by Akim Akimych and another prisoner; they did it with their own hands and with their own hands gave each of us his share. There was not the least objection, not the least envy of anyone; everyone was left pleased; there could even be no suspicion that the offerings might have been concealed or not distributed equally. Having settled his affairs in the kitchen, Akim Akimych proceeded to his vesting, dressed with all his propriety and solemnity, not leaving a single little hook unfastened, and, having dressed, at once set about praying in earnest. He prayed for quite a long time. Many prisoners were already standing in prayer, older ones for the most part. The young ones did not pray much: they might just cross themselves on getting up, even on a feast day. After praying, Akim Akimych came up to me and with a certain solemnity wished me a Merry Christmas. I immediately invited him for tea, and he invited me for his suckling pig. A little later Petrov came running to wish me a Merry Christmas. He seemed to have been drinking already, and though he came running breathlessly, he did not say much, but only stood in front of me for a short while in some expectation, then quickly left me for the kitchen. Meanwhile, the prisoners in the military barrack were preparing to receive the priest. This barrack was arranged differently from the others: the bunks in it stood along the walls and not in the middle of the room, as in the other barracks, so that it was the only room in the prison that was clear in the middle. It was probably done that way so that the prisoners could be gathered there in case of need. In the center of the room they placed a little table, covered it with a clean towel, stood an icon on it, and lit an icon lamp. A priest finally came with a cross and holy water. Having prayed and sung before the icon, he stood before the prisoners, and they all began to approach and kiss the cross with real veneration. Then the priest went around all the barracks and sprinkled them with holy water. In the kitchen he praised our prison bread, which was famous in town for its taste, and the prisoners decided at once to send him two fresh-baked loaves; an invalid was immediately dispatched to deliver them. The cross was seen off with the same veneration with which it had been met, and then almost at once the major and the commandant arrived. Among us the commandant was liked and even respected. He went around all the barracks accompanied by the major, wished everybody a Merry Christmas, stopped at the kitchen and tried the prison shchi. The shchi turned out to be fine; in honor of the day each prisoner was allotted nearly a pound of beef. On top of that there was millet kasha with plenty of butter. As he showed the commandant out, the major ordered the dinner to begin. The prisoners tried not to catch his eye. We didn't like his spiteful glance from behind his glasses, which even now he cast right and left, to see if there was any disorder, if anyone was to blame.

We began dinner. Akim Akimych's suckling pig was perfectly roasted. And I cannot explain how it happened, but right after the major's departure, some five minutes later, an extraordinary number of people turned out to be drunk, though five minutes earlier they had all been almost perfectly sober. Many glowing and shining faces appeared; balalaikas appeared. The little Pole with the fiddle, hired for the day, was already going around with some carouser and sawing away at merry dances. The conversation grew more drunken and noisy. But the dinner ended without any great disorders. Everyone had eaten his fill. Many of the old and staid men went to bed at once, which was what Akim Akimych did, evidently assuming that on a great feast day one must unfailingly sleep after dinner. The little old Starodubsky Old Believer, after dozing briefly, climbed onto the stove, opened his book, and prayed until late at night almost without interruption. It was painful for him to look at the "shame," as he referred to the general carousing of the prisoners. The Circassians all sat on the porch and with curiosity, but at the same time with a certain disgust, looked at the drunken men. I came across Nurra. "Yaman, yaman!"* he said to me, wagging his head in pious indignation. "Ah, yaman! Allah will be angry." Isai Fomich stubbornly and haughtily lit a candle in his corner and began to work, clearly showing that the feast was of no account to him. In corners here and there maidans began. There was no fear of the invalids, and sentries were posted in case the sergeant should come, though he tried not to notice anything himself. The guards officer came to the prison only three times during that whole day. But the drunkards hid themselves and the maidans were put away when he appeared, and it seemed he himself had decided to pay no attention to minor disorders. On that day a drunk man was considered a minor disorder. People gradually began to loosen up. Quarrels also began. But the great majority still remained sober, and they could look after the unsober. The carousers, however, were drinking beyond measure. Gazin was triumphant. He strutted with a self-contented air around his place on the bunk, under which he had boldly transferred the vodka he had kept hidden until then in the snow behind the barracks, in a secret place, and chuckled slyly, looking at the customers who kept flocking to him. He himself was sober and hadn't drunk a drop. He intended to carouse at the end of the feast, after emptying the prisoners' pockets of all their cash. Songs rang out in the barracks. But the drunkenness was already turning into a dazed stupor, and the songs were not far from tears. Many walked about with their own balalaikas, sheepskins thrown over their shoulders, fingering the strings with a dashing air. In the special section they even formed a chorus of about eight men. They sang nicely to the accompaniment of balalaikas and guitars. Of pure folk songs they sang only a few. I remember one, dashingly performed:

> *Last night, a young lass,*
> *I went to the feast.*

And here I heard a new version of this song, one I had never encountered before. Several lines were added at the end:

---

* "Bad, bad" in Tatar. *Translator.*

And I, a young lass,
Tidied up the house:
Washed the spoons in a tub,
Made shchi from the suds,
What I scraped from the doorposts,
I baked into pies.

They mostly sang prison songs, as we called them, well-known ones at that. One of them, "Once upon a time . . . ," was a comic song describing how a man used to make merry and live as a free gentleman, and had now landed in prison. It described how he used to liven up his "blamanzh with chempan," and now:

They dole me out some soggy cabbage,
And I just wolf it down.

This one, all too well known, was also popular:

As a lad I lived a merry life
With capital in my pocket,
Capital, yes, but I lost it all
And my freedom along with it . . .

and so on. Only among us it was pronounced "copital," not "capital," deriving *capital* from the word *kopit*, "to save." There were also mournful songs. One was in pure prison style, and also, I think, well known:

In the sky the dawn's light breaks;
Beats the morning drum.
A senior opens wide the gates,
The scribe with the roll call comes.

No one sees behind these walls
The painful life we bear,
But God the Father is with us all,
We'll not perish even here. Etc.

Another song was even more mournful, though with a beautiful tune, probably composed by some exile, with sickly sweet and quite illiterate words. I still remember a few lines from it:

No more I'll ever see again
The place where I was born;
Guiltless to suffering condemned,
Forever I'm forlorn.

From the roof a screech owl's call
Echoes through the hollow;
My heart is wrung, my spirits fall,
For there I cannot follow.

This song was often sung among us, not in chorus, but as a solo. Someone in his free time would go out to the porch of the barrack, sit down, brooding, his cheek propped on his hand, and start singing it in a high falsetto. You'd listen, and your heart would be wrung. We had some decent voices among us.

Meanwhile twilight was already coming. Sadness, anguish, and stupor showed painfully through the drinking and carousing. A man who had been laughing an hour earlier was now sobbing, having drunk to overflowing. Others had already managed to have a couple of fights. Still others, pale and barely keeping their feet, staggered around the barracks getting into quarrels. Those whose drunkenness was not of a provocative sort vainly looked for friends, so as to pour out their hearts to them and weep out their drunken grief. All these poor people had wanted to have fun, to spend the great feast joyfully—and Lord! how oppressive and sad this day was for nearly every one of them. Each of them saw it out as if he had been cheated of some hope. Petrov stopped to see me a couple of more times. He had drunk very little that whole day and was almost completely sober. But up to the very last hour he kept expecting that something simply had to happen, something extraordinary, festive, joyful. Though he didn't say it, you could see it in his eyes. He shuttled tirelessly from one barrack to another. But nothing special happened, and he met with nothing but drunkenness, senseless, drunken cursing, and heads stupefied by vodka. Sirotkin also wandered about all the barracks in his new red shirt, pretty, well scrubbed, and also as if quietly and naïvely expecting something. It was gradually becoming unbearable and disgusting in the barracks. Of course, there was also much that was funny, but I felt somehow sad and sorry for them all, I felt oppressed and stifled among them. Here are two prisoners arguing over who is going to stand whom to a drink. You can see they've been arguing for a long time and had even quarreled before then. One in particular has some long-standing grudge against the other. He's complaining and, moving his tongue thickly, is trying to prove that the other has dealt unfairly with him: some sheepskin jacket got sold, some money got hidden away sometime, last year, before Lent. There was something else besides . . . The accuser is a tall and muscular fellow, sensible, quiet, but with a yearning, when drunk, to make friends and pour out his grief. He scolds and states his claims as if wishing to make even firmer peace with his rival afterwards. The other is thickset, sturdy, short, with a round face, sly and cagey. He may have drunk more than his comrade, but he's only slightly tipsy. He has a strong character and a reputation for being rich, but for some reason it is to his advantage not to annoy his effusive friend right now, and so he takes him to the taverner. The friend insists that he must and is obliged to treat him, "if only you're an honest man."

The taverner, with a certain respect for the buyer and a shade of scorn for his effusive friend, who is not spending his own money but is being treated, produces the vodka and pours a glass.

"No, Stepka, you've got to," the effusive friend says, seeing that he's won out, "it's your duty."

"Well, I'm not going to waste my breath on you!" Stepka replies.

"No, Stepka, that's nonsense," the first one insists, taking the glass from the taverner, "'cause you owe me money; you've got no conscience, and your eyes aren't even yours, you borrowed 'em. You're a scoundrel, Stepka, so there—in a word, a scoundrel!"

"Well, quit whining, you're spilling your vodka! You asked for it, you got it, so drink it!" the taverner shouts at the effusive friend. "I won't stand over you till tomorrow!"

"I'm going to drink it, quit shouting! Merry Christmas, Stepan Dorofeich!" he says politely, with a slight bow, holding the glass in his hand and turning to Stepka, whom a moment earlier he had called a scoundrel. "May you keep your cheer for a hundred years, not counting what's past!" He drinks, grunts, and wipes his mouth. "Before, brothers, I could down a lot of vodka," he observes with grave dignity, as if addressing everybody and nobody in particular, "but now—must be I'm feeling my age. Thank you, Stepan Dorofeich."

"Don't mention it."

"So I come back to what I was saying to you, Stepka: besides you being a great scoundrel towards me, let me tell you . . ."

"And here's what I'll tell you, you drunken fish," Stepka, who has lost patience, interrupts him. "Listen and mark my every word: let's you and me divide the world in half, half for you and half for me. Go and don't come my way again. I'm sick of you!"

"So you won't give me back my money?"

"What's this money you keep on about, drunk man?"

"Eh, you'll come to give it back yourself in the next world—and I won't take it! I worked for my money, with sweat and calluses. You'll choke on my five kopecks in the next world."

"Giddap to the devil!"

"Quit giddapping me; I'm not a horse!"

"Get out, get out!"

"Scoundrel!"

"Mucker!"

And the swearing starts again, even worse than before the drinking.

Here are two friends sitting apart on the bunks. One is tall, thickset, beefy, a real butcher; his face is red. He's almost in tears, because he's very moved. The other is frail, scrawny, gaunt, with a long nose from which something seems to be dripping, and with little pig eyes fixed on the ground. He's a politic and educated man; he used to be a clerk and treats his friend somewhat haughtily, which the latter secretly finds very unpleasant. They've been drinking together all day.

"Me he dared!" the beefy friend shouts, grasping the clerk's head firmly with his left arm and rocking it back and forth. "Dared"— meaning struck. The beefy friend, a former sergeant, secretly envies his emaciated friend, and therefore they both flaunt the refinement of their style before each other.

"And I tell you that you're not right . . . ," the clerk begins dogmatically, stubbornly not raising his eyes to him and looking at the ground with dignity.

"Me he dared, do you hear!" his friend interrupts, pulling at his dear friend still more. "You're all that's left to me in the whole world now, do you hear? That's why it's to you alone I say: Me he dared! . . ."

"And I say again: such a flimsy excuse, dear friend, only heaps shame on your head!" the clerk objects in a thin and polite little voice. "And you'd better agree, dear friend, that all this drunkenness is due to your own inconstancy . . ."

The beefy friend shrinks back a little, stares dully with his drunken eyes at the self-satisfied little clerk, and suddenly, quite unexpectedly, with all his might, punches the clerk's little face with his enormous fist. Thus ends a whole day's friendship. The dear friend goes sprawling unconscious under the bunk . . .

Here one of my acquaintances from the special section comes into our barrack, an infinitely good-natured and jolly fellow, sensible, harmlessly mocking, and of extraordinarily simple appearance. He is the one who, on my first day in prison, during dinner in the kitchen, asked where the rich muzhik lived, claimed he had "anbishin," and drank tea with me. He's about forty, with a remarkably thick lower lip and a big, fleshy nose strewn with blackheads. He's holding a balalaika and casually fingering the strings. Behind him, as if in tow, followed an extremely small prisoner with a big head, of whom I knew very little as yet. However, nobody else paid any attention to him either. He was somehow strange, mistrustful, eternally silent and serious; he worked in the tailor's shop and obviously tried to live by himself, without dealing with anybody. But now, being drunk, he attached himself to Varlamov like his shadow. He followed after him in terrible agitation, waved his arms, beat his fist on the wall, on the bunk, and even all but sobbed. Varlamov seemed to pay no attention to him, as if he were not there beside him. It was remarkable that previously these two men had had almost no relations with each other; in occupation and in character they had nothing in common. They belonged to different categories and lived in different barracks. The little prisoner's name was Bulkin.

Seeing me, Varlamov grinned. I was sitting on my bunk by the stove. He stopped some distance away, facing me, pondered something, swayed, and came towards me with uneven steps, curving his whole body sideways somehow dashingly, and, lightly touching the strings, delivered a recitative, tapping his boot slightly:

Round her face, white her face,
Her voice has all a songbird's grace,
   My dearest little miss;
In her gown of satin bright
All garnished for the eye's delight,
   A pretty thing she is!

This song seemed to drive Bulkin out of his wits; he waved his arms and, turning to everybody, cried:

"It's all lies, brothers, it's all lies! He never says a word of truth, it's all lies!"

"To little old Alexander Petrovich!" said Varlamov, glancing at me with a mischievous laugh, and he almost came at me with his kisses. He was a bit drunk. The expression "To little old so-and-so . . . ," that is, "My respects to so-and-so," is used by simple folk all over Siberia, though it may refer to a man of twenty. The phrase "little old" stands for something honorable, respectable, even flattering.

"Well, Varlamov, how are you getting on?"

"Oh, one day at a time. Whoever's glad of the feast starts drinking bright and early; you must excuse me!" Varlamov said in a slight singsong.

"That's all lies, too! Again it's all lies!" Bulkin cried, pounding his fist on the bunk in some sort of despair. But it was as if Varlamov had promised himself not to pay the slightest attention to him, and there was an extraordinary comicality in that, because Bulkin had attached himself to Varlamov since morning for no reason at all, precisely because Varlamov "kept lying," as it somehow seemed to him. He trudged after him like a shadow, picked on his every word, wrung his hands, all but bloodied them banging on the walls and bunks, and suffered, visibly suffered, from the conviction that Varlamov "kept lying"! If he had had any hair on his head, he would probably have torn it out from grief. It was as if he had taken upon himself the duty of answering for Varlamov's actions, as if all of Varlamov's defects weighed on his conscience. But the thing was that the man didn't even look at him.

"It's all lies, lies, lies! Not a word of it fits with anything!" shouted Bulkin.

"What's that to you?" the prisoners responded, laughing.

"I must inform you, Alexander Petrovich, that I was very good-looking, and girls had a great liking for me . . . ," Varlamov suddenly began for no reason at all.

"Lies! More lies!" Bulkin interrupts with a shriek.

The prisoners guffaw.

"And I strutted before them: I wore a red shirt, velveteen trousers; I'd lie there like Prince Bottlekin, that is, drunk as a cobbler; in short— whatever you like!"

"Lies!" Bulkin confirms resolutely.

"And in those days I had my father's two-story stone house. Well, I squandered those two stories in two years; all I had left was the gate without the posts. Money's like pigeons: flies in and flies out again!"

"Lies!" Bulkin confirms still more resolutely.

"So some time ago I sent my relations a tearful letter from here, on the chance they'd send me some money. Because people said I'd gone against my parents. I'd been disrespectful! It was seven years ago I sent it."

"And still no answer?" I asked, laughing.

"No," he said, suddenly laughing himself and bringing his nose closer and closer to my face. "And I've got a sweetheart here, Alexander Petrovich . . ."

"You? A sweetheart?"

"Onufriev says to me the other day: 'Mine's pockmarked and ugly, but she's got lots of clothes; yours is pretty, but she's a beggar, goes around with a sack.'"

"And is it true?"

"It's true she's a beggar!" he replied and dissolved into inaudible laughter; there was also guffawing in the barrack. In fact, everybody knew he had been carrying on with some beggar woman and in the past six months had given her all of ten kopecks.

"Well, so what?" I asked, wishing finally to get rid of him.

He paused, gave me a sweet look, and uttered gently:

"So on that account won't you deign to buy me a little drink? All I've drunk today is tea, Alexander Petrovich," he added, sweetly accepting the money. "I've swilled so much tea I can hardly breathe, and it sloshes around in my belly like in a bottle . . ."

While Varlamov was taking the money, Bulkin's moral exasperation seemed to reach the final limits. He gesticulated like a desperate man and was all but weeping.

"God's people!" he shouted frenziedly, addressing the whole barrack. "Look at him! He keeps lying! Whatever he says, it's all lies, lies, lies!"

"What is it to you?" the prisoners shouted back, amazed at his rage. "You absurd man!"

"I won't let him lie!" Bulkin shouts, flashing his eyes and banging his fist on the bunk with all his might. "I don't want him to lie!"

Everybody guffaws. Varlamov takes the money, bows to me, and clownishly hurries out of the barrack, to the taverner, naturally. And here he seems to notice Bulkin for the first time.

"Well, come on!" he says to him, pausing on the threshold as if he really needed him for something. "Knob!" he adds scornfully, letting the aggrieved Bulkin go first and again beginning to strum his balalaika . . .

But why describe this muddle! The stifling day is finally over. The prisoners fall into heavy sleep on their bunks. In their sleep they talk and rave even more than on other nights. Here and there people still sit at maidans. The long-awaited feast is over. Tomorrow is an ordinary day again, and work again . . .

XI

The Performance

On the third day of Christmas, in the evening, the first performance in our theater took place.[1] A great deal of preliminary effort had probably gone into organizing it, but the actors took it all on themselves, so that the rest of us did not know where things were at, what precisely was being done, and did not even know very well what would be performed. For all those three days, the actors, going out to work, tried to collect as many costumes as they could. Baklushin, on meeting me, only snapped his fingers with pleasure. Apparently the major also turned out to be having a rather decent spell. However, we had no idea if he knew anything about the theater. If he knew, then had he allowed it formally, or had he only decided to say nothing, waving his hand at the prisoners' undertaking, and insisting, of course, that everything should be as orderly as possible? I think he knew about the theater; he could hardly not have known; but he did not want to interfere, realizing that it would be worse if he forbade it: the prisoners would start playing pranks, getting drunk, so that it was much better if they were busy with something. However, I am supposing that this was the major's reasoning, simply because it is the most natural, the most correct and sensible. You might even say that if the prisoners had not had the theater or some such occupation during the holidays, the authorities would have had to think it up themselves. But since our major was distinguished by a way of thinking completely opposite to the rest of mankind, it is very likely that I am sinning greatly in supposing he knew about the theater and allowed it. A man like the major always has a need to crush someone, to take something away, to deprive someone of his rights—in short, to restore order somewhere. In that respect he was known to the whole town. What did he care that precisely these constraints might lead to mischief in prison? There are punishments for mischief (so people like our major reason), and for these scoundrelly prisoners there is severity and an unrelenting, literal enforcement of the law—that's all it takes! These giftless enforcers of the law decidedly do not understand, and are incapable of understanding, that its literal enforcement alone, without thought, without an understanding of its spirit, leads straight to disorder and has never led to anything else. "The law says so; what more do you want?" they say, and are sincerely surprised that, in addition to the law, sound reasoning and a sober mind are also required of them. This last in particular seems to many of them a superfluous and outrageous luxury, an insufferable constraint.

But, be that as it may, the senior sergeant did not contradict the prisoners, and that was all they needed. I can positively say that the theater and gratitude for its being allowed were the reasons why there was not one serious disturbance in the prison during the holidays: not a single malignant quarrel, not a single theft. I myself was witness to how they quieted down some revelers or quarrelers solely on the grounds that the theater might be forbidden. The sergeant got the prisoners' word that everything would be quiet and they would behave well. They agreed gladly and religiously kept their promise; they were also very flattered that their word was trusted. It must be said, however, that it cost the authorities decidedly nothing to allow the theater; they made no contribution. No place was fenced off beforehand: the whole theater could be erected and dismantled in about a quarter of an hour. The performance lasted an hour and a half, and if orders came from above to end it, it could be done in a moment. The costumes were hidden in the prisoners' trunks. But before I tell how the theater was set up and precisely what sort of costumes these were, I will tell about the theater playbill, that is, precisely what they proposed to play.

There was no written playbill as such. One appeared, however, for the second and third performances, in Baklushin's hand, for the gentlemen officers and noble visitors in general, who honored our theater by their attendance even at the first performance. Namely, from among the gentlemen, the guards officer usually came, and once the commander of the guards himself came. One time the engineers officer also came. It was in case of such visitors that the playbill was produced. It was assumed that the fame of the prison theater would resound all through the fortress and even in town, the more so as it had no theater.

It was rumored that some amateurs got up one performance, but that was all. The prisoners were glad as children of the smallest success; they even became vainglorious. "Who knows," they thought and even said to themselves and to each other, "maybe the highest authorities will find out; they'll come and watch; then they'll see what sort of prisoners there are. This is no simple soldiers' performance, with some kind of dummies, with boats floating, with bears and goats walking around. We've got actors, real actors, who are playing in gentlemen's comedies. There's no such theater in town. They say there was a performance once at General Abrosimov's, and there'll be more; well, maybe they'll only outdo us with their costumes, but as for *dialogue*, maybe ours will do better! Maybe it'll get as far as the governor, and—devil knows!— he may want to come and see for himself. Since there's no theater in town . . ." In short, the prisoners' fantasy, especially after the first success, went to the ultimate degree during the holidays, all but to the giving of prizes or the shortening of their term at hard labor, though at the same time they began almost at once to laugh good-naturedly at themselves. In short, they were children, perfect children, though some of these children were forty years old. But even without the playbill, I knew the general content of the future performance. The first play was *Filatka and Miroshka, or The Rivals.*[2] A week before the performance, Baklushin boasted to me that the role of Filatka, which he had taken upon himself, would be performed as it had never been seen even in a *Saint* Petersburg theater. He strutted about the barracks, boasted mercilessly and shamelessly, but at the same time quite good-naturedly, and sometimes would suddenly go off into something "theaytrical," that is, from his role—and everybody would laugh, whether it was funny or not. Though it must be admitted that here, too, the prisoners were able to restrain themselves and keep their dignity: only the youngest folk, greenhorns with no control, went into raptures over Baklushin's antics and stories of the coming theater, or else the most important prisoners, whose authority was firmly established, so that they no longer had any fear of expressing their feelings directly, whatever they might be, even of the most naïve (that is, in prison terms, the most improper) nature. The rest listened to the talk and rumors silently, without disapproving, without contradicting, true, but trying their best to treat the talk of the theater with indifference and even in part with condescension. Only at the last moment, almost on the very day of the performance, did everybody begin to get interested: What's going to happen? How are our boys doing? What about the major? Will it turn out like the year before last? and so on. Baklushin assured me that the actors had been excellently chosen, each "suited to his place." That there would even be a curtain. That Filatka's bride would be played by Sirotkin—"and you'll see for yourself how he looks in a woman's dress!" he said, screwing up his eyes and clucking his tongue. The benevolent lady would have a dress with a falbala and a little pelerine, and a parasol in her hand, and the benevolent squire would come out in an officer's tunic with aiguillettes and with a cane. This play would be followed by another, a drama: *Kedril the Glutton.* The title intrigued me greatly; but though I kept asking about the play, I could not find out anything beforehand. All I found out was that it had been taken not from a book, but "from a manuscript"; that it had been obtained from some retired sergeant, who lived on the edge of town and probably once took part in its performance himself on some army stage. In our remote towns and provinces there indeed exist such theater plays, which nobody seems to know, which may never have been published anywhere, but which appeared of themselves from somewhere and constitute an indispensable part of every popular theater in certain regions of Russia. Incidentally, I have said "popular theater." It would be very good, very good indeed, if one of our researchers would undertake a new investigation, more thorough than previously, into popular theater, which is there, exists, and even may not be entirely insignificant. I refuse to believe that everything I saw later in our prison theater was invented by our own prisoners. There is a need here for a continuity of tradition, for methods and notions established once and for all, which are transmitted from generation to generation and through old memory. They must be sought among the soldiers, among factory workers in factory towns, and even among tradesmen in some poor, unknown little towns. They have also been preserved on estates and in provincial capitals among the house serfs in big landowners' houses. I even think that many old plays spread in manuscript all over Russia not otherwise than through house serfs. In the old days, landowners and the Moscow nobility had their own theaters with serf actors. And it was those theaters that saw the beginnings of our popular dramatic art, the signs of which are unmistakable. As for *Kedril the Glutton*, much as I wanted to, I could find out nothing before the performance except that evil spirits appear onstage and carry Kedril off to hell. But what does *Kedril* mean, and, finally, why Kedril and not Kiril? Was it a Russian or a foreign episode?—that I simply could not find out. It was announced that at the conclusion there would be a "pantermine with music." Of course, all this was very intriguing. There were some fifteen actors, all of them glib and gallant fellows. They banded together, held rehearsals, sometimes behind the barracks, in secret, in hiding. In short, they wanted to astonish us all with something extraordinary and unexpected.

On workdays the prison was locked up early, as soon as night fell. For Christmas an exception was made: it was not locked up until the evening drum. This privilege was granted strictly on account of the theater. During the holidays, a request was ordinarily sent each day, towards evening, from the prison to the guards officer, humbly begging him "to allow the theater and not lock up the prison until later," adding that there had been theater yesterday and they had locked up very late, but there had been no disorders. The guards officer reasoned like this: "There were in fact no disorders yesterday, and since they've given their word that there will be none today, it means they'll look after it themselves, and that's the surest of all. Besides, if the performance is not allowed, then most likely (who knows these convict folk!) they'll pull some dirty tricks on purpose out of spite and get the guards in trouble." Finally, there was this: standing guard was boring, and here was this theater, not just with soldiers, but with prisoners, and prisoners are interesting folk; it will be amusing to watch. And the guards officer always has the right to watch.

The duty officer will come: "Where's the guards officer?" "He went to the prison to count the prisoners and lock up the barracks"—a straight answer and a straight explanation. And so every evening during the holidays the guards officers allowed the theater and did not lock up the barracks until the evening drum. The prisoners knew beforehand that there would be no hindrance from the guards, and they were at ease.

Before seven Petrov came for me, and we went to the performance together. Almost everybody from our barrack went, except for the Old Believer from Chernigov and the Poles. Only for the very last performance, on the fourth of January, did the Poles get themselves to visit the theater, and that after many assurances that it was good, and amusing, and safe. The Poles' squeamishness did not bother the convicts in the least, and they were met very politely on the fourth. They were even shown to the best places. As for our Circassians, and for Isai Fomich in particular, they found the theater a sheer delight. Isai Fomich donated three kopecks each time, and the last time he put ten kopecks in the plate, and his face was a picture of bliss. The actors decided to collect whatever was donated, for theater expenses and for their own *fortification*. Petrov assured me that I would be shown to one of the best places, however packed the theater was, on the grounds that, being richer than the others, I would probably give more, and, besides, I was more of an expert than the rest. And so it happened. But first of all I'll describe the house and the way the theater was set up.

Our military barrack, in which the theater was set up, was about fifteen paces long. From the yard you went up to the porch, from the porch into the front hall, and from there into the barrack. This long barrack, as I've said, was arranged in a special way: the bunks stood along the walls, so that the middle of the room remained free. The half of the room closer to the entrance from the porch was allotted to the spectators; the other half, which communicated with another barrack, was allotted to the stage. First of all I was struck by the curtain. It stretched for about ten paces across the whole barrack. This curtain was such a luxury that it really was something to marvel at. Besides that, it was painted in oils: trees, arbors, ponds, and stars were depicted on it. It was a patchwork of linen, old and new, whatever people could give and sacrifice; of prisoners' old foot cloths and shirts, sewn together anyhow into one big sheet; and, finally, part of it, when they ran out of cloth, was simply made from paper, also begged sheet by sheet from various offices and departments. The painters—our "Briullov," A—v, outstanding among them—took care of painting and decorating it. The effect was astonishing. Such luxury delighted even the most sullen and fastidious of the prisoners, who, when it came to the performance, all turned out without exception to be as much children as the most fervent and impatient of them. Everybody was very pleased, even boastfully pleased. The lighting consisted of several tallow candles cut into pieces. In front of the curtain stood two benches from the kitchen, and in front of the benches three or four chairs found in the sergeants' room. The chairs were there just in case, for persons of the highest officer's ranks. The benches were for sergeants and engineering clerks, foremen and other folk who were superiors, though not of officer's rank, in case they dropped in on the prison. And so it happened: we were never lacking in visitors from outside all through the holidays; on some evenings there were more, on some less, and at the last performance there was not a single place on the benches left unoccupied. And, finally, behind the benches, came the prisoners, standing out of respect for the other visitors, caps off, in jackets or sheepskins, despite the stifling, steamy atmosphere of the room. Of course, the space intended for the prisoners was too small. Not only were some literally sitting on each other, especially in the back rows, but the bunks and wings were also occupied, and, finally, theater lovers turned up, who kept coming from the back, through the other barrack, and watched the performance behind the wings. The crowding in the front half of the barrack was unnatural and could have rivaled the crowding and crush I had seen not long before in the bathhouse. The door to the front hall was open; the temperature in the front hall was well below zero, but people were packed in there, too. For us, Petrov and me, they made way at once, almost right to the benches, where we could see much better than in the back rows. They saw me as something of a judge, a connoisseur, who had been in quite different theaters; they saw that Baklushin kept consulting me all the time and treated me with respect; so now I was well honored and well placed. Suppose the prisoners were vain and light-minded people in the highest degree, but that was all affectation. They could laugh at me, seeing that I was a bad helper to them at work. Almazov could look upon us gentlemen with contempt, flaunting before us his skill at baking alabaster. But mixed with their persecution and mockery of us there was something else: we had once been gentlemen; we belonged to the same estate as their former masters, of whom they could not have preserved a very good memory. But now, in the theater, they made way for me. They recognized that in this I was the better judge, that I had seen and knew more than they. Those who were least disposed towards me (this I know) now wished for my praise of their theater and without any self-abasement let me have the best place. I am judging now, recalling my impression then. It seemed to me then—I remember this—that in their just judgment of themselves there was no abasement at all, but a sense of their own dignity. The highest and most sharply characteristic feature of our people is this sense of justice and the thirst for it. There is no cocky habit in the people of being in the forefront everywhere and *at all costs*, whether a man is worthy of it or not. You need only peel off the external, superficial husk and look at the kernel more closely, attentively, without prejudice, and you will see such things in the people as you never anticipated. There is not much our wise men can teach the people. I will even say positively—on the contrary, they themselves ought to learn from them.

Petrov naïvely told me, when we were still just getting ready for the theater, that they would let me go to the front because I would also give more money. There was no fixed price: each gave what he could or what he wished. Almost everyone put in something, if only a half kopeck, when they passed the plate around. But if they let me go to the front partly for the sake of money, supposing I would give more than the others, again how much dignity there was in it! "You're richer than I am, so go to the front, and though we're all equal here, you'll put in more: consequently, a visitor like you is more welcome for the actors—you get the first place, because we're all here not for the money, but for respect, and consequently it's up to us to sort ourselves out." How much genuine, noble pride there is in that! It's not respect for money, it's respect for oneself. Generally, there was no particular respect for money, for wealth, in the prison, particularly if you looked at the prisoners without distinction, in the mass, as a group. I don't remember even one of them seriously demeaning himself for the sake of money, even if we consider each of them separately. There were cadgers, who also tried to get money out of me. But in this cadging there was more prankishness, more mischief, than real business; there was more humor and naïveté. I don't know if I'm making myself clear . . . But I've forgotten about the theater. To business.

Before the raising of the curtain, the whole room presented a strange and animated picture. First of all there was the crowd of spectators, pressed, squashed, squeezed on all sides, waiting patiently and with blissful faces for the performance to begin. In the back rows people were piled on top of each other. Many of them brought firewood from the kitchen: leaning a thick piece of firewood against the wall somehow, a man climbed up on it, propped himself on the shoulders of the one in front of him, and stood like that for two hours without changing his position, perfectly pleased with himself and his place. Others planted their feet on the lower step of the stove and stood it out the whole time in the same way, leaning on those in front of them. That was in the back rows, by the wall. On the sides, clambering onto the bunks, another packed crowd stood over the musicians. Those were good places. Some five men clambered up onto the stove itself and lay on it, looking down. That was sheer bliss! The windowsills along the opposite wall also swarmed with whole crowds of latecomers or those who had not found good places. Everyone behaved quietly and decorously. Everyone wanted to show himself from his best side before the gentry and visitors. On every face there was a look of the most naïve expectation. Every face was red and moist with sweat from the heat and the stuffiness. What a strange gleam of childlike joy, of sweet, pure pleasure, shone on those furrowed, branded brows and cheeks, in the gazes of these people, until then gloomy and sullen, in those eyes which sometimes shone with a terrible fire! They were all hatless, and their heads were all shaven on the right side. But now noise and bustle are heard on the stage. The curtain is about to rise. Now the orchestra starts to play . . . This orchestra is worth mentioning. To one side, on the bunks, some eight musicians had placed themselves: two violins (one found in the prison, the other borrowed from someone in the fortress, but the player was one of ours), three balalaikas, all homemade, two guitars, and a tambourine instead of a bass. The violins just screeched and squawked, the guitars were trash, but the balalaikas were superb. The swiftness of the fingers running over the strings certainly rivaled the cleverest sleight of hand. They kept playing dance tunes. In the most dancing passages the players rapped their knuckles on the soundboard of the balalaika; the tone, the taste, the execution, the handling of the instrument, the character given to the tune—all was their own, original, prisoner style. One of the guitarists also knew his instrument splendidly. This was that same gentleman who had killed his father. As for the tambourine player, he simply performed miracles: he would spin it on his finger, then pass his thumb over the skin, then we would hear rapid, resounding, and uniform taps, then suddenly it was as if this strong, distinct sound scattered into a countless number of jingling and rustling little sounds. Finally, two accordions also appeared. To tell the truth, until then I had no idea of what could be done with simple folk instruments; the harmony of sounds, the teamwork, and above all the spirit, the character of understanding and conveying the very essence of the tune, were simply amazing. For the first time then I fully understood precisely what was so endlessly exuberant and rollicking in these exuberant and rollicking Russian dance songs. Finally the curtain rose. Everybody stirred, shifted from one foot to the other, those in the back stood on tiptoe; someone fell off his log; one and all gaped their mouths and fixed their eyes, and total silence reigned . . . The performance began.

Beside me stood Alei in the group of his brothers and the other Circassians. They all became passionately attached to the theater and after that came every evening. Muslims, Tatars, and the like, as I've noticed more than once, are always passionate lovers of various spectacles. Beside them huddled Isai Fomich, who seemed to turn all ears and eyes as the curtain went up, in the most naïve, greedy expectation of wonders and delights. It would even have been a pity if his expectations had been disappointed. Alei's sweet face shone with such childlike, beautiful joy that, I confess, I found it terribly delightful to look at him, and I remember how, each time an actor pulled some funny and clever stunt, and there was a general burst of laughter, I involuntarily turned at once to Alei and tried to see his face. He didn't see me; what was I to him! Not far from me, on the left side, stood an older prisoner, eternally frowning, eternally displeased and grumbling. He, too, noticed Alei, and I saw him turn to look at him several times with a half smile: so sweet he was! He called him "Alei Semyonych," I don't know why. They began with *Filatka and Miroshka*. Filatka (Baklushin) was indeed magnificent. He played his role with astonishing precision. You could see that he had thought over each phrase, each movement. To each empty word, to each of his gestures, he was able to give a sense and significance that corresponded perfectly to the character of his role. Add to this diligence, to this study, an astonishing, unfeigned gaiety, simplicity, artlessness, and you would certainly agree, if you had seen Baklushin, that he was a natural-born actor of great talent. I had seen Filatka more than once in Moscow and Petersburg theaters, and I can say positively that the actors who played Filatka in the capitals played worse than Baklushin. Compared to him they were *paysans*, and not real muzhiks. They tried too hard to represent muzhiks. Above all Baklushin was moved by rivalry: everybody knew that in the second play the role of Kedril would be played by the prisoner Potseikin, an actor whom they all regarded for some reason as more gifted, as better than Baklushin, and Baklushin suffered from that like a child. How many times did he come to me in those last few days and pour out his feelings! Two hours before the performance, he was shaking as in a fever. When the crowd laughed and shouted: "Great, Baklushin! Fine fellow!"—his whole face lit up with happiness, genuine inspiration shone in his eyes. The scene of the kissing of Miroshka, when Filatka shouts beforehand "Wipe your mouth!" and then wipes his own, came out killingly funny. Everybody simply rolled with laughter. But most entertaining of all for me were the spectators; here everybody was unbuttoned. They gave themselves wholeheartedly to their pleasure. Shouts of encouragement rang out more and more often. Here a man nudges his neighbor and hastily tells him his impressions, not caring, and perhaps not even seeing, who is standing next to him; another, during some funny scene, suddenly turns rapturously to the crowd, quickly passes his gaze over them all, as if inviting them to laugh, waves his hand, and at once turns eagerly to the stage again. A third simply clucks his tongue and snaps his fingers, and, unable to stand quietly where he is, and since he cannot budge, keeps shifting from one foot to the other. By the end of the play the general merriment had reached the highest pitch. I am not exaggerating anything. Imagine prison, fetters, unfreedom, long sad years ahead, a life as monotonous as drizzling rain on a dreary autumn day—and suddenly all these downtrodden and confined men are allowed for one little hour to let go, to have fun, to forget the oppressive dream, to set up a whole theater, and what a theater: to the pride and astonishment of the whole town, as if to say, see what kind of prisoners we are! They were interested in everything, of course—the costumes, for instance. They were terribly curious, for instance, to see someone like Vanka Otpety, or Netsvetaev, or Baklushin in completely different clothes from what they had seen them in every day for so many years. "Why, he's a prisoner, that same prisoner, with the same clanking fetters, and here he comes out in a frock coat, a round hat, a cloak—a perfect civilian! Mustaches and hair stuck on. Look at him pulling a red handkerchief out of his pocket, fanning himself, acting the gentleman—a real gentleman, no more or less." And everybody is in ecstasy. The "benevolent squire" came out in an adjutant's uniform, a very old one, true, with epaulettes, a peaked cap with a little cockade, and made an extraordinary effect. There were two eager candidates for this role, and—would you believe it?—they quarreled terribly with each other, like little children, over who was going to play it: they both wanted to appear in an officer's uniform with aiguillettes! The other actors separated them and decided by a majority of votes to give the role to Netsvetaev, not because he was more handsome and presentable than the other, and therefore looked more like a gentleman, but because Netsvetaev persuaded them all that he would come out with a cane and swing it and trace on the ground with it like a real gentleman and the foremost dandy, which Vanka Otpety couldn't do, because he had never seen any real gentlemen. And indeed, when Netsvetaev came out before the public with his lady, all he did was trace quickly and nimbly on the ground with a thin rattan cane he had obtained somewhere, probably considering it a sign of the most lofty gentlemanliness, the utmost in foppishness and fashion. Probably sometime in his childhood, as a barefoot boy, a house serf, he had happened to see a well-dressed gentleman with a cane and to be captivated by his skill in twirling it, and the impression had remained forever indelible in his soul, so that now, at the age of thirty, he remembered it all as it had been, for the full captivation and fascination of the entire prison. Netsvetaev was so absorbed in what he was doing that he did not look anywhere or at anyone, even spoke without raising his eyes, and did nothing but follow his cane and its tip. The benevolent lady was also quite remarkable in her way: she appeared in an old, worn-out muslin dress that looked like a real rag, with bared arms and neck, a face terribly powdered and rouged, a calico nightcap tied under her chin, a parasol in one hand, and in the other a fan made of painted paper with which she ceaselessly fanned herself. The lady was met by a loud burst of laughter, and she herself could not help laughing several times. She was played by the prisoner Ivanov. Sirotkin, dressed up as a young girl, was very sweet. The couplets also came off well. In short, the play ended to the fullest and most general satisfaction. Of criticism there was none, nor could there be any.

The overture, "Hallway, My Hallway," was played once more, and the curtain rose again. This was *Kedril*. *Kedril* is something like *Don Juan*; at least at the end of the play devils carry both master and servant off to hell. A whole act was presented, but it was obviously a fragment; the beginning and end had been lost. Not the slightest sense or meaning. The action takes place somewhere in Russia, at an inn. The innkeeper shows a gentleman in an overcoat and a crumpled round hat to his room. They are followed by his servant Kedril with a suitcase and a chicken wrapped in blue paper. Kedril is wearing a sheepskin jacket and a lackey's visored cap. It's he who is the glutton. He is played by the prisoner Potseikin, Baklushin's rival; the master is played by the same Ivanov who played the benevolent lady in the first play. The innkeeper, Netsvetaev, warns them that there may be devils in the room, and disappears. The master, gloomy and preoccupied, mutters to himself that he's known that for a long time, and orders Kedril to unpack and prepare supper. Kedril is a coward and a glutton. Hearing about the devils, he turns pale and trembles like a leaf. He would run away, but he is afraid of his master. And, above all, he wants to eat. He is a sensualist, stupid, cunning in his own way, a coward, cheats his master at every step and at the same time is afraid of him. This is a remarkable type of servant, in whom the features of Leporello tell in some vague and remote way,[3] and he is indeed remarkably portrayed. Potseikin is decidedly talented, and, in my view, a still better actor than Baklushin. Naturally, when I met Baklushin the next day, I did not express my full opinion to him: I would have upset him too much. The prisoner who played the master also played rather well. He poured out some awful drivel, not resembling anything; but his diction was proper, glib, his gestures appropriate. While Kedril fusses about with the suitcases, the master pensively paces the stage and announces for all to hear that that evening marks the end of his wanderings. Kedril listens curiously, grimaces, speaks *a parte*, and makes the spectators laugh with every word. He's not sorry for his master; but he has heard about the devils; he wants to find out what's up, and so he starts talking and questioning. The master finally tells him that once, in some sort of trouble, he had asked Hell for help, and the devils had helped him, had rescued him; but that today was the end of the term, and maybe even today, as agreed, they would come for his soul. Kedril is badly frightened. But the master does not lose heart and tells him to make supper. On hearing about supper, Kedril revives, takes out the chicken, takes out the wine—and every now and then picks a piece off the chicken and tastes it. The public laughs. Then the door creaks, the wind beats at the shutters; Kedril trembles and hurriedly, almost unconsciously, stuffs into his mouth an enormous piece of chicken that he can't even swallow. Again laughter. "Is it ready?" shouts the master, pacing the room. "One moment, sir . . . I'm . . . getting it ready for you," says Kedril, and he sits down at the table himself and starts packing away his master's food. The public obviously loves the servant's quickness and cunning, and that the master is being made a fool of. It must be admitted that Potseikin really deserved praise. He pronounced the words "One moment, sir, I'm getting it ready for you" perfectly. Sitting at the table, he begins to eat greedily and flinches at the master's every step, hoping he won't notice his pranks; as soon as he turns around, Kedril ducks under the table and drags the chicken after him. He finally satisfies his initial hunger; it's time to think about the master. "Soon now, Kedril?" shouts the master. "Ready, sir!" Kedril responds pertly, suddenly realizing that there is almost nothing left for the master. In fact, there is only one drumstick on the plate. The master, gloomy and preoccupied, notices nothing and sits down at the table, and Kedril stations himself behind his chair with a napkin. Every word, every gesture, every grimace of Kedril's, when, turning to the public, he nods towards his nincompoop of a master, is met with irrepressible laughter from the spectators. But now, just as the master gets down to eating, the devils appear. Here it's impossible to understand anything, and the devils' entrance is somehow much too outlandish; a door opens in the wings and something in white appears, and in place of a head it has a lantern with a candle; another phantom, also with a lantern on its head, holds a scythe in its hands. Why the lanterns, why the scythe, why devils in white?—nobody can explain. However, nobody thinks about it. That's probably how it should be. The master addresses the devils quite bravely, shouting that he is ready to be taken. But Kedril is as scared as a rabbit; he crawls under the table, but, despite all his fears, doesn't forget to snatch the bottle from the table. The devils disappear for a moment; Kedril crawls out from under the table; but just as the master gets down to his chicken again, three devils burst into the room, pick him up from behind, and carry him off to Hell. "Kedril! Save me!" shouts the master. But Kedril's not about to do that. This time he takes the bottle, the plate, and even the bread under the table. Now he's alone—no devils, no master. Kedril creeps out, looks around, and a smile lights up his face. He squints slyly, sits down in his master's place, and, nodding to the public, says in a half whisper:

"Well, now I'm alone . . . without any master! . . ."

Everybody laughs at his being without a master; but now he adds in a half whisper, addressing the public confidentially and winking his little eye more and more merrily:

"The devils took my master! . . ."

The spectators' ecstasy is boundless! Besides the fact that the devils took his master, it was told in such a way, with such slyness, with such mockingly triumphant grimaces, that it really was impossible not to applaud. But Kedril's happiness does not last long. He has just taken possession of the bottle, filled his glass, and is about to drink, when the devils suddenly come back, sneak up behind him on tiptoe, and snitch-snatch him from both sides. Kedril shouts at the top of his lungs; he's so cowardly he doesn't dare turn around. He also cannot defend himself: his hands are taken up by the bottle and the glass, which he's unable to part with. His mouth gaping with terror, he sits for half a minute staring pop-eyed at the public, with such a hilarious expression of cowardly fright that he decidedly could have posed for a picture. They finally pick him up and carry him off; he holds on to the bottle, wiggles his legs, and shouts and shouts. You can still hear him shouting from backstage. But the curtain falls, and everyone laughs, everyone is in ecstasy . . . The orchestra strikes up the Kamarinskaya.

They begin softly, barely audibly, but the melody grows and grows, the tempo increases, dashing raps ring out on the soundboard of the balalaika . . . This is the Kamarinsky in full swing, and it truly would have been good if Glinka had happened to hear it in our prison.[4] The pantomime begins to the sound of the music. The Kamarinsky doesn't stop all through the pantomime. The scene is the interior of a cottage. A miller and his wife are onstage. The miller is mending a harness in one corner; in the other his wife is spinning hemp. The wife is played by Sirotkin, the miller by Netsvetaev.

I will note that our stage set is very sparse. In both this and the preceding piece, you fill in more with your imagination than you see with your eyes. Instead of a backdrop, they have stretched some sort of rug or horse blanket; to the sides are some trashy screens. The left side is not obstructed at all, and you can see the bunks. But the spectators are not demanding, and they agree to fill in the reality with their imagination, the more so as prisoners are quite good at it: "They say a garden, so consider it a garden, a room so it's a room, a cottage so it's a cottage—never mind, we don't stand on ceremony." Sirotkin looks very sweet in the costume of a young peasant wench. A few hushed compliments are heard among the spectators. The miller finishes his work, takes his hat and knout, goes to his wife, and explains with gestures that he has to leave, but that if she receives anybody in his absence, then . . . and he points to the knout. The wife listens and nods. She is probably well acquainted with this knout: the wench plays fast and loose with her husband. The husband leaves. The moment he steps out, his wife shakes her fist at his back. Then comes a knock; the door opens and a neighbor appears, also a miller, a muzhik in a kaftan and with a beard. In his hands a present, a red kerchief. The wench laughs; but the neighbor just goes to embrace her, when there is another knock on the door. Where to put him? She quickly hides him under the table and goes back to her spinning. Another admirer appears: this one is a clerk in a military uniform. So far the pantomime has gone flawlessly, the gestures have been exactly right. You might even wonder, watching these improvised actors, and involuntarily think to yourself: how much power and talent sometimes perishes in our Russia almost for nothing, in prison and in hardship! But the prisoner who played the clerk probably used to be in a provincial or home theater, and imagined that our actors, one and all, did not understand what they were doing and did not move the way one ought to move onstage. And so he performs as they say the heroes of classical theater used to perform in the old days: he takes a long stride and, before moving the other leg, suddenly stops, throws back his head and his whole body, looks around proudly, and—takes another stride. If such a gait was ridiculous in classical heroes, it was all the more so in a military clerk, in a comic scene. But our public thought it probably had to be so and accepted the long strides of the lanky clerk as an accomplished fact, without any particular criticism. The clerk has barely had time to reach the middle of the stage when more knocking is heard: the hostess is again all aflutter. Where to put the clerk? Into the trunk, which is thankfully open. The clerk slips into the trunk, and the wench closes the lid on him. This time a special guest appears, also an amorous one, but of a special sort. He is a Brahmin, even in his costume. Irrepressible laughter breaks out among the spectators. The prisoner Koshkin plays the Brahmin, and plays him beautifully. He has a Brahminish look. Through gestures he expresses the full extent of his love. He raises his hands to heaven, then presses them to his breast, his heart; but he has just managed to wax tender when there comes a loud knock on the door. You can tell by the knock that it's the master. The frightened wife is beside herself; the Brahmin rushes about frantically and begs to be hidden. She hastily puts him behind the cupboard and, forgetting to open the door, rushes to her spinning and spins, spins, not hearing her husband rapping on the door, in her fright twisting thread that isn't there and turning the spindle that she has forgotten to pick up from the floor. Sirotkin succeeded in portraying her fear very well. But the master kicks the door open with his foot and approaches his wife knout in hand. He has noticed and spied out everything, and holds up his fingers to say she has three of them hidden. Then he goes looking for them. The first to be found is the neighbor, whom he ushers out of the room with his fists. The cowardly clerk wanted to flee, raised the lid with his head, and thus gave himself away. The master whips him along with the knout, and this time the amorous clerk hops about in a none-too-classical way. There remains the Brahmin; the master spends a long time searching for him, finally finds him in the corner behind the cupboard, bows politely to him, and pulls him out into the middle of the room by his beard. The Brahmin tries to defend himself, shouts: "Curse you! Curse you!" (the only words spoken in the pantomime), but the husband doesn't listen and makes short work of him. The wife, seeing that it has now come around to her, drops the yarn and spindle and runs out of the room; the spinning-stool falls to the ground, the prisoners guffaw. Alei, without looking at me, tugs at my arm and shouts: "Look! The Brahmin! The Brahmin!" and laughs so he can hardly stand. The curtain falls. The next scene begins . . .

But there is no need to describe all the scenes. There were two or three more. They were all funny and unfeignedly merry. If the prisoners didn't write them themselves, they at least put a lot of their own into each of them. Almost every actor improvised, so that the next evening the same actor played the same scene slightly differently. The last pantomime, of a fantastic nature, concluded with a ballet. A dead man is being buried. The Brahmin and his numerous attendants perform various incantations over the coffin, but nothing helps. Finally, "The Sun Is Setting" rings out, the dead man rises, everybody joyfully begins to dance. The Brahmin dances with the dead man, and dances in a very special, Brahminish way. With that the theater ends, until the next evening. Our people all go their ways, cheerful, pleased, praising the actors, thanking the sergeant. No quarrels are heard. Everybody is somehow unusually pleased, even as if happy, and they fall asleep not as habitually, but almost with peace of mind—and why so, you wonder? And yet it's not a figment of my imagination. It's true, real. These poor men were allowed to live in their own way for a little while, to have fun like other people, to spend if only an hour of unprisonlike time—and they were morally changed, even if only for those few minutes . . . But now it's already deep night. I give a start for some reason and wake up: the old man is still praying on the stove and will go on praying till dawn; Alei is sleeping quietly next to me. I remember that as he was falling asleep he was still laughing, talking about the theater with his brothers, and I involuntarily lose myself in contemplating his peaceful, childlike face. I gradually remember everything: the past day, the holidays, this whole month . . . In fear I raise my head and look around at my sleeping comrades by the dim, flickering light of a two-penny prison candle. I look at their pale faces, their poor beds, at all this rank poverty and destitution—look at it intently—and it's as if I want to make sure that all this is not the continuation of an ugly dream, but the real truth. But this is the truth: I now hear someone moan; someone moves his arm clumsily and his chains clank. Another shudders in his sleep and starts to talk, while grandpa on the stove is praying for all "Orthodox Christians," and I can hear his measured, quiet, drawn-out "Lord Jesus Christ, have mercy on us! . . ."

"I'm not here forever, but only for a few years!" I think and lower my head to the pillow again.

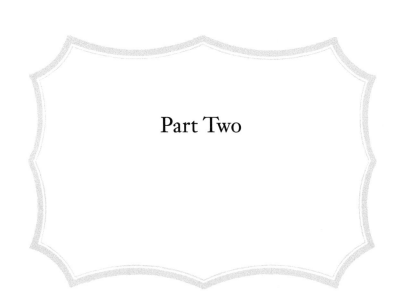

Part Two

I

The Hospital

Soon after the holidays, I fell ill and was sent to our military hospital. It stood apart, about a quarter mile from the fortress. It was a long one-story building, painted yellow. In the summer, when repair work was done, an extraordinary amount of ochre was expended on it. In the vast courtyard of the hospital there were offices, houses for the medical authorities, and other utility buildings. In the main building there were only wards. There were many wards, but for the prisoners there were only two in all, always very crowded, especially in summer, so that the beds often had to be pushed together. Our wards were filled with all sorts of "unfortunates." Our people went there, various sorts of military men on trial went there, held under various sorts of guard—already sentenced, awaiting sentence, and in transit; some were from the correctional company—a strange institution, to which delinquent or unreliable soldiers were sent from the battalions to have their behavior corrected, and from which, after two years or more, they usually came out such scoundrels as are rarely to be met with. Sick prisoners usually reported their sickness to the sergeant in the morning. They were entered into a book at once, and with that book the sick man was sent under convoy to the battalion infirmary. There a doctor made a preliminary examination of all the sick from all the military units billeted in the fortress, and those found to be actually sick were sent to the hospital. I was noted down in the book, and between one and two o'clock, when everybody had already gone from the prison to their afternoon work, I went to the hospital. A sick prisoner usually took with him as much money as he could, some bread, because he could not expect his ration in the hospital that day, a tiny pipe and a pouch of tobacco, a flint and steel. These last items were carefully hidden in a boot. I entered the grounds of the hospital not without a certain curiosity about this new variation, as yet unknown to me, on our prison life.

The day was warm, overcast, and sad—one of those days when such institutions as a hospital acquire an especially business-like, dreary, and sour look. The convoy and I went into the anteroom, where two copper bathtubs stood and where two patients from those on trial were already waiting, also under convoy. A medical attendant came in, looked us over lazily and with authority, and went still more lazily to report to the doctor on duty. The latter soon appeared; he examined us, treated us very kindly, and issued each of us a "chart of ills" on which our name was inscribed. The further description of the illness, the medications prescribed, the dosages, and so on, were left to the intern who was in charge of the prisoners' wards. I had already heard earlier that the prisoners could not praise their doctors too highly. "They're better than fathers!" was their reply to my questions, as I was leaving for the hospital. Meanwhile we changed. The clothes and linen we had come in were taken from us, and we were dressed in hospital linen, along with which they issued us long stockings, slippers, caps, and thick flannel robes of a brown color, lined with canvas or something like sticking plaster. In short, the robe was filthy to the utmost degree; but I appreciated it fully only when I was installed. Then they took us to the prisoners' wards, which were located at the end of a very long corridor, high-ceilinged and clean. The external cleanliness everywhere was very satisfactory; everything that first struck the eye was simply gleaming. However, it might well have seemed so to me after our prison. The other two men went to the ward on the left, I to the one on the right. At the door, fastened with an iron bolt, stood a sentry with a gun, a relief sentry beside him. A junior sergeant (from the hospital guard) ordered them to let me in, and I found myself in a long and narrow room, with beds lined up against both long walls, some twenty-two in number, of which three or four were as yet unoccupied. The beds were wooden, painted green, all too familiar to each of us in Russia—those same beds which, by a sort of predestination, simply cannot be without bedbugs. I placed myself in a corner on the window side.

As I've already said, there were also some of our convicts from prison there. Some of them already knew me or at least had seen me before. They were far outnumbered by those on trial or from the correctional company. The gravely ill, that is, those who could not get out of bed, were not so many. The rest, slightly ill or convalescent, either sat on their cots or paced up and down the room between the two rows of beds, where there was space enough for strolling. There was an extremely suffocating hospital smell in the ward. The air was infected with various unpleasant exhalations and the smell of medications, even though a wood stove burned almost all day long in one corner. My cot had a striped cover on it. I took it off. Under the cover I found a flannel blanket lined with canvas and coarse sheets of a highly dubious cleanness. Next to the cot stood a little table with a mug and a tin bowl on it. All this, for decency's sake, was covered by a small towel that had been issued to me. Under the little table was a shelf: there tea drinkers could keep a teapot, jugs of kvass, and so on; but among the patients there were very few tea drinkers. The pipes and tobacco pouches that almost everybody had, not excluding even the consumptives, were hidden under the cots. The doctors and other authorities almost never looked there, and if they did catch somebody with a pipe, they pretended not to notice. However, the patients were almost always cautious and went to smoke by the stove. Only during the night did they smoke right in bed; but nobody made the rounds of the ward at night, except sometimes the officer in charge of the hospital guard.

Until then I had never been in any hospital; all the surroundings were therefore completely new to me. I noticed that I aroused a certain curiosity. They had already heard about me and looked me over quite unceremoniously, even with a shade of some superiority, the way a new pupil at school or a petitioner in an office is looked over. To the right of me lay a man on trial, a clerk, the illegitimate son of a retired captain. He was charged with counterfeiting money and had been in the hospital for a year already, apparently not sick at all, but assuring the doctors that he had an aneurysm. He achieved his goal: he avoided hard labor and corporal punishment and a year later was sent to Tobolsk, to be kept somewhere near a hospital. He was a sturdy, thickset fellow of about twenty-eight, a great crook and legalist, by no means stupid, extremely casual and self-assured, morbidly vain, who had quite seriously convinced himself that he was the most honest and truthful man in the world and even not guilty of anything at all, and remained forever convinced of it. He spoke to me first, started questioning me with curiosity, and told me in great detail about the external rules of the hospital. Before all, naturally, he informed me that he was a captain's son. His greatest wish was to seem like a nobleman or at least "from the gentry." After him a patient from the correctional company came up to me and began assuring me that he had known many earlier exiled noblemen, calling them by first name and patronymic. He was already a gray-haired soldier; it was written on his face that he was lying about it all. His name was Chekunov. He was obviously trying to suck up to me, probably suspecting I had money. Noticing my packet of tea and sugar, he immediately offered his services in finding a teapot and making tea for me. M—cki had promised to send me a teapot from the prison the next day, with one of the prisoners who went to work in the hospital. But Chekunov took care of it all. He found some sort of kettle, even a bowl, boiled the water, brewed the tea—in short, he served me with extraordinary zeal, which at once drew some venomous remarks at his expense from one of the patients. This patient, who lay across from me, was a consumptive by the name of Ustyantsev, a soldier on trial, the same one who, fearing punishment, drank a jug of vodka infused with a lot of snuff, which gave him consumption; I mentioned him earlier. Until then he had been lying there silently and breathing with difficulty, studying me intently and seriously, and following Chekunov with indignation. An extraordinary, bilious gravity gave an especially comic tinge to his indignation. Finally, he could not restrain himself:

"Look at the flunkey! He's found a master!" he said with pauses and in a voice gasping from weakness. He was living out his last days.

Chekunov turned to him with indignation:

"Who's a flunkey?" he said, glaring contemptuously at Ustyantsev.

"You're a flunkey!" the man replied in a self-assured tone, as if he had every right to scold Chekunov and had even been attached to him for that purpose.

"Me a flunkey?"

"Yes, you. Listen, good people, he doesn't believe it! He's surprised!"

"What's it to you! Look, he's alone, like he has no hands. They're not used to being without servants, we know that. Why shouldn't I serve him, you shaggy-mugged clown?"

"Who's shaggy-mugged?"

"You're shaggy-mugged."

"Me shaggy-mugged?"

"Yes, you!"

"And you're a beauty, eh? If I'm shaggy-mugged . . . you've got a face like a crow's egg!"

"You *are* shaggy-mugged! God's already killed you, so lie down and die! But no, he goes on picking! Well, what are you picking for?"

"What for! No, I'd rather bow to a boot than to a bast shoe. My father never bowed and told me not to! I . . . I . . ."

He wanted to continue, but was seized by a terrible coughing fit for several minutes, spitting blood. Soon the cold sweat of exhaustion stood out on his narrow forehead. The coughing hindered him, or he would have gone on talking; you could see by his eyes how he wanted to keep up the abuse; but in his weakness he could only wave his hand . . . So that in the end Chekunov forgot about him.

I sensed that the consumptive's anger was directed more at me than at Chekunov. Nobody would have been angry at Chekunov or looked at him with particular contempt for his wish to be of service and earn a kopeck by it. Everybody understood that he did it simply for money. On this account simple folk are not that touchy and have a keen perception of things. What Ustyantsev did not like was me myself, he did not like my tea, and that I, as a gentleman, even if in fetters, seemed unable to get along without a servant, though I never asked or wished for any servant. In fact, I always wanted to do everything myself, and I especially did not wish to give the impression that I was a softy, a sissy, who plays the lord. I even took some pride in that, while we're at it. But still—and I decidedly do not understand how this always happened—I could never say no to the various attendants and servants who latched on to me and finally took complete possession of me, so that in reality they were my masters and I their servant; but in appearance it somehow came out by itself that I was in fact a gentleman, who could not do without servants and playing the lord. That, of course, vexed me very much. But Ustyantsev was a consumptive, irritable man. The other patients maintained an air of indifference, even with a certain shade of haughtiness. I remember that everybody was preoccupied with one particular circumstance: from the prisoners' conversation I learned that a convict was to be brought that evening, who at the moment was being punished by running the gauntlet. The prisoners awaited the new man with some curiosity. They said, however, that the punishment was a light one— only five hundred strokes.

I gradually took in my surroundings. As far as I could tell, most of those who were really sick had scurvy or eye infections—the local diseases in those parts. There were several of them in the ward. Others of the really sick had fevers, various sores, chest ailments. Here it was not like in the other wards, here all diseases were heaped together, even the venereal. I said "*really* sick," because there were some who came *just like that*, without any illness, "for a rest." The doctors admitted them willingly, out of compassion, especially when there were many empty beds. Confinement in the guardhouses and prisons seemed so bad compared with the hospital that many prisoners gladly came to lie there, despite the stuffiness and the locked ward. There were even special lovers of lying in bed and of hospital life in general; they came mostly from the correctional company. I studied my new comrades with curiosity, but, I remember, one man from our prison, who was already dying, especially aroused my curiosity, also a consumptive and also in his last days, who was lying two beds away from Ustyantsev and was thus almost opposite me. His name was Mikhailov; I had seen him in the prison just two weeks before. He had been ill for a long time, and should have come long ago to be treated; but with some sort of stubborn and completely needless patience he had mastered himself, held out, and only during the holidays had gone to the hospital, to die in three weeks of terrible consumption, as if he just burned up. I was shocked now by his dreadfully altered face—a face that had been one of the first I noticed on entering the prison; it had somehow leaped into my eyes then. Next to him lay a soldier from the correctional company, already an old man, a dreadful and repulsive sloven . . . But I'm not going to go through all the patients . . . I remembered about this old cadger now only because he also made a certain impression on me then and in one minute managed to give me a rather full understanding of certain peculiarities of the convicts' ward. The old fellow, I remember, had a bad cold then. He sneezed all the time and went on sneezing for the whole next week, even in his sleep, somehow in volleys of five or six sneezes at a time, punctiliously saying each time, "Lord, what a punishment!" At the moment he was sitting on his bed and greedily filling his nose with snuff from a little paper packet, so as to sneeze more forcefully and punctiliously. He sneezed into a cotton handkerchief, his own, checkered, washed a hundred times and extremely faded, in the process wrinkling his little nose peculiarly, forming countless fine wrinkles, and exhibiting the stumps of old, blackened teeth along with red, slobbery gums. Having finished sneezing, he opened the handkerchief, attentively examined the abundant phlegm accumulated in it, and immediately smeared it on his brown hospital robe, so that all the phlegm remained on the robe, while the handkerchief was only left a little damp. He did that for the whole week. This meticulous, niggardly preservation of his own handkerchief to the detriment of the hospital robe did not stir up any protest on the patients' part, though one or the other of them might have to wear the same robe after him. But our simple folk are strangely unsqueamish and unfastidious. As for me, I cringed at that moment, and with disgust and curiosity at once began involuntarily to inspect the robe I had just put on. Here I noticed that it had long been attracting my attention by its strong smell; it had already had time to warm up on me and smelled more and more strongly of medicines, plasters, and, it seemed to me, some sort of pus, which was no wonder, since from time immemorial it had never left patients' shoulders. It may be that the canvas lining on the back had been washed occasionally, I don't know for certain. But at the present time that lining was steeped in all sorts of unpleasant juices, lotions, fluid drained from pierced Spanish flies, and so on. What's more, men who had just run the gauntlet very often arrived in the prisoners' wards with lacerated backs; they were treated with lotions, and then the robe, put on right over the wet shirt, could not possibly help being tainted: everything stayed on it. And all the time I was in prison, all through those several years, whenever I happened to be in the hospital (which was pretty often), I put a robe on each time with timorous mistrust. I especially disliked the big and remarkably fat lice I sometimes met with in these robes. The prisoners delighted in executing them, so that when an executed beast popped under a prisoner's thick, clumsy nail, you could even judge the extent of the satisfaction it gave him by the look on the hunter's face. We also had a strong dislike of bedbugs, and it happened that the whole ward sometimes rose up to exterminate them on a long, dull winter night. And though, apart from the heavy stench, everything in the ward was externally as clean as possible, the inner, the lining cleanliness, so to speak, was nothing to boast of. The patients were used to it and even considered that it had to be that way, and the rules themselves were not conducive to any special cleanliness. But I'll speak of the rules later . . .

As soon as Chekunov served me tea (made, be it said in passing, from the ward's water, which was fetched once a day and somehow all too soon went bad in our atmosphere), the door opened with some noise and the soldier who had just run the gauntlet was brought in under reinforced convoy. It was the first time I had seen a flogged man. Later they were brought in often, some were even carried (after a very severe flogging), and each time it afforded the patients great diversion. Such men were usually met among us with an exceedingly stern expression of the face and even with a certain slightly forced seriousness. However, the reception depended in part on the degree of importance of the crime and, consequently, on the number of strokes. A very badly beaten and, reputedly, greater criminal enjoyed greater respect and greater attention than some little runaway recruit, for instance, like the one just brought in now. But in the one case as in the other, neither special compassion nor any especially irritable remarks were offered. They silently helped the unfortunate man and took care of him, especially if he could not do without help. The medical attendants knew they were entrusting the beaten man to experienced and skillful hands. The help usually consisted of frequent and necessary changes of sheets or shirts moistened with cold water, with which they covered the torn back, especially if the punished man was unable to look after himself, and also in deftly pulling out the splinters that often remained in the wounds from rods broken over the back. This last operation was usually very unpleasant for the patient. But generally I was always amazed by the extraordinary staunchness with which the punished men endured pain. I've seen many of them, sometimes very badly beaten, and almost none of them moaned! Only it was as if their faces changed completely, turned pale; their eyes burned; their gaze wandered, became troubled;

their lips trembled, so that the poor men would bite them on purpose, sometimes until they bled. The soldier who came in was a lad of about twenty-three, strong, muscular, with a handsome face, tall, well-built, swarthy. His back, however, had suffered a proper beating. His body was bared to the waist; a wet sheet was thrown over his shoulders, which made him tremble all over as if in a fever, and for about an hour and a half he paced up and down the ward. I studied his face: it seemed he was not thinking of anything at that moment; he had a strange and wild look; his gaze wandered; he obviously had difficulty fixing it attentively on anything. It seemed to me that he looked intently at my tea. The tea was hot; steam rose from the cup, and the poor man was chilled and trembling, his teeth were chattering. I invited him to drink some. He turned to me silently and sharply, took the cup, drank it standing and without sugar, very hurriedly and somehow trying especially not to look at me. Having drunk it all, he silently set the cup down and, without even nodding to me, started pacing up and down the ward again. He couldn't be bothered with words and nods! As for the prisoners, at first for some reason they all avoided any conversation with the punished recruit; on the contrary, having begun by helping him, it was as if they then tried not to pay any more attention to him, perhaps wishing to leave him in peace as far as possible and not bother him with any further questions and "sympathizings," with which he seemed to be perfectly content.

Meanwhile it grew dark, the night lamp was lit. It turned out that some of the prisoners even had their own candlesticks, though not very many. Finally, after the doctor's evening visit, the sergeant of the guard came in, counted all the patients, and locked the ward, having brought in a night tub beforehand . . . I was surprised to learn that this tub would remain there all night, though there was a real lavatory just outside in the corridor, only two steps from our door. But such was the established order. During the day a prisoner could be let out of the ward, though for no more than one minute; but at night it was out of the question. The convicts' wards were not like the ordinary ones, and a sick prisoner bore his punishment even in sickness. Who originally established this order I don't know; all I know is that there was no real order in it and that the whole useless essence of formalism was nowhere expressed more fully than, for instance, in this case. This order, naturally, did not come from the doctors. I repeat: the prisoners could not praise their doctors highly enough, looked upon them as fathers, respected them. Everyone saw kindness from them, heard gentle words; and a prisoner, having been rejected by the whole world, valued that, because he could see how unfeigned and sincere those gentle words and that kindness were. They might not have been; no one would have asked questions if the doctors had treated them differently, that is, more rudely and inhumanly: consequently, they were kind out of genuine humanity. And, naturally, they understood that a sick man, whether or not he was a prisoner, needs such a thing, for instance, as fresh air, like any other sick man, even of the highest rank. The patients in other wards, the convalescents, for instance, could freely walk through the corridors, getting good exercise, breathing air which was not as poisoned as the air in the wards, stifling and always inevitably filled with suffocating exhalations. It is horrible and disgusting now to imagine to what extent the air, which was already poisoned to begin with, must have become poisoned at night, when they brought in that tub, considering the warm temperature of the ward and certain illnesses, with which it is impossible to avoid going. If I said just now that the prisoner bore his punishment even in sickness, I naturally did not and do not suppose that it was set up that way only for the sake of punishment. Naturally, that would be senseless slander on my part. There is no point in punishing sick men. And if so, then it goes without saying that some strict, harsh necessity probably forced the authorities to take measures so harmful in their consequences. What sort? But here is the vexing thing, that nothing else can begin to explain the necessity of this measure, and many other measures besides, so incomprehensible that it is impossible not only to explain them, but even to imagine an explanation. How explain such pointless cruelty? Can you picture a prisoner who comes to the hospital, purposely pretending to be sick, deceives the doctors, goes out to the latrine at night, and escapes under cover of darkness? To seriously demonstrate all the absurdity of such reasoning is almost impossible. Escape where? Escape how? Wearing what? During the day they let men out one by one; they could do the same at night. At the door stands a sentry with a loaded gun. The lavatory is literally two steps from the sentry, but despite that the patient is accompanied by a second sentry, who never takes his eyes off him all the while. There is only one window in the place, with double frames, as in winter, and with iron bars. In the yard outside the window, right by the windows of the prisoners' ward, another sentry paces all night. To get through the window, you would have to break the frames and the bars. Who would allow that? Suppose he kills the second sentry beforehand, so that he doesn't make a peep and nobody hears anything. But, even allowing for that absurdity, the window and bars still have to be broken. Notice that here, right next to the sentry, sleep the guards of the ward, and ten paces away, by the other prisoners' ward, stands another sentry with a gun, beside him a second sentry and other guards. And where will he escape to in the winter, wearing stockings, slippers, a hospital robe, and a nightcap? And if so, if there is so little danger (that is, really none at all), why put such a heavy burden on the sick, maybe in the last days and hours of their life, sick men for whom fresh air is more necessary than for healthy people? What for? I never could understand it . . .

And, while we're at it, once we've asked "What for?" I can't help remembering now another perplexity that stuck up in front of me for many years in the guise of a most mysterious fact, which I also failed to explain in any way. I can't help saying a few words about it, before I go on with my description. I'm speaking of the fetters, from which no illness saved a man condemned to hard labor. Even consumptives died before my eyes in fetters. And yet everybody was used to it, everybody considered it something accomplished, irrefutable. I doubt that anybody even stopped to think about it, since it never even once entered the head of any of our doctors all through those several years to petition the authorities to unfetter the gravely ill prisoners, especially the consumptives. Granted, the fetters themselves are not God knows how heavy. They weigh between eight and twelve pounds. For a healthy man, it's not burdensome to carry ten pounds. I was told, however, that after several years fetters begin to make your legs wither. I don't know if it's true, though, by the way, there is some probability of it. A weight, even a small one, even just ten pounds, attached permanently to your leg, does make the limb abnormally heavy, and in the long run may have a detrimental effect . . . But granted it's all right for a healthy man.

Is it the same for a sick one? Granted, it's all right for an ordinary sick man. But, I repeat, is it the same for the gravely ill, is it the same, I repeat, for the consumptives, whose arms and legs are withering away even without that, so that every straw feels heavy? And, truly, if the medical authorities had obtained that relief just for the consumptives alone, that in itself would have been a real and great benefit. Granted, they say a prisoner is an evildoer and unworthy of any benefits; but need one aggravate the punishment for someone who has already been touched by the finger of God? And it is impossible to believe it is done for the sake of punishment alone. Even the court spares consumptives from bodily punishment. Consequently, here again there is some secret, important measure, taken as a salutary precaution. But what sort?—it's impossible to grasp. It's impossible in fact to fear that a consumptive will escape. Who could conceive of that, especially bearing in mind a certain degree in the development of the illness? To pretend to have consumption, to deceive the doctors in order to escape, is impossible. It's not that sort of illness; you can see it at a glance. And by the way: can it be that they put a man in leg fetters only so that he won't escape or so as to hinder him from escaping? Not at all. Fetters are simply a dishonor, a shame and a burden, physical and moral. At least they're supposed to be. They can never hinder anybody from escaping. With no great effort, the most unskillful, the most clumsy of prisoners is able to saw them off or knock the rivet out with a stone very quickly. Leg fetters are decidedly no precaution against anything; and if so, if they are prescribed for a condemned convict only as a punishment, then again I ask: why punish a dying man?

And now, as I write this, I vividly recall one dying man, a consumptive, that same Mikhailov, who lay almost opposite me, not far from Ustyantsev, and who died, I remember, four days after my arrival in the ward. Maybe I began talking about consumptives now inadvertently repeating the impressions and thoughts that occurred to me then on the occasion of his death. Mikhailov himself, however, I knew very little. He was still a very young man, of about twenty-five, not more, tall, slender, and of extremely pleasing appearance. He lived in the special section and was strangely taciturn, always somehow quietly, somehow peacefully sad. As if he was "withering away" in prison. So at least the prisoners, among whom he left good memories of himself, put it afterwards. I remember only that he had beautiful eyes, and I truly don't know why I remember him so distinctly. He died at around three o'clock in the afternoon, on a clear and frosty day. I remember the sun's strong, slanting rays piercing the green, slightly frosted windows of our ward. A whole stream of them poured onto the unfortunate man. He died unconscious and agonized painfully for a long time, several hours on end. Since morning his eyes had stopped recognizing those who approached him. They wanted to make it somehow easier, seeing that it was very painful for him; he breathed with difficulty, deeply, hoarsely; his chest rose high, as if he could not get enough air. He threw off his blanket, all his clothes, and finally began tearing at his shirt; even that seemed too heavy to him. They helped him to take off his shirt. It was frightening to look at that long, long body with its legs and arms withered to the bone, with its sunken stomach, protruding chest, sharply outlined ribs like a skeleton's. All that was left on him was a wooden cross with an amulet and the fetters, through which it seemed he could now have drawn his withered leg. Half an hour before his death, we all became as if hushed, began talking almost in whispers. Those who walked, stepped inaudibly. We talked little, about unrelated things, and only glanced every once in a while at the dying man, who was wheezing more and more. Finally, his wandering and shaky hand found the amulet on his chest and began tearing it off, as if it, too, was a burden to him, bothered him, weighed him down. We took the amulet off as well. About ten minutes later he died. We knocked on the door to let the guard know. A watchman came in, looked dully at the dead man, and went for the medical attendant. The medical attendant, a kindly young fellow, somewhat excessively preoccupied with his appearance, which, by the way, was rather pleasing, came soon; with rapid steps, which rang out loudly in the hushed ward, he went up to the dead man, and with a particularly casual air, as if purposely devised for the occasion, took his pulse, waved his hand, and went out. The guard was informed at once: the criminal was an important one, from the special section; even his death had to be acknowledged with special ceremony. While waiting for the guard, one of the prisoners, in a quiet voice, expressed the thought that it would not be a bad thing to close the dead man's eyes.

Another listened to him attentively, silently went to the dead man, and closed his eyes. Seeing the cross lying there on the pillow, he picked it up, looked at it, and silently put it back on Mikhailov's neck; put it back and crossed himself. Meanwhile the dead face was stiffening; a ray of light played over it; the mouth was half open, two rows of white young teeth gleamed from under the thin lips stuck to the gums. Finally the sergeant of the watch came, wearing a saber and a helmet, followed by two guards. He approached, stepping more and more slowly, looking in perplexity at the hushed prisoners gazing at him sternly from all sides. A step away from the dead man, he stopped in his tracks, as if frightened. The completely naked, withered corpse, with nothing on it but fetters, shocked him, and he suddenly undid the chin strap, took off his helmet, which was by no means called for, and made a large sign of the cross. He had a stern, gray, old soldier's face. I remember at that same moment Chekunov was standing there, also a gray-haired old man. All this time he had been looking silently and fixedly at the sergeant's face and studying his every gesture with some strange attention. But their eyes met, and for some reason Chekunov's lower lip suddenly trembled. He twisted it somehow strangely, bared his teeth, and nodding quickly, as if accidentally, towards the dead man, said to the sergeant:

"He had a mother, too!"—and walked away.

I remember it was as if those words pierced me . . . And what made him speak them and how did they enter his head? But here they started lifting the body, lifted it together with the cot; the straw crunched, the fetters, amidst the general silence, clanked loudly against the floor . . . They were picked up. The body was carried out. Suddenly everybody started talking loudly. The sergeant, already in the corridor, was heard sending someone for the blacksmith. The dead man had to be unfettered . . .

But I've strayed from my subject . . .

II

Continuation

The doctors made the round of the wards in the morning; between ten and eleven they all appeared together in our ward, accompanying the head doctor, and an hour and a half before them we were visited by our intern. At that time our intern was a knowledgeable young doctor, gentle, affable, whom the prisoners liked very much, and in whom they found only one shortcoming: "much too meek." He was indeed somehow untalkative, even as if embarrassed with us, all but blushing, changing doses at the patient's first request, and he even seemed ready to prescribe medicines for them at their own request. However, he was a nice young man. It must be admitted that in Russia many doctors enjoyed the love and respect of simple folk, and that, as far as I have observed, is perfectly true. I know that my words will seem paradoxical, especially considering the universal mistrust all simple Russian folk have for medicine and for foreign drugs. Indeed, a simple man suffering for several years from a very grave illness will sooner be treated by a wise woman or his own homemade folk remedies (which are by no means to be scorned) than go to a doctor or lie in a hospital. But, besides that, there is one extremely important circumstance here that has no relation to medicine: namely, the universal mistrust among all simple folk of everything that bears the stamp of the administrative, the official; besides that, people are frightened and prejudiced against hospitals by various fears, by tall tales, often absurd, but occasionally based on some reality. But above all they are frightened by the German rules in hospitals,[1] by having strangers around during the whole course of an illness, the strictness concerning food, stories of the persistent severity of medical attendants and doctors, of the dissecting and disemboweling of corpses, and so on. Then, too, simple folk reason, the treatment will be done by gentlefolk, because doctors are gentlefolk all the same. But on closer acquaintance with doctors (not without exceptions, but for the most part), all these fears disappear very quickly, which, in my opinion, redounds directly to the credit of our doctors, predominantly the young ones. The greater part of them are able to earn the respect and even the love of simple folk. I am writing at least of what I myself saw and experienced more than once and in many places, and I have no grounds for thinking it should differ all that often in other places. Of course, in some little corners doctors do take bribes, profit greatly from their hospitals, all but ignore their patients, even forget about medicine altogether. That is still so; but I'm talking about the majority or, rather, about the spirit, the tendency, that is being realized in medicine now, in our day. Those others, apostates from the cause, wolves in a flock of sheep, whatever justification they offer, however they try to justify themselves, say, for example, by the *environment*, to which they, too, are prey in their turn, they will always be wrong, especially if, along with that, they have also lost their humanity. Humanity, kindness, brotherly compassion for a sick man are sometimes more necessary to him than any medicine. It is time we stopped complaining apathetically that we are prey to the environment. Granted, it does prey on us in many ways, but not in all ways, and often some clever swindler who knows his business skillfully conceals and justifies not only his weakness, but often simply his baseness, by the influence of the environment, especially if he has a gift for fine talk or writing. However, I've wandered from my theme again; I only wanted to say that simple folk are mistrustful, and more hostile to medical administration than to doctors. Learning how they are in reality, they quickly lose many of their prejudices. To this day other circumstances in our clinics are in many ways not in keeping with the spirit of simple folk, to this day they are hostile in their rules to the habits of our people and are unable to gain their full trust and respect. So at least it seems to me from some of my own impressions.

Our intern usually stopped before each patient, examined him and talked with him seriously and extremely attentively, prescribed medicines, doses. Sometimes he himself noticed that the sick man was not sick at all; but since the prisoner had come to rest from work or to lie on a mattress instead of bare boards, and, finally, at least in a warm room, not in the damp guardhouse, where dense crowds of the accused, pale and haggard, were kept in a cramped space (the accused, all over Russia, are almost always pale and haggard—a sign that their conditions and their inner state are almost always worse than with the condemned), our intern calmly wrote them down as having some sort of *febris catarrhalis** and let them stay there sometimes even for a week. We all laughed at this *febris catarrhalis*. We knew very well that it was adopted among us, by a sort of mutual agreement between doctor and patient, as a formula for designating a feigned illness—"spare cramps," as the prisoners themselves translated it. Sometimes a sick man abused the doctor's softheartedness and prolonged his stay until he was driven out by force. You should have seen our intern then: he seemed to grow timid, as if he were ashamed to tell the patient directly to get well and ask to be discharged, though he had full right to discharge him without any discussion or cajoling, quite simply by writing on his chart: *Sanat est.†* At first he would hint to him, then he would all but plead: "Isn't it time? You're nearly well, the ward is crowded," and so on and so forth, until the sick man became ashamed of himself and finally asked to be discharged. The head doctor, though a humane and honest man (the patients also liked him very much), was incomparably more stern and resolute than the intern, even on occasion displayed a stern severity, and for that he was somehow particularly respected among us. He would appear after the intern, in the company of all the hospital doctors; he also examined each man individually, lingered particularly over the gravely ill, was always able to give them a kind, encouraging, often even heartfelt word, and generally made a good impression. He never rejected or sent away those who came with "spare cramps"; but if the patient persisted, he quite simply discharged him: "Well, brother, you've stayed here a good while, rested up, off you go now, enough's enough." Those who persisted were usually lazy men, unwilling to work, especially during the work-filled summertime, or accused men awaiting punishment. I remember they had to use particular severity, even cruelty, on one of these persistent ones to persuade him to get discharged. He had come with an eye infection; his eyes were red, he complained of a sharp, stinging pain in them. They started treating him with Spanish flies, leeches, sprayed his eyes with some caustic liquid, and so on, but the infection still did not go away, his eyes would not clear. The doctors gradually realized that the infection was feigned:

---

* Literally "catarrhal fever" (Latin). *Author.*
† "Healthy" (Latin). *Author.*

there was a persistent slight inflammation, which did not get worse, but would not be cured, it remained the same, the case looked suspicious. The prisoners had all long known that he was pretending and deceiving people, though he never admitted it himself. He was a young fellow, even a handsome one, but he made an unpleasant impression on us all: secretive, suspicious, frowning, never talked to anyone, glanced about furtively, shied away from everyone, as if he suspected everyone. I remember it even occurred to some of us that he might get up to something. He had been a soldier, had been caught stealing a large sum, and was to be given a thousand strokes and sent to a prisoners' company. To put off the moment of punishment, as I've mentioned before, condemned men sometimes resorted to horrible escapades: they would stick a knife into one of their superiors or their own fellow prisoners on the eve of the punishment, there would be a new trial, the punishment would be put off for a month or two, and their goal would be achieved. Never mind that in two months they will be punished two or three times more severely; if only the terrible moment has now been put off for at least a few days, then come what may—so dispirited the unfortunate men sometimes are. It was already being whispered among us that we should be wary of him; he might just stab somebody during the night. However, that was only talk; nobody took any special precautions, not even those whose cots were next to his. They saw, however, that at night he rubbed his eyes with lime from the plaster and with something else, so that in the morning they were red again. Finally, the head doctor threatened him with a seton. When a stubborn eye infection lasts for a long time, and all medical resources have already been tried, doctors resort to a strong and painful treatment to save vision: they give the patient a seton, as with horses. But even then the poor fellow would not agree to recover. His character was either stubborn or all too cowardly: a seton is not as painful as the gauntlet, but still it is very painful. You gather up the skin on the back of the patient's neck, as much as you can hold, pierce the gathered flesh through with a knife, producing a wide and long wound across the entire nape, and pass a linen tape through this wound, a rather wide one, almost a finger's breadth; then each day, at an appointed time, you draw this tape through the wound, as if cutting it once again, so that it goes on festering and doesn't heal. The poor man stubbornly endured this torture for several days, though with terrible suffering, and only then finally agreed to be discharged. His eyes became perfectly well overnight, and, as soon as his neck healed, he went to the guardhouse, so as to go the next day and get his thousand strokes.

Of course, the moment before punishment is hard, so hard that I may sin in calling this fear fainthearted and cowardly. It must be hard, if a man will accept a double or triple punishment, only not carried out at once. However, I have also mentioned those who asked to be discharged sooner, their backs still not healed from the first rods, so as to run through the remaining strokes and be finally done with their sentence; being kept under sentence in the guardhouse is, of course, incomparably worse than prison. But, besides the difference of temperaments, a great role in the resoluteness and fearlessness of some men is played by an ingrained habit of receiving blows and punishments. Manifold beatings somehow strengthen a man's spirit and back, and he comes to look upon punishment skeptically, almost as a minor inconvenience, and no longer fears it. Generally speaking, that is true. One of our prisoners from the special section, a baptized Kalmyk,[2] Alexander, or Alexandra, as he was called among us, a strange fellow, wily, fearless, and at the same time very good-natured, told me about how he went through his four thousand, laughed and joked as he told it, but at once swore seriously that if, from childhood, from the most tender childhood, he had not grown up under the lash, the scars from which literally never left his back during all his life in the horde, he would not have survived those four thousand. He told it as if he blessed this upbringing under the lash. "I was beaten for everything, Alexander Petrovich," he told me once, sitting on my cot in the evening before the lights were brought in, "for everything and anything, whatever it might be, beaten for fifteen years on end, from the first day I can remember, several times a day; anybody who liked beat me; so in the end I got pretty used to it." How he ended up a soldier, I don't know; I don't remember, though he may have told me; he was an eternal runaway and tramp. I only remember his story of how terribly frightened he was when they sentenced him to four thousand rods for murdering an officer. "I knew I'd be badly punished and that I might not survive the gauntlet, and

though I was used to the lash, four thousand was no joke! And with all
the officers angry besides! I knew, I knew for sure, that I wouldn't get
off lightly, that I wouldn't make it; they wouldn't let me go through. At
first I tried getting baptized, I thought maybe they'd pardon me, and
though my people told me then that nothing would come of it, that
they wouldn't pardon me, I thought: All the same I'll try it, all the same
they may take pity on a Christian. So I got myself baptized and at the
holy baptism I was named Alexander, but the strokes stayed the same;
they didn't take a single one away; I even got offended. So I thought
to myself: just wait, I'll dupe you all well and good. And guess what,
Alexander Petrovich—I duped them! I was terribly good at pretending
to be dead, that is, not really dead, but as if my soul was about to leave
my body. They led me out; they took me through a thousand: it burns, I
shout; they led me through another; well, I think, this is the end of me,
the wits have all been knocked out of me, my legs are giving way; I col-
lapse on the ground: my eyes go dead, my face is blue, no breath, foam
at the mouth. The doctor came over: he's dying, he says. They carried
me to the hospital, and I revived at once. So then they led me out two
more times, and they were angry, very angry at me, but I duped them
two more times: I'd only just gone through the third thousand, played
dead, but when I started through the fourth, each blow pierced me like a
knife through the heart, each blow felt like three, they beat so painfully!
They were ferocious with me. That measly last thousand (blast it! . . .)
was worth the first three, and if I hadn't died before the end (there were
only two hundred left), they'd have beaten me to death right there, but
I stuck up for myself: I duped them and played dead again, and again
they believed it, and how could they not believe it, even the doctor
believed it, so for those last two hundred they put all their rage into it,
they beat me so that another time two thousand would be easier, but
no, tough luck, they didn't finish me off, and why didn't they? Again,
because I grew up under the lash since childhood. That's why I'm alive
today. Oh, I've been beaten, beaten in my lifetime!" he added at the
end of his story, as if in sorrowful reflection, as if trying to remember
and count up how many times he had been beaten. "Ah, no," he added,
interrupting the momentary silence, "there's no counting all my beatings; and how could they be counted! There aren't enough numbers."
He glanced at me and laughed, but so good-naturedly that I couldn't

help smiling back. "You know, Alexander Petrovich, even now when I dream at night, it's always of being beaten: I don't have any other dreams." In fact, he often shouted at night, shouted at the top of his lungs, so that the prisoners shook him awake at once: "What are you shouting for, you devil!" He was a strapping fellow, short, fidgety and cheerful, about forty-five years old, got along well with everybody, and though he was very fond of stealing and was very often beaten for it, who among us did not get caught stealing and get beaten for it?

I will add one thing to that: I was always astonished at the extraordinary good-naturedness, the complacency, with which all these beaten men told about how they were beaten and about those who beat them. Often not even the slightest shade of spite or hatred could be heard in such stories, which sometimes shook my heart and made it beat hard and fast. They would tell about it and laugh like children. M—cki, on the other hand, told me about his punishment; he was not a nobleman and got five hundred. I learned of it from others and asked him myself if it was true and how it went. He replied somehow curtly, as if with some inner pain, trying not to look at me, and his face turned red; half a minute later he looked at me, and the fire of hatred flashed in his eyes, his lips trembled with indignation. I felt that he could never forget this page from his past. But the others, almost all of them (I cannot guarantee there were no exceptions), looked at it quite differently. It cannot be, I sometimes thought, that they consider themselves wholly guilty and deserving of punishment, especially if their offense was not against their own, but against the authorities. The majority of them did not blame themselves at all. I've already said that I did not notice any pangs of conscience, even in those cases when the crime was against their own kind. To say nothing of crimes against the authorities. It sometimes seemed to me that in this latter case they had their own special, so to speak, practical or, better, factual view of the matter. It took account of fate, the irrefutability of the fact, and it was not so much thought out as unconscious, like a sort of faith. For instance, though a prisoner is always inclined to feel himself justified in his crimes against the authorities, so that the very question of it is unthinkable for him, all the same in practical terms he was aware that the authorities viewed his crimes quite differently, which meant that he had to take his punishment and be quits. Here the struggle was mutual. At the same time the criminal knows and has no doubt that he is vindicated by the court of his own milieu, his own simple folk, who will never (this, too, he knows) condemn him definitively, and for the most part will vindicate him outright, as long as his offense is not against his own, his brothers, his fellow simple folk. His conscience is at peace, which makes him strong and morally untroubled, and that is the main thing. It's as if he feels that he has something to support him, and therefore he does not hate, but takes what has happened to him as an inescapable fact, which did not begin with him, will not end with him, and will continue for a long, long time amidst the ongoing, passive, but persistent struggle. What soldier personally hates a Turk when he makes war on him? And yet the Turk cuts him down, stabs him, shoots at him. However, not all the stories were so cool-headed and indifferent. The story of Lieutenant Zherebyatnikov, for instance, was told with a certain shade of indignation, though not all that great. I became acquainted with this Lieutenant Zherebyatnikov during my first stay in the hospital—from the prisoners' stories, naturally. Then one day I saw him in the flesh, when he stood guard over us. He was a man of about thirty, tall, fat, flabby, with ruddy, fat-bloated cheeks, white teeth, and a booming Nozdryovian laugh.[3] You could see by his face that this was the most unreflective man in the world. He passionately loved whipping and punishing with rods, when he happened to be appointed the executor. I hasten to add that already then I regarded Lieutenant Zherebyatnikov as a monster among his kind, and so did my fellow prisoners. There were others besides him, in the old days, of course, in those recent old days of which "the memory is fresh, but hard to believe,"[4] who loved performing their task zealously and diligently. But for the most part it was done naïvely and with no special enthusiasm. Whereas the lieutenant was something like a refined gourmet in performing the task. He loved, he passionately loved performing his art, and loved it solely for the art's sake. He took pleasure in it, and, like a jaded Roman patrician, glutted with pleasures, he invented for himself various subtleties, various perversions, in order to arouse and pleasantly tickle his fat-bloated soul at least somewhat. Here they lead out a prisoner for punishment; Zherebyatnikov is the executor; one glance at the long row of people lined up with thick sticks already inspires him. He walks self-contentedly down the rows and insistently repeats that everyone should perform his task zealously, conscientiously, or else . . . The soldiers know the meaning of this "or else" . . . But now they bring the criminal himself, and if he is not yet acquainted with Zherebyatnikov, if he has not yet heard all there is to know about him, then here, for example, is the trick he will play on him. (Naturally, this is one of a hundred little tricks; the lieutenant's inventiveness was inexhaustible.) Every prisoner, at the moment when he is stripped and his arms are tied to the gun stocks, by which the sergeants will then pull him down the whole green street—every prisoner, following the general custom, begins at that moment to beg the executor in a tearful, plaintive voice to soften the punishment and not aggravate it by unnecessary severity: "Your Honor," the unfortunate man cries, "have mercy, be a father to me, I'll pray to God for you all my life, don't destroy me, be merciful!" That is just what Zherebyatnikov would be waiting for; he stops the procedure at once and, also with a sensitive look, starts talking with the prisoner:

"My friend," he says, "what am I to do with you? It's not me, it's the law that's punishing you!"

"Your Honor, everything's in your hands! Be merciful!"

"Do you think I don't feel sorry for you? Do you think it's a pleasure for me to watch you get beaten? I'm also a human being! Am I a human being or not, in your opinion?"

"For sure, Your Honor, it's a known thing; you're fathers, we're children. Be a father to me!" cries the prisoner, beginning to hope.

"But, my friend, judge for yourself; you've got a mind to judge with: I myself know that out of humanity I should look upon you, a sinner, indulgently and mercifully . . ."

"It's the veritable truth you're so kindly speaking, Your Honor!"

"Yes, to look mercifully, no matter what a sinner you are. But here it's not me, it's the law! Think! I serve God and the fatherland; I'll be taking a heavy sin on myself if I relax the law, think about that!"

"Your Honor!"

"Well, all right! So be it, just for you! I know I'm sinning, but so be it . . . I'll take pity on you this time, I'll lighten the punishment. Well, but what if I'm actually doing you harm by it? I show you mercy now, I lighten the punishment, and you count on it being the same the next time and commit another crime—what then? It'll be on my conscience . . ."

"Your Honor! I'll swear by anything you like! As if before the throne of the Lord in heaven . . ."

"Well, enough, enough now! But you swear to me that you'll behave yourself in the future?"

"Lord strike me dead, and torment me in the next world, if I . . ."

"Don't swear, it's a sin. I'll take your word for it. Do you give me your word?"

"Your Honor!!!"

"Well, listen then, I'll have mercy on you only for the sake of your orphan's tears. Are you an orphan?"

"An orphan, Your Honor, alone as could be, no father, no mother . . ."

"Well, then, for the sake of your orphan's tears; but watch out, it's the last time . . . Take him," he adds in such a tender-hearted voice that the prisoner no longer knows what kind of prayers he can pray to God for such mercifulness. But now the dread procession starts, he is led along; the drum thunders, the first rods are raised . . . "Lay into him!" Zherebyatnikov shouts at the top of his lungs. "Burn him! Thrash, thrash! Scorch him! More, more! Lay into the orphan, lay into the rogue! Roast him, roast him!" And the soldiers thrash with all their might, sparks fly out of the poor man's eyes, he begins to shout, and Zherebyatnikov runs down the line after him, laughs, laughs his head off, holds his sides splitting with laughter, he can't straighten up, so that in the end you even pity the dear heart. And he's delighted, he's amused, and only rarely does his loud, healthy, resounding laughter break off, and again you hear, "Thrash him, thrash him! Scorch the rogue, scorch the orphan! . . ."

And here are some other variations he came up with: a prisoner is led out for punishment; again he begins to plead. This time Zherebyatnikov doesn't play-act, doesn't mug, but goes in for frankness:

"You see, my dear fellow," he says, "I'm going to punish you properly, because you deserve it. But here's what I'll do for you, if you like: I won't tie you to the gun stocks. You'll go it alone, only in a new way: run through the whole line as fast as you can! Then even if every rod hits you, the thing will be shorter, don't you think? Want to give it a try?"

The prisoner listens with perplexity, with mistrust, and reflects.

"Why not?" he thinks. "Maybe it really will be easier; I'll run as hard as I can, and the torture will be five times shorter, and maybe not every rod will hit me."

"Very well, Your Honor, I agree."

"And I agree, too, so go to it! Watch out, don't gawk!" he shouts to the soldiers, knowing beforehand, however, that not a single rod will miss the guilty back; the soldier who misses also knows very well what he risks. The prisoner sets off running as fast as he can down the "green street," but, naturally, doesn't make it past the fifteenth row; the rods, like drumsticks, like lightning, all at once, suddenly crash down on his back, and the poor man, screaming, falls as if he's been cut down, as if he's been hit by a bullet. "No, Your Honor, better stick to the law," he says, slowly getting up from the ground, pale and frightened, and Zherebyatnikov, who knew the whole trick beforehand and what would come of it, roars with laughter. But it's impossible to describe all his amusements and all that the prisoners told about him!

In a somewhat different way, in a different tone and spirit, they told about a certain Lieutenant Smekalov, who fulfilled the duties of commandant in our fortress before our major was appointed to the post. Though they told about Zherebyatnikov rather indifferently, with no special anger, all the same they did not admire his feats, did not praise him, but obviously scorned him. They even somehow haughtily despised him. But Lieutenant Smekalov was remembered among us with joy and delight. The thing was that he was not at all some sort of special enthusiast of whipping; the pure Zherebyatnikovian element was totally lacking in him. But at the same time he had nothing against whipping; the whole point was that his flogging itself was remembered among us with a sort of sweet love—so well the man knew how to please the prisoners. How, though? How did he earn such popularity? True, our people, perhaps like all the Russian people, are ready to forget the whole torture for one kind word; I'm speaking of this as of a fact, without analyzing it this time from one side or the other. It was not difficult to please these people and acquire popularity among them. But Lieutenant Smekalov had acquired a *special* popularity—so that even the way he whipped was remembered with all but tenderness. "He was more than a father," the prisoners used to say, and they would even sigh, comparing their memories of their former temporary superior,

Smekalov, with the present major. "He's all heart!" He was a simple man, maybe even kind in his own way. But it can happen that there is not only a kind, but even a magnanimous man among the authorities; and what then?—nobody likes him, and sometimes they simply laugh at him. The thing is that Smekalov was somehow able to do it so that everybody among us took him as *their* man, and that is a great skill, or, more precisely, an inborn ability, which even those who possess it do not stop to think about. Strangely enough, there are even some among them who are not kind people at all, and yet they sometimes acquire great popularity. They are not squeamish, they are not disgusted by the people under them—there, it seems to me, is where the reason lies! You see nothing of the clean-handed little squire in them, you catch no whiff of the fine lord, but they have a sort of special, inborn, common-folk smell, and, my God, how sensitive the people are to that smell! What won't they give for it! They are even ready to exchange the most merciful man for the most severe, so long as he gives off their own homespun smell. And what if the man with their smell is also really kindhearted, though in his own way? Then he's priceless! Lieutenant Smekalov, as I've already said, sometimes punished painfully, but he was somehow able to do it so that not only was no one angry, but, on the contrary, even now, in my time, when it was all long past, they remembered his *little tricks* during the whipping with laughter and delight. However, he had few tricks, for lack of artistic fantasy. In truth, there was just one trick, one only, with which he got by with us for almost a whole year; but maybe it was so dear to them precisely because it was the only one. There was much naïveté in that. For instance, they bring in a guilty prisoner. Smekalov himself comes to the punishment, comes with a smile, with a joke, straightaway asks the guilty man about something, about something irrelevant, about his personal life, his home life, his prison life, and not at all with any sort of aim, not to play up to him, but simply *because he really wants to know about these things*. The birches are brought, and a chair for Smekalov; he sits down, even lights his pipe. He had a long-stemmed pipe. The prisoner begins to plead . . . "No, brother, lie down, there's no point . . . ," says Smekalov; the prisoner sighs and lies down. "Well, my dear man, so you know the Lord's Prayer by heart?" "How could I not, Your Honor, I'm a Christian, I learned it as a child." "Well, recite it, then." And the prisoner knows what to recite, and knows ahead of time what will come of the recital, because the same trick has already been repeated some thirty times before with other prisoners. And Smekalov himself knows that the prisoner knows it; he knows that even the soldiers standing with raised birches over the prostrate victim have also been hearing about this same trick for a long time, and still he repeats it again—it has pleased him so much once and for all, maybe precisely because he made it up, out of literary vanity. The prisoner begins to recite, the men with the birches stand waiting, while Smekalov even leans forward, raises his arm, and stops smoking his pipe, waiting for a certain little word. After the first line of the well-known prayer, the prisoner finally reaches the words "our daily *bread.*" No more is needed. "Stop!" cries the inflamed lieutenant, and instantly, with an inspired gesture, addressing the man with the raised birch, cries: "Give him the birch *instead!*"

And he dissolves in loud laughter. The soldiers standing around also grin: the flogger grins, even the flogged man all but grins, though at the command "instead" the birch is already whistling through the air, to cut an instant later like a razor into his guilty body. And Smekalov is delighted, delighted precisely because he worked it out so well—and *himself* composed that "our daily bread" and "birch instead"—it's apt and it rhymes. And Smekalov goes away after the punishment perfectly pleased with himself, and the whipped man also goes away all but pleased with himself and Smekalov, and, lo and behold, half an hour later he's already telling the whole prison how, just now, the already thirty times repeated trick was repeated for the thirty-first time. "He's all heart! A funny man!"

On occasion the memories of the kindly lieutenant even smacked of a sort of Manilovism.[5]

"You're going along, you know, brothers," some little prisoner tells, and his whole face smiles at the memory, "you're going along and he's sitting by the window in his dressing gown, sipping tea, smoking his pipe. You take your hat off. 'Where you going, Aksenov?'

"'To work, Mikhail Vassilyich, to the workshop first off,' and he laughs to himself . . . All heart he is! Heart's the only word!"

"And try finding the likes of him!" adds one of his listeners.

III

Continuation[*]

I have begun talking about punishments, as well as about the various performers of these interesting duties, essentially because, having gone to stay in the hospital, I only then received a first visual notion of all these things. Until then I had known of them only by hearsay. All the convicts punished by flogging from all the battalions, all the prison sections, and all the military units stationed in our town and its environs were brought to our two wards. In that first time, when I so greedily observed everything that went on around me, all these procedures that were strange to me, all these men punished or preparing to be punished, naturally made the strongest impression on me. I was disturbed, confused, and frightened. I remember that right then I suddenly and impatiently started going into all the details of these new phenomena, listening to other prisoners' conversations and stories about the subject, asking them questions myself, seeking solutions. I wished, among other things, to know for certain all the degrees of sentences and executions, all the nuances of these executions, the prisoners' own view of it all; I tried to picture to myself the psychological state of the men going to punishment. I've already said it was a rare man who preserved his equanimity in the face of punishment, not excepting even those who had previously been much and repeatedly beaten. Here the condemned man is generally overcome by an acute but purely physical fear, involuntary and irrepressible, which crushes all of a man's moral essence. Later, too, all through those several years of prison life, I could not help observing those men who, having lain in hospital after the first half of their punishment and healed their backs, were discharged from the hospital so as to undergo the next day the remaining half of the strokes

[*] All that I am writing here about punishments and floggings was so in my time. Now I hear that it has all changed and is still changing. *Author.*

allotted to them. This dividing of the punishment in half always takes place on orders from the doctor who is present at the punishment. If the number of strokes fixed for the crime is great, so that the prisoner cannot bear them all at once, they divide the number into two or even three parts for him, depending on what the doctor says at the time of the punishment itself, that is, whether the man being punished can continue to run the gauntlet, or it would put him in danger of his life. Usually five hundred, a thousand, or even fifteen hundred are dealt out all at once; but if the sentence is for two or three thousand, the punishment is divided into two or even three parts. Men who, once their backs had healed after the first half, left the hospital to undergo the second half, were usually gloomy, sullen, and taciturn on that day and the day before. A certain mental stupor, a certain unnatural distraction could be noticed in them. Such a man does not get into conversation and is mainly silent; most curious of all is that the prisoners themselves never talk with such a man or try to discuss what awaits him. No unnecessary words, no comforting; they even try generally to pay little attention to him. That, of course, is better for the condemned man. There are exceptions, such as Orlov, for instance, of whom I have already told. After the first half of the punishment, all that vexed him was that his back took a long time to heal and that he could not be discharged sooner, the sooner to undergo the rest of the strokes, be sent with a party to the place of exile appointed for him, and escape on the way. But this man was entertaining a purpose, and God knows what he had in mind. He was a man of passion and great vitality. He was very pleased, in a state of intense excitement, though he restrained his feelings. The thing was that before the first half of his punishment he thought he would not survive the rods and was sure to die. Various rumors had already reached him about the authorities' measures while he was awaiting sentence; already then he was preparing for death. But, having undergone the first half, he took heart. He arrived in the hospital beaten half to death; I had never seen such welts; but he came with joy in his heart, with the hope that he would be left alive, that those rumors were false, that he had, after all, survived the rods, so that now, after awaiting sentence for so long, he began to dream of the road, escape, freedom, the fields and forests . . . Two days after he was discharged from the hospital, he died in that same hospital, on his former cot, not having withstood the second half. But I have already mentioned that.

And yet those very prisoners who had such a hard time in the days and nights before their punishment, endured that same punishment manfully, not excluding the most fainthearted of them. I rarely heard any moaning, even during the night of their arrival, not even from those who had been very badly beaten. The people generally are able to endure pain. On the subject of pain I made many inquiries. I sometimes wanted to find out for certain how great this pain was, what it might finally be compared with. I truly don't know why I kept getting at that. I remember only one thing, that it was not out of idle curiosity. I repeat, I was disturbed and shaken. But no one I asked could give me a satisfactory answer. It burns, it scorches like fire—that was all I could find out, and that was the sole answer I got from all of them. It burns, that's all. In that first time, having become close with M—cki, I put these questions to him. "It hurts very much," he said, "and the feeling is of burning, like fire; as if your back is being roasted over a very hot fire." In short, everybody said exactly the same thing. However, I remember, I made a strange observation then, on the correctness of which I will not especially insist; but it was strongly corroborated by the general opinion of the prisoners: it was that the birch, if applied in large quantity, was the worst punishment of all in use among us. At first glance, that would seem absurd and impossible. And yet five or even four hundred strokes of the birch can beat a man to death; and more than five hundred almost certainly. Even a man of the strongest constitution cannot survive a thousand strokes at one time. Whereas a man can endure five hundred rods without any danger to his life. He can endure a thousand rods without danger to his life, even if he's not a man of strong constitution. Even two thousand rods cannot kill a man of average strength and healthy constitution. The prisoners all said that the birch is worse than the rod. "The birch smarts more," they said, "it's a greater torment." Of course, the birch is more tormenting than the rod. It chafes more, it has more effect on the nerves, excites them immeasurably, shocks them impossibly. I don't know how it is now, but in the still recent old days there were gentlemen for whom the possibility of whipping their victim afforded something reminiscent of the Marquis de Sade and Brinvilliers.[1] I think there is something both sweet and painful in this sensation that makes these gentlemen's hearts swoon. There are people, like tigers, who have a thirst for licking blood. A man who has once experienced this power, this unlimited lordship over the body, blood, and spirit of a man just like himself, created in the same way, his brother by the law of Christ; a man who has experienced this power and the full possibility of inflicting the ultimate humiliation upon another being bearing the image of God, somehow involuntarily loses control of his sensations. Tyranny is a habit; it is endowed with development, and develops finally into an illness. I stand upon this, that the best of men can, from habit, become coarse and stupefied to the point of brutality. Blood and power intoxicate: coarseness and depravity develop; the most abnormal phenomena become accessible and, finally, sweet to the mind and feelings. Man and citizen perish forever in the tyrant, and the return to human dignity, to repentance, to regeneration, becomes almost impossible for him. What's more, the example, the possibility, of such self-will has a contagious effect on the whole of society: power is seductive. A society that looks indifferently upon such a phenomenon is itself infected at its foundation. In short, the right of corporal punishment, granted to one man over another, is one of the plagues of society, one of the most powerful means of annihilating in it any germ, any attempt at civility, and full grounds for its inevitable and ineluctable corruption.

The executioner is shunned in society, but the gentleman executioner is far from being shunned. Just recently the contrary opinion has been expressed, but as yet only in books, abstractly. Even those who express it have not yet managed to extinguish this need for despotism in themselves. Even every manufacturer, every entrepreneur must inevitably feel a sort of rousing pleasure in the fact that his worker sometimes depends entirely, with his entire family, on him alone. That is certainly so; a generation does not tear itself away so quickly from the inheritance sitting in it; a man does not renounce so quickly what has entered his blood, what was passed on to him, so to speak, with his mother's milk. Such precocious revolutions do not happen. To acknowledge one's guilt and ancestral sin is little, very little; it is necessary to break with them completely. And that cannot be done so quickly.

I have spoken of the executioner. The characteristics of the executioner can be found in embryo in almost every contemporary man. But the brutish characteristics of men do not develop equally. If in their development they overpower all the other characteristics in someone, such a man, of course, becomes ghastly and deformed. Executioners are of two kinds: some are voluntary, others are forced, obliged. The voluntary executioner is, of course, inferior in all respects to the forced one, who, nevertheless, is so repugnant to the people, repugnant to the point of horror, of loathing, of an unaccountable, all but mystical fear. Whence comes this almost superstitious fear of one executioner and such indifference, all but approval, of the other? There are examples that are utterly strange: I have known people who were even good, even honest, even respected in society, and yet, for example, they could not take it calmly if a man who was being punished did not cry out under the lashes, did not plead and beg for mercy. Punished men must unfailingly cry out and plead for mercy. That's how it's done; it's considered both proper and necessary, and once, when the victim did not want to cry out, the officer, whom I knew, and who might have been considered a kind man in other respects, even became personally offended. At first he was going to punish the man lightly, but, not hearing the usual "Your Honor, dear father, have mercy, I'll pray to God eternally," and so on, he flew into a rage and gave him fifty extra lashes, wishing to get cries and pleas from him—and he got them. "Impossible, sir, it's rudeness," he answered me very seriously. As for the real executioner, the forced, the obliged one, this much is known: he is a prisoner who has been tried and sentenced to exile, but has been kept behind as an executioner; he first works as an apprentice to another executioner, and, having learned from him, is kept in the prison for good, where he is held separately, in a separate room, and even manages his own household, but almost always goes around under convoy. Of course, a living man is not a machine; though an executioner beats out of duty, sometimes he also gets carried away, but even if he finds some satisfaction in beating, he almost never feels a personal hatred for his victim. The deftness of the stroke, the knowledge of his profession, the desire to show off before his comrades and the public, tickle his vanity. He does it for the sake of art. Besides, he knows very well that he is a universal outcast, that superstitious fear meets him and accompanies him everywhere, and there is no guaranteeing that this does not influence him, does not increase his ferocity, his brutish inclinations. Even children know that he has "renounced his father and mother." Strangely enough, all the executioners I've happened to see were developed men, with sense, with intelligence, and with an extraordinary vanity, even pride. Whether that pride develops in them as a reaction to the universal contempt for them; whether it is increased by the awareness of the fear they inspire in their victims and the feeling of lordship over them—I don't know. It may even be that the very showiness and theatricality of the situation in which they appear before the public on the scaffold contributes to the development of a certain arrogance in them. I remember, it so happened that for a certain period of time I met frequently with an executioner and observed him closely. He was a fellow of medium height, muscular, lean, about forty years old, with a rather pleasant and intelligent face and curly hair. He was always extraordinarily grand, calm; outwardly he bore himself like a gentleman, always answered briefly, reasonably, and even affably, but with a sort of lofty affability, as if he were swaggering before me. Guards officers frequently addressed him in my presence and, truly, even with a certain sort of respect for him. He was aware of that, and before a superior he deliberately redoubled his politeness, dryness, and sense of personal dignity. The more affably a superior spoke to him, the more unyielding he himself seemed, and though he never departed from the most refined politeness, I'm certain that at such moments he considered himself immeasurably above the superior who was speaking to him. It was written on his face. Sometimes it happened that, on a very hot summer day, he would be sent under convoy with a long, thin pole to kill off stray dogs in town. In that little town there were an extraordinary number of dogs that did not belong to anyone and that multiplied with unusual speed. In the hot weather they became dangerous, and the executioner would be sent, on orders from the authorities, to exterminate them. But even this humiliating duty apparently did not humiliate him in the least. You should have seen with what dignity he strolled about the streets of the town, accompanied by the weary convoy, the very sight of him scaring away the passing women and children, and how calmly and even haughtily he looked at everyone he met. However, executioners have a comfortable life. They have money, they eat very well, drink vodka. The money comes from bribery. A civilian who has been tried and sentenced to corporal punishment by a court will first of all give something to the executioner, even if it's the last he has. But with some, with rich offenders, they take it themselves, setting the amount depending on the prisoner's probable means, take as much as thirty roubles, sometimes even more. With the very rich there may even be a lot of bargaining. The executioner cannot, of course, punish very weakly; for that he would have to answer with his own back. But still, for a certain bribe, he promises the victim that he will not beat him very painfully. His offer is almost always accepted; if not, the punishment is indeed barbaric, and that is wholly within his power. It can happen that he imposes a considerable sum even on a very poor man; relations come, bargain, bow and scrape, and too bad if they don't satisfy him. On such occasions he is greatly helped by the superstitious fear he inspires. What wonders don't they tell about executioners! However, the prisoners themselves assured me that an executioner can kill with one blow. But, first of all, when has that been tested? However, maybe so. They spoke of it all too affirmatively. An executioner himself assured me that he could do it. It was also said that he could hit a criminal's back with a full swing, but in such a way that not even the smallest welt would rise up after the blow, and the criminal would not feel the slightest pain. However, all too many stories are known about all these tricks and subtleties. But even if an executioner takes a bribe for punishing lightly, he still has to give the first blow with a full swing and with all his might. That even became a custom among them. He can soften the subsequent blows, especially if he has been paid beforehand. But the first blow—whether he's been paid or not—is his. I truly don't know why they do it that way. Is it to inure the victim at once to the further blows, reckoning that after a very heavy blow the lighter ones will not seem so painful, or is it simply a wish to show off before the victim, to put fear into him, to disconcert him from the start, so that he understands whom he's dealing with—to display himself, in short? In any case, before the start of the punishment, the executioner feels himself in an excited state of mind, feels his power, is conscious of being the master; he is an actor in that moment; the public looks at him with wonder and horror, and it is certainly not without pleasure that he cries out to his victim before the first blow: "Hold on, it'll burn!"—the usual and fatal words on those occasions. It is hard to conceive how far human nature can be distorted.

During that first time in the hospital, I listened avidly to all these prisoners' stories. Lying there was terribly boring for us. The days were all so much alike! In the morning we were somewhat diverted by the doctors' visit, soon followed by dinner. Naturally, in such monotony, meals provided considerable diversion. The rations differed, depending on the patient's illness. Some got only soup with some sort of grain; others only thin gruel; still others only farina, which a great many of them fancied. From lying there a long time, the prisoners grew soft and acquired a taste for good food. The convalescent and nearly well were given a piece of boiled beef, or "bull," as we called it. Best of all was the scurvy ration—beef with onion, horseradish, and so on, sometimes with a dram of vodka. Bread, also going by the illness, was black or half-white, and properly baked. This officialism and nicety in prescribing rations only made the patients laugh. Of course, in some illnesses a man would not eat anything. But those who did have an appetite ate whatever they liked. Some exchanged their rations, so that a ration suited to one illness would go to a completely different one. Others who were on a mild diet bought beef or the scurvy ration, drank kvass or hospital beer, buying it from those to whom it was prescribed. Some even downed two rations. These rations were sold or resold for money. A ration of beef was priced rather high; it cost five paper kopecks. If there was nobody in our ward to buy from, a guard was sent to the other prisoners' ward, or else to the soldiers' "free" wards, as we called them. People willing to sell were always found. They were left with bread alone, but they made money. Poverty was, of course, universal, but those who had a bit of cash sent to the market for kalachi, or even for sweets and the like. Our guards carried out all these errands quite disinterestedly. After dinner came the most boring time; some slept from having nothing to do, some chatted, some quarreled, some told stories aloud. If no new patients were brought, it was still more boring. The arrival of a new man almost always produced a certain impression, especially if no one was acquainted with him. We looked him over, tried to find out who and what he was, where from, and what his case was. Those who were in transit aroused special interest; they always had something to tell, though not about their intimate affairs; of that, if they did not bring it up themselves, they were never asked, but only where they were from, who they had come with, how the journey had been, where they were going, and so on. Some, on hearing a new story, would remember as if in passing something of their own about various transits, parties, executors, and party heads. Those punished with rods also appeared at around that time, towards evening. They always made a rather strong impression, as, by the way, has already been mentioned; but they were not brought every day, and on those days when there weren't any, some sort of listlessness came over us, as if we were terribly sick of each other's faces, and we even began to quarrel. We were even glad of the crazy ones, who were brought for testing. The trick of pretending to be crazy in order to avoid punishment was occasionally used by the convicts. Some were quickly exposed, or, rather, they themselves decided to change the politics of their actions, and a prisoner, after acting up for two or three days, suddenly, for no reason at all, would become sensible, quiet down, and glumly ask to be discharged. Neither the prisoners nor the doctors reproached or shamed such a man by reminding him of his recent antics; they silently discharged him, silently sent him away, and in two or three days he would come back to us after his punishment. Such cases, however, were generally rare. But the genuine madmen brought for testing were truly a divine punishment for the whole ward. Some of these madmen, jolly, lively, shouting, dancing, singing, were first greeted by the prisoners with all but delight. "Here's some fun!" they said, looking at a grimacing fellow who had just been brought in. But I found it terribly difficult and painful to see these poor wretches. I could never look indifferently at madmen.

However, the continual grimacing and restless antics of the madman, who was greeted with laughter when he was brought in, soon simply wearied us all, and after two days we were at the end of our patience. One of them was kept with us for three weeks, and we were ready to go running out of the ward. As if on purpose, just then another madman was brought in. This one made a particular impression on me. It happened during the third year of my term. In the first year, or, rather, in the first months of my prison life, in the spring, I went with a party to work as a carrier for the kiln makers in a brickyard a mile and a half away. The kilns had to be repaired for the coming summer's brickmaking. That morning, at the factory, M—cki and B. introduced me to Sergeant Ostrozhski, who was the resident overseer there. He was a Pole, an old man of about sixty, tall, lean, of a most seemly and even majestic appearance. He had been serving in Siberia from way back, and though he was of simple stock and had come as a soldier in the onetime army of 1830,[2] M—cki and B. loved and respected him. He was always reading the Catholic Bible. I used to talk with him, and he spoke so kindly, so sensibly, told such interesting stories, had such a good-natured and honest look. After that I did not see him for two years, and only heard that he was under investigation for something, and suddenly they brought him into our ward as a madman. He came in shrieking, guffawing, and started dancing around the ward with the most indecent, clownish gestures. The prisoners were delighted, but for me it was so sad . . . After three days, none of us knew what to do with him. He quarreled, fought, shrieked, sang songs, even during the night, did such repulsive things every moment that we all felt simply nauseated. He was not afraid of anybody. They put him in a strait-jacket, but that only made things worse for us, though without it he picked quarrels and got into fights with just about everybody. During those three weeks the whole ward sometimes rose up as one man and asked the head doctor to transfer our treasure to the other prisoners' ward. There, after two days, they begged in turn that he be transferred back to us. And since we happened to have two madmen at once, both restless and quarrelsome, our two wards kept taking turns exchanging madmen. But they both turned out worse. We all breathed freely when they were finally taken away somewhere . . .

I also remember another strange madman. Once during the summer they brought in a convict, a robust and very clumsy-looking fellow of about forty-five, with a face disfigured by smallpox, with small, red, puffy eyes and an extremely dark and sullen look. They put him next to me. He turned out to be a very docile fellow, didn't speak to anybody, and sat there as if pondering something. It was getting dark, and he suddenly turned to me. Straight off, without further preliminaries, but looking as if he were letting me in on a great secret, he began telling me that one of these days he was supposed to get two thousand, but now it wouldn't happen, because Colonel G.'s daughter had interceded for him. I looked at him in perplexity and replied that in such cases, it seemed to me, a colonel's daughter was in no position to do anything. I had not yet guessed what was up; he had not been brought in as a madman, but as an ordinary patient. I asked him what he was sick with. He said he didn't know, that he had been sent here for some reason, but that he was in perfectly good health, and the colonel's daughter was in love with him; that once, two weeks ago, she had been driving past the guardhouse, and just then he had looked out the barred window. She had seen him and fallen in love at once. And she had come to the guardhouse three times after that on various pretexts; the first time she had dropped in with her father to see her brother, an officer, who was standing guard just then; another time she had come with her mother to hand out alms, and, passing by, had whispered to him that she loved him and would rescue him. It was strange with what fine detail he told me this whole absurdity, which, of course, was born entirely in his poor, deranged head. He had a sacred belief in his deliverance from punishment. He spoke calmly and affirmatively of this young lady's passionate love for him, and, not to mention the overall absurdity of the story, it was quite wild to hear this romantic account of a lovelorn maiden from a man approaching fifty, with such a doleful, distressed, and ugly physiognomy. It is strange what the fear of punishment could do to this timid soul. Maybe he really had seen someone from the window, and the madness being prepared in him by fear, growing with every hour, all at once found its outlet, its form. This unfortunate soldier, who in his whole life may never once have given a thought to young ladies, suddenly thought up a whole novel, instinctively clutching at that straw at least. I heard him out silently and told the other prisoners about it. But when the others began to ask questions, he became chastely silent. The next day the doctor questioned him at length, and since he told him that he was not sick at all, and on examination that turned out to be so, he was discharged. But we found out that they had written sanat on his medical chart only when the doctors had left the ward, so that it was impossible to tell them what was wrong with him. And we ourselves had not yet fully figured out the main thing. Yet the whole affair consisted in a mistake made about him by the authorities, who sent him to us without explaining why. There was some sort of carelessness here. And maybe even those who sent him were still only guessing and were not at all convinced of his madness, but acted on obscure rumors and sent him for testing. However it was, two days later the unfortunate man was taken out to be punished. It seems he was very shocked by the unexpectedness; until the last minute he didn't believe he would be punished, and when they led him between the rows, he began to shout "Help!" In the hospital this time, for lack of cots, he was placed not in ours but in the other ward. But I inquired about him and learned that for all eight days he did not say a word to anyone, was confused and extremely sad . . . Then, after his back healed, he was transferred somewhere. I at least never heard anything more about him.

As for treatment and medications in general, as far as I could observe, the slightly ill almost never followed prescriptions and took medications, but the gravely ill and the truly ill in general liked very much to be treated, and took their mixtures and powders conscientiously; but most of all they liked external treatments. Cupping glasses, leeches, poultices, and bloodletting, which our simple folk love and believe in so much, were accepted among us willingly and even with pleasure. One strange circumstance interested me. These same people, who were so patient in enduring the most agonizing pain from rods and birches, often complained, winced, and even moaned from mere cupping glasses. Either they had gone very soft, or they were simply shamming—I really don't know how to explain it. True, our cupping glasses were of a special kind. Our intern once upon a time had lost or broken the little instrument for making instant cuts in the skin, or else it broke by itself, so that he was forced to make the necessary incisions with a lancet. Around twelve incisions were made for each cupping glass. With the instrument it was painless. Twelve little knives struck suddenly, instantly, and caused no pain. But incisions with the lancet were another matter. A lancet cuts comparatively very slowly; you feel the pain; and since, for example, for ten cupping glasses a hundred and twenty such incisions have to be made in all, of course, it hurts badly. I experienced it, but though it was painful and annoying, still it was not so bad that you couldn't keep yourself from moaning. It was even funny sometimes to watch some hale and hearty fellow squirm and begin to whine. Generally, it can be compared with a man who is firm and even calm in some serious matter, but mopes and fusses at home when he has nothing to do, won't eat what he's offered, curses and shouts; everything is wrong, everybody annoys him, is rude to him, torments him— in short, it's too much of a good thing, as we sometimes say of such gentlemen, though they are also to be met with among simple folk, and in our prison, with its mutual general cohabitation, even all too often. It happened that the men in his ward would start teasing such a sissy, or else would simply scold him; he would then shut up, as if in fact he had just been waiting for them to scold him so as to shut up. Ustyantsev especially disliked that and never missed a chance to quarrel with a sissy. He generally never missed a chance to wrangle with anybody. It was a pleasure for him, a need, owing to his illness, naturally, and in part to his dull-wittedness. He used first to stare earnestly and intently, and then in a sort of calm, assured voice would begin to deliver his exhortation. He made everything his business; it was as if he had been attached to us to keep an eye on the order or the general morality.

"Pokes his nose into everything," the prisoners would say, laughing. They spared him, however, and avoided abusing him, but only laughed sometimes.

"Talked a heap! Three cartloads or more."

"A heap, did I? No hats off to a fool, you know. Why's he shouting because of a lancet? If you like it hot, you can like it not—I mean, take what comes."

"What's it to you?"

"No, brothers," one of our prisoners interrupted, "the cupping glasses are nothing; I've been through it; but there's no worse pain than when they pull you by the ear for a long time."

Everybody laughed.

"And you've had yours pulled?"

"You don't think so? Sure I have!"

"So that's why your ears stick out like that."

This little prisoner, Shapkin, indeed had very long ears sticking out on both sides. He was a tramp, still a young fellow, sensible and quiet, who always spoke with some serious, hidden humor, which lent a good deal of comedy to some of his stories.

"Why on earth should I think you've had your ears pulled? How would I think that up, you numbskull?" Ustyantsev mixed in again, addressing Shapkin with indignation, though the man had not been speaking to him, but to everyone in general. But Shapkin did not even look at him.

"And who did it?" someone asked.

"Who? The police chief, that's who. It was back when I was a tramp. We arrived in K. then, there were two of us, me and another man, also a tramp, Efim, no last name. On our way, we picked up a little something from a peasant in the village of Tolmina. There's this village, Tolmina. Well, so we come and look around: let's pick up a little something here, too, and make tracks. Where the winds blow free is the place for me, but in town it's creepy, you know. Well, so first of all we come to a pot-house. We look around. A man comes up to us, a real shambles, all out at the elbows, in German clothes. Yack, yack.

" 'And, if I may ask,' he says, 'have you got documents?'*

" 'No,' we say, 'no documents.'

" 'Well, there. Same for us, sir. I've got a couple of chums here,' he says. 'We're also under General Cuckooshkin.† So I make bold to ask, we've done a bit of carousing and haven't had a red cent coming in. Favor us with a half bottle.'

" 'With the greatest pleasure,' we say. Well, so we drank. And here they pointed us to a piece of business, breaking and entering, that is, in our line. There was this house on the edge of town, and a rich trades-man lived there, heaps of goods, so we decided to call on him during the night. Only that same night, at the rich merchant's, all five of us got caught. They took us to the police station, then to the chief in person. 'I'll question them myself,' he says. He comes out with his pipe, they carry a cup of tea behind him, a strapping fellow, with side-whiskers. He sits down. And here they brought in three more besides us, also tramps. Your tramp's a funny man, brothers: he doesn't remember a thing, you can split him three ways up, he forgets everything, doesn't know anything. The police chief made straight for me: 'Who are you?'

---

* I.e., passports. *Author.* [Meaning "internal" passports, required of all Russian people moving from their registered place of residence. *Translator.*]

† That is, in the forest, where the cuckoo sings. He means to say that they are also tramps. *Author.*

He roared it out, like from a barrel. Well, you know, I said the same as everybody: 'I don't remember anything, Your Honor,' I say, 'I've forgotten it all.'

" 'Hold on,' he says, 'I'll talk more with you, your mug's familiar,' and he claps his blinkers on me. And I'd never seen him before. He turns to another man:

" 'Who are you?'

" 'Go-off Wavin, Your Honor.'

" 'So your name is Go-off Wavin?'

" 'That's right, Your Honor.'

" 'Well, fine, so you're Go-off Wavin. And you?' To a third man, that is.

" 'Me After-im, Your Honor.'

" 'Yes, but what's your name?'

" 'That's my name, Your Honor: Me After-im.'

" 'Who called you that, you scoundrel?'

" 'Good people, Your Honor. You know, Your Honor, the world is not without good people.'

" 'And who are these good people?'

" 'They've gone clean out of my head, Your Honor, I ask you kindly to forgive me.'

" 'You've forgotten them all?'

" 'Forgotten them all, Your Honor.'

" 'Still, you had a father and mother, didn't you? . . . Do you remember them at least?'

" 'It must be supposed I did, Your Honor, but anyhow they've also gone clean out of my head. Maybe I did, Your Honor.'

" 'Where have you lived up to now?'

" 'In the woods, Your Honor.'

" 'Always in the woods?'

" 'Always in the woods.'

" 'Well, and in winter?'

" 'Never saw any winter, Your Honor.'

" 'And you, what's your name?'

" 'Axe, Your Honor.'

" 'And yours?'

"'Grind Don't Gape, Your Honor.'

"'And yours?'

"'Grind-away No-fear, Your Honor.'

"'None of you remembers anything?'

"'We don't remember anything, Your Honor.'

"He stands there, laughs, and they look at him, grinning. Well, another time you'd get your teeth bashed in, worse luck. And they're all such sturdy, beefy fellows.

"'Take them to jail,' he says, 'I'll deal with them later. But you stay,' he says, meaning me. 'Come here, sit down!' I look: a table, a chair, paper, a pen. I think: What's he up to? 'Sit in the chair,' he says, 'take the pen, write!'—and he grabs me by the ear and pulls it. I look at him like the devil at a priest: 'I don't know how, Your Honor.' 'Write!'

"'Have mercy, Your Honor.' 'Write the way you know how!'—and all the while he pulls my ear, goes on pulling it, and suddenly twists it! Well, brothers, I'll tell you, it would have been better if he'd given me three hundred birches. Sparks flew out of my eyes. 'Write, I told you!'"

"What, he went foolish?"

"No, he didn't. But a short time before, in T—k, a clerk had pulled a fast one: filched some government money and made off with it, and his ears also stuck out. Well, they made it known far and wide. And I seemed to fit the description, so he tested me to see if I knew how to write."

"What a business, lad! And it hurt?"

"I'll say it did."

General laughter rang out.

"Well, and did you write?"

"How was I supposed to write? I started moving the pen, went on moving it, moving it over the paper, and he gave up. Well, he boxed my ears a dozen times, naturally, and with that let me go—to jail, I mean."

"So you do know how to write?"

"I used to, but when they started writing with pens, I lost the knack . . ."

It was in such stories, or, better, in such blather, that our boring time was sometimes spent. Lord, how boring it was! The days were long, suffocating, all exactly alike. Oh, for some book or other! And yet I went to the hospital often, especially in the beginning, sometimes because I was sick, sometimes just to lie there; to get away from the prison. It was hard there, still harder than here, morally harder. Malice, hostility, quarreling, envy, eternal carping at us gentry, spiteful, threatening faces! Here in the hospital we were all on more of an equal footing, lived more amicably. The saddest time in the whole course of the day came at evening, by candlelight, and the beginning of night. We go to bed early. The bright spot of a dim night-light shines far away by the door, but our end is in semidarkness. It grows more stinking and stuffy. Someone is unable to fall asleep, sits up, and stays for an hour and a half on his bed, bowing his head in its nightcap, as if thinking about something. You look at him for a whole hour and try to guess what he's thinking about, so as to kill your own time somehow as well. Or else you start dreaming, remembering the past, painting broad and bright pictures in your imagination; you recall details such as you would never recall or feel at any other time than now. Or else you guess about the future: How will it be to get out of prison? Where to go? When will it be? Will you ever return to your native parts? You think and think; hope begins to stir in your soul . . . Or sometimes you simply start counting: one, two, three, and so on, so as to somehow fall asleep in the midst of this counting. I sometimes counted up to three thousand and didn't fall asleep. Here somebody begins to toss. Ustyantsev coughs his putrid, consumptive cough and then moans weakly and each time says: "Lord, I'm a sinner!" And it is strange to hear this sickly, broken, and whining voice amidst the general silence. And somewhere there in a corner men are also not sleeping and are conversing from their cots. One starts telling something about his past, about far away, about long ago, about being a tramp, about his children, about his wife, about the way things used to be. And you can feel just from his far-off whispering that nothing he is talking about will ever come back to him, and he himself, the storyteller, is a cut-off slice. The other man listens. You hear only a quiet, measured whisper, like water murmuring somewhere far away . . . I remember hearing a story once on a long winter night. At first glance it seemed to me like a feverish dream, as if I were lying in a fever and dreaming it all up in the heat of delirium . . .

IV

Akulka's Husband

It was already late at night, past eleven o'clock. I had fallen asleep, but suddenly woke up. The dim little flame of the distant night-light barely lit up the ward . . . Almost everyone was asleep by then. Even Ustyantsev was asleep, and in the silence you could hear his heavy breathing and the phlegm wheezing in his throat with every breath. In the distance, in the entryway, the heavy footsteps of the approaching relief guard were suddenly heard. A rifle butt banged on the floor. The door opened; the corporal, stepping carefully, counted the patients. A moment later the ward was locked, a new sentry was posted, the guard moved off, and again the former silence. Only now did I notice that, not far away from me, to the left, two men were not asleep and seemed to be whispering to each other. This happened in the wards: sometimes men would lie next to each other for days and months without saying a word, and suddenly would somehow get to talking at an inviting hour of the night, and one would start laying out his whole past before the other.

They had evidently been talking for a long time already. I hadn't caught the beginning, nor could I make it all out now; but I gradually got used to it and began to understand everything. I couldn't sleep; what else could I do but listen? . . . One was heatedly telling his story, half lying on the bed, his head raised and his neck stretched towards his comrade. He was obviously flushed, agitated; he wanted to tell his story. His listener, sullen and perfectly indifferent, was sitting up on his cot, his legs stretched out, occasionally mumbling something in reply or as a sign of sympathy for the storyteller, but as if more out of propriety than in reality, and filling his nose with snuff from a horn every other minute. This was the corrective-company soldier Cherevin, a man of about fifty, a sullen pedant, a cold reasoner, and a conceited fool. The storyteller, Shishkov, was still a young lad, under thirty, a civil convict, who worked in the tailor's shop. I had paid little attention to him before then; and later, too, in the whole time of my prison life, I somehow never felt like taking an interest in him. He was an empty and crotchety man. Sometimes he was silent, lived sullenly, behaved rudely, didn't talk for weeks. And sometimes he would suddenly get mixed up in some incident, start gossiping, get excited over trifles, shuttle between the barracks bearing news, telling tales, working himself up. He would get beaten and fall silent again. He was a cowardly and flimsy fellow. Everybody seemed to treat him with scorn. He was short, lean; his eyes were somehow restless, and sometimes as if dully pensive. Occasionally he told about something: he would start hotly, with ardor, even wav-ing his arms—and suddenly break off, or turn to something else, get carried away by new details, and forget what he began with. He often railed at people, and when he did, he always reproached the man for something, for some sort of guilt before him, spoke with feeling, all but wept . . . He was rather good at playing the balalaika and liked playing it, and on holidays he even danced, and danced well, when he was made to . . . Making him do something was quick work . . . Not that he was all that obedient, but he liked to force his way into comradeship and to be obliging out of comradeship.

For a long time I could not grasp what his story was about. It also seemed to me at first that he kept straying from his theme and getting sidetracked. He may have noticed that Cherevin could not have cared less about his story, but it seemed he wanted purposely to convince himself that his listener was all attention, and it might have pained him greatly if he had been convinced of the contrary.

". . . He'd go out to the market," he continued, "everybody bows to him, does him honor—rich is the word."

"He was a merchant, you say?"

"Yes, a merchant. The tradesmen among us were plain poor. Naked as could be. The women went to the riverside, outside town, to fetch water for their vegetable patches; they slogged and slogged, and come autumn they didn't have enough for a cabbage soup. Ruination. Well, he had a big holding, kept hired men to work the land, three of them, and then again he had his beehives, dealt in honey and in cattle, too, so he was held in great respect in our parts. He was awful old, seventy, bones gone heavy, gray-haired, big as anything. He'd go out to the market in his fox-skin coat, and everybody'd honor him. They really felt it, I mean. 'Greetings, dear Ankudim Trofimych!' 'And greetings to you,' he'd say. He didn't scorn anybody. 'Long life to you, Ankudim Trofimych!' 'And how are you doing?' he'd ask. 'Oh, we're doing all right, as soot is white. And you?' 'Well enough for all my sins,' he says, 'blowing smoke against the wind.' 'Long life to you, Ankudim Trofimych!' He didn't scorn anybody, you see, and when he spoke, his every word was as good as gold. He was read up on the scriptures, literate, always reading some holy book. He'd sit his old woman down in front of him: 'Listen now, wife, and understand!'—and he'd start explaining. And this old woman wasn't all that old, she was already his second wife, for the sake of children, I mean, because he'd had none by the first. Well, but by the second, by Marya Stepanovna, he had two sons not yet full-grown, the youngest, Vasya, begotten when he was sixty, plus Akulka, his daughter, the oldest of them all, who was eighteen."

"Your wife, is it?"

"Hold on. To begin with it's Filka Morozov who'll do his bit. 'Divvy up,' he says to Ankudim. 'Give me the whole four hundred roubles— am I your hired man or something? I don't want to deal with you, and I don't want to take your Akulka. I'm now going on a binge,' he says. 'My parents are dead now, so I'll drink up the money and then get myself recruited as a soldier, and in ten years I'll come back to you a field marshal.' Ankudim gave him the money, that is, settled accounts with him for good—because his father and the old man had dealt on the same capital. 'You're done for,' he says. And Filka says, 'Well, maybe I'm done for and maybe I'm not, but with you, old graybeard, a man learns to sup milk from an awl. You want to economize on a split kopeck, you pick up all kinds of trash in case it might be good in your kasha. I spit on all that. You save and save, and dig your own grave. I've got character,' he says. 'And anyhow I won't take your Akulka; I've already slept with her as it is . . .'

" 'What?' says Ankudim. 'You dare to disgrace the honest daughter of an honest father? When did you sleep with her, you snake's lard, you pike's blood?' And he was shaking all over. Filka told about it himself.

" 'Not just me,' I say, 'I'll make it so your Akulka won't marry anybody now, nobody'll take her, and Mikita Grigoryich won't take her now, because now she's dishonored. She and me have been going at it ever since fall. And I wouldn't agree now for a hundred crayfish. Go on, try giving me a hundred crayfish on the spot—I won't agree . . .'

"And what a binge the fine lad gave us! The earth was groaning, the town was booming with it! He collected some chums, caroused for three months, squandered the whole pile of money. 'Once I've gone through all the money,' he'd say, 'I'll throw in the house, I'll throw in everything, and then either get myself recruited or go and become a tramp!' He was drunk from morning till night, and drove around in a carriage and pair with little bells. And the girls were awfully fond of him. He played the *torban*[1] very well."

"So he and Akulka had dealings even before?"

"Wait, hold on. I had also buried my father by then, and my mother baked gingerbread, we worked for Ankudim, and that's what fed us. It was a wretched life. Well, we also had a little plot beyond the woods, sowed wheat on it, but after my father that all ended, because I also went on a binge, brother. I used to beat money out of my mother . . ."

"That's not good, to beat her. It's a great sin."

"I used to be drunk, brother, from morning till night. Our house was still so-so, passable, a bit rotten, but ours, though you could go chasing hares in it. We used to sit hungry for whole weeks, chewing on a rag. My mother used to harp and carp at me; but what did I care! . . . I never left Filka Morozov's side then, brother. Was with him from morning till night. 'Play the guitar for me and dance,' he says, 'and I'll lie here and throw money at you, because I'm the most rich man!' And what didn't he do! He only didn't take stolen goods: 'I'm not a thief,' he says, 'I'm an honest man.' 'Let's go,' he says, 'and smear tar on Akulka's gate;[2] because I don't want Akulka to marry Mikita Grigoryich. That's dearer to me now than custard,' he says. The old man had wanted to marry the girl off to Mikita Grigoryich even before. Mikita was also an old man, a widower, went around in spectacles, doing deals. As soon as he heard there were rumors about Akulka, he backed out: 'It would be a great dishonor to me, Ankudim Trofimych,' he says, 'and, besides, I don't wish to marry in my old age.' So we tarred Akulka's gate. How they thrashed her, how they thrashed her for that at home . . . Marya Stepanovna shouted: 'I'll skin you alive!' And the old man: 'In the old days, under the honorable patriarchs, I'd have chopped her up and burned her,' he says, 'but now there's darkness and corruption in the world.' The neighbors all down the street could hear Akulka howling away: they whipped her from morning till night. And Filka shouts to the whole market: 'There's this fine wench Akulka, we share a bottle. You walk bright, you dress in white, tell me who you'll love tonight? I'll shove it in their noses,' he says, 'they'll remember.' At that time I once ran into Akulka carrying water buckets and called out: 'Greetings, Akulina Kudimovna! I salute Your Ladyship, you walk bright, you live so free, write down the good man's name for me!'—that's all I said; and she just looked at me, she had such big eyes, and herself grown thin as a sliver. As she was looking at me, her mother thought she was having a laugh with me and shouted from the gateway: 'What are you grinning for, you shameless hussy!'—and that same day she thrashed her again. She used to thrash her for a whole solid hour. 'I'll whip the daylights out of her,' she'd say, 'because she's no daughter of mine anymore.'"

"Meaning she was a wanton."

"You just listen, uncle. So me and Filka kept on drinking then, and my mother comes to me, and I'm lying there: 'What are you doing, you scoundrel, lying there?' she says. 'You filthy robber,' she says. She scolded me, I mean. 'Get married,' she says, 'get married to that Akulka. They'll be so glad to give her to you now, they'll give you three hundred roubles in cash.' I say to her: 'But now she's dishonored before the whole world.' 'You're a fool,' she says. 'Marriage covers up everything; it's even better if she comes out guilty before you for her whole life. And we could set ourselves up with that money,' she says. 'I've already talked with Marya Stepanovna. She heard me out.' And I say, 'I want twenty roubles in cash on the table, then I'll marry her.' And, believe it or not, I was dead drunk right up to the wedding. And here again Filka Morozov threatened me: 'You, Akulka's husband, I'm going to break all the ribs in you, and, if I like, I'll sleep with your wife every night.' And I say: 'You're lying, dog's-meat!' And then he shamed me up and down the street. I came running home: 'I don't want to get married,' I say, 'unless they lay out another fifty roubles on the spot!'"

"And they gave her to you?"

"To me? Why not? We weren't dishonorable. My father was ruined only towards the end on account of a fire, but before that we lived richer than them. Ankudim says to me: 'You're naked beggars.' And I answer: 'So they didn't put enough tar on your gate?' And he says to me: 'Why go bullying us? Prove she's dishonored, we can't gag every mouth. God's here, the doorway's there,' he says, 'don't take her. Only give back the money you took.' Then me and Filka decided to send Mitry Bykov to tell him I was going to dishonor him now before the whole world, and right up to the wedding, brother, I was dead drunk. I only sobered up to get married. When they brought us back from the church, they sat us down, and Mitrofan Stepanych, her uncle, that is, said: 'Though it's without honor, it's solid. The deed's done, and there's an end to it.' The old man, Ankudim, was also drunk and began to cry—sat there with tears running down his beard. Well, brother, here's what I did then: I put a whip in my pocket, I'd prepared it before the wedding, and figured I'd have some fun now with Akulka, teach her to go getting married by dishonest trickery, and let people know I didn't take her like a fool . . ."

"That's it! Meaning so she feels it in the future . . ."

"No, uncle, you just keep still. In our parts they take you to a separate room right after the wedding, and meanwhile go on drinking. So they left me and Akulka in the room. She sat there so white, not a drop of blood in her face. She was scared, I mean. Her hair was also as white as flax. She had big eyes. And she used to be silent all the time, not a peep out of her, as if a mute girl was living in the house. Really strange. And what might you think of this, brother: I had the whip ready and laid it there by the bed, but it turned out, brother mine, that she wasn't guilty of anything before me."

"You don't say!"

"Not of anything; as honest a girl as could be, from an honest house. But in that case, brother, why had she suffered such torments? Why had Filka Morozov dishonored her before the whole world?"

"Right."

"I got down on my knees to her then, right there by the bed, clasped my hands, and said: 'Akulina Kudimovna, dearest, forgive me,

I'm a fool that I also took you for that kind of woman. Forgive me,' I say, 'I'm a scoundrel!' She sits before me on the bed, looks at me, puts both hands on my shoulders, laughs, and at the same time the tears are flowing; she cries and laughs . . . Then I went out to them all: 'Well,' I say, 'let me meet Filka Morozov now—and he won't be long for the world!' And the old folk don't know who to pray to: her mother all but fell at her feet, howling. And the old man said: 'If only we'd known, my beloved daughter, this is not the sort of husband we'd have found for you.' And how we went to church together the first Sunday—me in an astrakhan hat, a fine broadcloth kaftan, velveteen balloon trousers; her in a new hare-skin coat, a silk kerchief—that is, me worthy of her, and her worthy of me: that's how we went! People admire us: I'm what I am, and Akulinushka, though she can't be praised above others, also can't be put down, she's in the first ten . . ."

"Well, good."

"Well, listen now. The day after the wedding, though I was drunk, I escaped from the guests; I got out and went running to the market, shouting: 'Give me that do-nothing Filka Morozov, give him here, the scoundrel!' Well, but then I was drunk; so three men took me by force near the Vlasovs' house and brought me home. And talk went around town. The girls in the market talk among themselves: 'Girlies, smarties, you know what? Akulka turned out honest!' A little while later Filka says to me in front of people: 'Sell your wife—you'll get drunk. There's this soldier here, Yashka,' he says, 'he got married just for that: didn't sleep with his wife, but stayed drunk for three years instead.' I say to him: 'You're a scoundrel!' 'And you,' he says, 'are a fool. You were drunk when you got married. What could you understand about these things?' I came home and shouted: 'You married me off drunk!' My mother fell upon me. 'Your ears are stuffed with gold, mother,' I say. 'Give me Akulka!' So I start whacking her around. I whacked her, brother, whacked her, for two hours I whacked her, till my legs gave out under me. For three weeks she didn't get out of bed."

"Of course," Cherevin observed phlegmatically, "if you don't beat 'em, they'll . . . But did you catch her with her lover?"

"No, I didn't catch her," Shishkov remarked after a pause and as if with effort. "But it hurt me a lot, people kept teasing me, and Filka was the ringleader of it all. 'Your wife's no slattern,' he says, 'she's a perfect pattern.' He invited us as guests; here's what he came out with: 'His spouse is a merciful soul, noble, polite, well-mannered, good in every way, that's how it is for him now! And have you forgotten, my lad, how you yourself smeared her gate with tar?' I was sitting there drunk, and he just grabbed me right then by the hair, grabbed me, bent me down: 'Dance,' he says, 'Akulka's husband, I'm going to hold you by the hair like this, and you dance for my entertainment!' 'You scoundrel, you!' I shout. And he says to me: 'I'll come to you with my chums and flog your wife Akulka with birches right in front of you as much as I like.' After that, believe it or not, I was afraid to leave the house for a whole month: he'll come and dishonor me, I thought. And on account of that I started beating her . . ."

"But why beat her? The hands are bound, the tongue's unbound. It's no good, so much beating. Punish her, teach her, but then be kind to her. That what a wife's for."

Shishkov was silent for a while.

"It hurt me," he began anew. "And again I got into this habit: some days I'd beat her from morning till night; she got up wrong, she doesn't walk proper. If I didn't beat her, I got bored. She'd sit looking out the window and crying . . . She cried all the time. I felt sorry for her, but still I beat her. My mother would harp and carp at me on account of her: 'Scoundrel,' she'd say, 'meat for Siberia!' 'I'll kill her,' I shouted, 'and nobody dares to say anything to me now, because I got married off by trickery.' At first old man Ankudim showed up to defend her: 'God knows you don't amount to much yourself,' he says. 'I'll get the best of you!' But then he gave up. But Marya Stepanovna turned all humble. She came once and pleaded in tears: 'I've come to you with a bother-some thing, Ivan Semyonych,' she says, 'a small point, but a big favor. Show us some daylight, dear man.' She bows down. 'Humble yourself, forgive her! Wicked people have slandered our daughter. You yourself know that you married an honest girl . . .' She bows down at my feet, weeps. But I bully her: 'I don't want to listen to you now! I'll do what-ever I want now to all of you, because I'm not my own master now; and Filka Morozov,' I say, 'is my chum and my best friend . . .'"

"So you went carousing together again?"

"Forget it! You couldn't get near him. He was drunk as a fish. He ran through all he had and leased himself out to a merchant, to go for a soldier in place of his older son. And in our parts, once a man's leased out, then till the day he's taken everything in the house has to fall down before him, and he's master over it all. He gets paid in full when they take him, but till then he lives in the house, sometimes as long as six months, and the things he does to his hosts—saints alive! I'm going for a soldier in place of your son, he says, meaning I'm your benefactor, so you all have to respect me, or else I'll back out. So Filka let all hell break loose at the merchant's, slept with the daughter, pulled the master's beard every day after dinner—did whatever he liked. Took a steam bath every day, and had them make the steam from vodka, and had the women carry him in their arms to the bathhouse. He comes back from carousing, stands outside: 'I don't want to go through the gate, pull down the fence!'—so in another place, beside the gate, they have to pull down the fence to let him in. Finally, it was over, they took him, sobered him up. People, people from everywhere came pouring into the street: Filka Morozov's going for a soldier! He bows on all sides. And just then Akulka was coming from the kitchen garden; when Filka saw her, just by our gate, 'Wait!' he shouted, leaped out of the cart, and bowed to the ground before her: 'My soul,' he says, 'my berry, for two years I've loved you, and now they're taking me for a soldier with all the music. Forgive me,' he says, 'honest daughter of an honest father, because I'm a scoundrel before you—the guilt is all mine!' And again he bowed to the ground. Akulka first stopped, as if she was frightened, and then bowed low to him and said: 'Forgive me, too, good youth, and I know of no evil in you.' I followed her into the cottage: 'What's that you said to him, dog's-meat?' And, believe it or not, she looked at me and said: 'I love him now more than the whole world.'"

"So, then! . . ."

"I didn't say a word to her that whole day . . . Only towards evening, I said: 'Akulka, now I'm going to kill you!' That night I didn't sleep, I went out to the front hall to drink some kvass, and here dawn began to break. I went back inside. 'Akulka,' I say, 'get ready to go to our plot.' I'd been planning to go there even before, and mother knew we'd be going. 'That's the way,' she says. 'It's the busy season, and I hear the hired man's been laid out three days with a stomach ache.' I silently hitched up the cart. Once you leave our town, it's forest for ten miles, and beyond the forest is our plot. We went two miles through the forest, I stopped the horse: 'Get out, Akulina,' I say, 'your end has come.' She looks at me, gets frightened, stands in front of me, says nothing. 'I'm sick of you,' I say. 'Pray to God!' I grabbed her by the hair; she had such long, thick braids, I wound them around my hand, held her between my knees, drew my knife, pulled her head back, and slashed her throat . . . She screamed, the blood spurted, I dropped the knife, threw my arms around her from the front, lay on the ground, embraced her and cried out over her, howled and wailed; she cries out, and I cry out; she's trembling, thrashing around in my arms, and the blood, the blood just gushes out at me, gushes out—at my face, my hands. I abandoned her, fear came over me, I abandoned the horse and ran, ran, came running home the back way, into the bathhouse: we had this old, unused bathhouse; I crouched under a shelf and sat there. I went on sitting there till nightfall."

"And Akulka?"

"She must've gotten up after I left and also went home. They found her afterwards a hundred steps from the place."

"So you didn't finish her off."

"No . . ." Shishkov paused for a moment.

"There's this vein," Cherevin observed, "if it, this same vein, isn't cut through first off, then however much a man struggles, and however much blood he loses, he won't die."

"But she did die. They found her dead in the evening. Informed the authorities, started searching for me, and found me that night in the bathhouse . . . Must be the fourth year I'm living here," he added after a pause.

"Hm . . . Of course, if you don't beat them—no good'll come of it!" Cherevin observed coolly and methodically, taking out his snuff horn again. He began sniffing, at length and with pauses. "And then again, lad," he went on, "you yourself come out so-o-o stupid. I also caught my wife with a lover once. So I invited her to the shed; doubled up the reins. 'Who's your master?' I say. 'Who's your master?' And I thrashed her with the reins, thrashed and thrashed her, for an hour and a half I thrashed her, till she cried out: 'I'll wash your feet, I will, and drink the water.' Her name was Ovdotya."

V

Summertime

But here it is already the beginning of April, here Holy Week is already approaching.[1] The summer work also gradually begins. The sun gets warmer and brighter with each day; the air smells of spring and has a stimulating effect on the organism. The coming beautiful days excite the fettered man, too, and in him, too, give rise to certain desires, yearnings, longings. It seems the pining for freedom is still stronger under a bright ray of sunlight than on a gray winter or autumn day, and that is noticeable in all prisoners. It is as if they are glad of the bright days, and at the same time some sort of impatience, of impulsiveness, intensifies in them. Indeed, I noticed that in the spring quarrels seemed to become more frequent in prison. Noise, shouts, din were heard more frequently, scandals broke out; and at the same time you would notice somebody at work somewhere gazing pensively and intently into the blue distance, there on the other side of the Irtysh, where the boundless stretch of the free Kirghiz steppe, a thousand miles of it, begins; you would hear somebody sigh deeply, with his whole chest, as if the man were longing to breathe in that faraway, free air and relieve his crushed, fettered soul. "Ah, well!" the prisoner finally says and all at once, as if shaking off his dreams and broodings, impatiently and sullenly picks up his spade or the bricks that have to be carried from one place to another. A minute later he has already forgotten his sudden sensation and begins to laugh or curse, according to his character; or else, with an extraordinary ardor out of all proportion with the need, he suddenly throws himself into his work assignment, if he has been given one, and begins to work—to work with all his might, as if he wishes to stifle in himself by heavy work something that is weighing on him and crushing him from inside. These are all strong folk, for the most part in the flower of their youth and strength . . . Fetters are heavy at that time of life! I am not poeticizing now and am convinced of the truth of my observations.

Besides the fact that, in warm weather, bathed in bright sunlight, when with your whole soul, with your whole being, you hear and feel nature resurrecting around you with boundless force, you feel all the more oppressed by the locked prison, the convoy, and the will of others; besides that, in this time of spring, across Siberia and across all Russia, with the first lark, the tramp's life begins: God's people escape from the jails and take refuge in the forests. After stuffy holes, after courts, fetters, and rods, they wander about entirely by their own will, wherever they like, wherever it looks more inviting and free; they drink and eat wherever and whatever they can, whatever God sends them, and at night they fall peacefully asleep in forest or field, with no great cares, with no prison anguish, like forest birds, saying good night before sleep only to the stars in heaven, under God's eye. It is sometimes a hard, hungry, exhausting life "serving General Cuckooshkin." Who says it's not! At times you go for whole days without a glimpse of bread; you have to lie low, to hide from everybody; you're forced to pilfer and rob, and sometimes even to kill. "Like exile, like child: where the eye falls, the hand follows"—so they say in Siberia about exiles. The phrase can be applied to tramps in its full force and even with a bit more added. It is rare that a tramp is not a robber, and he is almost always a pilferer, naturally more from necessity than by vocation. There are inveterate tramps. Some run away even after they have finished their term in prison and have already settled. It would seem they should be pleased to be settled and secure, but no! they're drawn somewhere, they're called away somewhere. Life in the forest, a life poor and terrible, but free and full of adventures, has something tempting about it, a sort of mysterious enchantment for those who have once experienced it, and— lo and behold—the man runs away, even a modest, conscientious man, who has promised to become a good, sedentary man and a sensible householder. A man may even marry, have children, live in the same place for five years, and suddenly, one fine morning, disappear somewhere, leaving his wife, children, and the whole neighborhood in bewilderment. One of these runaways was pointed out to me in prison. He had not committed any particular crimes, at least I never heard anything of the sort said of him, but he kept running away, all his life he was on the run. He had been to the southern border of Russia beyond the Danube, and in the Kirghiz steppe, and in eastern Siberia, and in the Caucasus—he had been everywhere. Who knows, maybe under different circumstances he would have become a sort of Robinson Crusoe with his passion for traveling. However, it was others who told me all this about him; he himself spoke little in prison, and then only said what was strictly necessary. He was a very small, puny muzhik, already about fifty years old, extremely docile, with an extremely calm and even stupid face, calm to the point of idiocy. In summer he liked to sit in the sun and would invariably hum some little song to himself, but so softly that it couldn't be heard five steps away. The features of his face were somehow wooden; he ate little, mostly bread; he never bought a single kalach or sup of vodka; it is doubtful that he ever had any money, doubtful that he even knew how to count. He regarded everything with perfect calm. He sometimes fed the prison dogs from his own hands, though none of us fed the prison dogs. Russian people generally don't like feeding dogs. It was said that he had been married, even twice; it was said that he had children somewhere . . . Why he landed in prison, I have no idea. We were all expecting him to slip away from us, too; but either his time hadn't come, or the years overtook him, and so he lived his life, regarding somehow contemplatively this whole strange milieu that surrounded him. However, there was no way to be certain; though you might wonder, why would he escape, and what would he gain by it? But meanwhile, all the same, on the whole, the forest, the tramp's life, is paradise compared to prison. It is so understandable; there can even be no comparison. Though it's hard still, it's your own will. That is why every prisoner in Russia, wherever he may be locked up, becomes somehow restless in spring, with the first welcoming rays of spring sunshine. By no means everybody intends to escape: one can say for certain that, difficulty and accountability considered, only one in a hundred ventures upon it; but the other ninety-nine at least dream of how it would be to escape and where they would escape to; they can at least unburden their hearts by the mere wish, by picturing the mere possibility. Some can at least recall how they escaped once long ago . . . I am speaking now of convicted prisoners. Those awaiting sentence, naturally, venture to escape far more often and in greater numbers. Convicts already serving a term escape, if at all, only at the beginning of their prison life. Having spent two or three years at hard labor, a prisoner comes to value those years and gradually accepts the thought that it is better to finish his term in legal fashion and go free as a settler than to venture upon such a risk and such ruin in the case of failure. And failure is so possible. Maybe only one in ten succeeds in *changing his lot.* Among convicted prisoners, those sentenced to very long terms also risk escaping more often than others. Fifteen or twenty years seem like an eternity, and a man sentenced to such a term is permanently prepared to dream of changing his lot, even if he has already knocked off ten years in prison. Finally, branding somewhat hinders a man from risking escape. "Changing one's lot" is a technical term. So, at interrogations, if a prisoner has been caught escaping, he answers that he wanted "to change his lot." This slightly bookish expression applies literally to the case. Every runaway has in mind not so much freeing himself completely—he knows that that is almost impossible—as either getting into another institution, or ending up as a settler, or going to trial again for a new crime—committed while he was a tramp—in short, anywhere you like, only not in the old place he's so sick of, not in the former prison. All these runaways, if in the course of the summer they don't happen to find some extraordinary place to spend the winter; if, for instance, they don't find someone who shelters runaways and makes a profit from it; if, finally, they don't get hold, sometimes by means of murder, of some passport with which they can live anywhere—by autumn all these runaways, if they're not caught before then, for the most part turn up in dense crowds in the towns and prisons, as tramps, and spend the winter behind bars, not without hope, of course, of escaping again in the summer.

Spring had its effect on me as well. I remember how I would sometimes look greedily through the chinks in the paling and stand for a long time, my head pressed against our fence, peering intently and insatiably at the grass greening on our prison rampart, while the distant sky turned a deeper and deeper blue. My restlessness and anguish increased with every day, and prison was becoming ever more hateful to me. The hatred which I, as a nobleman, experienced constantly from the prisoners during the first years became unbearable to me. It poisoned my whole life with its venom. In those first years, I often went to stay in the hospital, without any illness, solely so as not to be in the prison, so as to rid myself of that persistent, relentless, universal hatred. "You've got iron beaks, you've pecked us to death!" the prisoners would say to us, and how I used to envy the simple folk who came to the prison! They at once became comrades with everybody. And therefore spring, the phantom of freedom, the general rejoicing in nature, also told on me somehow sadly and irritably. At the end of Lent, I think in the sixth week, I had to prepare for communion.[2] Already in the first week, the senior sergeant had divided all the prisoners into seven shifts, for the number of weeks of Lent, to prepare in turn. So there happened to be about thirty men in each shift. I liked the week of preparation very much. Those preparing were relieved of work. We went to the church, which was not far from the prison, two or three times a day. I hadn't been to church for a long time. The services of the Great Lent, so familiar from far-off childhood in my parents' home, the solemn prayers, the bowing to the ground—all this stirred in my soul the distant past, brought back to me the impressions of my childhood years, and I remember having a very pleasant feeling when, in the morning, over ground slightly frozen the night before, we would be taken under armed convoy to the house of God. The convoy, however, did not enter the church. Inside the church, we stood in a compact group just by the door, in the last place, so that we only heard the vociferous deacon and occasionally, through the crowd, glimpsed the priest's black vestment and bald spot. I remembered how, in my childhood, standing in the church, I sometimes looked at the simple folk thickly crowding by the entrance and obsequiously parting before a pair of thick epaulettes, before a fat squire or a spruced-up but extremely pious lady, who unfailingly went to the first places and were ready every moment to fight for them. There, by the entrance, it seemed to me then, they were not praying as we were, they were praying humbly, zealously, bowing to the ground, and with a full awareness of their own lowliness.

Now I, too, had to stand in that same place, and not even in that place; we were shackled and disgraced; everybody shunned us, everybody even seemed to fear us, we were given alms each time, and, I remember, I was somehow even pleased by that, some sort of refined, peculiar sensation told itself in that strange satisfaction. "If so, let it be so!" I thought. The prisoners prayed very assiduously, and each of them each time brought his beggarly kopeck to church for a candle or the collection. "I'm also a human being," he may have thought or felt as he gave it. "Before God we're all equal . . ." We took communion at the early liturgy. When the priest holding the chalice recited the words ". . . but like the thief accept me,"[3] almost everybody fell to the ground, their fetters clanking, as if taking these words literally to their account.

But now Easter came. From the authorities we received one egg and a piece of fancy white bread. Alms from town again poured into the prison. Again the priest visited with the cross, again the authorities visited, again hearty shchi, again drunkenness and loafing—all exactly the same as at Christmas, with the difference that it was now possible to stroll in the prison yard and warm yourself in the sun. It was somehow more bright, more spacious than in winter, but somehow more anguished. The long, endless summer day became somehow especially unbearable during the holidays. Ordinarily the day was shortened by work.

The summer work indeed turned out to be much harder than the winter. The work went mostly into engineering constructions. Prisoners built, dug the earth, laid bricks; others were employed in the metalworking, joinery, and painting sections, repairing government buildings. Still others were sent to make bricks. This last work was considered the hardest of all. The brickyard was two or three miles from the fortress. Every day during the summer, at six o'clock in the morning, a whole party of prisoners, some fifty men, set off to make bricks. Unskilled laborers were chosen for this work, that is, not craftsmen or men versed in any trade. They took bread with them, because the place was far away and it was not worth going home to eat and thus doing an extra six miles, so they ate in the evening on returning to the prison. A task was set for the whole day, and one that would take the prisoner an entire working day to finish. First you had to dig up and transport the clay, bring the water yourself, knead the clay in a pit with your feet, and finally make it into a great many bricks, something like two hundred, if not even two hundred and fifty. I went to the brickyard only twice. People came home in the evening tired, worn out, and reproached the others all summer with the fact that they were doing the hardest work.

That, it seems, was their consolation. In spite of which, some even went there with a certain eagerness: first of all, the work was outside town, the place was open, free, on the bank of the Irtysh. In any case, you could look around more cheerfully; here was no hateful prison routine! You could smoke freely and even lie down for half an hour with the greatest pleasure. As for me, I either went to the workshop as before, or to the alabaster, or, finally, was used in the capacity of a brick carrier on a building site. In this last case I once had to carry bricks from the bank of the Irtysh to the building site of a barrack some five hundred feet away, over the fortress rampart, and that work went on for two months in a row. I even liked it, though the rope that the bricks had to be carried with constantly chafed my shoulders. But I liked it that this work was obviously developing my strength. At first I could lug only eight bricks, each brick weighing about twelve pounds. But later I got up to twelve or even fifteen bricks, and that made me very happy. In prison you need as much physical as moral strength to endure all the material inconveniences of that cursed life.

And I wanted to go on living after prison as well . . .

However, I liked lugging bricks not only because the work strengthened my body, but also because it took place on the bank of the Irtysh. I mention that bank so often because only from there could I see God's world, the pure, clear distance, the unpopulated, free steppe, which made a strange impression on me by its emptiness. Only on that bank could you turn your back to the fortress and not see it. All our other workplaces were inside the fortress or next to it. From the very first days I conceived a hatred for that fortress and especially for some of its buildings. Our major's house seemed to me some sort of cursed, repulsive place, and I glanced at it with hatred every time I passed by. On the bank you could forget yourself: you looked at that boundless, empty vastness exactly as an inmate looks out of his prison window at freedom. Everything there was dear and sweet to me: the bright, hot sun in the bottomless blue sky, and the far-off song of a Kirghiz, carried here from the Kirghiz side. You peer into it for a long time and finally make out the poor, sooty yurt of some native; you make out smoke by the yurt, a Kirghiz woman who is bustling about with her two sheep. It is all poor and wild, but free. You make out a bird in the blue, transparent air, and intently follow its flight for a long time: now it skims over the water, now it disappears into the blue, now it reappears as a fleeting dot . . . Even the poor, stunted flower I found in early spring in a crevice of the stony bank, even that somehow morbidly held my attention. The anguish of that whole first year at hard labor was unbearable, and it made me bitter and irritable. In that first year, because of that anguish, I did not notice many things around me. I closed my eyes and did not want to look. Among my malicious, hateful fellow convicts, I did not notice the good people, capable of thinking and feeling, despite all the revolting crust that covered them outside. Amidst the biting words, I sometimes did not notice a friendly and affectionate word, which was the dearer for being uttered without any purpose, and often straight from a heart that had perhaps suffered and endured more than mine. But why enlarge on that? I was extremely glad if I came back home dead tired: I might fall asleep! Because sleeping was a torment for us in summer, maybe even worse than in winter. True, the evenings were sometimes very nice. The sun, which never left the prison yard all day, would finally go down. Coolness would come, and after it the almost cold (comparatively speaking) steppe night. The prisoners, waiting to be locked in, would wander in groups around the yard. True, the main body of them crowded mostly in the kitchen. There some vital prison question was always raised, there was talk of one thing or another, some rumor was occasionally discussed, most often absurd, but which aroused an extraordinary attention in these people estranged from the world. Once, for instance, news came that our major was to be thrown out. Prisoners are as gullible as children; they themselves know that this news is nonsense, that it has been brought by a well-known bab-bler and "absurd" man—the prisoner Kvasov, whom they decided long ago not to believe, and whose every other word is a lie—and yet they all seize upon the news, talk it over, amuse themselves, and end by get-ting angry with themselves, being ashamed of themselves, for having believed Kvasov.

"So who's going to throw him out?" shouts one. "He's got a thick neck all right, he'll deal with it."

"But there's got to be superiors above him!" another objects, a hot-tempered fellow and no fool, a man who had seen all the sights, but a debater such as the world has never known.

"A raven won't peck out a raven's eye," a third observes sullenly, as if to himself, a gray-haired man, sitting alone in a corner finishing his shchi.

"As if those superiors are going to come and ask you if they should replace him or not?" a fourth adds indifferently, lightly strumming a balalaika.

"And why not?" the second retorts fiercely. "I mean, if all the poor people ask for it, then we've all got to speak up if they start questioning. With us everybody shouts all right, but when it gets down to business, they back out!"

"And what else?" says the balalaika player. "That's prison for you!"

"And the other day," the debater goes on, not listening and all afire, "there was flour left over. We scraped it up, the last drops of it, I mean; sent it to be sold. But no, he found out; the foreman denounced us; they took it away; economy, you know. Is that fair or not?"

"Who do you want to complain to?"

"Who to? To the isspector that's coming."

"What isspector's that?"

"It's true, brothers, an isspector's coming," says the sprightly young fellow, a literate man, a former scribe, who has read *The Duchess of La Vallière* or something of the sort. He is always jovial and amusing, but is respected for having a certain practical knowledge and worldly wear and tear. Paying no attention to the general curiosity aroused by the future inspector, he goes straight to the cooky and asks him for some liver. Our cookies often dealt in things of that sort. For instance, they would buy a big piece of liver on their own money, fry it, and then sell it in small pieces to the prisoners.

"Kopeck, half a kopeck?" asks the cooky.

"Cut me a kopeck's worth: let people envy me!" the prisoner answers. "It's a general, brothers, one of those generals from Petersburg, coming to look over all Siberia. It's a sure thing. They said so at the commandant's."

The news causes an unusual stir. For a quarter of an hour, questions go around: who precisely, which general, of what rank, and is he superior to the local generals? Prisoners are terribly fond of talking about ranks, authorities, who is superior among them, who can make others kowtow to him and who must do the kowtowing, and they even argue and curse and all but get into fights over it. What's the profit in it? you wonder. But a detailed familiarity with generals and authorities of all sorts was a measure of a man's knowledge, understanding, and former, pre-prison significance in society. In prison, conversation about the higher authorities is generally considered the most refined and important.

"So it turns out to be true, brothers, that they're coming to replace the major," observes Kvasov, a small, red-faced man, hot-tempered and extremely muddle-headed. He had been the first to bring the news about the major.

"He'll sweeten him up," the sullen, gray-haired prisoner, who had already dealt with his shchi, objects curtly.

"That he will," says another. "He's stashed away plenty of loot for himself! Before us he was a battalion commander. A while ago he wanted to marry the archpriest's daughter."

"But he didn't. They showed him the door, meaning he's a poor man. What kind of suitor is he? He got up from his chair—and that was it for him! He blew it all at cards during Holy Week. Fedka told us."

"Yes, he's a tight-fisted one, yet his money's all gone."

"Eh, brother, I was married, too. When a poor man marries, even the nights are too short!" observed Skuratov, turning up at this point in the conversation.

"Oh, yes! You're just the one we've been talking about," observed the casual former scribe. "And you are a great fool, Kvasov, let me tell you. Do you really think our major could sweeten up a general like him, and that a general like him would come from Petersburg to inspect a major? You're stupid, lad, that's what I say."

"You mean because he's a general he won't take?" someone in the crowd remarked skeptically.

"It's a known thing he won't, and if he does take, it'll be fat."

"Sure it'll be fat; to go with his rank."

"Generals always take," Kvasov observes resolutely.

"So you've tried it, have you?" Baklushin, suddenly coming in, says scornfully. "I bet you've never even seen a general!"

"I have, too!"

"Liar."

"Liar yourself."

"If he's seen one, boys, let him say now, in front of everybody, which general he knows. Well, speak up, because I know all the generals."

"I've seen General Ziebert," Kvasov replied somewhat hesitantly.

"Ziebert? There's no such general. This Zeeber must have looked you in the back when he was maybe still a lieutenant colonel, and you got so scared you imagined he was a general."

"No, you listen to me," Skuratov shouts, "because I'm a married man. There actually was such a general in Moscow. Ziebert, of German stock, but a Russian. He went to a Russian priest for confession every year during the Dormition fast,[4] and kept drinking water, brothers, just like a duck. Every day he drank forty glasses of Moskva River water. It was a cure for some illness, they said; his vallay told me so himself."

"He must've got a bellyful of carp from all that water," observes the prisoner with the balalaika.

"Well, enough from you! We're talking business here, and they . . . Who's this isspector, brothers?" a fidgety prisoner, Martynov, an old military man, a former hussar, asks solicitously.

"They're a bunch of liars!" one of the skeptics observes. "Where do they get it, and where do they put it? And it's all trash!"

"No, it's not trash!" Kulikov, who up to now has remained majestically silent, says dogmatically. He is a fellow of around fifty, of extremely handsome looks and with a contemptuously majestic and weighty manner. He is aware of it and is proud of it. He is part Gypsy, a veterinarian, earns money in town by treating horses, and trades in vodka in the prison. He is an intelligent man and has seen a lot. He utters a word like he's giving you a rouble.

"It's true, brothers," he calmly goes on, "I already heard it last week; a general's coming, a very important one, to inspect the whole of Siberia. He'll take sweeteners, that's a known thing, only not from our Eight-eyes: he won't even dare go near him. There's generals and generals, brothers. There's all kinds. Only I'm telling you, in any case our major'll stay just where he is. That's for sure. We've got no tongues, and the superiors won't denounce one of their own. The inspector'll look the prison over, and then just leave, and report that everything's in good order . . ."

"So there, brothers, and the major's turned coward: he's been drunk since morning."

"And in the evening a different wagonload drives up. Fedka said so."

"You can't wash a black dog white. What, is it the first time he's drunk?"

"No, what is it then, if the general doesn't do anything either! No, enough of going along with his foolery!" the agitated prisoners say among themselves.

Word of the inspector immediately spreads through the prison. People wander about the yard and impatiently give each other the news. Others purposely keep silent, preserving their equanimity, and thereby obviously trying to give themselves greater importance. Still others remain indifferent. Prisoners with balalaikas sit themselves on the porches of the barracks. Some go on chattering. Others strike up songs. But generally everyone that evening is in a state of extreme agitation.

After nine o'clock we were all counted, driven into the barracks, and locked up for the night. The nights were short; they woke us up between four and five, and we never fell asleep before eleven. Until then there would always be bustle, talk, and sometimes maidans, as in winter. During the night it was unbearably hot and stuffy. Though a bit of nighttime coolness wafts in through the open sash of the window, the prisoners thrash about on their cots all night as if in delirium. Fleas swarm in myriads. They thrive among us in winter, too, and in quite sufficient numbers, but, starting in spring, they multiply at such a rate that, though I had heard about it before, having had no actual experience of it, I had refused to believe it. And the closer to summer, the more vicious they become. True, you can get used to fleas, as I experienced myself; but all the same it doesn't come easy. Sometimes they torment you so much that you finally lie there as if in a fever, and you feel yourself that you're not asleep, but only delirious. Towards morning, when the fleas themselves finally calm down, as if in a swoon, and you really do seem to fall into a sweet sleep in the morning coolness—the pitiless rat-a-tat of the drum suddenly resounds by the prison gate, and reveille begins. Cursing, you listen, wrapping your sheepskin around you, to the loud, distinct sounds, as if counting them, and meanwhile, through sleep, the unbearable thought enters your head that it will be the same tomorrow, and the day after tomorrow, and for several years on end, all the way till freedom. But when will you be free, you think, and where is this freedom? And meanwhile you've got to wake up; the everyday walking and jostling begins . . . People get dressed, hurry to work. True, you can catch another hour of sleep at noon.

It was true what they said about the inspector. The rumors were confirmed more and more each day, and finally everybody knew for certain that an important general was coming from Petersburg to inspect the whole of Siberia, that he had already arrived, that he was already in Tobolsk. Each day new rumors reached the prison. News also came from town: we heard that everybody was frightened, aflutter, wanting to put on a good show. They said the high authorities were preparing receptions, balls, fêtes. Whole groups of prisoners were sent to level the streets in the fortress, raze the bumps, paint the fences and posts, plaster, patch—in short, they wanted to fix up in no time everything that had to be on show. Our men understood very well what it was about and discussed it among themselves ever more heatedly and fervently. Their fantasy reached colossal proportions. They even planned to present a *grievance*, if the general began asking about their contentment. And meanwhile they argued and quarreled among themselves. The major was nervous. He came to the prison more often, shouted more often, attacked people more often, locked them in the guardhouse more often, and kept a sharper eye on cleanliness and good order. At that time, as if on purpose, a little incident took place in the prison, which, however, did not upset the major in the least, as one might have expected, but, on the contrary, even afforded him pleasure. During a fight, one prisoner stabbed another in the chest with an awl, just near the heart.

The prisoner who committed the crime was named Lomov; the wounded man was known among us as Gavrilka; he was one of the inveterate tramps. I don't remember if he had any other name; we always called him Gavrilka.

Lomov was a well-to-do peasant from the K—sk district of T— province. The Lomovs lived together as a family: the old father, his three sons, and their uncle Lomov. They were wealthy muzhiks. The talk all over the province was that they had a capital of about three hundred thousand in banknotes. They farmed, dressed hides, traded, but most of all they engaged in usury, the harboring of tramps and stolen goods, and other artful dodges. Half the peasants of the district owed them money and were in bondage to them. They were reputed to be intelligent and cunning muzhiks, but in the end they became self-conceited, especially when a very important person in that area began to stop with them on his travels, made the personal acquaintance of the old man, and came to admire him for his shrewdness and resourcefulness. They suddenly got the notion that there was no more holding them back, and they started taking bigger and bigger risks in various illegal ventures. Everybody murmured against them; everybody wished the earth would swallow them; but they stuck their noses up more and more. Police chiefs and assessors meant nothing to them. Finally they came a cropper and were ruined, though not for anything bad, not for their secret crimes, but on a false accusation. They had a big farmstead, called a *zaïmka* in Siberia, some seven miles from the village. Once towards autumn they had six Kirghiz workers living there, in bondage to them from long ago. One night all these Kirghiz workers were murdered. An inquiry began. It went on for a long time. In the course of it many other bad things were uncovered. The Lomovs were accused of killing their workers. They told about it themselves, and the whole prison knew it: the suspicion was that they owed these workers too much, and since they were stingy and greedy, despite their great fortune, they murdered the Kirghiz to get out of paying what they owed. During the investigation and trial their entire fortune went up in smoke. The old man died. The children were scattered. One of the sons and his uncle landed in our prison for twelve years. And what then? They were completely innocent of the Kirghiz's deaths. Later, here in our prison, Gavrilka appeared, a notorious rogue and tramp, a merry and glib fellow, who took this whole affair upon himself. Though I never heard that he had confessed to it, the whole prison was fully convinced that those Kirghiz were his doing. While still a tramp, Gavrilka had had dealings with the Lomovs. He came to the prison on a short sentence as a runaway soldier and tramp. He and three other tramps had murdered the Kirghiz; they had thought to profit greatly by robbing the farmstead.

The Lomovs were not liked among us, I don't know why. One of them, the nephew, was a fine fellow, intelligent and easy to get along with; but his uncle, who stabbed Gavrilka with the awl, was a stupid and cantankerous muzhik. He had quarreled with many people before then, and had been properly beaten. Everybody liked Gavrilka for his merry and easy character. Though the Lomovs knew he was a criminal and they had come there by his doing, they didn't quarrel with him; however, they also never kept company with him; nor did he pay any attention to them. And suddenly he had a quarrel with the uncle Lomov over a certain disgusting wench. Gavrilka started boasting of her favors; the muzhik got jealous and one fine noonday stabbed him with an awl.

Though the Lomovs had been ruined by their trial, in prison they lived like rich men. They obviously had money. They owned a samovar, drank tea. Our major knew about that and hated both Lomovs to the utmost degree. He picked on them and tried to get at them, as was obvious to everyone. The Lomovs explained it by the major's desire to extract a bribe from them. But they gave him no bribes.

Of course, if Lomov had stuck the awl in a little deeper, he would certainly have killed Gavrilka. But the affair ended decidedly with nothing but a scratch. It was reported to the major. I remember how he came galloping, breathless and obviously pleased. He treated Gavrilka with astonishing tenderness, just like his own son.

"Well, my friend, can you make it to the hospital or not? No, better hitch up a horse for him. Hitch up a horse at once!" he shouted breathlessly to the sergeant.

"But, Your Honor, I don't feel a thing. He just pricked me a little, Your Honor."

"You don't know, you don't know, my dear fellow; you'll see . . . It's a dangerous spot; everything depends on the spot; he hit you right by the heart, the villain! And you, you," he roared at Lomov, "now I'm going to get you! . . . To the guardhouse!"

And he really did get him. Lomov was put on trial, and though the wound turned out to be just a slight prick, the intention was obvious. The criminal's term at hard labor was extended, and he got a thousand rods. The major was quite pleased . . .

Finally, the inspector arrived.

The day after his arrival in town he came to us in the prison. It was a Sunday. Several days earlier, we already had everything scrubbed, polished, licked clean. The prisoners were freshly shaved. Their clothes were clean and white. In the summer, according to regulations, everybody wore white linen jackets and trousers. On the back of each a black circle some four inches in diameter was sewn. The prisoners spent a whole hour being taught how to respond if the exalted person happened to greet them. Rehearsals were held. The major rushed about like a madman. An hour before the general's appearance we were all standing in our places like statues, arms at our sides. Finally, at one o'clock in the afternoon, the general came. He was an important general, so important that it seemed all the official hearts must have been fluttering all over western Siberia on account of his arrival. He entered sternly and majestically; after him a large suite of attending local officials came pouring in; a few generals, colonels. There was one civilian, a tall and handsome gentleman in a tailcoat and low boots, who also came from Petersburg and bore himself with extreme ease and independence. The general often addressed him, and highly courteously. This aroused extraordinary interest among the prisoners: a civilian, but such esteem, and that from such a general! Afterwards we found out his name and who he was, but meanwhile there were a great many rumors. Our major, laced up tight, with an orange collar, bloodshot eyes, a purple face covered with blackheads, did not seem to make an especially favorable impression on the general. Out of special respect for the exalted visitor, he had removed his glasses. He stood at a distance, drawn up to attention, his whole being expressing a feverish anticipation of the moment when he would be needed for something, so as to fly and carry out his excellency's wishes. But he was not needed for anything. The general silently went about the barracks, looked into the kitchen, apparently tried the shchi. They pointed me out to him: So-and-so, they said, a nobleman.

"Ah!" replied the general. "And how is he behaving himself now?"

"Satisfactorily so far, Your Excellency," they replied to him.

The general nodded and two minutes later left the prison. The prisoners, of course, were bedazzled and bemused, but all the same were left in some perplexity. Any grievance against the major was, naturally, out of the question. And the major had been quite certain of it beforehand.

VI

Prison Animals

The buying of Gnedko,* which took place soon afterwards, occupied and entertained the prisoners far more pleasantly than the exalted visit. We were supposed to have a horse in the prison to deliver water, take away sewage, and so on. A prisoner was appointed to look after him. He also drove him, under convoy naturally. There was quite enough work for our horse, both morning and evening. Gnedko had already served us for a very long time. He was a good horse, but a bit worn out. One fine morning, just before St. Peter's Day,[1] having delivered the evening barrel, Gnedko collapsed and died a few minutes later. We were sorry for him, everybody gathered around, talked, argued. Those among us who were former cavalrymen, Gypsies, veterinarians, and so on, even displayed on the occasion a great deal of specific knowledge in the horse line, even quarreled among themselves, but failed to resurrect Gnedko. He lay dead, with a swollen belly which everybody considered it his duty to poke with his finger; they reported to the major about God's will being done, and he decided that a new horse should be bought at once. On St. Peter's Day, in the morning, after the liturgy, when we were all there in full house, the horses up for sale were brought. It went without saying that the buying would be entrusted to the prisoners themselves. There were real connoisseurs among us, and to dupe two hundred and fifty men, who had previously been occupied only with that, was difficult. Kirghiz, horse traders, Gypsies, townsfolk turned up. The prisoners waited impatiently for the appearance of each new horse. They were happy as children. Most of all they were flattered that here they were, just like free men, just like they really were buying a horse for *themselves*, out of *their own* pocket, and had every right to do so. Three horses were led in and led out again, before they

---

* Literally "bay boys," from *gnedoi* ("bay"). *Translator.*

settled on the fourth. The entering traders looked around with some amazement and as if timidly, and even glanced now and then at the convoy soldiers who brought them in. A crowd of two hundred such people, shaven, branded, in fetters, and at home in their convicts' nest, the threshold of which nobody ever crosses, inspired its own sort of respect. Our men outdid each other in various stratagems for testing each horse. They examined them all over, felt them everywhere, and did it with such a businesslike, serious, and preoccupied air as if the very well-being of the prison depended on it. The Circassians even leaped onto the horses' backs; their eyes glowed, and they chattered rapidly in their incomprehensible language, baring their white teeth and nodding their swarthy, hook-nosed faces. Some of the Russians simply riveted all their attention on their debate, as if they wanted to jump into their eyes. They didn't understand the words, so they wanted to guess by the look in their eyes what had been decided: would the horse do, or not? To an outside observer such strained attention might even seem odd. Why, you wonder, should some prisoner, and a run-of-the-mill, humble, downtrodden prisoner at that, who doesn't dare make a peep even before his own fellow prisoners, get so especially hot and bothered here? As if he were buying a horse for himself, as if it were not all the same to him which one they bought? Besides the Circassians, the former Gypsies and horse traders distinguished themselves most: they were granted the first place and the first word. Here a sort of noble duel even took place between two of them—the prisoner Kulikov, a former Gypsy, a horse thief and trader; and a self-taught veterinarian, a cunning Siberian muzhik recently arrived in prison, who had already managed to win away all of Kulikov's town practice. The thing was that our self-taught prison veterinarians were highly valued by the whole town, and not only tradesmen and merchants, but even the highest ranks turned to the prison when their horses were sick, though the town had several real veterinarians. Before the arrival of Yelkin, the Siberian muzhik, Kulikov knew no rivals, had a large practice, and, naturally, received monetary rewards. He played the Gypsy and charlatan to the hilt, and knew much less than he pretended. In terms of income, he was an aristocrat among us. By his experience, his intelligence, his courage and resolution, he had long since inspired an involuntary respect for himself in all the inmates of the prison. He was listened to and obeyed among us. But he spoke little: he spoke as if he was giving a rouble, and that only in the most important cases. He was decidedly a showoff, but there was much real, unfeigned energy in him. He was already on in years, but very handsome, very intelligent. He treated us noblemen with a sort of refined courtesy, and at the same time with extraordinary dignity. I think if he were dressed up and brought in the guise of a count to some club in the capital, he would find his bearings, play whist, speak excellently well, not much, but with great weight, and the whole evening might go by without anyone figuring out that he was not a count, but a tramp. I'm speaking seriously: so intelligent he was, sharp, and quick on the uptake. Then, too, he had the fine manners of a dandy. He must have seen all sorts of sights in his life. However, his past was shrouded in the darkness of the unknown. He lived in our special section. But with the arrival of Yelkin, who, though a muzhik, was a very cunning muzhik, some fifty years old, a schismatic, Kulikov's veterinary fame was eclipsed. In some two months Yelkin won away almost all of his town practice. He cured, and very easily, horses that Kulikov had given up on long ago. He even cured the ones that the town veterinarians had given up on. This little muzhik came to us along with some others for false coinage. He just had to get involved, in his old age, as a partner in such doings! He told us, laughing at himself, that from three real gold pieces they only managed to produce one false one. Kulikov was somewhat offended by his veterinary successes, and his own fame among the prisoners even began to fade. He kept a mistress on the outskirts, wore a velveteen waistcoat, had a silver ring, an earring, and his own boots with trimming, and suddenly, for lack of income, he was forced to become a taverner, and therefore everybody expected that now, at the buying of the new horse, the enemies might, for all they knew, get into a fight. They all waited with curiosity. Each had his own party. The leaders of both parties were beginning to get worked up and exchanged some curses. Yelkin himself had already twisted his cunning face into a most sarcastic smile. But it turned out otherwise: Kulikov never thought of cursing, but acted masterfully without that. He began by yielding, he even listened respectfully to his rival's critical opinions, but, catching him on one word, modestly and insistently pointed out to him that he was mistaken, and before Yelkin had time to gather his wits and defend himself, proved that he was mistaken precisely on this point and on that. In short, Yelkin was quite unexpectedly and artfully thrown off, and though he still had the upper hand, Kulikov's party also remained pleased.

"No, boys, you know, you won't throw him off so quickly, he can stand up for himself!" they said.

"Yelkin knows more!" observed the others, but somehow yieldingly. Both parties suddenly began to speak in an extremely yielding tone.

"It's not that he knows more, he just has a lighter hand. But Kulikov won't be fazed when it comes to livestock."

"The fellow won't be fazed!"

"That he won't . . ."

The new Gnedko was finally chosen and bought. He was a nice little horse, young, handsome, strong, and with an extremely kind, cheerful look. Naturally, in all other respects he turned out to be irreproachable. There was some bargaining: the asking price was thirty roubles, our men offered twenty-five. They bargained hot and long, offering less, then giving way. In the end they found it funny themselves.

"Are you taking the money from your own purse, or what?" said some. "Why this bargaining?"

"Sparing the treasury, are you?" cried others.

"All the same, brothers, all the same it's the collective's money . . ."

"The collective's! No, obviously, fools like us aren't planted, we spring up by ourselves . . ."

In the end a bargain was struck for twenty-eight roubles. It was reported to the major, and the purchase was concluded. Naturally, bread and salt were brought out at once, and the new Gnedko was led into the prison with honor. It seemed there was not a prisoner who on that occasion did not pat him on the neck or stroke his muzzle. On that same day Gnedko was harnessed to bring in water, and everybody watched with curiosity as the new Gnedko hauled his barrel. Our water carrier, Roman, kept glancing at the new horse with extraordinary self-satisfaction. He was a muzhik of about fifty, of staid and taciturn character. But then, all Russian coachmen tend to be of extremely staid and even taciturn character, as if it were indeed true that the constant handling of horses endows a man with a special staidness and even importance. Roman was quiet, gentle with everybody, unloquacious, took snuff from a pouch, and from time immemorial had always looked after the prison Gnedkos. The newly purchased one was the third. We were all convinced that a bay coat suited the prison, that it was the right color for *our house*. Roman maintained the same thing. Never, for instance, would we have bought a piebald. The post of water carrier was, by some right, permanently reserved for Roman, and none of us would ever have thought of disputing that right with him. When the previous Gnedko fell dead, it never entered anyone's head, not even the major's, to accuse Roman of anything: it was the will of God, that was all, and Roman was a good coachman. Gnedko soon became the prison favorite. The prisoners, though they were stern folk, often came to pet him. Coming back from the river, Roman used to lock the gate that the sergeant had opened for him, and Gnedko, going into the prison yard, would stand with the barrel and wait for him, looking at him sidelong. "Go by yourself!" Roman would shout to him, and Gnedko would at once go on alone, get as far as the kitchen, and stop, waiting for the cooks and the slop men with their pails to come and fetch water. "Smart boy, Gnedko!" the men would shout to him. "Brought it by himself! . . . Does what he's told."

"It's really so: a brute, but he understands!"

"Good boy, Gnedko!"

Gnedko shakes his head and snorts, as if he really does understand and is pleased to be praised. And somebody inevitably brings out bread and salt for him. Gnedko eats and again nods his head, as if to say: "I know you, I do! I'm a nice horse, and you're a good man!"

I also liked to give Gnedko bread. It was somehow pleasant to look at his pretty muzzle and feel his soft, warm lips on my palm as they promptly picked up the offering.

Generally, our prisoners were capable of loving animals, and if they had been allowed to, they would eagerly have raised lots of domestic livestock and birds in prison. And what, it seems, could have softened and ennobled the stern, brutal character of the prisoners more, for instance, than such an occupation? But it was not allowed. Neither our regulations nor the place permitted it.

During my time, however, chance brought several animals to our prison. Besides Gnedko, we had dogs, geese, the billy goat Vaska, and for a while an eagle also lived with us.

In the quality of permanent prison dog, as I have already said before, we had Sharik, an intelligent and kind dog, with whom I was permanent friends. But since among simple folk dogs are generally considered unclean animals to whom no attention should be paid, almost nobody among us paid any attention to Sharik. The dog just lived there, slept in the yard, ate kitchen scraps, and aroused no special interest in anybody, though he knew everybody and considered everybody in the prison his master. When the prisoners returned from work and he heard the shout "Corporal!" by the guardhouse, he ran to the gate, affectionately greeted each party, wagging his tail and affably trying to catch the eye of each man who came through the gate, waiting for at least some affection. But in the course of many years, he got no affection from anyone except me. Because of that, he loved me most of all. I don't remember how it was that another dog, Belka, later turned up in the prison. A third, Kultyapka, I myself brought back from work one day, still a puppy. Belka was a strange creature. She had been run over by a cart, and her back was curved inwards, so that when she ran, it looked from a distance as if two white animals grown together were running. Besides, she was all mangy, with festering eyes; her tail was bare, almost without fur, and permanently tucked between her legs. Insulted by fate, she had obviously decided to submit. She never barked or growled at anybody, as if she didn't dare. She lived mostly behind the barracks, in hopes of food; if she happened to see one of us, she would immediately roll over on her back, while still some steps away, in a sign of submission, as if to say: "Do what you like with me, you can see I have no thought of resisting." And each prisoner she rolled over in front of would kick her with his boot, as if he considered it his unfailing duty: "Take that, you creep!" he would say. But Belka didn't even dare to yelp, and if the pain really got to her, she would produce a muted, plaintive yowl. She rolled over in the same way in front of Sharik and in front of any other dog, when she went outside the prison on business of her own. She would roll over and lie there submissively when some big, lop-eared dog came rushing at her roaring and barking. But dogs like submissiveness and obedience in their own kind. The fierce dog would immediately calm down, pause somewhat pensively over the obedient dog lying legs up in front of him, and slowly, with great curiosity, begin to sniff all parts of her body. What could the trembling Belka have been thinking at that moment? "Is the robber going to tear me apart?" probably went through her head. But, having sniffed her over attentively, the dog would finally abandon her, finding nothing of particular interest in her. Belka would jump up at once and again go hobbling behind the long line of dogs accompanying some Zhuchka or other. And though she knew for certain that she would never become closely acquainted with Zhuchka, this hobbling along at a distance was still a comfort to her in her misfortunes. She had obviously stopped thinking about honor. Having lost any future career, she lived only for the sake of food and was fully aware of it. I once tried to pet her; this was so new and unexpected for her that she suddenly sank to the ground on all four paws, trembled all over, and began to squeal loudly from tender feeling. I patted her often out of pity. She couldn't see me without squealing. She would catch sight of me and squeal, squeal painfully and tearfully. It ended with her being torn to pieces by other dogs on the rampart behind the prison.

Kultyapka was of a totally different character. Why I brought him from the workshop to the prison while still a blind puppy, I don't know. I enjoyed feeding him and raising him. Sharik immediately took Kultyapka under his protection and slept with him. When Kultyapka began to grow up, he allowed him to nip his ears, tear at his fur, and play with him, the way grown-up dogs usually play with puppies. Strangely, Kultyapka almost didn't grow in height, but all in length and breadth. His fur was shaggy, of a light mousy color; one ear stood up, the other hung down. He was of an ardent and rapturous character, like all puppies, who, from joy at seeing their master, would squeal, bark, come to lick his face, and are ready to lose control of all their other feelings in front of you: "Proprieties mean nothing, if only you see my rapture!" Wherever I might be, at the shout "Kultyapka!" he would suddenly appear from around the corner, as if from nowhere, and with squealing rapture would come flying to me, rolling like a ball and turning somersaults on the way. I became terribly fond of the little monster. It seemed that fate had prepared only pleasures and joys for him in his life. But one fine day the prisoner Neustroev, whose occupation was stitching women's shoes and dressing skins, took special note of him. Something suddenly struck him. He called Kultyapka over, felt his fur, and rolled him over affectionately on the ground. Kultyapka, suspecting nothing, squealed with delight. But the next morning he disappeared. I looked a long time for him; he had vanished without a trace; and only two weeks later was it all explained: Neustroev had taken a great liking to Kultyapka's fur. He had skinned him, dressed the hide, and used it to line the velvet winter half boots the auditor's wife had commissioned from him. He showed me the half boots when they were ready. The fur had come out astonishingly well. Poor Kultyapka!

Many people in our prison were occupied with dressing hides and often brought in dogs with good pelts, who instantly vanished. Some had been stolen, and some had even been bought. I remember I once saw two prisoners behind the kitchen. They were deliberating on something and bustling about. One of them was holding a magnificent big dog, obviously of a valuable breed, on a rope. Some scoundrel of a lackey had stolen him from his master and sold him to our shoemakers for thirty silver kopecks. The prisoners were about to hang him. This could all be done very handily: they would remove the hide and throw the body into the big and deep refuse pit, which was in the farthest corner of the prison and stank terribly in summer, when the heat was intense. It was occasionally cleaned. The poor dog seemed to understand the fate being prepared for him. He glanced questioningly and uneasily at the three of us in turn and only occasionally ventured to wag his bushy tail, which he kept between his legs, as if wishing to soften us by this sign of his trust in us. I quickly left, and they, naturally, finished their business successfully.

Geese also came to us somehow by chance. Who brought them, and whom they actually belonged to, I don't know, but for some time they amused the prisoners greatly and even became known in town. They were hatched in the prison and kept in the kitchen. When the brood grew up, the whole gaggle of them got into the habit of going out to work with the prisoners. As soon as the drum roll sounded and the inmates moved towards the gates, our geese would rush honking after us, spreading their wings, jump one after the other over the high threshold of the gateway, and unfailingly make for the right flank, where they would line up waiting for the assignments to be made. They always joined the biggest party and grazed somewhere nearby while the work went on. As soon as the party headed back from work to the prison, they also got up to go. Rumor spread through the fortress that the geese were going to work with the prisoners. "Look, the prisoners are coming with their geese!" people meeting them would say. "How did you train them to do it?" "Here's for your geese!" someone else would add, giving them alms. But in spite of all their devotion, they were all slaughtered for some festive meal.

On the other hand, our billy goat, Vaska, would never have been slaughtered, had it not been for a special circumstance. I also don't know where he came from and who brought him, but suddenly a small, white, very pretty little goat turned up in the prison. After a few days we all got to love him, and he became our general entertainment and even delight. A reason was found for keeping him: it was necessary to keep a goat in the prison stables.[2] However, he didn't live in the stables, but first in the kitchen, and then all over the prison. He was a most graceful and frolicsome creature. He came running when called, jumped onto the benches and tables, butted the prisoners, was always merry and amusing. Once, when he had already cut good-sized horns, the Lezgin Babai, sitting on the barrack porch one evening in a group of other prisoners, decided to butt heads with him. They butted each other's foreheads for a long time—that being the prisoners' favorite amuse-ment with the goat—when Vaska suddenly leaped onto the upper step of the porch, and the moment Babai looked away, he instantly reared up, pressing his front hoofs to his body, and hit Babai on the back of the head with all his might, sending him tumbling off the porch, to the delight of all those present and of Babai first of all. In short, everybody was terribly fond of Vaska. When he began to grow up, a general and serious conference was held, as a result of which a certain operation was performed on him, which our veterinarians knew perfectly well how to do. "Otherwise he'll smell of goat," the prisoners said. After that Vaska grew terribly fat. And they fed him as if for the slaughter. In the end he grew into a fine, big billy goat, with the longest horns and of an extraordinary corpulence. He waddled when he walked. He also got into the habit of going to work with us, to the amusement of the prisoners and the public we met. Everybody knew the prison goat Vaska. Sometimes, if they were working, for instance, on the riverbank, the prisoners would tear off flexible willow branches, gather leaves of some sort, pick some flowers on the ramparts, and decorate Vaska with it all: weave the branches and flowers around his horns, hang garlands all over his body. Vaska always used to go back to the prison at the head of the prisoners, adorned and decked out, and they walked behind him as if priding themselves before the passersby. This admiration of the goat went so far that some of them even came up with a childish idea: "Why not gild Vaska's horns?" But they only talked about it, and didn't do it. However, I remember asking Akim Akimych, our best gilder after Isai Fomich, if you could in fact gild a goat's horns. He first looked the goat over attentively, then considered seriously and replied that maybe you could, but it wouldn't last and besides was completely useless. The matter ended there. Vaska would have lived a long time in the prison and died, probably, of shortness of breath, but one day, coming back from work at the head of the prisoners, adorned and decked out, he ran into the major driving in his droshky. "Stop!" he bellowed. "Whose goat is that?" It was explained to him. "What? A goat in the prison, and without my permission? Sergeant!" The sergeant appeared at once and was ordered to slaughter the goat immediately. To skin him, sell the hide at the market, add the money to the official prison purse, and put the meat into the prisoners' shchi. There was much talk and regret in the prison, but they did not dare disobey. Vaska was slaughtered over our refuse pit. One of the prisoners bought all of the meat, paying a rouble and a half into the prison purse. The money was spent on kalachi, and the man who had bought Vaska sold him in pieces to his fellows for roasting. The meat turned out in fact to be remarkably tasty.

An eagle, a karagush (a breed of small steppe eagles), also lived with us in prison for a time. Somebody brought him to the barrack wounded and suffering. The prisoners all stood around him; he couldn't fly; his right wing hung down, and one leg was dislocated. I remember how fiercely he looked around at the curious crowd and opened his hooked beak, prepared to sell his life dearly. When they had looked at him enough and began to disperse, he hobbled off, limping, skipping on his one leg and flapping his good wing, to the farthest end of the prison, where he huddled in a corner, pressing himself close to the palings. There he lived for some three months, and in all that time he never left his corner. At first people often went to look at him and set the dog on him. Sharik attacked him fiercely, but was obviously afraid to get close, which amused the prisoners greatly: "He's wild, he won't give himself up!" they said. Later Sharik also began to hurt him badly; his fear left him, and when they set him on, he managed to catch him by the injured wing. The eagle defended himself with all his might, claws and beak, and huddled in his corner, gazing proudly and wildly, like a wounded king, at the curious who came to look at him. In the end they all got tired of him; they abandoned him and forgot him, and yet each day you could see scraps of raw meat and a crock of water beside him. Somebody must have been looking after him. At first he refused to eat, didn't eat for several days; in the end he started to take food, but never from men's hands or in front of them. I happened to watch him more than once from a distance. Seeing no one and thinking he was alone, he sometimes ventured to leave his corner and hobble along the fence, some twelve paces from his place, then went back, then went out again, as if doing it for exercise. Catching sight of me, he hurried back to his place at once, limping and skipping with all his might, and, throwing back his head, opening his beak, all ruffled up, at once prepared for battle. I couldn't soften him with any affection: he bit and thrashed, refused to take beef from me, and all the while I stood over him, looked me fixedly in the eye with his angry, piercing gaze. Solitary and angry, he awaited death, trusting no one and making peace with no one. At last, it was as if the prisoners remembered him, and though no one had bothered with him, though no one had even mentioned him for two months, it was as if they all suddenly felt compassion for him. They said the eagle ought to be taken out. "Let him die, but not in prison," some said.

"Right, he's a free, tough bird, he's not used to prison," others agreed.

"Meaning he's not like us," somebody added.

"What blather: he's a bird, and we're men."

"The eagle, brothers, is the king of the forests . . . ," Skuratov began, but this time nobody listened to him. One day, after lunch and the drum roll to go back to work, they took the eagle, holding his beak tight, because he began to struggle fiercely, and carried him out of the prison. They came to the ramparts. The twelve men who made up the party were curious to see where the eagle would go. Strangely, they were all pleased at something, as if they were getting a share of his freedom.

"Look at this dog's-meat: you do him good, and he keeps biting!" said the man who was holding him, looking at the angry bird almost with love.

"Let him go, Mikitka!"

"Can't fob him off with any humbuggery. Got to give him freedom, downright free freedom!"

They threw the eagle from the rampart into the steppe. It was late autumn, a cold and gloomy day. Wind whistled over the bare steppe and rustled through the yellow, withered clumps of steppe grass. The eagle went straight off, waving his injured wing and as if hurrying to get away from us wherever his legs would carry him. The prisoners followed with curiosity the way his head kept flashing up from the grass.

"See him go!" one said thoughtfully.

"And he doesn't look back!" added another. "Hasn't looked back once, brothers, he's running for it!"

"So you thought he'd come back to thank us?" observed a third.

"Freedom, right enough. He's feeling his freedom."

"Meaning liberty."

"Can't see him anymore, brothers . . ."

"What're you standing there for! March!" the convoy shouted, and we all silently trudged off to work.

VII

The Grievance

In beginning this chapter, the editor of the late Alexander Petrovich Goryanchikov's notes considers it his duty to make the following report to the reader.

In the first chapter of *Notes from a Dead House*, a few words were said about a certain parricide from the nobility. Among other things, he was held up as an example of the callousness with which prisoners sometimes speak of the crimes they have committed. It was also said that the murderer had not confessed his crime before the court, but that, judging by what people told who knew all the details of his story, the facts were so clear that it was impossible not to believe in his crime. The same people told the author of the *Notes* that the criminal's behavior had been totally dissolute, that he had fallen into debt and had killed his father out of a craving for his inheritance. However, the whole town where this parricide had formerly served told the same story. Of this last fact the editor of the *Notes* has rather reliable information. Finally, we are told in the *Notes* that in prison the murderer was always in the most excellent, the merriest spirits; that he was a whimsical, light-minded man, unreasonable in the highest degree, though by no means a fool, and that the author of the *Notes* never noticed any particular cruelty in him. And right there the words are added: "Of course, I did not believe in that crime."

The other day the editor of *Notes from a Dead House* received information from Siberia that the criminal was indeed in the right and had suffered ten years of hard labor for nothing; that his innocence had been revealed in court, officially. That the real criminals had been found and had confessed, and the unfortunate man had already been released from prison. The editor can in no way doubt the truthfulness of this news . . .

There is nothing more to add. There is no point in talking and expanding upon all the depths of the tragic in this fact, upon the ruining of a still young life under such a terrible accusation. The fact is all too clear, all too shocking in itself.

We also think that if such a fact turns out to be possible, then the possibility itself adds another new and extremely striking feature to the description and full portrayal of the *Dead House*.

And now let us go on.

I have already said earlier that I finally adjusted to my situation in prison. But this "finally" was accomplished with great strain and suffering, and all too gradually. In fact, it took me nearly a year, and that was the hardest year of my life. That is why it has been stored away all of a piece in my memory. It seems to me that I remember each hour of that year in succession. I have also said that other prisoners, too, could not *get used* to that life. I remember often reflecting to myself during that first year: "What, how are they, can they really be at peace?" These questions preoccupied me very much. I have already mentioned that the prisoners all lived as if they were not at home, but in an inn, on a march, at some sort of stopping place. Even people sent up for life fidgeted or pined away, and each of them certainly dreamed of something almost impossible. This eternal restlessness, manifesting itself silently but visibly; this strange fervor and impatience of sometimes involuntarily expressed hopes, at times so unfounded that they were more like raving, and, what was most striking of all, that often dwelt in the most practical-seeming minds—all this gave the place an extraordinary appearance and character, so much so that these features may have constituted its most characteristic qualities. You somehow felt, almost from the first glance, that there was none of this outside prison. Here everyone was a dreamer, and that jumped into your eyes. You felt it painfully, precisely because this dreaminess lent the majority of the prisoners a gloomy and dismal, somehow unhealthy look. The great majority were silent and spiteful to the point of hatred, and did not like to openly display their hopes. Simple-heartedness and candor were held in contempt. The more unrealizable the hopes were, and the more the dreamer himself felt that unrealizability, the more stubbornly and chastely he concealed them within himself, but renounce them he could not. Who knows, maybe some were secretly ashamed of them. In the Russian character there is so much of the positive and sober-minded, so much inner mockery of oneself first of all . . . Maybe it was because of this constant secret dissatisfaction with themselves that there was so much impatience in these people in everyday relations with each other, so much resentment and mockery of each other. And if, for instance, someone of a more naïve and impatient sort should suddenly pop up among them and express aloud what was in all of their minds, should start dreaming and hoping, he would immediately be rudely checked, cut short, derided; but I suspect that the most zealous of the persecutors would be precisely those who themselves perhaps went still further in their dreams and hopes. The naïve and simple-minded, as I've already said, were generally looked upon among us as the most banal fools and were treated with contempt. Each man of us was so gloomy and vain that he had contempt for anyone who was kind and without vanity. Apart from these naïve and simple-minded babblers, all the rest, that is, the silent ones, were sharply divided into the good and the wicked, the gloomy and the bright. There were incomparably more of the gloomy and wicked; if there happened to be some among them who were talkative by nature, they were all inevitably restless gossips and anxious enviers. They minded everybody else's business, yet never exposed their own soul, their own secret business, to anybody. It wasn't the fashion, it wasn't done. The good—a very small group—were quiet, silently kept their expectations to themselves, and, naturally, were more inclined than the gloomy to have hopes and to believe in them. However, it seems to me that there was also a category in the prison of those in total despair. One such, for instance, was the old man from the Starodubsky settlements; in any case there were very few of them. The old man looked calm (I've already spoken of him), but, judging by certain signs, I suspect his inner state was terrible. However, he had his own salvation, his own way out: prayer and the idea of martyrdom. Having gone out of his mind, the Bible-reading prisoner, whom I have already mentioned and who attacked the major with a brick, was probably also one of those in despair, those whose last hope had abandoned them; and since it is impossible to live with no hope at all, he invented a way out for himself in a voluntary, almost artificial martyrdom. He declared that he had attacked the major without anger, but solely from a wish to embrace suffering. And who knows what psychological process had gone on in his soul then! No living man lives without some sort of goal and a striving towards it. Having lost both goal and hope, a man often turns into a monster from anguish . . . The goal of all of us was freedom and getting out of prison.

However, here I am now trying to sort our whole prison into categories; but is that possible? Reality is infinitely diverse compared to all, even the most clever, conclusions of abstract thought, and does not suffer sharp and big distinctions. Reality tends towards fragmentation. We, too, had our own particular life, of whatever sort, but at least we had it, and not only an official, but an inner life of our own.

But, as I've already partly mentioned, I could not and did not even know how to penetrate to the inner depths of this life at the beginning of my time in prison, and therefore all its external manifestations tormented me with an inexpressible anguish. Sometimes I would simply begin to hate these men, who were sufferers the same as I was. I even envied them and blamed fate. I envied them for being in any case among their own kind, with comrades, and able to understand each other, though in fact they were all as sick of it as I was and loathed this comradeship under the lash and stick, this forced association, and each inwardly turned away from it all. I repeat again, this envy that visited me in moments of anger had its legitimate grounds. Indeed, they are decidedly wrong who say that for a nobleman, an educated man and so on, the hardship in our prisons and labor camps is exactly the same as for any muzhik. I know, I heard of that supposition just recently, I read about it. The grounds for this idea are just, humane. We're all people, all human beings. But the idea is too abstract. It loses sight of a great many practical considerations that cannot be understood otherwise than in reality itself. I say this not because the noble and the educated supposedly feel things more refinedly, more painfully, because they are more developed. It is difficult to submit the soul and its development to any given standard. Even education itself is not a measure in this case. I will be the first to testify that in the most uneducated, in the most downtrodden milieu of these sufferers I have met with features of the most refined inner development. In prison it sometimes happened that you would know a man for several years and think he was a beast, not a man, and despise him. And suddenly a chance moment would come when his soul, on an involuntary impulse, would open up and you would see in it such riches, feeling, heart, such a clear understanding of his own and others' suffering, as if your own eyes had been opened, and in the first moment you would not even believe what you saw and heard. The reverse also happens: education sometimes goes along with such barbarity, such cynicism, that you loathe it, and however kind or well-disposed you may be, you can find neither excuses nor justifications for it in your heart.

I also say nothing about the change of habits, way of life, food, and so on, which for a man of a higher social stratum are, of course, harder than for a muzhik, who had often gone hungry in freedom, and in prison at least ate his fill. I will not argue about that either. Let's suppose that, for a man of at least some strength of will, these are all trifles compared with other discomforts, though as a matter of fact the change of habits is not at all a minor and trifling thing. But there are inconveniences before which all this pales so much that you pay no attention either to the filthy surroundings, or to the constraints, or to the meager, sloppy food. The most clean-handed lordling, the softest softy, after working the whole day by the sweat of his brow, as he never worked in freedom, will eat coarse bread and soup with cockroaches. You can get used to that, too, as is mentioned in a comic prisoner's song about a former lordling who lands in hard labor:

> *They dole me out some soggy cabbage,*
> *And I just wolf it down.*

No, more important than all this is that every newcomer to prison, two hours after his arrival, becomes the same as all the others, *at home*, as rightfully a master in the prison association as any other. They all understand him, and he understands them all, is known to them all, and they all consider him *one of theirs*. Not so with a *nobleman*, a gentleman. No matter how fair, kind, intelligent he is, for years on end the whole mass of them will hate and despise him; they will not understand him and, above all, will not trust him. He is not a friend and not a comrade, and even if over the years he reaches a point where they no longer insult him, still he will never be one of them and will be eternally, painfully

conscious of his estrangement and solitude. This estrangement sometimes happens without any malice on the part of the prisoners, but just
so, unconsciously. He's not one of us, that's all. Nothing is more terrible
than to live in a milieu that is not your own. A muzhik transferred from
Taganrog to the port of Petropavlovsk will at once find there a Russian muzhik exactly like himself, and will at once fall in with him, and
in a couple of hours they may well start living in the most peaceable
fashion in the same cottage or hut. Not so for the noblemen. They are
separated from simple people by the deepest abyss, and that can be *fully*
noticed only when the *nobleman* suddenly, by force of external circumstances, is really in fact deprived of his former rights and turned into a
simple man. Otherwise, though you may have to do with the people all
your life, though you may come together with them for forty years on
end, through the service, for instance, in conventional administrative
forms, or even just so, in a friendly way, as a benefactor and in a certain
sense a father—you will never know their real essence. It will all be an
optical illusion, and nothing more. Oh, I know that everybody, decidedly everybody, reading my remarks will say I am exaggerating. But I
am convinced that they are right. I became convinced of it, not through
books, not by speculation, but in reality, and I had quite enough time to
verify my conviction. Maybe later on everyone will come to know how
true it is . . .

Events, as if on purpose, confirmed my observations from the very
first step and had a nervous and morbid effect on me. During that first
summer, I wandered about the prison almost entirely alone. I have
already said that my state of mind was such that I was even unable to
appreciate and distinguish those convicts who were capable of liking
me and who did like me later on, though we never came to be on an
equal footing. There were comrades for me from the nobility, but this
comradeship did not lift the whole burden from my soul. I couldn't bear
the sight of it all, yet there was no escape from it. Here, for instance, is
one of those occasions which, right from the first, gave me to understand most fully my estrangement and the peculiarity of my position
in the prison. Once, that same summer, already approaching August,
on a clear and hot day, past noon, when everybody was resting as usual
before the after-dinner work, the whole prison suddenly arose as one
man and began to form up in the prison yard. I knew nothing about

it until that very moment. In those days I was sometimes so absorbed in myself that I hardly noticed what was going on around me. And yet the prison had been in smoldering unrest for some three days already. That unrest may have begun much earlier, as I realized only afterwards, inadvertently recalling something from the prisoners' talk, and along with that the increasing quarrelsomeness, gloominess, and especially the bitterness noticeable in them in recent days. I had ascribed it to the hard work, the long, boring summer days, involuntary dreams of the forests and the free life, the short nights when you couldn't get enough sleep. Maybe it all came together now in one outburst, but the pretext for the outburst was the food. For several days recently there had been loud complaints, indignation in the barracks and especially when we came together in the kitchen for dinner and supper; they were displeased with the cooks, even tried to replace one of them, but immediately chased out the new one and brought back the old one. In short, everybody was in some sort of agitated state.

"The work's hard, and they feed us tripe," somebody in the kitchen would start grumbling.

"If you don't like it, order blancmange," another would pick up.

"I really like shchi with tripe, brothers," a third picks up. "It's smacking good."

"And if they feed you the same tripe all the time, will it be smacking good?"

"Now's the time for meat, of course," says a fourth. "We slave away at the brickyard; when your lesson's over, you want to grub up. And what kind of food is tripe?"

"And if it's not tripe, it's awful."*

"Just take this awful, for instance. Tripe and awful, over and over again. Some food that is! Is it fair or isn't it?"

"Yeah, the feed's bad."

"He must be lining his pocket."

"That's none of your business."

"And whose is it, then? It's my belly. The whole lot of us should make a grievance, that would do it."

"A grievance?"

---

* That is, offal. The prisoners mockingly call it "awful." *Author.*

"Yes."

"As if you haven't been thrashed enough for these grievances. Blockhead!"

"That's right," another, who has been silent up to now, adds gruffly. "No hurry, no worry. What'll you put into your grievance, tell us that first, big brain."

"All right, I'll tell you. If everybody was to go, then I'd talk with everybody. Poverty, I mean. Some of us eat what's their own, and some only sit down to prison food."

"What a sharp-eyed envier! Ogling other people's goods!"

"Don't let your mouth lust for another man's crust. The early to rise feast more than their eyes."

"More than their eyes! . . . I could haggle with you over it till my hair turns gray. So you're a rich man, since you just sit there with folded arms?"

"Rich Ignát has a dog and a cat."

"No, really, brothers, why just sit there? I mean, enough of putting up with their foolery. They're skinning us alive. Why not go to them?"

"Why not? Must be you want it all pre-chewed and put in your mouth; you must be used to eating it chewed. Because it's prison—that's why!"

"So it comes down to: the people bleed, and the generals feed."

"That's it. Eight-eyes has grown fat. Bought himself a pair of grays."

"And he's sure no lover of drink."

"The other day he had a fight with the veterinarian over cards."

"Trumped each other all night. Our man kept his fists at it for two hours. Fedka told me."

"That's why we get shchi with awful."

"Ah, you fools! It's not our business to stick our noses out."

"But let's all go and see what he can say to justify himself. We'll stand on it."

"Justify! He'll punch you in the teeth, and that'll be it."

"And take you to court, too . . ."

In short, everybody was agitated. Our food was indeed bad at that time. And one thing was added to another. But the main thing was the general mood of anguish, the eternally suppressed suffering. Convicts are quarrelsome and rebellious by nature; but they rarely rebel all together or in a big group. The reason for that is eternal disagreement. Each of them felt it himself: that is why there was more bickering than doing among us. And yet this time the agitation did not go for nothing. They began to gather in groups, talked in the barracks, swore, angrily recalled our major's whole administration, and tried to get to the bottom of it all. Some were particularly agitated. In any situation like that, instigators, ringleaders, always turn up. The ringleaders in such cases, that is, in cases of grievance, are generally quite remarkable people, and not only in prison, but in all associations, teams, and the like. They are a special type, everywhere alike. They are hotheaded people, yearning for justice, and, in the most naïve and honest way, convinced of its inevitable, indisputable, and, above all, immediate possibility. These people are not stupider than others, some of them are even very intelligent, but they are too hotheaded to be clever and calculating. In all these cases, if there are men who are able to guide the masses deftly and come out winners, they constitute another type of guide and natural leader of the people, a type extremely rare among us. But those I'm now talking about, the instigators and ringleaders of grievances, almost always come out losers and afterwards populate the prisons and labor camps. They lose because of their hotheadedness, but because of their hotheadedness they also have influence on the masses. In the end, people follow them eagerly. Their ardor and honest indignation affect everybody, and in the end even the most irresolute join them. Their blind confidence in success seduces even the most inveterate skeptics, though that confidence sometimes has such flimsy, childish foundations that an outsider might wonder how anyone could follow them. The main thing is that they march in the forefront, and march fearing nothing. They rush straight ahead like bulls, horns down, often without knowing what it's about, without prudence, without that practical Jesuitism with which even the most mean and besmirched man sometimes wins the battle, achieves his goal, and comes out of the water dry. They inevitably break their horns. In ordinary life these people are bilious, peevish, short-tempered, and intolerant. Most often they are also terribly narrow-minded, which, however, partly constitutes their strength. The most vexing thing in them is that, instead of heading straight for the goal, they often rush off on a tangent, and instead of the main thing, end in trifles. And that's what destroys them. But the masses understand them; in that lies their strength . . . However, a couple of words must be said about what is meant by a *grievance* . . .

In our prison there were several men who had come there on account of grievances. They were the ones who were most agitated. Especially one, Martynov, who had formerly served as a hussar, a hot-headed, restless, and suspicious man, though an honest and truthful one. Another was Vassily Antonov, a man somehow cold-bloodedly irritable, with an insolent gaze, a haughty, sarcastic smile, extremely developed views, though also honest and truthful. But I cannot run through them all; there were many of them. Petrov, by the way, kept darting back and forth, listening to all the groups, spoke little, but was obviously agitated and was the first to rush out of the barrack when the lining up began.

Our prison sergeant, who performed the duties of a sergeant major among us, came out at once in fright. Having lined up, the people politely asked him to tell the major that the convicts wished to talk to him and to make personal requests with regard to certain points. Following the sergeant, the invalids all came out and lined up on the other side opposite the convicts. The commission given to the sergeant was extraordinary and plunged him into terror. But he did not dare not to report to the major immediately. First, once the convicts had risen up, it could lead to something worse. Our authorities were all somehow intensely fearful of the convicts. Second, even if nothing came of it, if they all thought better of it and dispersed, then, too, the sergeant would immediately have to report everything that had happened to the authorities. Pale and trembling with fear, he hastened to the major without even trying to question and admonish the prisoners himself. He could see that they would not speak to him now.

Knowing absolutely nothing, I, too, went out to line up. I learned all the details of the affair later. At the moment I thought some sort of roll call was going on; but, not seeing the guards who conducted the roll call, I was surprised and started looking around. The faces were agitated and annoyed. Some were even pale. Everyone in general was preoccupied and silent in anticipation of how they would have to talk to the major. I noticed that many of them looked at me with extreme astonishment, but silently turned away. They clearly found it strange that I lined up with them. They evidently did not believe that I should also present the grievance. Soon, however, almost everyone around me began to address me again. They all looked at me questioningly.

"What are you doing here?" Vassily Antonov asked loudly and rudely. He was standing further away from me than the others and until then had always addressed me formally and politely.

I looked at him in perplexity, still trying to understand what it all meant, and already guessing that something unusual was going on.

"Really, what are you doing standing here? Go back to the barrack," said one young fellow from the military, with whom until then I had not been acquainted at all, a kind and quiet lad. "This is none of your business."

"But they're lining up," I answered him. "I thought it was a roll call."

"So he dragged himself out, too," one man shouted.

"Iron beak!" said another.

"Fly squashers!" said a third with inexpressible contempt. This new nickname set off a general guffawing.

"They keep him in the kitchen as a favor," yet another added.

"It's all paradise for them. We're at hard labor, and they eat kalachi and buy pork. Go eat your own food; don't butt in here."

"This is not the place for you," said Kulikov, coming up to me casually. He took me by the arm and led me out of the ranks.

He was pale himself, his dark eyes flashed, and he was biting his lower lip. He was not waiting cool-headedly for the major. Incidentally, I was terribly fond of looking at Kulikov on occasions like this, that is, on all those occasions when he had to make a show of himself. He was a terrible poseur, but he also did his job. I think he would have gone to execution with a certain chic and jauntiness. Now, when everybody spoke rudely to me and swore at me, he redoubled his politeness to me, obviously on purpose, and at the same time his words were somehow especially, even haughtily, insistent, suffering no objection.

"We're here on our own business, Alexander Petrovich, and you have nothing to do with it. Go away somewhere, wait it out . . . All your kind are in the kitchen, go there."

"To the back of beyond, and good riddance!" somebody joined in.

Through the open kitchen window I did, in fact, make out our Poles; however, it seemed to me that there were many people there besides them. Puzzled, I went to the kitchen. Laughter, cursing, and hooting (which replaced whistling among the convicts) followed after me.

"He didn't like it! . . . Hoo-hoo-hoo! Sic him! . . ."

Never before had I been so insulted in the prison, and at the time it was very painful for me. But I had happened upon such a moment. In the entry to the kitchen I ran into T—ski,[1] a nobleman, a firm and magnanimous young man, without much education, and terribly fond of B. The convicts set him apart from all the others and even liked him somewhat. He was brave, manly, and strong, and it somehow showed in his every gesture.

"What is it, Goryanchikov?" he shouted to me. "Come here!"

"But what's going on there?"

"They're presenting a grievance, didn't you know? Naturally, they won't succeed: who's going to believe convicts? They'll look for the instigators, and if we're there, naturally, they'll heap the blame for the mutiny on us first of all. Remember what we came here for. They'll simply get beaten, but we'll go on trial. The major hates us all and would gladly do us in. He'll use us to vindicate himself."

"And the convicts will put all the blame on us," added M—cki, as we entered the kitchen.

"There's no fear they'll feel sorry!" T—ski added.

Besides the noblemen, there were many other people in the kitchen, some thirty in all. They had all stayed behind, not wishing to present the grievance—some out of cowardice, others being absolutely convinced of the total uselessness of any grievance. There was also Akim Akimych, the inveterate and natural enemy of all such grievances, as interfering with the regular flow of work and good conduct. He waited silently and quite calmly for the end of the affair, not troubled in the least about the outcome, but, on the contrary, perfectly convinced of the inevitable triumph of order and the will of the authorities. There was also Isai Fomich, standing in extreme perplexity, head bent, listening greedily and fearfully to our talk. He was in great anxiety. There were all the prison's simple Poles, who also sided with the noblemen. There were a few timid Russians, ever silent and downtrodden folk. They didn't dare to come out with the rest, and waited sadly for how the affair would end. There were, finally, a few gloomy and perpetually stern prisoners, not timid folk. They stayed behind from the stubborn and disdainful conviction that it was all nonsense and nothing but harm would come of the affair. But it seemed to me that all the same they now felt somehow awkward, that they did not look entirely self-assured. Though they understood that they were perfectly right about the grievance, as was confirmed afterwards, all the same they were conscious of being outcasts of a sort, who had abandoned their group, as if betraying their comrades to the major. Yelkin also turned up here, that same clever little Siberian muzhik, who was sent up for false coinage and took away Kulikov's veterinary practice. The old man from the Starodubsky settlements was also there. Decidedly all of the cooks to a man stayed in the kitchen, probably from the conviction that they also constituted part of the administration, and consequently it was improper for them to come out against it.

"However," I began, addressing M—cki uncertainly, "except for these, almost everybody's come out."

"What's that to us?" muttered B.

"We'd risk a hundred times more if we came out; and for what? *Je haïs ces brigands.*[*] And can you possibly think even for a moment that their grievance will get anywhere? Why poke your nose into such an absurdity?"

"Nothing will come of it," one of the convicts, a stubborn and embittered old man, put in. Almazov, who happened to be right there, hastened to yes him in reply.

"Nothing will come of it—except they'll give some fifty men a whipping."

"Here comes the major!" somebody shouted, and they all eagerly rushed to the windows.

The major came flying in, angry, infuriated, red-faced, in spectacles. Silently but resolutely he approached the front line. In these cases he

---

[*] "I hate these brigands" in French. *Translator.*

was indeed brave and did not lose his presence of mind. However, he was almost always half-drunk. Even his greasy visored cap with its orange band and his dirty silver epaulettes had something sinister about them. He was followed by the scribe Dyatlov, an extremely important person, essentially in charge of everything in our prison, and even having influence over the major, a clever fellow, who knew very well what he was about, but not a bad man. The prisoners were pleased with him. Following him came our sergeant, who had obviously already had time to receive a frightful roasting and was expecting ten times worse; after him came the convoy, three or four men, not more. The prisoners, who seemed to have been standing with their caps off ever since they sent for the major, now all straightened up and put themselves in order; each of them shifted from one foot to the other, after which they all froze in place, awaiting the first word, or, better, the first shout from the high authority.

It followed immediately; by the second word our major was roaring at the top of his lungs, this time even with a sort of shriek: he was already quite enraged. Through the windows we could see him running up and down the line of men, dashing about, asking questions. However, we were too far away to hear his questions or the prisoners' replies. All we could catch were his shrieking shouts:

"Mutineers! . . . run the gauntlet . . . Instigators! You're an instigator! You're an instigator!" He fell upon someone.

The reply could not be heard. But after a minute we saw a prisoner separate himself and head for the guardhouse. After another minute, a second headed off behind him, then a third.

"All of you on trial! I'll show you! Who's there in the kitchen," he shrieked, seeing us in the open windows. "Get them all out here! Drive them out here now!"

The scribe Dyatlov came to us in the kitchen. In the kitchen he was told that we had no grievances. He went back immediately and reported to the major.

"Ah, so they haven't!" he said two tones lower, obviously glad. "Never mind, bring them out here!"

We came out. I felt it was somehow shameful for us to come out. And indeed we all walked hanging our heads.

"Ah, Prokofiev! Yelkin, too, and that's you, Almazov . . . Stand here, stand here in a group," the major said to us in a sort of hurried but soft voice, glancing at us benignly. "M—cki, you're here as well . . . Make a list, Dyatlov! Make a list right now of all the contented and discontented, all to a man, and bring me the paper. I'll put you all . . . on trial! I'll show you rogues!"

The list had its effect.

"We're content!" one voice from the crowd of discontents called out sullenly, but somehow not very resolutely.

"Ah, you're content! Who's content? Whoever's content, step forward!"

"We're content, we're content!" several voices joined in.

"You're content! So you've been stirred up? So there were instigators, mutineers? All the worse for them! . . ."

"Lord, what is this?!" someone's voice came from the crowd.

"Who's that, who's that who shouted, who was it?" the major bellowed, rushing to where the voice came from. "It was you who shouted, Rastorguev? To the guardhouse!"

Rastorguev, a tall, puffy-faced young fellow, stepped out and slowly headed for the guardhouse. He was not the one who had shouted, but since he had been pointed out, he did not protest.

"You've got too fat a life!" the major yelled after him. "Look at his bloated mug! . . . I'll search you all out! Those who are content, step forward!"

"We're content, Your Honor!" several dozen voices said gloomily; the rest remained stubbornly silent. But that was all the major needed. It was obviously most advantageous for him to finish the affair quickly and in some sort of reconciliation.

"Ah, so now you're *all* content!" he said hastily. "I saw that . . . I knew it. It's instigators! Obviously, there are instigators among them!" he went on, turning to Dyatlov. "This must be looked into in more detail. But now . . . now it's time for work. Beat the drum!"

He was present himself for the assigning. The prisoners silently and sadly went off to work, content at least to quickly get out of his sight. But after the assigning, the major immediately visited the guardhouse and dealt with the "instigators," though not very severely. Even hastily.

One of them, it was said later, begged forgiveness, and he forgave him at once. It was clear that the major was not quite himself and maybe had even turned coward. A grievance is a ticklish thing in any case, and though the prisoners' complaint essentially could not be called a grievance, because it had been presented not to the higher authorities, but to the major himself, all the same it was somehow not right, not good. It was especially embarrassing that they had all risen up at once. The affair had to be quashed at all costs. The "instigators" were soon released. The food improved the very next day, though not for long. For the first few days, the major started visiting the prison more often and found disorders more often. Our sergeant went around preoccupied and confused, as if he still could not get over his astonishment. As for the prisoners, they could not calm down for a long time after that, though they were not as agitated as before, but were silently anxious and somehow puzzled. Some were even downcast. Others spoke gruffly, though not loquaciously, about the whole affair. Many jeered at themselves somehow bitterly and aloud, as if punishing themselves for the grievance.

"So, brother, take that and eat it!" one would say.

"If you laugh it off, you'll work it off!" another adds.

"Where's the mouse that ever belled the cat?" a third remarks.

"It takes a big stick to convince our kind, that's a known thing. Just as well he didn't beat us all."

"Next time know more and blab less, you'll be better off for it!" somebody observed angrily.

"So you're teaching us, teacher?"

"Sure I'm teaching you."

"Who are you to pop up like this?"

"So far I'm still human, what about you?"

"A dog's bone, that's what you are."

"That's what *you* are."

"All right, all right, enough of that! Stop the racket!" others shouted at the arguers from all sides . . .

That same evening, that is, on the same day as the grievance, on coming back from work, I met Petrov behind the barracks. He was looking for me. Coming up to me, he muttered something, some two or three vague exclamations, but soon fell absentmindedly silent and walked along mechanically beside me. This whole affair still weighed painfully on my heart, and it seemed to me that Petrov might clarify it somewhat for me.

"Tell me, Petrov," I asked him, "aren't your people angry with us?"

"Who's angry?" he asked, as if coming to his senses.

"The prisoners, with us . . . with the noblemen?"

"Why should they be?"

"Well, because we didn't come out for the grievance."

"And why should you present a grievance?" he asked, as if trying to understand me. "You eat your own food."

"Ah, my God! But some of yours eat their own food, and they still came out. We should have, too . . . out of comradeship."

"But . . . but what kind of comrade are you for us?" he asked in perplexity.

I glanced at him quickly: he decidedly did not understand me, did not understand what I was getting at. But I understood him perfectly at that moment. For the first time now, a certain thought that had long been vaguely stirring in me and pursuing me finally became clear, and I suddenly understood something that I had realized only poorly till now. I understood that I would never be accepted as a comrade, even if I was a prisoner a thousand times over, even unto ages of ages, even in the special section. It was Petrov's look at that moment that especially remained in my memory. In his question, "What kind of comrade are you for us?" such unfeigned naïveté, such simple-hearted perplexity, could be heard. I thought: isn't there some sort of irony, malice, mockery in these words? Nothing of the sort: you're simply not a comrade, that's all. You go your way, and we go ours; you have your business, and we have ours.

And indeed I was thinking that after the grievance they would simply chew us up and make life impossible for us. Not at all: we did not hear the slightest reproach, not the slightest hint of reproach, no particular increase of malice. They simply nagged at us a little on occasion, as they had nagged at us before, and nothing more. However, they were also not angry in the least with all those who did not wish to present a grievance and remained in the kitchen, nor with those who were the first to shout that they were content with everything. Nobody even mentioned it. This last especially I could not understand.

VIII

Comrades

I was, of course, more drawn to my own kind, that is, to the "noblemen," especially at first. But of the three former Russian noblemen who were in our prison (Akim Akimych, the spy A—v, and the one who was considered a parricide), I only kept company and talked with Akim Akimych. I confess, I approached Akim Akimych, so to speak, out of despair, in moments of the most intense boredom, and when there was no prospect of approaching anyone else but him. In the previous chapter I was trying to sort all our people into categories, but now, as I recall Akim Akimych, I think one more category can be added. True, it was made up of him alone. It is the category of the totally indifferent convicts. The totally indifferent, that is, those to whom it was all the same whether they lived in freedom or in prison, naturally did not and could not exist among us, but Akim Akimych seems to have made the exception. He even set himself up in prison as if he intended to live there all his life: everything around him, starting with his mattress, pillows, utensils, was arranged so solidly, so firmly, so durably. Of the camp-like, the temporary, no trace could be noticed in him. He still had many years of prison ahead of him, but I doubt that he ever thought of getting out. But if he was reconciled with reality, then, of course, it came not from the heart, but rather from subordination, which for him, however, were one and the same. He was a kind man and even helped me in the beginning with advice and some services; but sometimes, I regret to say, he involuntarily drove me, especially at first, into unparalleled anguish, intensifying still more my state of mind, which was already anguished without that. Yet it was out of anguish that I got to talking with him. I would be thirsting for some living word, even if bitter, even if impatient, even if angry: we could at least be angry together at our fate; but he would keep silent, glue up his little lanterns, or tell me about some review they had held in such-and-such year, and who

had been the division commander, and what his first name and patronymic were, and whether he had been pleased with the review or not,
and how the riflemen's signals had been changed, and so on. And all
with such a level, sedate voice, like drops of water dripping. He even
showed almost no animation when he told me that, for taking part in
some action in the Caucasus, he had been awarded a Saint Anne on
the sword.[1] Only his voice became somehow unusually imposing and
solemn at that moment; he lowered it slightly, even to a sort of myste-
riousness, when he uttered "Saint Anne," and for some three minutes
after he remained somehow especially silent and solemn . . . In that first
year I had my stupid moments when (and always somehow suddenly) I
would begin almost to hate Akim Akimych, without knowing why, and
to silently curse my fate for having placed me head to head with him on
the bunks. Usually an hour later I was already reproaching myself for
it. But that was only during the first year; later on I became completely
reconciled with Akim Akimych in my soul and was ashamed of my former stupidity. Outwardly, as I recall, we never quarreled.

Besides these three Russians, there were eight other noblemen
in our prison during my time. With certain of them I became quite
close and even took pleasure in it, but not with all. The best of them
were somehow sickly, exclusive, and intolerant in the highest degree.
With two of them I simply stopped speaking later on. Only three
of them were educated: B—ski,[2] M—cki, and old Zh—ski,[3] who
had formerly been a mathematics professor somewhere—a kind and
good old man, a great eccentric, and it seems, despite his education, extremely narrow-minded. M—cki and B—ski were quite different. With M—cki I got on well from the first; I never quarreled with
him, respected him, but could never love him or become attached to
him. He was a deeply mistrustful and embittered man, but was able to
control himself astonishingly well. It was this all too great ability that I
disliked in him: you somehow felt that he would never open his whole
soul to anyone. However, I may be mistaken. His was a strong nature
and noble in the highest degree. His extreme, even somewhat Jesuitic
adroitness and prudence in dealing with people betrayed his deep, hidden skepticism. And yet his was a soul suffering precisely from this dual-
ity: skepticism and a deep, unwavering belief in certain of his personal

convictions and hopes. However, despite all his worldly adroitness, he was in implacable enmity with B—ski and his friend T—ski. B—ski was a sickly man, somewhat inclined to consumption, irritable and nervous, but essentially very kind and even magnanimous. His irritability sometimes reached the point of extreme intolerance and capriciousness. I could not bear his character and later on broke with B—ski, though I never ceased to love him; while with M—cki I didn't quarrel, and yet I never loved him. Having broken with B—ski, it so happened that I had at once to break with T—ski as well, that same young man I mentioned in the previous chapter, telling about our grievance. That was a great pity for me. T—ski, though uneducated, was kind, manly—in short, a nice young man. The thing was that he loved and respected B—ski so much, revered him so much, that he considered those who fell out ever so slightly with B—ski to be almost his own enemies. Later on, it seems, he broke with M—cki, too, over B—ski, though he refrained for a long time. However, they were all morally sick, bilious, irritable, mistrustful. That was understandable: it was very hard for them, much harder than for us. They were far from their native land. Some of them were sentenced to long terms, ten or twelve years, but the main thing was that they had a deeply prejudiced view of everyone around them, saw only brutality in the convicts, and could not, even would not, see a single good feature in them, anything human, which was also quite understandable: this unfortunate point of view had been imposed on them by force of circumstances, by fate. It was clear that they were choking with anguish in prison. With the Circassians, with the Tatars, with Isai Fomich, they were gentle and affable, but they turned away from all the other convicts with loathing. Only the Starodubsky Old Believer earned their full respect. It is remarkable, however, that during all the time I spent in prison, not one of the convicts reproached them either with their origin, or with their faith, or with their way of thinking, something that can be met with in our simple folk with regard to foreigners, primarily Germans, though very rarely. However, at Germans they may only laugh; the German embodies in himself something deeply comical for the Russian people. The convicts treated our foreigners respectfully, much more so than they did us Russians, and never *touched* them. But it seems they never wished to notice it and take it into consideration. I began talking about T—ski. It was he who, when they were being transferred from their first place of exile to our fortress, carried B—ski in his arms almost all the rest of the way, when the man, who was of weak health and constitution, got worn out after barely half a day's march. They had been sent first to U—gorsk.⁴ There, they told us, they had had it good, that is, much better than in our fortress. But they had started some sort of correspondence—completely innocent, by the way—with other exiles in another town, and for that it was found necessary to transfer the three of them to our fortress, under the closer scrutiny of our high authorities. Their third comrade was Zh—ski. Before their arrival, M—cki had been alone in the prison. How he must have pined away during his first year in exile!

This Zh—ski was that same eternally prayerful old man I have already mentioned. Our political prisoners were all young men, some even very young; only Zh—ski was already fifty and then some. He was, of course, an honest man, but somewhat strange. His comrades B—ski and T—ski disliked him very much, even did not speak to him, saying that he was stubborn and quarrelsome. I don't know how right they were in this case. In prison, as in any place where people bunch together not of their own free will but by force, they are more likely to quarrel and even to hate each other than in freedom. Many circumstances contribute to that. However, Zh—ski was indeed a rather obtuse and perhaps even unpleasant man. None of his other comrades got along with him either. Though I never quarreled with him, I was not particularly close to him. His subject, mathematics, he did seem to know. I remember he kept trying to explain to me in his half-Russian tongue some special astronomical system he had invented. I was told that he had published it at one time, but the whole learned world had only laughed at him. It seems to me that he was somewhat deranged. He spent whole days on his knees praying to God, which earned him the general respect of the whole prison, and which he enjoyed until the day of his death. He died in our hospital after a serious illness, before my eyes. However, the convicts respected him from his first steps in the prison, after his episode with our major. On the road from U—gorsk to our fortress they hadn't shaved, and their beards had grown, so that when they were brought straight to the major, he became furiously indignant at this breach of subordination, for which, however, they were not to blame.

"Just look at them!" he bellowed. "Like tramps, robbers!"

Zh—ski, who had a poor understanding of Russian then and thought they were being asked whether they were tramps or robbers, replied:

"We are not tramps, we are political criminals."

"Wha-a-at?! Insolence? That's insolence!" the major bellowed. "To the guardhouse! A hundred lashes, right now, this minute!"

The old man was punished. He lay down unprotestingly under the lashes, bit his hand, and endured the punishment without the slightest cry or moan, not stirring. Meanwhile B—ski and T—ski had gone into the prison, where M—cki was already waiting for them by the gate and threw himself on their necks, though he had never seen them before. Shaken by the major's reception, they told him all about Zh—ski. I remember M—cki telling me about it: "I was beside myself," he said. "I didn't know what was happening to me, and was trembling as if in a fever. I waited for Zh—ski by the gate." He was supposed to come straight from the guardhouse, where they punished him. Suddenly the door opened: Zh—ski, not looking at anybody, with a pale face and pale, trembling lips, passed through the convicts gathered in the yard, who had already learned that a nobleman was being punished,[5] went into the barrack, straight to his place, and, not saying a word, knelt down and began praying to God. The convicts were struck and even moved. "When I saw that gray-haired old man," said M—cki, "who had left his wife and children behind in his native land, when I saw him on his knees praying, after being shamefully punished—I rushed behind the barracks and for a whole two hours was as if oblivious; I was beside myself . . ." The convicts began to respect Zh—ski greatly after that and always treated him deferentially. They especially liked it that he had not cried out under the lashes.

But the whole truth needs to be told: it is by no means possible to judge by this example the way the authorities in Siberia treated exiles from the nobility, whoever those exiles might be, Russians or Poles . . . This example only shows that you could run into a bad man, and, of course, if that bad man was an independent and senior commander somewhere, then the exile's lot, if by chance this bad commander took a particular dislike to him, would be very uncertain. But it is impossible not to admit that the highest authorities in Siberia, upon whom the tone and disposition of all the other commanders depend, are very scrupulous with regard to exiled noblemen, and in some cases even try to grant them indulgence, in comparison with the rest of the prisoners, those from the people. The reasons for that are clear: these highest authorities, first of all, are noblemen themselves; second, it has happened before that certain noblemen have refused to lie down under the lashes and have attacked the executioners, which has led to horrors; and third, and, it seems to me, most important, a long time back, some thirty-five years ago, a large group of exiled noblemen appeared in Siberia suddenly, all at once, and those exiles, in the course of thirty years, had managed to establish and prove themselves so well all over Siberia, that in my time the authorities, by long-standing, inherited habit, willy-nilly looked upon noble criminals of a certain category with different eyes than upon all other exiles.[6] Following the highest authorities, the lower commanders also habitually looked with the same eyes, taking this view and tone from above, obeying it, submitting to it. However, many of these lower commanders viewed things stupidly, privately criticized the orders from above, and would have been only too glad if they could have ordered things their own way without interference. But that was not entirely allowed them. I have firm grounds for thinking so, and here is why. The second category of penal servitude, to which I belonged and which consisted of prisoners held under military authority, was incomparably harder than the other two categories, that is, the third (in the mills), and the first (in the mines). It was harder not only for the noblemen, but for all the prisoners, precisely because both the authorities and the structure of this category were military, very much like the penal companies in Russia. Military authorities are more strict, the rules are tighter, you're always in chains, always under convoy, always under lock and key: and that does not hold so much for the other two categories. So at least said all our prisoners, and there were some connoisseurs among them. They would all gladly have gone to the first category, considered the hardest by the law, and they even dreamed of it many times. Of the penal companies in Russia, all of our people who had been there spoke with horror and insisted that there was no place harder than the penal companies in Russian fortresses, and that Siberia was paradise compared with life there. Consequently, if in such strict detention as in our prison, in the presence of military authorities, before the eyes of the governor-general himself, and, finally, in view of those occasions (which sometimes occurred) when certain semi-official outsiders, from malice or zeal for service, secretly informed the proper quarters that such-and-such disloyal commanders were showing leniency towards such-and-such category of criminals—if in those quarters, I say, noble criminals were viewed with somewhat different eyes than other convicts, how much more leniently must they have been viewed in the first and third categories. Consequently, from the prison I was in, it seems to me that I can judge in this respect about the whole of Siberia. All the rumors and stories that reached me on this score from exiles of the first and third categories confirmed my conclusion. Indeed, the authorities in our prison kept an attentive and wary eye on all of us noblemen. There was decidedly no indulgence towards us with regard to work and keeping: the same work, the same fetters, the same locks, in short, everything the same as for all the prisoners. And there was no way to lighten it. I know that in that town, in that *recent long-past* time,[7] there were so many informers, so many intrigues, so much undermining of each other, that the authorities were naturally afraid of denunciations. And at that time what more terrible denunciation could there be than that the authorities were granting indulgence to a certain category of criminals! Thus, they were all afraid, and we lived in the same way as all the convicts, but with respect to bodily punishment there were certain exceptions. True, we would be flogged quite handily if we deserved it, that is, if we trespassed in some way. That was demanded by the duty of service and equality in the face of corporal punishment. But all the same they would not flog us just like that, for nothing, casually, while with simple prisoners that sort of casual treatment, naturally, did take place, especially under certain subaltern commanders and enthusiasts for giving orders and reprimands on any convenient occasion. It was known to us that the commandant, on learning about the incident with old Zh—ski, was very indignant and told the major to keep himself on a shorter tether in the future. So everyone told me. It was also known among us that the governor-general himself, who trusted our major and rather liked him as an efficient and more or less capable man, on learning of this incident, also reprimanded him. And our major took that into consideration. How he would have liked, for instance, to get at M—cki, whom he hated owing to A—v's slander, but he never could flog him, though he sought pretexts, persecuted him, and lay in wait for him. Soon the whole town knew about the incident with Zh—ski, and public opinion was against the major; many reprimanded him, some even with unpleasantness. I remember now my first encounter with the major. We, that is, myself and another exile from the nobility who had entered prison with me, had already been frightened in Tobolsk by stories of the man's unpleasant character. At that time there were old-timers there, noblemen who had spent twenty-five years in exile, who met us with deep sympathy and stayed in touch with us all the while we were in the transit prison, warned us against our future commander, and promised to do all they could, through people they knew, to protect us from his persecution. In fact, the governor-general's three daughters, who had come from Russia and were visiting their father at that time, received letters from them and, it seems, spoke in our favor to him. But what could he do? He merely told the major to be a bit more discriminating. It was past two in the afternoon when we, that is, my comrade and I, arrived in this town, and the convoy led us straight to our lord and master. We stood in the anteroom waiting for him. Meanwhile the prison sergeant had already been sent for. As soon as he appeared, the major also came out. His purple, malicious, and blackhead-covered face had an extremely depressing effect on us: like a malicious spider pouncing on a poor fly caught in its web.

"What's your name?" he asked my comrade. He spoke quickly, sharply, abruptly, and obviously wanted to make an impression on us.

"So-and-so."

"Yours?" he went on, turning to me and fixing me with his spectacles.

"So-and-so."

"Sergeant! To prison with them at once; give them a civilian shave in the guardhouse, immediately, half the head; fetters to be redone tomorrow. What are these overcoats? Where did you get them?" he asked suddenly, turning his attention to the gray coats with yellow circles on the back issued to us in Tobolsk, in which we had appeared before his serene countenance. "It's a new uniform! It must be some sort of new uniform . . . Still in the planning stage . . . from Petersburg . . . ," he said, turning us around, first one, then the other. "Nothing with them?" he suddenly asked our convoy gendarme.

"Their own clothes, sir," the gendarme replied, somehow instantly snapping to attention, even with a slight start. Everybody knew him, had heard about him, was afraid of him.

"Take it all away. Leave them only the underwear, if it's white, but if it's colored, take it away. The rest will all be sold at auction. The money set down as general income. A prisoner has no private property," he went on, looking at us sternly. "See that you behave yourselves! That I hear nothing! Or else. . . . cor-por-al pun-ish-ment! For the slightest misstep—the bir-r-rches! . . ."

Being unused to such a reception, I was almost ill all that evening. However, the impression was intensified by what I saw in the prison; but of my entry into the prison I have told already.

I mentioned just now that no one granted us or dared to grant us any indulgence, any lightening of the workload compared with other prisoners. Once, though, an attempt was made: for a whole three months, B—ski and I went to work as clerks in the engineering office. But that was done hush-hush, and done by the engineering officers. That is, all the others who needed to know, most likely did know, but made it look as if they didn't. This took place under the commander G—kov. Lieutenant Colonel G—kov fell on us as if from heaven, spent a very short time with us—no more than six months, if I'm not mistaken, or even less than that—and went back to Russia, having made an extraordinary impression on all the prisoners. He was not so much loved by the prisoners as adored by them, if it is possible to use that word here. How he did it I don't know, but he won them over from the first. "A father! A father! Better than a real one!" the prisoners kept saying all the while he managed the engineering section. It seems he was a terrible carouser. Small of stature, with a bold, self-assured gaze. But along with that, he was affectionate with the prisoners, all but tender, and indeed literally loved them like a father. Why he loved the prisoners so much I cannot say, but he could not see a prisoner without saying some affectionate, cheerful word to him, without laughing with him, joking with him, and, above all—there was not a drop of anything official in it, nothing to suggest any inequality or purely official benevolence. He was our comrade, our own man in the highest degree. But, despite all his instinctive democratism, the prisoners never once made the misstep of being disrespectful or familiar with him. On the contrary. A prisoner would simply beam all over when he met the commander and, taking off his hat, would watch smiling as the man approached him. And if he began to speak, it was like being given a rouble. There really are such popular people. He was a fine fellow to look at, with a straight, dashing stride. "An eagle!" the prisoners used to say of him. He could not, of course, make things easier for them; he was only in charge of the engineering works, which, as under all the other commanders, followed their own habitual, pre-established, lawful course. Except that, chancing upon a party at the works, and seeing that the job was done, he would not hold them for the extra time and would let them go before the drum. But what was likeable in him was his trust in the prisoners, the absence of petty touchiness and irritability, the complete absence of other insulting forms in official relations. If he had lost a thousand roubles and the foremost of our thieves had found them, I think he would have returned them to him. Yes, I'm sure of it. With what deep sympathy the prisoners learned that their eagle-commander had quarreled mortally with our hated major. This happened in the first month after his arrival. Our major had once served with him. They met as friends after many years and began carousing together. But something suddenly snapped between them. They quarreled, and G—kov became his mortal enemy. There was even a rumor that they fought on this occasion, which could happen with our major: he often fought. When the prisoners heard that, their joy was boundless. "Eight-eyes can't get along with such a man! He's an eagle, and our major's a . . ." and here they usually put in an unprintable word. We were all terribly interested in who had beaten whom. If the rumor of their fight had turned out to be false (which it might have been), I believe our prisoners would have been very upset. "No, the commander must have won," they said. "He's small but spunky, and they say the other one hid from him under the bed." But G—kov soon left, and the prisoners fell into dejection again. True, our engineer commanders were all good to us: in my time there were three or four, "but they don't make them all like that one," the prisoners said. "He was an eagle, an eagle and a defender." So this

G—kov loved us noblemen very much, and towards the end he told B—ski and me to come to the office sometimes. After his departure, that was established in a more regular fashion. Among the engineers there were people (one especially) who sympathized very much with us. We went, copied papers, our handwriting even began to improve, when an order suddenly came from the higher authorities that we were to return immediately to our former work: someone had managed to denounce us! However, it was a good thing: we were both getting quite sick of the office. After that, for some two years B—ski and I went almost inseparably to the same jobs, most often to the workshops. We chattered away, talked of our hopes, our convictions. He was a nice man; but his convictions were sometimes very strange, exceptional. Often in a certain category of very intelligent people, completely paradoxical notions sometimes establish themselves. But they have suffered so much for them, have paid so dear a price for them, that to tear themselves away from them is too painful, almost impossible. B—ski took every objection with pain and responded to me caustically. However, in many things maybe he was more right than I was, I don't know; but we finally parted ways, and that was very painful for me: we had shared much together.

Meanwhile M—cki was somehow becoming more and more sad and gloomy with the years. Anguish was overcoming him. Earlier, during my first time in prison, he had been more communicative; his soul had all the same broken through more often and more fully. When I arrived, it was already his third year at hard labor. In the beginning he was interested in many things that had gone on in the world during those two years, and of which he had no notion, being in prison; he asked questions, listened, showed emotion. But towards the end, with the years it all somehow started to concentrate inside him, in his heart. The coals were covering over with ashes. He became more and more embittered. *"Je haïs ces brigands,"* he often repeated to me, looking with hatred at the convicts, whom I had already come to know more closely, and none of my arguments in their favor had any effect on him. He did not understand what I was saying, though he occasionally agreed absent-mindedly; but the next day he would repeat again: *"Je haïs ces brigands."* By the way, he and I often spoke in French, and for that one of the supervisors at work, the engineer soldier Dranishnikov, for who knows what reason, nicknamed us "medicos." M—cki became animated only when he remembered his mother. "She's old, she's sick," he said to me. "She loves me more than anything in the world, and here I don't know whether she's alive or not. It was already enough for her, knowing that I had run the gauntlet . . ." M—cki was not a nobleman and before his exile had suffered corporal punishment. Remembering it, he clenched his teeth and tried to look away. Lately he had begun to go about alone more and more. One morning, between eleven and twelve, he was summoned to the commandant. The commandant came out to him with a cheerful smile.

"Well, M—cki, what did you dream about last night?" he asked.

"I gave such a start," M—cki told us when he came back. "As if I'd been stabbed through the heart."

"I dreamed I got a letter from my mother," he replied.

"Better, better!" the commandant retorted. "You're free! Your mother petitioned . . . Her petition has been granted. Here's her letter, and here's the order about you. You'll be leaving prison straightaway."

He came back to us pale, not yet recovered from the news. We congratulated him. He pressed our hands with his trembling, cold hands. Many of the prisoners also congratulated him and were glad of his good luck.

He was released as a settler and stayed in our town. They soon gave him a job. At first he often came to our prison and, whenever he could, told us various bits of news. He was mainly very interested in politics.

Of the other four, that is, besides M—cki, T—ski, B—ski, and Zh—ski, two were still very young men, sent up for short terms, little educated, but honest, simple, direct. The third, A—chukovsky, was all too simple-minded and there was nothing special in him, but the fourth, B—m, a man already on in years, made a very nasty impression on us all. I don't know how he ended up in such a category of criminals, and he himself denied it. His was a coarse, petty bourgeois soul, with the habits and principles of a shopkeeper grown rich by cheating on kopecks. He was without any education and was interested in nothing except his trade. He was a house painter, but an outstanding one, a magnificent one. The authorities soon learned of his abilities, and the whole town started asking B—m to paint their walls and ceilings. In two years he painted nearly all the government apartments. The apartment owners paid him personally, and his life was not a poor one. But the best thing of all was that his other comrades were sent to work with him. Of the three who always went with him, two learned his trade, and one of them, T—zewski, began to paint no worse than he. Our major, who also occupied a government house, sent for B—m in his turn and ordered him to paint all the walls and ceilings for him. Here B—m outdid himself: even the governor-general's was not painted so well. The house was wooden, one-storied, quite decrepit, and badly peeling on the outside, but the inside was painted like a palace, and the major was delighted … He rubbed his hands and said that now he would certainly get married: "With such lodgings, it's impossible not to get married," he added very seriously. He was more and more pleased with B—m, and through him with the others who worked along with him. The work went on for a whole month. During that month, the major totally changed his opinion about all our group and began to patronize them. It went so far that he once suddenly summoned Zh—ski to him outside the prison.

"Zh—ski!" he said, "I offended you. I was wrong to flog you, I know it. I repent. Do you understand that? I, *I*, I—repent!"

Zh—ski replied that he understood that.

"Do you understand that I, *I*, your superior, summoned you in order to ask your forgiveness? Do you feel that? Who are *you* next to me? A worm! Less than a worm: you're a prisoner! While I, by God's grace,* am a major. A major! Do you understand that?"

Zh—ski replied that he understood that, too.

"Well, so now I'm making peace with you. But do you feel it, do you feel it fully, in all its fullness? Are you capable of understanding and feeling it? Just think: I, I, a major … ," and so on.

Zh—ski himself recounted this whole scene to me. It meant there was some human sense in this drunken, cantakerous, and disorderly man. Considering his notions and development, such an act could be

---

* The literal expression, employed in my time, however, not only by our major, but by many petty commanders, mainly those who had risen from the ranks. *Author.*

seen as almost magnanimous. However, his drunken state may have contributed much to it.

His dream was not realized: he did not get married, though he was completely set on it, once the decoration of his lodgings was finished. Instead of marrying, he wound up in court and was ordered to hand in his resignation. Here all his old sins were dragged in as well. Earlier, as I recall, he had been the mayor of this town . . . The blow fell on him unexpectedly. In the prison the news caused boundless rejoicing. It was a holiday, a celebration! They say the major howled like an old woman and drowned himself in tears. But there was nothing to be done. He resigned, sold his pair of grays, then all his possessions, and even fell into poverty. We would run into him afterwards in a shabby civilian frock coat and a visored cap with a little cockade. He looked spitefully at the prisoners. But all his fascination went away as soon as he took off his uniform. In uniform he was a terror, a god. In a frock coat he suddenly became a complete nothing and smacked of the lackey. It's astonishing how much a uniform does for these people.

IX

The Escape

Soon after our major's replacement, radical changes took place in our prison. Hard labor was abolished and instead of it a penal company of the military department was formed, on the pattern of the Russian penal companies. This meant that exiled convicts of the second category were no longer brought to our prison. It began to be populated from then on only by prisoners from the military department, meaning people not stripped of their civil rights, the same as all other soldiers, only punished, who came for short terms (six years at the most), and, upon leaving prison, joined their battalions again as the same privates they had been before. However, those who returned to prison after a second crime were punished, as before, with a twenty-year sentence. With us, however, even prior to that change there had been a section of prisoners of the military category, but they lived with us because there was no other place for them. Now the whole prison became of this military category. Needless to say, the previous convicts, the real civil convicts, stripped of all their rights, branded, and with half their heads shaved, remained in the prison until the end of their full terms; no new ones came, and those who remained gradually served their terms and went away, so that after some ten years there could not have been a single convict left in our prison. The special section also remained in the prison, and from time to time serious criminals from the military department were still sent to it, pending the opening of the heaviest hard labor in Siberia. Thus life went on for us essentially as before: the same keeping, the same work, and almost the same rules, only the authorities were changed and became more complex. A staff officer was appointed, a company commander, and on top of that four subalterns who took turns on duty in the prison. The invalids were also abolished; instead of them twelve sergeants and a quartermaster were established. Divisions of ten were introduced, corporals from among the prisoners themselves were introduced, nominally, to be sure, and needless to say Akim Akimych at once found himself a corporal. This whole new establishment and the whole prison with all its officials and prisoners remained as before in the jurisdiction of a commandant as the highest superior. That was all that happened. Naturally, the prisoners were very agitated at first, discussed, tried to fathom, to figure out their new superiors; but when they saw that essentially everything remained as before, they calmed down at once, and our life went on in the old way. But the main thing was that we were rid of the former major; it was as if we all relaxed and cheered up. Frightened looks disappeared; each of us knew now that in case of need he could talk things over with the superior, that only by mistake could an innocent man be punished instead of a guilty one. Vodka even went on being sold among us in the same way and on the same basis as before, despite the fact that sergeants had been put in place of the former invalids. These sergeants for the most part turned out to be decent and sensible men who understood their position. Some of them, however, at first tried to show bravado and, of course, from inexperience, thought of treating the prisoners like soldiers. But soon they, too, understood what it was all about. Others who took too long in understanding were shown the essence of the matter by the prisoners themselves. There were some rather sharp clashes: for instance, they would tempt a sergeant, get him drunk, and after that announce to him, as among friends, of course, that he had drunk with them, and consequently . . . In the end, the sergeants looked indifferently or, better, looked away, when the bladders were smuggled in and the vodka was sold. What's more, just like the former invalids, they went to the market and brought the prisoners kalachi, beef, and all the rest—that is, whatever they could do without great shame. Why all these changes had to take place, what the penal company was set up for—I don't know. It happened during my last years in prison. But I was fated to live two more years under these new rules . . .

Must I make note of all that life, of all my years in prison? I don't think so. If I were to write out in order, in sequence, all that happened and that I saw and experienced in those years, I could, naturally, write three or four times more chapters than I have written so far. But such a description would, willy-nilly, become too monotonous. The adventures would all come out too much in the same tone, especially if the reader has managed, from the chapters I've already written, to form for himself at least a somewhat satisfactory notion of prison life in the second category. I wanted to present the whole of our prison and all that I lived through during those years in one graphic and vivid picture. Whether I have achieved that goal, I don't know. And that is not entirely for me to judge. But I'm convinced that I can stop here. Besides, I myself sometimes get sick at heart from these memories. And I can hardly remember everything. The subsequent years have somehow been erased from my memory. I've completely forgotten many circumstances, I'm sure of that. I remember, for instance, that all those years, essentially so like one another, went by sluggishly, drearily. I remember that those long, boring days were as monotonous as rainwater dripping from the roof drop by drop. I remember that only the passionate desire for resurrection, renewal, a new life, gave me the strength to wait and hope. And I finally pulled myself together: I waited, I counted off each day, and, though there were a thousand left, I counted off each one with delight, bade farewell to it, buried it, and, with the coming of the new day, rejoiced that it was no longer a thousand, but nine hundred and ninety-nine. I remember that in all that time, despite having hundreds of fellow prisoners, I was in terrible solitude, and I finally came to love that solitude. Spiritually alone, I revisited all my past life, went through everything down to the smallest detail, pondered my past, judged myself alone strictly and implacably, and sometimes even blessed my fate for having sent me this solitude, without which neither that judgment of myself nor that strict review of my past life could have been. And what hopes then throbbed in my heart! I thought, I resolved, I swore to myself that in my future life there would be no such mistakes, no such falls, as there had been before. I outlined a program for the whole of my future and resolved to follow it firmly. A blind faith arose in me that I would and could fulfill it all . . . I waited, I called for freedom to come quickly; I wanted to test myself anew, in a new struggle. At times I was seized by a convulsive impatience . . . But it pains me to remember now about the state of my soul then. Of course, all this concerns just me alone . . . But I have written about it, because it seems to me that everyone will understand it, because the same thing should happen with anyone, if he does time in prison, in the flower of his youth and strength.

But why talk of that! . . . I'd better tell something more, so as not to break off too abruptly.

It occurred to me that someone might well ask: Can it be that no one could possibly escape from the prison, and that in all those years no one did escape? I've already noted that a prisoner who has spent two or three years in prison begins to value those years and willy-nilly comes to reckon that it is better to serve the rest with no trouble, no danger, and get out, finally, to live in legitimate fashion as a settler. But such a reckoning only enters the head of a prisoner sentenced to a relatively short term. A long-timer might well be ready to risk it . . . But that somehow didn't happen among us. I don't know whether they were too cowardly, or the surveillance was especially strict, military, or the location of our town was in many ways unfavorable (on the steppe, exposed)—it's hard to say. I think all those causes had their influence. Indeed, it would have been quite difficult to escape from our prison. And yet one such case did occur while I was there: two men risked it, and they were even from among the most important criminals.

After the major was replaced, A—v (the one who spied for him in the prison) was left completely alone, without protection. He was still a very young man, but his character had strengthened and formed itself with the years. Generally he was a bold, resolute, and even very clever man. He would have gone on spying and dealing in various underground ways even if they had granted him freedom, but now he would not have gotten caught so stupidly and improvidently as he had been before, paying for his stupidity with hard labor. Among us he did some faking of passports. I cannot speak positively, however. I heard it from our prisoners. They said he did work of that sort while he was still going to the major's kitchen and, naturally, derived what profit he could from it. In short, it seems he would have tried anything to change his lot. I had occasion to learn something of his soul: his cynicism reached the point of outrageous insolence, of the coldest mockery, and aroused an insurmountable loathing. It seems to me that if he had badly wanted a drink of vodka, and could not have obtained it otherwise than by cutting somebody's throat, he would certainly have cut it, provided it could have been done on the quiet, so that nobody knew. He learned calculation in prison. It was to this man that Kulikov, a prisoner in the special section, turned his attention.

I have already spoken of Kulikov. He was no longer a young man, but passionate, strong, of great vitality, with extraordinary and varied abilities. There was strength in him, and he still wanted to live; such people keep this wish to live into deep old age. And if I should start wondering why none of us tried to escape, then Kulikov would naturally be one of the first I would wonder about. But Kulikov did try. Who had more influence on whom, A—v on Kulikov or Kulikov on A—v, I don't know, but they were worthy of each other and were mutually suited to this affair. They became friends. I believe Kulikov counted on A—v to prepare the passports. A—v was a nobleman, from good society—that promised a certain diversity in their future adventures, once they made it back to Russia. Who knows how they arranged things and what their hopes were; but their hopes certainly went beyond the usual routine of Siberian vagrancy. Kulikov was a born actor, he had many different roles to choose from in life; he could hope for many things, at least for diversity. Prison must be oppressive for such people. They arranged to escape.

But it was impossible to escape without a convoy soldier. They had to persuade a convoy soldier to join them. There was a Pole serving in one of the battalions stationed in our fortress, an energetic man and perhaps deserving of a better lot, a man already on in years, trim, serious. In his youth, having only just come to serve in Siberia, he had deserted out of a deep longing for his native land. He was caught, punished, and spent two years in the penal companies. When they sent him back to the ranks, he thought better of it and began to serve zealously, with all his might. For distinguished service he was made a corporal. He was an ambitious, self-confident man, and knew his own worth. He looked, he spoke like a man who knew his own worth. During those years I met him several times among our convoy soldiers. The Poles told me a thing or two about him as well. It seemed to me that the former longing had turned into a concealed, smoldering, perpetual hatred in him. This was a man capable of anything, and Kulikov was not mistaken in choosing him as a comrade. His name was Koller. They made arrangements and fixed the day. It was in the month of June, in the hot days. The climate in that town was rather steady; in summer the weather was invariably hot, and that played into the hands of tramps.

Naturally, they could not set out straight from the fortress: the whole town stands in the open, exposed on all sides. There is no forest for a great distance around. They had to change into ordinary clothes, and for that they had to get to the outskirts, where Kulikov had long had a hideout. I don't know if their friends on the outskirts were in on the secret. It must be supposed that they were, though later on, during the trial, that was not fully explained. That year in one corner of the outskirts a young and quite comely girl nicknamed Vanka-Tanka, who showed great promise and later partly fulfilled it, was just beginning her career. She was also called "Fire." It seems she played a certain part here. Kulikov had been bankrupting himself on her for a whole year. Our lads came out to the morning roll call and deftly arranged to be sent with the prisoner Shilkin, a stove maker and plasterer, to plaster some empty battalion barracks, which the soldiers had long since left for the camps. A—v and Kulikov went with him as porters. Koller turned up as convoy, and since two convoy soldiers were needed for three prisoners, Koller, as a veteran and corporal, was readily entrusted with a young recruit to be trained and instructed in convoy duties. Which means that our jailbreakers had a very strong influence on Koller and gained his trust, since after many years of service and some success recently, he, an intelligent, solid, prudent man, decided to follow them.

They came to the barracks. It was six o'clock in the morning. There was nobody there besides them. After working for about an hour, Kulikov and A—v told Shilkin they were going to the workshop, first, to see someone, and, second, at the same time to pick up some tool they turned out to be lacking. Shilkin had to be handled cleverly, that is, as naturally as possible. He was a Muscovite, a stove maker by profession, from Moscow tradesmen, cunning, devious, intelligent, taciturn. Outwardly he was frail and haggard. He should have gone around all the time in a waistcoat and dressing gown, Moscow style, but fate had worked otherwise, and after long wanderings he had settled with us permanently in the special section, that is, in the category of the most terrible military criminals. How he earned such a career I don't know; but I never noticed any particular displeasure in him; he always behaved himself peaceably and steadily; only he occasionally got drunk as a cobbler, but then, too, he behaved well. He was not, of course, in on the secret, but he had sharp eyes. Needless to say, Kulikov winked at him, meaning they were going to get vodka stashed away in the workshop the day before. Shilkin was touched by that; he parted with them without any suspicions and remained alone with the recruit, while Kulikov, A—v, and Koller went to the outskirts.

Half an hour went by; the absent men did not come back, and Shilkin, suddenly realizing it, fell to thinking. The fellow had gone through hell and high water. He began to recollect: Kulikov had seemed to be in a special mood, A—v had seemed to exchange whispers with him twice, Kulikov had at least winked at him a couple of times, he had seen that; now he remembered it all. In Koller, too, he had noticed something: at least, as he was leaving with them, he began giving instructions to the recruit on how to behave in his absence, and that had somehow been not entirely natural, at least from Koller. In short, the more Shilkin remembered, the more suspicious he became. Meanwhile, time was passing, the men did not come back, and his uneasiness reached the utmost limits. He realized very well how much at risk he was in this affair: the authorities might turn their suspicions on him. They might think he had knowingly allowed his comrades to leave, by mutual arrangement, and if he were slow to report the disappearance of Kulikov and A—v, those suspicions would be still more justified. There was no time to lose. Then he remembered that Kulikov and A—v had become somehow especially close lately, had often whispered together, had often walked behind the barracks, away from all eyes. He remembered that even then he had already thought something about them . . . He looked searchingly at his convoy; the soldier yawned, leaning on his gun, and picked his nose in the most innocent way, so that Shilkin did not deign to impart his thoughts to him, but simply told him to follow him to the engineering workshop. In the workshop they had to inquire whether the men had come there. It turned out that no one there had seen them. All of Shilkin's doubts were dispelled: "They might simply have gone to drink and carouse in the outskirts, which Kulikov sometimes did," Shilkin thought, "but here even that can't be so. They would have told me, because there was no point in concealing it from me." Shilkin dropped his work and, without stopping at the barracks, went straight to the prison.

It was already nearly nine o'clock when he appeared before the master sergeant and told him what was going on. The master sergeant got scared and even refused to believe it at first. Naturally, Shilkin told it all to him only in the form of a surmise, a suspicion. The master sergeant rushed straight to the major. The major rushed immediately to the commandant. Within a quarter of an hour all the necessary steps had been taken. It was reported to the governor-general himself. The criminals were important ones, and on account of them there might be a severe dressing-down from Petersburg. Rightly or not, A—v was reckoned a political prisoner; Kulikov was from the "special section," that is, an archcriminal, and a military one to boot. There had never yet been an instance of anyone escaping from the special section. It was recalled, incidentally, that according to the rules each prisoner of the special section was supposed to have two convoy guards, or at least one each. This rule had not been observed. The affair thus proved to be an unpleasant one. Messengers were sent to all the townships, to all the surrounding areas, to inform them about the escapees and leave their descriptions everywhere. Cossacks were sent to pursue them, to catch them; letters were written to the neighboring districts and provinces . . . In short, they were all panic-stricken.

Meanwhile, another sort of excitement began in the prison. The prisoners, as they came back from work, learned at once what was happening. The news had already spread everywhere. Everyone took it with a sort of extraordinary, secret joy. Everyone's heart leaped . . . Besides the fact that this incident disrupted the monotonous life of the prison and stirred up the anthill, an escape, and such an escape, echoed somehow intimately in every soul and touched long-forgotten strings; something like hope, daring, the possibility of changing their lot, stirred in all hearts. "So people can escape: why, then . . . ?" And at this thought each man took courage and looked defiantly at the others. In any case they all suddenly became somehow proud and began to glance haughtily at the sergeants. Naturally, the authorities swooped down on the prison at once. The commandant himself came. The prisoners took courage and looked on boldly, even somewhat contemptuously, and with a sort of silent, stern gravity, as if to say: "We know how to handle things." Needless to say, our men foresaw at once that there would be a general visit from the authorities. They also foresaw that there would certainly be searches, and everything was hidden beforehand. They knew that in such cases the authorities always become wise after the fact. And so it happened: there was great turmoil; they rummaged through everything, searched everywhere, and—found nothing, naturally. The prisoners were sent to their afternoon work under a reinforced convoy. In the evening, guards looked into the barracks every other minute; the people were counted up one more time than usual; in the process they miscounted twice more than usual. That led to more fuss: we were all driven out to the yard and counted over again. Then we were counted yet another time in the barracks . . . In short, there was a great fuss.

But the prisoners didn't turn a hair. They all looked extremely independent and, as always happens in such cases, behaved themselves with extraordinary decorum all that evening, meaning: "There's no finding fault with anything." Needless to say, the authorities were thinking "Did the escapees not leave some accomplices behind in the prison?" and ordered the guards to keep their eyes and ears open. But the prisoners only laughed. "As if you'd leave accomplices behind in a job like that!" "A job like that is done on tiptoe, or not at all." "And is Kulikov the kind, is A—v the kind, as not to hide all traces in such a job? It was masterfully done, no loose ends. These folk have gone through hell and high water; they can get through a locked door all right!" In short, Kulikov and A—v grew in fame; everybody was proud of them. The feeling was that their deed would go down to the furthermost generations of prisoners, outliving the prison itself.

"Masterful folk," said some.

"See, people thought you couldn't escape from here. But they escaped! . . . ," others added.

"Escaped, yes!" a third offered, looking around with some authority. "But who escaped? . . . The likes of you, was it?"

At another time, a prisoner to whom these words were addressed would certainly have responded to the challenge and defended his honor. But now he modestly kept silent. "In fact, not everybody's like Kulikov and A—v; prove yourself first . . ."

"And really, brothers, what are we doing living here?" A fourth, modestly sitting by the kitchen window, broke the silence, speaking in a slight singsong from some sort of limp but secretly self-satisfied feeling, propping his cheek in his palm. "What are we here? We live, but we're not people; we die, but we're not dead men. E-ech!"

"The thing's not a boot. You can't kick it off. Why 'e-ech'?"

"Yes, but Kulikov . . . ," one of the hotheads, a young greenhorn, tried to mix in.

"Kulikov!" another picked up at once, contemptuously narrowing his eyes at the greenhorn. "Kulikov! . . ."

By which he meant: How many Kulikovs are there?

"And A—v, too, brothers, he's a slick one, oh, he's a slick one!"

"You said it! He'll wind Kulikov around his little finger. He'll give 'em all the slip!"

"I'd like to know how far they've gone by now, brothers . . ."

And the conversation turned at once to how far they might have gone, and what direction they might have taken, and where it would be best for them to go, and what was the nearest township. There were people who knew the area. They were listened to with curiosity. They spoke of the inhabitants of the neighboring villages and decided that they were unreliable folk. They lived close to town, they knew what was what; they would not let the prisoners off, they would catch them and turn them in.

"The muzhiks here are a wicked bunch, brothers. O-o-oh, what muzhiks!"

"Untrustworthy folk!"

"Salt-eared Siberians.[1] Keep away from them, they'll kill you."

"Well, but our lads . . ."

"Depends on who gets the upper hand. And there's no flies on ours."

"If we don't die first, we'll hear."

"And what do you think? Will they catch them?"

"I think they'll never catch them in their lives!" another hothead picks up, banging his fist on the table.

"Hm. Well, it all depends on what turn it takes."

"And here's what I think, brothers," Skuratov puts in. "If I was a tramp, never in their lives would they take me!"

"You, hah!"

Some start laughing, others make a show of not wanting to listen. But Skuratov is already wound up.

"Never in their lives would they take me!" he goes on energetically.

"I often think about it to myself, brothers, and marvel at myself: seems I'd just squeeze through a crack and wouldn't be taken."

"You'd most likely get hungry and go to the peasants for bread."

General guffawing.

"For bread? Nonsense!"

"What are you wagging your tongue for? You and Uncle Vasya killed the cow's death,* that's what you came here for."

The guffawing grows louder. The serious ones look still more indignant.

"That's nonsense!" shouted Skuratov. "It's Mikitka who blabbed about me, and not about me, but about Vaska, and I just got dragged into it. I'm a Muscovite and a well-tried tramp since childhood. A clerk, when he was teaching me to read, used to yank my ear and say: 'Repeat after me: "Have mercy on me, God, according to Thy great mercy" and so on . . .' And I'd repeat after him: 'Have the police on me according to Thy mercy' and so on . . . I've been acting like that ever since I was a kid."

Everybody guffawed again. But that was just what Skuratov wanted. He couldn't help playing the fool. They soon dropped him and took up the serious discussion again. It was mainly the old men and the knowledgeable ones who did the talking. The younger and humbler people were glad enough just to look on, and thrust their heads forward to listen. A large crowd gathered in the kitchen; naturally, there were no sergeants there; there would have been no talk in their presence. Among those who were especially pleased I noticed the Tatar Mametka, a short man with high cheekbones, an extremely comical figure. He spoke almost no Russian and understood almost nothing of what the others said, but he also thrust his head from behind the crowd and listened, listened with delight.

"So, Mametka, yakshi?"† Skuratov, rejected by all and having nothing to do, latched on to him.

"Yakshi, oh, yakshi!" Mametka babbled, becoming all animated, nodding his funny head at Skuratov. "Yakshi!"

"They won't take them? Yok?"‡

---

* That is, killed a peasant man or woman on the suspicion that they had loosed a spell on the wind which caused cattle to die. There was one such murderer in the prison. *Author.*

† "Good?" in Tartar. *Translator.*

‡ "No" in Tartar. *Translator.*

"Yok, yok!" And Mametka started babbling again, this time waving his arms.

"Meaning yours lies, mine never tries, is that it?"

"It, it, yakshi!" Mametka agreed, nodding his head.

"Well, so, yakshi!"

And, smacking him on the hat and pulling it down over his eyes, Skuratov walked out of the kitchen in the merriest of spirits, leaving Mametka in some astonishment.

The strictness in the prison continued for a whole week, as did the intensifying pursuit and search in the vicinity. I don't know how, but the inmates received at once and in detail all the news of the authorities' maneuvers outside the prison. For the first few days, all the news was in favor of the escapees: there was no trace of them, they had vanished, and that was all. Our people only chuckled. All worry about the fate of the escapees vanished. "They won't find anything, they won't take anybody!" they said smugly.

"Nothing left! Off like a shot!"

"Bye-bye, don't cry, back soon!"

We knew that all the local peasants were on their feet and were keeping watch on all the suspicious places, all the woods, all the ravines.

"Nonsense," our people said, chuckling, "they must have somebody they're staying with now."

"No doubt about it!" said others. "Men like them prepare everything beforehand."

They went further in their suppositions: they started saying that the escapees may have been sitting on the outskirts all along, waiting in some cellar until the "halarm" died down and their hair grew back. Live there half a year, a year, and then go away . . .

In short, everybody was even in a sort of romantic state of mind. Then suddenly, some eight days after the escape, a rumor went around that their trail had been found. Naturally, the absurd rumor was rejected at once with contempt. But that same evening the rumor was confirmed. The prisoners began to worry. The next morning there was talk in town that they had already been caught and were in transit. After dinner still more details were learned: they had been caught fifty miles away, in such-and-such village. Finally, precise news was received. The sergeant major, coming back from the major's, announced positively that in the evening they would be brought straight to the prison guardhouse. Doubt was no longer possible. It is hard to describe the impression this news made on the prisoners. At first it was as if everybody became angry, then dejected. Then a certain tendency to mockery peeped through. They began to laugh, not at the pursuers now, but at the pursued—a few at first, then almost everybody, except for several serious and firm ones, who thought independently and could not be thrown off by mockery. They looked contemptuously at the light-minded masses and held their peace.

In short, as much as Kulikov and A—v had been exalted before, so they were humiliated now, even with delight. It was as if they had offended everybody in some way. The story, told with a contemptuous look, was that they had wanted very much to eat, that they had been unable to bear their hunger and had gone into a village to ask the muzhiks for bread. That was the last degree of humiliation for tramps. However, these stories were not true. The escapees had been tracked down; they had hidden in the forest; people had surrounded the forest on all sides. Seeing there was no possibility of saving themselves, they surrendered. There was nothing else they could do.

But when they were actually brought by the gendarmes in the evening, bound hand and foot, the whole prison poured out to the fence to see what would be done to them. Naturally, they saw nothing but the major's and the commandant's carriages by the guardhouse. The escapees were kept in solitary, chained up, and the next day they were put on trial. The mockery and scorn of the prisoners soon ceased of themselves. They learned the details of the affair, learned that there had been nothing else to do but surrender, and they all started earnestly following the course of the trial.

"They'll slap a thousand on them," some said.

"A thousand, hah!" said others. "They'll finish them off. A—v may get a thousand, but the other one they'll finish off, brother, because he's from the special section."

They guessed wrong, though. A—v was given a mere five hundred; they took into consideration his satisfactory former behavior and the fact that this was his first offense. Kulikov, I believe, got fifteen hundred. The punishment was carried out rather mercifully. As sensible people, they did not implicate anyone at the trial, testified clearly, precisely, said they had escaped straight from the fortress, and had not stopped off anywhere. I was sorry most of all for Koller: he lost everything, his last hopes, went through the most, two thousand I believe, and was sent somewhere as a prisoner, only not to our prison. A—v was punished lightly, sparingly; the doctors had a hand in that. But he swaggered and said loudly in the hospital that now he would try anything, he was ready for anything, and there was nothing he wouldn't do. Kulikov behaved as always, that is, gravely, decently, and, on coming back to the prison after his punishment, looked as if he had never left. But that was not how the prisoners looked at him: though Kulikov had always and everywhere known how to stand up for himself, in their hearts the prisoners somehow ceased to respect him, began to treat him somehow more familiarly. In short, after this escape Kulikov's glory faded considerably. Success means so much to people . . .

X

Leaving Prison

All this happened during my last year at hard labor. That last year is almost as memorable for me as the first, especially my very last days in prison. But there's no need to speak of details. I remember only that during that last year, despite my great impatience to finish my term quickly, life was easier for me than in all the previous years of exile. First of all, by then I had many friends and acquaintances among the prisoners, who had decided once and for all that I was a good man. Many of them were devoted to me and sincerely loved me. The pioneer almost burst into tears, seeing me and my comrade off from prison, and when, after leaving, we then spent a whole month in a government building in that town, he came to visit us almost every day, just to have a look at us. However, there were also persons who remained stern and unfriendly to the end, for whom it was apparently hard to say a word to me—God knows why. There seemed to be some sort of barrier between us.

During that last time I generally had more privileges than in all my time in prison. It turned out that I had some acquaintances and even old schoolmates among the military personnel in town. I renewed relations with them. Through them I could have more money, could write home, and could even have books. For several years I hadn't read a single book, and it is hard for me to give an account of the strange and at the same time exciting impression that the first book I read in prison made on me. I remember I started reading it in the evening, when the barracks had been locked, and went on reading all night until dawn. It was an issue of a magazine. It was as if news of that world came flying to me; all my former life rose up clear and bright before me, and I tried to guess from my reading if I had fallen far behind that life, if they had lived through much without me, what stirred them now, what questions now occupied them. I picked at words, read between the lines, tried to find hidden meanings, allusions to former things; I searched for traces of what had stirred people before, in my time, and how sad it was for me now to find how much of a stranger I actually was to the new life, how much of a cut-off slice. I would have to get used to the new, to acquaint myself with the new generation. I especially threw myself into articles that appeared over a familiar name, that of a man formerly close to me . . . But new names could already be heard: new active figures appeared, and I eagerly hurried to acquaint myself with them and was vexed that I had the prospect of so few books and it was so difficult to get hold of them. Formerly, under the former major, it had even been dangerous to bring books to the prison. In case of a search, there were bound to be questions: "Where did these books come from? Where did you get them? So you have connections? . . ." What could I reply to such questions? And therefore, living without books, willy-nilly I went deeper into myself, asked myself questions, tried to resolve them, sometimes suffered over them . . . But it can't all be told like this! . . .

I had entered prison in winter and therefore in winter I was also to be set free, on the same day of the month as I had arrived. With what impatience I waited for winter, with what delight at the end of summer I watched the leaves withering on the trees and the grass fading on the steppe! But now summer was over, the autumn wind began to howl; now the first snowflakes came fluttering . . . It finally settled in, that long-awaited winter! My heart would sometimes start pounding hollowly, heavily, in great anticipation of freedom. But, strangely, the more time passed and the nearer the end came, the more and more patient I grew. By the very last days I was even astonished and reproached myself: it seemed to me that I had become completely cool and indifferent. Many prisoners, meeting me in the yard during our free time, got to talking with me, to congratulating me:

"So, dear Alexander Petrovich, soon, soon you'll be out there in freedom. You'll leave us all alone."

"And what about you, Martynov, will it be soon now?" I replied.

"Me? Don't ask! I've got seven more years to waste away here . . ."

And sighing to himself, he would stop, gaze off absent-mindedly, as if peering into the future . . . Yes, many of them congratulated me sincerely and joyfully. It seemed to me that they all began to treat me more affably. I was evidently already ceasing to be one of them; they were taking leave of me. K—chinsky, a Polish nobleman, a quiet and meek young man, liked, as I did, to walk a lot in the yard during our free time. He hoped, by fresh air and exercise, to preserve his health and make up for all the harm of the stuffy nights in the barrack. "I'm waiting impatiently for you to get out," he once said with a smile, running into me during a walk. "You'll leave, and *then I'll know* that I have exactly a year left till I get out."

I will note here in passing that, owing to dreaminess and long estrangement, freedom seemed to us in prison somehow freer than true freedom, that is, as it actually exists in reality. The prisoners exaggerated the notion of actual freedom, and that is quite natural, quite proper to every prisoner. Some ragged little officer's orderly was considered almost a king among us, all but the ideal of the free man compared to prisoners, because he went about unshaven, without fetters and without a convoy.

On the eve of the very last day, at dusk, I walked *for the last time* along the fence around our whole prison. How many thousands of times I had walked along that fence in all those years! There, behind the barracks, I had wandered during my first year at hard labor, alone, orphaned, crushed. I remember counting then how many thousands of days I had left. Lord, how long ago it was! Here, in this corner, our eagle had lived in captivity; here Petrov had often come to meet me. Now, too, he did not abandon me. He came running and, as if guessing my thoughts, silently walked beside me and looked as if he were surprised at something. I was mentally saying good-bye to the blackened log beams of our barracks. How they had shocked me with their unfriendliness *then*, in that first time! They, too, must have aged now compared to back then; but I didn't notice it. And how much youth was buried uselessly within these walls, how much great strength perished here for nothing! I must say it all: these people are extraordinary people. They are perhaps the most gifted, the strongest of all our people. But their mighty strength perishes for nothing, perishes abnormally, unlawfully, irretrievably. And who is to blame?

That's just it: who is to blame?

Early the next morning, before the men went out to work, when dawn was just beginning to break, I went around all the barracks to say good-bye to all the prisoners. Many strong, callused hands reached out to me affably. Some pressed mine in quite a comradely way, but those were few. Others understood very well that I was about to become a totally different man from them. They knew I had acquaintances in town, that from here I would go straight to those *gentlemen* and sit down with those gentlemen as an equal. They understood that and though they said good-bye to me affably, affectionately, it was hardly as to a comrade, but as if to a squire. Some turned away from me and sternly refused to answer my good-bye. A few even looked at me with a sort of hatred.

They beat the drum, and everybody headed off to work, while I stayed home. That morning Sushilov had gotten up almost earlier than anybody and bustled about with all his might to prepare tea for me in time. Poor Sushilov! He wept when I gave him my old prison clothes, shirts, under-fetters, and some money. "It's not that, not that!" he said, trying hard to control the trembling of his lips. "But to lose you, Alexander Petrovich? How can I go on here without you?!" I said good-bye for the last time to Akim Akimych as well.

"It will be your turn soon!" I said to him.

"I'll be here a long time, a long time yet, sir," he murmured, shaking my hand. I threw myself on his neck and we kissed.

Ten minutes after the prisoners went out, we also left the prison, never to return—I and my comrade, with whom I had first come there. We had to go straight to the blacksmith, to have our fetters removed. But now no armed convoy came with us: we went with a sergeant. The fetters were removed by our fellow prisoners in the engineering workshop. I waited while they unfettered my comrade, then approached the anvil myself. The smiths turned my back to them, raised my leg, placed it on the anvil . . . They fussed about, wanted to do it better, more skillfully . . .

"The rivet, turn the rivet first of all! . . . ," the older one commanded. "Put it this way, right . . . Now hit it with the hammer . . ."

The fetters fell off. I picked them up . . . I wanted to hold them in my hand, to look them over for the last time. It was as if I marveled now that they had just been on my legs.

"Well, go with God, go with God!" the prisoners said, their voices abrupt, coarse, but as if pleased at something.

Yes, with God! Freedom, a new life, resurrection from the dead . . . What a glorious moment!

Appendix: The Peasant Marey[1]

But I think all these *professions de foi* are very boring to read, and so I'll tell you a story; though it is not even a story, but only a distant memory, which for some reason I would like to tell about precisely here and now, at the conclusion of our treatise on the people. I was only nine years old then . . . but, no, I'd better start with when I was twenty-nine.

It was the second day of the Easter holiday. The air was warm, the sky blue, the sun high, "warm," bright, but my soul was very dark. I was wandering behind the barracks, staring at and counting the palings of the stout prison stockade, but I didn't want to count them, though I had the habit. It was the second day of "holiday making" in the prison; the convicts were not sent to work, there were lots of drunks, cursing and quarreling broke out every moment in all the corners. Vile, outrageous songs, card-playing maidans under the bunks, some convicts, sentenced by their own comrades for excessive violence, already beaten half to death and covered with sheepskin coats on the bunks until they revived and came to, knives already drawn several times—all this, in two days of holiday, had tormented me to the point of illness. I never could bear the people's drunken carousing without loathing, especially here, in this place. During those days even the superiors did not look in on the prison, did not carry out searches, did not hunt for vodka, realizing that once a year even these outcasts had to be allowed some merriment, and that otherwise it would be worse. Finally, anger began to burn in my heart. I ran into the Pole M—cki, a political prisoner; he gave me a dark look, his eyes flashed and his lips trembled: *"Je haïs ces brigands!"* he rasped in a half whisper and walked on by. I returned to the barrack, though a quarter of an hour earlier I had fled from it half-crazed, when six hefty muzhiks at once had fallen on the drunken Tatar Gazin and set about beating him so as to quiet him down; they beat him absurdly, such blows could have killed a camel; but they knew that this Hercules was hard to kill, and so they beat him without second thoughts. Now, on returning, I noticed the unconscious Gazin at the back of the barrack, on a bunk in a corner, showing almost no signs of life; he lay under a sheepskin coat, and everyone passed him by silently: though they firmly hoped he would come to the next morning, still "who knows, after such a beating, a man might just up and die." I made my way to my place, facing a barred window, and lay on my back, my hands behind my head and my eyes shut. I liked to lie like that: a sleeping man wasn't bothered, and meanwhile you could dream and think. But I did not dream; my heart beat uneasily, and M—cki's words rang in my ears: "*Je haïs ces brigands!*" However, why describe impressions; even now I sometimes dream at night of that time, and for me no dreams are more tormenting. Perhaps it will also be noticed that until today I have almost never spoken in print about my life at hard labor; I wrote *Notes from a Dead House* fifteen years ago, through a fictional character, a criminal who had supposedly murdered his wife. Incidentally, I will add as a detail that since then a great many people have thought and maintain even now that I was sent to Siberia for murdering my wife.

I indeed forgot myself little by little and sank imperceptibly into memories. During all my four years in prison, I was constantly remembering my whole past and, it seems, living through all my former life again in memories. These memories arose of themselves; I rarely called them up by my own will. It would start with some point, some line, sometimes imperceptible, and then would gradually grow into a complete picture, some strong and complete impression. I analyzed these impressions, lent new features to what had been lived through long ago, and, above all, retouched them, ceaselessly retouched them, and in that lay all my amusement. This time for some reason I suddenly remembered an insignificant moment from my early childhood, when I was only nine years old—a moment which it seemed I had completely forgotten; but I was especially fond then of memories from my earliest childhood. I remembered one August on our country estate: the day was dry and clear, but slightly cold and windy; summer was coming to an end, and I would soon have to go back to Moscow and be bored again all winter over French lessons, and I felt so sorry to leave the country. I walked past the barns, went down into the ravine, climbed up to the Losk—as we called the thick bushes that went from the other side of the ravine all the way to the woods. And so I hide myself deep in the bushes and hear, as if not far away, some thirty paces, a solitary peasant plowing in the clearing. I know he's plowing up a steep hill, and it's hard going for the horse, and once in a while I hear him shout "Hup, hup!" I know almost all our peasants, but I don't know which of them is plowing now, and it's all the same to me, I'm wholly immersed in my own business, I'm also busy: I break off a hazel switch for whipping frogs; hazel switches are so pretty and so fragile, a far cry from birch ones. I'm also interested in bugs and beetles, I collect them, some are very fancy; I also like the little, nimble red-and-yellow lizards with black spots, but I'm afraid of snakes. However, you come upon snakes much more rarely than lizards. There are few mushrooms here; I have to go to the birch grove for mushrooms, and I'm about to go there. And never in my life have I loved anything so much as the forest, with its mushrooms and wild berries, its bugs and little birds, hedgehogs, squirrels, with its damp smell of rotten leaves, which I love so much. And even now, as I write, I can sense so well the smell of the birch grove on our estate: such impressions stay with you all your life. Suddenly, amid the deep silence, I clearly and distinctly heard a cry: "A wolf's coming!" I screamed and, beside myself with fear, shouting at the top of my voice, rushed out to the clearing, straight to the plowing peasant.

It was our peasant Marey. I don't know if there is such a name, but everybody called him Marey—a man of about fifty, thickset, rather tall, with a lot of gray in his broad, dark brown beard. I knew him, but until then had almost never had occasion to speak to him. He even stopped his little mare, hearing my cry, and when I ran to him and clutched his plow with one hand and his sleeve with the other, he could tell how frightened I was.

"A wolf's coming!" I shouted, gasping for breath.

He raised his head and involuntarily looked around, almost believing me for a moment.

"Where's the wolf?"

"There was a shout ... Somebody just shouted: 'A wolf's coming! ... ,'" I babbled.

"Now, now, what wolf? You imagined it. See? There can't be any wolf!" he murmured, encouraging me. But I clutched his coat still more tightly, trembling all over, and was probably very pale. He looked at me with an uneasy smile, obviously worried and anxious about me.

"You're really frightened—ay, ay!" He shook his head. "Enough now, my dear. There's a good lad!"

He reached out and suddenly stroked my cheek.

"Well, enough now, Christ be with you, cross yourself." But I wouldn't cross myself; the corners of my lips twitched, and I think he was especially struck by that. He gently reached out his thick, dirt-covered finger with its black nail and gently touched my quivering lips.

"Really now," he smiled at me with a long and somehow motherly smile. "Lord, what's all this, really now, ay, ay!"

I finally understood that there was no wolf and that I had imagined the cry "A wolf's coming!" The cry had been very clear and distinct, but I had imagined such cries once or twice before (not only about wolves), and I was aware of it. (Later, along with my childhood, these hallucinations went away.)

"Well, I'll go now," I said, looking at him questioningly and timidly.

"Well, off with you, then, and I'll keep an eye on you. I won't let the wolf get you!" he added with the same motherly smile. "Well, off you go, and Christ be with you"—and he made the sign of the cross over me and over himself. I went, turning to look back almost every ten steps. While I went, Marey stood by his little mare watching me and nodding to me each time I looked back. I must confess I was a little ashamed before him for being so afraid, but I kept going, still very frightened of the wolf, until I reached the top of the other slope of the ravine and the first barn; there my fear fell away completely, and suddenly, out of nowhere, our yard dog Volchok came rushing to me. With Volchok there, I felt totally reassured and turned to Marey for the last time. Though I couldn't see his face clearly, I felt that he was still smiling tenderly at me and nodding his head. I waved to him, he waved back to me and touched up his little mare.

"Hup, hup!" his distant cry came again, and again the little mare pulled her plow.

I recalled all this at once, I don't know why, but with an astonishing precision of detail. I suddenly came to and sat up on the bunk, and, I remember, I still had the quiet smile of remembrance on my face. For another minute I went on remembering.

On coming home from Marey then, I didn't tell anyone about my "adventure." And what sort of adventure was it? And about Marey I also very soon forgot. Meeting him occasionally afterwards, I never even spoke to him, not only about the wolf, but about anything at all, and now suddenly, twenty years later, in Siberia, I remembered this whole encounter with such clarity, to the very last detail. Which means that it had embedded itself in my soul imperceptibly, on its own and without my will, and I suddenly remembered it when it was needed; I remembered that tender, motherly smile of the poor serf, his signs of the cross, the way he shook his head: "You're really frightened, lad!" And especially that thick, dirt-covered finger of his, with which he had touched my quivering lips gently and with timid tenderness. Of course, anyone would reassure a child, but here, in this solitary encounter, something quite different happened, as it were, and if I had been his own son, he could not have given me a look shining with more radiant love—and who made him do it? He was our own serf, and I was his little master; no one would learn how tender he had been with me and reward him for it. Was it that he loved little children so much? There are such people. This had been a solitary encounter, in an empty field, and maybe only God above had seen what deep and enlightened human feeling, what refined, almost feminine tenderness could fill the heart of a coarse, brutishly ignorant Russian serf, who back then was not yet expecting or even dreaming of his freedom. Tell me, is that not what Konstantin Aksakov meant when he spoke of the lofty education of our people?[2]

And so, when I got off my bunk and glanced about, I remember suddenly feeling that I could look at these unfortunate men with totally different eyes, and that suddenly, by some miracle, all the hatred and anger in my heart had vanished completely. I went about peering into the faces I met. This shaved and disgraced muzhik, drunk and with a branded face, bellowing out his hoarse, drunken song, why, he also could be that same Marey: I could not look into his heart. That same evening I met M—cki again. Poor man! He certainly could not have had memories of any Mareys or any other view of these people than *"Je haïs ces brigands!"* No, those Poles endured more than we did then!

Notes

PART ONE

INTRODUCTION

1. **the capitals:** It was customary to refer to two capitals of Russia—the old capital, Moscow, and the newer capital, St. Petersburg, founded by Peter the Great in 1703.
2. **a settler in the town of K.:** On finishing their term at hard labor, prisoners were required to settle in Siberia rather than return to European Russia, and were thus known as "settlers." The town of K. is the Siberian town of Kuznetsk (later Novokuznetsk), over six hundred miles east of Omsk, where the prison was located. Dostoevsky married his first wife there in 1857, three years after his release.

I. THE DEAD HOUSE

1. **not to remember evil against him:** It was a Russian custom on bidding farewell to bow in four directions and ask forgiveness of all those present by repeating the formula "Do not remember evil against me."
2. **"stroll down the green street":** Prison jargon for running the gauntlet.
3. **kalachi:** A kalach (pl. kalachi) is a purse-shaped loaf of fine white bread.

II. FIRST IMPRESSIONS

1. **the Irtysh:** A major river in western Siberia, which rises in the Altai Mountains and flows through Omsk on its way to join the Ob.
2. **shchi:** Cabbage soup prepared with or without meat and other ingredients; one of the staples of the Russian diet.
3. **the bird Kagan:** A legendary bird of Russian folklore, said to bring happiness.
4. **"a pantry whore":** Dostoevsky recorded these phrases in notes taken while he was in prison; they mean "a petty thief, who tried to escape and was caught."

5. **kvass:** A slightly fermented, mildly alcoholic drink popular in Russia and other Slavic countries, made from rye bread.

6. **in the Caucasus:** The Russian conquest of the Caucasus took place between 1817 and 1864. In the Russian army, *junker* (borrowed from the German) was a low rank of noncommissioned officer.

7. **"One's a cantonist":** Cantonists were sons of Russian conscripts and other military personnel, who were trained for military service in special schools known as "cantonist schools" and were obliged to serve afterwards. The Circassians are a Caucasian ethnic group; they strongly opposed the Russian conquest and were the last to sign a treaty with the imperial forces in 1864. The schismatics (raskolniki in Russian) were and are members of the religious group known as the Old Believers, who broke with the Russian Orthodox Church in protest against reforms carried out by the patriarch Nikon between 1652 and 1666.

8. **a holy fool:** A "holy fool" ("fool in God" or "fool for Christ") could be a harmless village idiot, but there are also saintly persons or ascetics whose saintliness is expressed as "folly."

9. **the stove:** Russian wood-burning stoves were large and rather elaborate structures, which included special shelves designed for sleeping or reclining.

III. FIRST IMPRESSIONS

1. **M—cki:** Alexander Mirecki (b. 1820) was a Polish revolutionary, who was sentenced to ten years at hard labor for participating in the "Greater Poland Uprising" of 1846, one of the many uprisings that took place following the partition of Poland among Russia, Prussia, and Austria in 1772.

2. **Starodubsky settlements:** During the eighteenth century, a large number of Old Believers moved from Vietka on the river Sozh in Belarus to Starodub, in the Ukrainian district of Chernigov.

3. **taverners:** The Russian word here is tselovalnik ("kisser"), from tselovat', "to kiss." Permission to sell vodka involved the ritual of kissing the cross and vowing not to dilute the drink.

4. **from *sirota*, "orphan.":** After the conquest of the Tatar capital Kazan by Ivan the Terrible in 1552, many Tatar princes embraced Christianity and were received at court in Moscow. Seeking favors and rewards, they pretended to be poor, and thus earned the nickname "orphans from Kazan."

5. **"four thousand":** According to the regulations of 1839 and 1855, the maximum number of strokes a man could be sentenced to was six thousand, but in practice it was unofficially lowered to three thousand, and in 1856 it was reduced to one thousand.

6. **Nerchinsk:** The town of Nerchinsk is in Eastern Siberia, about 140 miles from the Chinese border. The Russians built a fortress there in 1654, and by the late eighteenth century it was receiving large numbers of convicts sentenced to hard labor.

IV. FIRST IMPRESSIONS

1. *maidan:* "Maidan," in many eastern languages, means an open space, a market or meeting place; it also came to mean a gambling house and, in prison jargon, simply a game of cards. The word derives ultimately from Arabic.

2. **two Lezgins, one Chechen, and three Daghestan Tatars:** The Lezgins and Chechens are peoples that have been living since the Bronze Age in the area of the Caucasus—the Lezgins on what is now the border between southern Daghestan and northeastern Azerbaijan, and the Chechens in the northern Caucasus. The Tatars were originally a nomadic Turkic people from the area between China and Mongolia; they joined with the forces of Genghis Khan and in 1239 invaded Daghestan, where they settled.

3. **"how well he speaks":** "Isa" is how Jesus is known in Islam; the words Alei repeats are from the Sermon on the Mount (Matthew 5–7), the longest single discourse in the Gospels, containing the essentials of Christ's teaching.

4. **Gogol's little Jew Yankel:** Nikolai Gogol (1809–52) published his novella about Ukrainian Cossack life, *Taras Bulba*, in 1835. Yankel the Jew is a character in the novella, who is saved by Taras Bulba and later helps him against the Poles. Gogol describes him as looking like a plucked chicken.

V. THE FIRST MONTH

1. **a moral Quasimodo:** Quasimodo, the hero of Victor Hugo's *Hunchback of Notre Dame*, was only physically deformed. A—v's full name, as we know from Dostoevsky's notes, was Pavel Aristov.

2. **Briullov:** Karl Briullov (1799–1852) was a major Russian portraitist and historical painter. His masterpiece, *The Last Day of Pompeii* (1830–33), brought him great fame in Russia and Europe.

VI. THE FIRST MONTH

1. **those who also suffered in exile:** When Dostoevsky's party stopped in Tobolsk on the way to Omsk, it was met by the wives of some of the Decembrists, who had been exiled twenty-five years earlier. One of them, Natalya Dmitrievna Fonvizina (1805–69), gave Dostoevsky a Gospel, the only book allowed in prison, which he kept for the rest of his life. The Decembrists were members of a group of reformist aristocrats in Petersburg who staged an uprising on December 14, 1825, after the sudden death of the emperor Alexander I, demanding that Russia become a constitutional monarchy. The revolt was brutally suppressed, five leaders were executed, and more than a hundred others were exiled to Siberia. Their wives chose to accompany them. Dostoevsky wrote some important letters to Natalya Dmitrievna after his release.

2. **Nastasya Ivanovna:** The woman's real name was Natalya Stepanovna Kryzhanovskaya, as Dostoevsky records in his notes; she lived in Omsk and exchanged letters with him.

3. **the greatest egoism:** This notion, known as "rational egoism," was propounded by the materialist philosopher and utopian socialist Nikolai Chernyshevsky (1828–89) in *The Aesthetic Relations of Art to Reality* (1855) and particularly in *The Anthropological Principle in Philosophy*, published in 1860, just as Dostoevsky was working on his *Notes from a Dead House*.

4. **the pioneers:** Soldiers who went ahead of an advancing army, preparing roads, bridges, and so on; also known as sappers.

VII. NEW ACQUAINTANCES. PETROV

1. **a president:** Louis-Napoléon Bonaparte (1808–73), the nephew of Napoléon I, was elected president of the Second Republic in 1848; in 1851 he staged a coup d'état and in 1852 took the throne as Napoléon III, establishing the Second Empire.

2. **the countess La Vallière:** Louise de la Baume le Blanc (1644–1710) became one of the mistresses of Louis XIV, who made her Duchess of La Vallière. She gives her name to the middle volume of *Le Vicomte de Bragelonne* (1847–50), the last of the three d'Artagnan novels by Alexandre Dumas (1802–70).

VIII. RESOLUTE MEN. LUCHKA

1. **"to Ch—ov":** That is, the city of Chernigov, capital of Chernigov province in the northern Ukraine. K—v, mentioned a moment later, is Kiev, the Ukrainian capital.

2. **the image of God:** See Genesis 1:26: "And God said, Let us make man in our image, after our likeness." This is the most fundamental notion of Judeo-Christian anthropology.

IX. ISAI FOMICH. THE BATHHOUSE. BAKLUSHIN'S STORY

1. **as they crossed the Red Sea:** See Exodus 12–14, the story of the flight of the Jews from Egypt.

2. **a garrison battalion in R.:** That is, in Riga, now the capital of Latvia, but annexed to the Russian Empire by Peter the Great in the early eighteenth century.

3. **the zertsalo:** A three-sided pyramid of mirrored glass topped by a two-headed eagle, which stood on the desk of every Russian official. It was introduced by Peter the Great as a symbol of law and order, each face of the zertsalo being engraved with words from one of his decrees.

X. CHRISTMAS

1. **the breaking of the fast:** In the Orthodox Church, Christmas (the Feast of the Nativity) is preceded by the forty-day Advent fast.

2. **they always spread hay:** There was a custom of spreading hay on the floor for Christmas, to suggest the manger in which Christ was born (see Luke 2:11–16).

XI: THE PERFORMANCE

1. **the first performance:** In his memoirs, *At Hard Labor 1846–57*, Szymon Tokarzewski, one of the Poles imprisoned at Omsk, mentions that "the improvised actors asked the writer Fyodor Dostoevsky to give directions when necessary on how to speak theatrically."
2. ***Filatka and Miroshka, or The Rivals:*** A popular vaudeville by P. G. Grigoryev (1807–54), first produced in Petersburg in 1831.
3. **Leporello:** Don Giovanni's manservant in Mozart's opera.
4. **the Kamarinskaya:** The Kamarinskaya is a fast Russian folk dance. The composer Mikhail Glinka (1804–57) wrote a famous Kamarinskaya for orchestra, first performed in 1848.

PART TWO

II. CONTINUATION

1. **the German rules:** For the simple Russian folk, "German" meant anything foreign or simply unfamiliar.
2. **a baptized Kalmyk:** The Kalmyks are a western Mongol people who settled north of the Caucasus on the west coast of the Caspian Sea. Their national religion is Buddhism.
3. **Nozdryovian laugh:** Nozdryov is a loud, boastful character from Gogol's *Dead Souls.*
4. **"the memory is fresh":** A quotation from the play *Woe from Wit*, by the poet and diplomat Alexander Griboedov (1795–1829). Many lines from the play became proverbial.
5. **Manilovism:** Manilov is a softhearted, sentimental, and futile landowner in Gogol's *Dead Souls.*

III. CONTINUATION

1. **the Marquis de Sade and Brinvilliers:** Donatien Alphonse François, Marquis de Sade (1740–1814), is most famous as a writer of novels combining philosophy, eroticism, and violence—hence the word *sadism.* Marie Madeleine Dreux d'Aubray, Marquise de Brinvilliers (1630–76), was a notorious poisoner: having tested her potions first on poor hospital patients and her own chambermaid, she proceeded to poison her father, two brothers, and sister. She was arrested, tried, and beheaded.
2. **the onetime army of 1830:** That is, the army of the Polish uprising of 1830, known as the November Uprising, and of the resulting Polish-Russian war of 1830–31.

IV. AKULKA'S HUSBAND

1. *torban:* A Ukrainian musical instrument, a combination of the European bass lute (theorbo) and the zither.
2. **smear tar on Akulka's gate:** A traditional way of publicly shaming a girl who has "lost her virtue."

V. SUMMERTIME

1. **Holy Week:** The week from Palm Sunday to Easter, following the Great Lent.
2. **prepare for communion:** A time of fasting, prayer, and confession before taking the sacrament of the Eucharist.
3. **"but like the thief accept me":** A fused quotation of two phrases from the prayer before communion: "accept me today as a communicant" and "like the thief will I confess Thee."
4. **"the Dormition fast":** The two-week fast preceding the feast of the Dormition (Assumption) of the Mother of God, celebrated on August 15.

VI. PRISON ANIMALS

1. **St. Peter's Day:** That is, June 29, the feast day of Saints Peter and Paul.
2. **a goat in the prison stables:** Goats have traditionally been kept in stables because of their calming influence on skittish horses.

VII. THE GRIEVANCE

1. **T—ski:** That is, Szymon Tokarzewski (1821–1900), whose memoirs of his years in the Omsk prison and his relations with Dostoevsky were written in 1857.

VIII. COMRADES

1. **Saint Anne on the sword:** The Order of St. Anne was founded in 1735 by Karl Friedrich, Duke of Schleswig-Holstein, in honor of his wife, Anna Petrovna, daughter of the Russian emperor Peter the Great. The fourth (lowest) class of the order was a medal attached to the hilt of the sword.
2. **B—ski:** B—ski, elsewhere referred to as B., is the Polish revolutionary Joszef Boguslawski.
3. **Zh—ski:** Zh—ski is Joszef Zhochowski (1800–51), also a revolutionary, whose death sentence had been commuted to ten years at hard labor in Omsk.
4. **U—gorsk:** That is, Ust-Kamenogorsk, a fortress and trading post established by Peter the Great in what is now eastern Kazakhstan.
5. **a nobleman was being punished:** One of the privileges of the Russian nobility was freedom from corporal punishment, but there could be exceptions, as in this case. Hence the convicts' interest.

6. **a large group of exiled noblemen:** The reference is to the Decembrists (see the first note to part one, chapter VI).

7. **that *recent long-past* time:** The peculiar wording and emphasis are a left-handed appeasement of the censors, who would not have approved the book for publication if they thought it referred to present evils.

IX. THE ESCAPE

1. **Salt-eared Siberians:** The epithet "salt-eared" was originally applied to inhabitants of the region of Perm, in eastern Russia near the Urals. Legend held that the men who worked in the salt mines there had their ears pickled from carrying sacks of salt, which turned them big and red.

APPENDIX: THE PEASANT MAREY

1. **The Peasant Marey:** Dostoevsky included this reminiscence in the February 1876 number of his *Writer's Diary*, which he published periodically from 1873 to 1876 and again from 1877 to 1881.

2. **Konstantin Aksakov:** Konstantin Aksakov (1817–1860) was one of the major figures of the Slavophile movement, which sought continuity with the traditions and values of early Russian history and opposed the influence of western European ideas. He wrote a thesis on the question of the historical and religious mission of the Russian peasant.

A NOTE ABOUT THE AUTHOR

Fyodor Mikhailovich Dostoevsky (1821–1881) is best known for the series of novels he wrote in the last twenty years of his life—*Notes from Underground, Crime and Punishment, The Idiot, Demons, The Adolescent,* and *The Brothers Karamazov*—which made him one of the major figures of Western literature. These works were all nourished by and partly foreshadowed in *Notes from a Dead House* (1862), the author's semifictional account of his own experiences as a political prisoner in Siberia from 1850 to 1854.

A NOTE ABOUT THE TRANSLATORS

Together, Richard Pevear and Larissa Volokhonsky have translated works by Dostoevsky, Tolstoy, Chekhov, Gogol, Bulgakov, and Pasternak. They were twice awarded the PEN/Book-of-the-Month Club Translation Prize (for Dostoevsky's *The Brothers Karamazov* and Tolstoy's *Anna Karenina*), and their translation of Dostoevsky's *Demons* was one of three nominees for the same prize. They are married and live in France.

A NOTE ON THE TYPE

This book was set in Janson, a typeface long thought to have been made by the Dutchman Anton Janson, who was a practicing typefounder in Leipzig during the years 1668 to 1687. However, it has been conclusively demonstrated that these types are actually the work of Nicholas Kis (1650–1702), a Hungarian, who most probably learned his trade from the master Dutch typefounder Dirk Voskens. The type is an excellent example of the influential and sturdy Dutch types that prevailed in England up to the time William Caslon (1692–1766) developed his own incomparable designs from them.

Typeset by Scribe,
Philadelphia, Pennsylvania

Printed and bound by Berryville Graphics,
Berryville, Virginia

Designed by Soonyoung Kwon